A

Diane Gaston's d͏ romance novels. G͏ dream and has ne͏ won Romance's h͏ the National Readers Choice Award, Holt Medallion, Golden Quill, and Golden Heart. She lives in Virginia with her husband and three very ordinary house cats. Diane loves to hear from readers and friends. Visit her website at: http://dianegaston.com

Regency Reputations

Regency Reputations:

The Masquerade Club

DIANE GASTON

MILLS & BOON

First Published in Great Britain 2021
By Mills & Boon, an imprint of HarperCollins*Publishers*
1 London Bridge Street, London, SE1 9GF

www.harpercollins.co.uk

HarperCollins*Publishers*
1st Floor, Watermarque Building,
Ringsend Road, Dublin 4, Ireland

REGENCY REPUTATIONS: THE MASQUERADE CLUB ©
2022 Harlequin Books S.A.

A Reputation for Notoriety © 2013 Diane Perkins
A Lady of Notoriety © 2014 Diane Perkins

ISBN: 978-0-263-30426-8

MIX
Paper from
responsible sources
FSC™ C007454

A REPUTATION
FOR NOTORIETY

In fond memory of my Aunt Loraine, who taught me to enjoy life, no matter what.

Prologue

London—June 1819

Rhys noticed the woman as soon as she appeared in the game room doorway. Taller than fashionable, she held her head high as she perused the room. Her face was half covered by a black mask reminiscent of those he'd seen in Venice, crowned with feathers and painted with gilt filigree. A large garnet was set between the eyes. Visible still were her full lips, tinted and enticing.

In her deep red gown, matching the reds, greens and golds of the game room, she might have been an item he'd personally selected. He watched as she moved gracefully through the room, stepping carefully as if uncertain the space worthy of her. Did she intend to play hazard? Or one of the other games? He was keen that this woman should admire what he'd done to the gaming hell and enjoy herself.

He wanted her to return.

Rhys intensely wished for this gaming house to be a success. He would settle for nothing less than it becoming London's most desirable place to gamble, a place both gentlemen and ladies would be eager to attend. Not for the

profit it would earn, but to show he could be the best at
whatever he tackled.

The challenge exhilarated him, in a way he'd not experienced since the stimulation of battle. Only this time
there was no carnage in its wake.

This time there was a beautiful woman here to enjoy
herself and it was his job to see that she did.

She paused in the middle of the room and he quickly
made his way to her.

'Good evening, madam.' He bowed. 'I am Mr Rhysdale,
the proprietor of this establishment. It will be my pleasure
to assist you. What game do you wish to play?'

She lifted her eyes to him. Through the black mask he
saw they were an intriguing green. Her hair, a walnut-
brown laced with gold, was loosely piled on her head.

Who was she?

'Mr Rhysdale.' She nodded and her voice was surpris-
ingly soft and reticent. 'I would like to play whist, but I
do not have a partner.'

How he would relish partnering her himself, but he did
not play in his own gaming house. He would have to find
a gentleman willing to be her partner, but he'd find no enjoyment in the task. His friend Xavier would play cards
with her if Rhys asked, but women much too easily succumbed to Xavier's handsome features. No, Rhys would
not pass her on to Xavier.

Rhys wanted her for himself.

Chapter One

London—May 1819, one month earlier

Rhys and his friend Xavier sat at a table in the dining room of Stephen's Hotel. They had just been served their food when Rhys glanced towards the doorway.

Two men stood there, scanning the dining room.

Rhys knew them. Had known them since childhood. Viscount Neddington, né William Westleigh, and his brother Hugh, the legitimate sons of Earl Westleigh.

His brothers.

Rhys turned back to his food.

Xavier put down his fork with a clatter. 'What the devil?' He inclined his head towards the doorway. 'Look who is here.'

Rhys glanced up. 'They are looking for someone.'

Stephen's Hotel catered to military men, or former military men like Rhys and Xavier. Not the usual stamping ground of the Westleighs.

Rhys waited for the inevitable moment one of the Westleighs would notice him and slip his gaze away as if Rhys had never existed. Over the years when their paths had crossed, Neddington and Hugh always tried to act as if he'd never existed. Certainly that was their wish.

Ned, the elder, taller brother, turned his head in Rhys's direction. Their eyes locked, but this time Ned did not look away. This time he nudged his brother and the two walked straight for Rhys's table.

'They are headed here,' Rhys told Xavier.

His friend blew out a breath. 'I'll be damned…'

Rhys continued to hold Ned's gaze. Rhys always stood his ground with the Westleighs.

They stopped at the table.

'Rhys.' Ned inclined his head in an effort, Rhys supposed, to appear cordial.

'Gentlemen.' Rhys would be damned if he'd greet them by name and pretend an intimacy that had never existed. He gestured towards Xavier. 'My friend, Mr Campion.'

'We are acquainted.' Ned bowed in acknowledgement.

'We are indeed.' Xavier's tone was sarcastic.

Rhys cut another piece of meat. 'Are you merely paying your respects, or do you seek me out?'

'We seek you out,' Hugh replied, his voice taut and anxious.

Xavier glanced from one man to the other, obviously curious as to the purpose of this unusual visit.

Rhys made his expression neutral. Years of card-playing taught him to conceal his thoughts and emotions. He certainly had no intention of revealing anything to a Westleigh. He lifted a piece of beef into his mouth.

'Forgive us for interrupting your dinner.' Ned's tone was conciliatory, if somewhat stiff. 'We need a word with you.'

They *needed* a word with him? Now this was unique.

Rhys deliberately kept his attention to his plate, but he gestured to the empty chairs at the table. 'Have a seat.'

Hugh, shorter and always more hot-headed, emitted an indignant sound.

'We would prefer to speak in private.' Ned seemed anxious to avoid offending Rhys in any way.

Xavier straightened. If his friend were carrying a sword, Rhys suspected he'd have drawn it.

Rhys gazed at the two men, seeing only the boys they once were. The bitter memory of their first encounter, when Rhys was nine, flashed through his mind. He'd confronted them with what he'd just learned—that they shared a father.

That moment, like countless others from their childhoods, had resulted in flying fists and bloody noses.

Rhys stared into eyes identical to his. Dark brown, framed by thick eyebrows. Like his, Ned's and Hugh's hair was close-cut and near-black. Rhys might be taller and thicker-muscled, but if he stood side by side with these two men, who could ever deny they were brothers?

He exchanged a glance with Xavier, whose lips thinned in suspicion.

Rhys shrugged. 'Wait for me in the parlour off the hall. I'll come to you as soon as I've finished eating.'

Ned bowed curtly and Hugh glowered, but both turned and walked away.

Xavier watched their retreat. 'I do not trust them. Do you wish me to come with you?'

Rhys shook his head. 'There never was a time I could not take on both Westleighs.'

'Just the same, I dislike the sound of this,' Xavier countered. 'They are up to something.'

Rhys took another bite of his food. 'Oh, they are up to something. On that we agree. But I will see them alone.'

Xavier shot him a sceptical look.

Rhys took his time finishing his meal, although he possessed no more appetite for it. In all likelihood this would be an unpleasant interview. All encounters with Ned and Hugh were unpleasant.

Xavier clapped him on his shoulder before parting from him in the hall. 'Take care, Rhys.'

Rhys stepped into the parlour and Ned and Hugh turned to him. They'd remained standing.

He gestured. 'Follow me to my rooms.'

He led them up the two flights of stairs to his set of rooms. The door opened to a sitting room and as soon as Rhys led the men in, his manservant appeared.

'Some brandy for us, MacEvoy.'

MacEvoy's brows rose. MacEvoy, a man with an even rougher history than Rhys, had been his batman during the war. Obviously he recognised Hugh Westleigh from the battlefield.

'Please sit.' Rhys extended his arm to a set of chairs. It gave him a perverse pleasure that his furnishings were of fine quality, even if the items had been payment for various gambling debts. Rhys was doing well, which had not always been true.

MacEvoy served the brandy and left the room.

Rhys took a sip. 'What is this about, that you must speak with me now? You've made such a point of avoiding me all these years.'

Ned glanced away as if ashamed. 'We may not have… spoken to you, but we have kept ourselves informed of your whereabouts and actions.'

Ned was speaking false. Rhys would wager his whole fortune that these two had never bothered to discover what had happened to him after his mother had died and their father had refused any further support. The earl had left him penniless and alone, at a mere fourteen years of age.

No use to contest the lie, however. 'I'm flattered,' he said instead.

'You've had a sterling military record,' Ned added.

Hugh turned away this time.

'I lived,' Rhys said.

Hugh had also been in the war. The two former officers had come across each other from time to time in Spain, France and finally at Waterloo, although Hugh had been in a prestigious cavalry regiment, the Royal Dragoons. Rhys ultimately rose to major in the 44th Regiment of Foot. After the disastrous cavalry charge at Waterloo, Rhys had pulled Hugh from the mud and saved him from a French sabre. They said not a word to each other then, and Rhys would not speak of it now. The moment had been fleeting and only one of many that horrendous day.

Ned leaned forwards. 'You make your living by playing cards now, is that not correct?'

'Essentially,' Rhys admitted.

He'd learned to play cards at school, like every proper schoolboy, but he'd become a gambler on the streets of London. Gambling had been how he'd survived. It was still how he survived. He had become skilled at it out of necessity, earning enough to purchase his commission. Now that the war was over his winnings fed the foundation of a respectable fortune. Never again would his pockets be empty and his belly aching with hunger. He would be a success at…something. He did not know yet precisely what. Manufacturing, perhaps. Creating something useful, something more important than a winning hand of cards.

Hugh huffed in annoyance. 'Get on with it, Ned. Enough of this dancing around.' Hugh had always been the one to throw the first fist.

Ned looked directly into Rhys's eyes. 'We need your help, Rhys. We need your skill.'

'At playing cards?' That seemed unlikely.

'In a manner of speaking.' Ned rubbed his face. 'We have a proposition for you. A business proposition. One we believe will be to your advantage, as well.'

Did they think him a fool? Eons would pass before he'd engage in business with any Westleigh.

Rhys's skin heated with anger. 'I have no need of a business proposition. I've done quite well...' he paused '...since I was left on my own.'

'Enough, Ned.' Hugh's face grew red with emotion. He turned to Rhys. 'Our family is on the brink of disaster—'

Ned broke in, his voice calmer, more measured. 'Our father has been...reckless...in his wagering, his spending—'

'He's been reckless in everything!' Hugh threw up his hands. 'We are punting on the River Tick because of him.'

Earl Westleigh in grave debt? Now that was a turn of affairs.

Although aristocrats in severe debt tended to have abundantly more than the poor in the street. Ned and Hugh would never experience what Rhys knew of hunger and loneliness and despair.

He forced away the memory of those days lest he reveal how they nearly killed him.

'What can this have to do with me?' he asked in a mild tone.

'We need money—a great deal of it—and as quickly as possible,' Hugh said.

Rhys laughed at the irony. 'Earl Westleigh wishes to borrow money from me?'

'Not borrow money,' Ned clarified. 'Help us make money.'

Hugh made an impatient gesture. 'We want you to set up a gaming house for us. Run the place. Help us make big profits quickly.'

Ned's reasonable tone was grating on Rhys's nerves. On Hugh's, too, Rhys guessed.

Ned continued. 'Our reasoning is thus—if our father can lose a fortune in gaming hells, we should be able to recover a fortune by running one.' He opened his palms. 'Only *we* cannot be seen to be running one, even if we knew how. Which we do not. It would throw too much suspicion on our situation, you see, and that would cause our creditors to become impatient.' He smiled at Rhys. 'But *you* could do it. You have the expertise and…and there would not be any negative consequences for you.'

Except risking arrest, Rhys thought.

Although he could charge for membership. Call it a club, then it would be legal—

Rhys stopped himself. He was not going to run a gaming hell for the Westleighs.

'We need you,' Hugh insisted.

Were they mad? They'd scorned him his whole life. Now they expected him to help them?

Rhys drained the contents of his glass and looked from one to the other. 'You need me, but I do not need you.'

Hugh half rose from his chair. 'Our father supported you and your mother. You owe him. He sent you to school. Think of what would have happened if he had not!'

Rhys glared at him, only a year younger than his own thirty years. 'Think of what my mother's life might have been like if the earl had not seduced her.'

She might have married. She might have found respectability and happiness instead of bearing the burden of a child out of wedlock.

She might have lived.

Rhys turned away and pushed down the grief for his mother. It never entirely left him.

Ned persisted. 'Rhys, I do not blame you for despising

our father or us, but our welfare is not the main issue. Countless people, some known to you, depend upon our family for their livelihood. The servants. The tenant farmers. The stable workers. The village and all its people in some fashion depend upon the Westleigh estate to be profitable. Too soon we will not be able to meet the expenses of planting. Like a house of cards, everything is in danger of collapsing and it is the people of Westleigh who will suffer the most dire of consequences.'

Rhys curled his fingers into fists. 'Do not place upon my shoulders the damage done by the earl. It has nothing to do with me.'

'You are our last resort,' Hugh implored. 'We've tried leasing the estate, but in these hard times, no one is forthcoming.'

Farming was going through difficult times, that was true. The war left much financial hardship in its wake. There was plenty of unrest and protest around the country about the Corn Laws keeping grain prices high, but, without the laws, more farms would fold.

All the more reason the earl should have exercised prudence instead of profligacy.

'Leave me out of it.'

'We cannot leave you out of it!' Hugh jumped to his feet and paced the room. 'We need you. Do you not hear me? You must do this for us!'

'Hugh, you are not helping.' Ned also rose.

Rhys stood and faced them both. 'Words *our* father once spoke to me, I will repeat to you. *I am under no obligation to do anything for you.*' He turned away and walked over to the decanter of brandy, pouring himself another glass. 'Our conversation is at an end.'

There was no sound of them moving towards the door. Rhys turned and faced them once again. 'You need to leave me, gentlemen. Go now, or, believe me, I am quite capable of tossing you both out.'

Hugh took a step towards him. 'I should like to see you try!'

Ned pulled him away. 'We are leaving. We are leaving. But I do beg you to reconsider. This could bring you a fortune. We have enough to finance the start of it. All we need is—'

Rhys lowered his voice. 'Go.'

Ned dragged his brother to the door. They gathered their hats and gloves and left the rooms.

Rhys stared at the door long after their footsteps faded in the hallway.

MacEvoy appeared. 'Do you need anything, sir?'

Rhys shook his head. 'Nothing, MacEvoy. You do not need to attend me.'

MacEvoy left again and Rhys downed his brandy. He poured himself another glass, breathing as heavy as if he'd run a league.

He almost wished Hugh had swung at him. He'd have relished planting a fist in the man's face, a face too disturbingly similar to his own.

A knock sounded at the door and Rhys strode over and swung it open. 'I told you to be gone!'

'Whoa!' Xavier raised his hands. 'They are gone.'

Rhys stepped aside. 'What were you doing? Lurking in the hallway?'

'Precisely.' Xavier entered the room. 'I could not wait a moment longer to hear what they wanted.'

Rhys poured another glass of brandy and handed it to his friend. 'Have a seat. You will not believe this, I assure you…'

Sending away the Westleighs ought to have been the end of it. Rhys ought to have concentrated on his cards that night rather than observe the workings of the gaming hell on St James's Street. He ought to have slept well without his thoughts racing.

Over the next few days, though, he visited as many gambling establishments as he could, still playing cards, but taking in everything from the arrangements of the tables, the quality of the meals, the apparent profitability of the various games.

'Why this tour of gaming hells?' Xavier asked him as they walked to yet another establishment off of St James's. 'A different one each night? That is not your habit, Rhys. You usually stick to one place long enough for the high-stakes players to ask you to play.'

Rhys lifted his shoulders. 'No special reason. Call it a whim.'

His friend looked doubtful.

Rhys did not wish to admit to himself that he was considering his half-brothers' offer, although all the people who had been kind to his mother in the village kept rising to his memory. He could almost envision their suffering eyes if Westleigh Hall was left in ruins. He could almost feel their hunger.

If he pushed the faces away, thoughts of how much money he could make came to the fore. The Westleighs would be taking the risk, not Rhys. For Rhys it was almost a safe bet.

If only it had been anyone but the Westleighs.

Rhys sounded the knocker on the door of an innocuous-appearing town house. A huge bear of a man in colourful livery opened the door. Rhys had not been to this house in perhaps a year, but it appeared unchanged.

'How do you do, Cummings?' he said to the liveried servant. 'I have been gone too long from here.'

'G'd evening, Mr Rhysdale,' Cummings responded in his deep monotone. He nodded to Xavier. 'Mr Campion.'

Cummings might act the doorman, but he'd be better described as the gatekeeper, allowing only certain people in, chucking out any patron who became rowdy or combative.

Cummings took their hats and gloves. 'Nothing has changed here. Except some of the girls. They come and go. The game room is up the stairs. Same as always.'

Rhys was not interested in the girls, who often sold their favours on the side.

He glanced around the hall. Nothing appeared changed.

Three years ago he'd been a frequent patron of this place. He, like so many gentlemen at that time, had been intrigued by a masked woman who came to play cards and often did quite well. She'd been a mystery and that intensified her appeal. Soon the men were wagering on which of them would bed her first, all properly written down in the betting book. Rhys had not been interested in seducing a woman just to win a bet.

He shook his head. He had not thought of that masked woman in years. Who had won her? he wondered.

He turned back to Cummings. 'And Madame Bisou. Is she here tonight?' Madame Bisou owned this establishment.

'Aye. She should be in the game room.' Cummings turned away to store their hats.

Rhys and Xavier climbed the stairs and entered the game room, all a-bustle with activity as the time approached midnight. The hazard table was in the centre of the room, encircled by eager players. The familiar sound of dice shaken in a cup and shouts of 'Seven!' reached Rhys's ears, followed by the roll of the dice on the green baize and more shouting. Now and again a patron might win big, but the odds always favoured the bank, as they did in faro and *rouge et noir.* The two faro tables stood against one wall, nearly obscured by players; the other side held the games of *rouge et noir.* Rhys avoided all these games, where winning was almost completely dependent on luck. He confined himself to games of skill.

'I thought you came to play cards.' Xavier nudged him.

'I have,' he responded. 'But I have not been here in a year. I am taking stock of the room.'

At that moment, a buxom woman with flaming red hair hurried towards them. 'Monsieur Rhysdale. Monsieur Campion. How good it is to see you. It has been *trop longtemps,* no?'

Rhys smiled both at the pleasure of seeing her again and at her atrocious French accent. 'Madame Bisou!' He leaned over to give her a kiss on the cheek and whispered in her ear, 'How are you, Penny?'

'*Très bien, cher,*' she responded, but her smile looked stressed. She turned to greet Xavier before Rhys could ask more.

In those difficult London days of his youth Madame Bisou had been Penny Jones, a decade older than he and just as determined to free herself from the shackles of poverty. They'd both used what God had provided them: Rhys, his skill at cards—Penny, her body. But she did not spend all the money she earned on gin like so many of the other girls. She'd saved and invested and finally bought this place. She'd been running it for almost ten years.

'Why has it been so long since you have been here?' She took Rhys's hand and squeezed it.

'I am asking myself that same question.' Rhys smiled at her, genuinely glad to see an old friend.

Her tone changed to one of business. 'What is your

pleasure today, gentlemen? Do you wish a woman? Or a game of chance?'

Xavier answered her. 'A game of whist, if we can manage it.'

Rhys would have preferred merely to watch the room for a little while, but Penny found them two willing high-stakes partners.

When the play was over, Rhys and Xavier collected their winnings, more modest than most nights, but Rhys had to admit to being distracted. They moved on to the supper room. One of the girls began a flirtation with Xavier. Rhys spied Penny sitting in a far corner.

He walked over to her. 'It is not like you to sit alone, Penny. Is something amiss? Might I help?'

She sighed wearily and appeared, for the moment, much older than her forty years. 'I have lost the heart for this, Rhys. I wish I could just walk away from it all….'

Rhys's heart beat faster. 'Are you thinking of selling the business?'

'How can it be done? I cannot advertise.' Her gaming hell was illegal. 'I am too weary to even think how to accomplish it.'

This was unlike her. Penny always found a way to do precisely as she wished.

Rhys's nostrils filled with the scent of opportunity.

Fate was shoving him in the direction he must go. He was the solution to Penny's problems. He could save his old village. He could enrich his coffers.

All he must do was sell his soul to the devil.

His father.

The next day Rhys presented himself at the Westleigh town house. He'd not told Xavier his intention. He'd not wanted to be talked out of it.

It was well before the fashionable hour for making calls. Probably well before Ned and Hugh rose. It was half-past nine, a time working men and women were well into their day while the wealthy still slept. But Rhys needed to do this first thing or risk the chance of changing his mind.

The footman who answered the door led him to a drawing room off the hall. Unfortunately, the room was dominated by a huge portrait of the earl. Painted with arms crossed, the image of Earl Westleigh stared down, his expression stern and, Rhys fancied, disapproving.

Let his image disapprove. Rhys knew his own worth. He was determined the world should know it soon enough.

Still the earl's presence in this house set his nerves on edge. Would he join Ned and Hugh for this interview? Rhys half hoped so. He would relish standing in a superior position to this man who once held power over his life.

But it was far more likely the earl would do anything possible to avoid his bastard son.

Rhys's brothers, to their credit, did not keep him waiting long. He heard their hurried footsteps and their hushed voices before they entered the room.

Ned walked towards him as if he would offer his hand to shake, but he halted and gestured to a chair instead. 'Shall we sit?'

Hugh held back and looked solemn.

Rhys calmly looked from one to the other. 'I believe I'll stand.'

His response had the desired effect. Both men shifted uncomfortably.

'Are we to assume your presence here to mean you have reconsidered our offer?' Ned asked.

Rhys inwardly grimaced. Ned called it an offer? 'I came to further the discussion of whether I am willing to rescue you and our father from penury.'

'Why?' Hugh demanded in a hot voice. 'What changed your mind?'

Rhys levelled a gaze at him. 'Call it an attack of family loyalty, if you like. I did not say I've changed my mind.'

Ned placed a stilling hand on Hugh's arm, but spoke to Rhys. 'What do you wish to discuss?'

Rhys shrugged. 'Well, for one, it takes a great deal of money to start a gaming establishment. Will I be expected to invest my own money? Because I would not stake my fortune against something so risky.'

'How is it risky?' Hugh cried. 'The house always has the advantage. You know that.'

'The house can be broken,' Rhys countered. 'It is all chance.' Rhys succeeded at cards by reducing chance.

'But it is not likely, is it?' Hugh shot back.

Ned's eyes flashed a warning to Hugh, before he turned to Rhys again. 'The monetary investment will be ours.' He lowered his voice. 'It is now or never for us, Rhys. We've scraped the last of our fortune to bank this enterprise. All we want from you—all we need from you—is to run it.'

They must truly be desperate to devise a plan like this, especially as it involved him. Desperate or mad.

'A gaming house will not make much money right away unless it can quickly build a reputation. It must distinguish itself from other places. Give gamblers a reason to attend.' Rhys paused. 'You want to attract the high-stakes gamblers who have money to throw away.'

'It must be an honest house,' Hugh snapped. 'No rigged dice. No marked cards.'

Rhys gave him a scathing look. 'Are you attempting to insult me, Hugh? If you do not think me an honest man, why ask me to run it?'

Hugh averted his gaze.

'No cheating of any kind,' Rhys reiterated. 'And no

prostitution. I will tolerate neither.' He'd keep the girls at Madame Bisou's employed, but he'd have nothing to do with them selling their bodies.

'We are certainly in agreement with all you say,' Ned responded.

Rhys went on. 'Within the parameters of honesty, I must be given free rein in how the house is run.'

'Of course,' Ned agreed.

'Wait a moment.' Hugh glared. 'What precisely do you mean by free rein?'

'I mean I decide how to run it,' Rhys responded. 'There will be no countering of what I choose to do.'

'What do you choose to do?' Hugh shot back.

Rhys kept his tone even. 'I will make this house the one every wealthy aristocrat or merchant wants to attend. I want to attract not only wealthy men, but ladies, as well.'

'Ladies!' Hugh looked appalled.

'We all know ladies like to gamble as well as gentlemen, but ladies risk censure for it, so I propose we run the house like a masquerade. Anyone may come in costume or masked. That way they can play without risk to their reputation.' This had worked for the masked woman who'd come to Madame Bisou's and caused such a stir those years ago. No one had ever learned who she was.

Rhys had thought this all through. It had been spinning in his mind ever since Ned and Hugh first proposed he run a gambling house. He would call it the Masquerade Club. Members could join for a nominal fee. They could dress in masquerade as long as they purchased their counters with the coin in their pockets. If they sought credit or were forced to sign a promissory note, they must reveal their identity.

He continued explaining to Ned and Hugh. 'This is my plan thus far. It is not up to negotiation. If I come up with a better idea, I will implement it and I will not confer with you beforehand.'

'See here—' Hugh began.

Ned waved a hand. 'Leave it, Hugh. As long as it is honest and profitable, what do we care how the place is run?' He turned to Rhys. 'Anything else?'

'I want half the profit.'

'Half?' Hugh shouted.

Rhys faced him again. 'You risk money, but it is my reputation that will be at risk. We can charge a nominal subscription and call it a gaming club, but there is still the risk that it will be declared illegal. I must be compensated for that risk.' Besides, he intended to give Penny a portion of his profits, as part of the sale, and Xavier, too, if he was willing to help.

'I think your terms are agreeable,' Ned responded. 'Shall we discuss how much money you need to get started?'

Rhys nodded, but tapped a finger against his lips. 'I do have a question.'

Ned looked up suspiciously. 'What is it?'

'Does the earl know you wish me to do this?'

The brothers exchanged glances.

'He knows,' Ned answered.

And was not happy about it, Rhys guessed. Something Rhys counted upon. Besides earning a profit, Rhys wanted the gaming house to provide him another pay-off. He wanted to rub the earl's nose in the fact that it was his bastard son who pulled him from the brink of ruin. Rhys wanted revenge against the man who sired him and never, ever, acknowledged that fact, who had instead turned him away without a penny, not caring if he lived or died.

He tapped on the back of a chair with his fingertips.

'Very well, my *brothers*—' he spoke sarcastically '—I agree to run your gaming house.'

The two men who so resembled him visibly relaxed.

'On one more condition,' Rhys added.

Hugh rolled his eyes. Ned looked nervous.

'Our *father*—' Rhys spoke this word with even greater sarcasm '—Earl Westleigh, that is—must publicly acknowledge me as his son. It must seem as if I am accepted into the family as one of you, an equal member. I must be included in family functions and social occasions. I must be treated as one of the family.' What better revenge than this?

Ned and Hugh gaped back at him with horrified expressions. Apparently the idea of accepting him as a brother was as anathema to them as it would be to the earl.

'That is my condition,' Rhys reiterated.

Ned glanced away and silence stretched between them.

Finally he raised his eyes to Rhys. 'Welcome to the family, brother.'

Chapter Two

Rhys accomplished the sale and reopening of the gaming hell within three weeks of calling upon his half-brothers. He changed the décor and the menu and retrained all the workers. Madame Bisou's became the Masquerade Club and news of its opening travelled swiftly by word of mouth.

The first days had been stressful, but each night the numbers of patrons had grown, as had the profit, which made the Westleighs less fraught with worry. Rhys could count on one of them—Hugh mostly—to come in the guise of an ordinary patron. Rhys knew they were keeping tabs on what he had created.

He'd been watching for one of them when he spied the beautiful masked woman who had just told him she wished to play whist.

Rhys had experienced his share of affairs with women. He and Xavier had enjoyed some raucous nights in Paris with willing *elegantes,* but rarely, if ever, had he been so intrigued as with this woman.

Her posture was both proud and wary, and she had come to the gaming house alone, in itself a courageous act for a woman. What's more, her lips were moist and pink and her voice like music to his ears.

'How might a lady find a willing partner?' she asked. What man could refuse her?

For the first time since opening the gaming house, Rhys regretted that he could not play cards. He would have relished being her partner and showing her his skill.

As it was, he must find her another man—to partner her in whist.

He bowed. 'Give me a moment to fulfil your desire.' A serving girl walked by with a tray of port. He took one glass and handed it to her. 'Refresh yourself in the meantime and take a look at all the house has to offer.'

He quickly scanned the room and spied Sir Reginald, a harmless man who frequented gaming hells and flirted with the ladies, but rarely followed through. His card playing was competent, if not inspired. Sir Reginald would be forgiving if she turned out to be a poor player, but would not disappoint if she was skilled.

Rhys could not imagine her not being skilled at whatever she tried. He wanted her to enjoy herself. He wanted her to like the Masquerade well enough to return.

He brought the unmasked Sir Reginald to her. 'Madam, may I present Sir Reginald.'

Sir Reginald bowed gallantly. 'It will be my privilege to partner you.'

She smiled at Sir Reginald, her pink lips parting to reveal pretty white teeth. Handing Rhys her empty glass as if he were a servant, she accepted Sir Reginald's arm and walked with him to a card table with two other men. After speaking with the men, the lady and Sir Reginald sat. One of the other men dealt the cards.

Rhys had no intention of being so easily dismissed by this mysterious masked woman. He had other duties to occupy him at the moment, but, before she left, he intended to speak with her again.

* * *

Celia Gale breathed a sigh of relief to finally be seated at a card table, staring at diamonds, hearts, clubs and spades.

Entering the game room had been like crossing through the gates of hell. It had taken all her courage to do something so potentially damaging to her reputation. A lady, even a baron's widow, did not go gambling alone in the dead of night.

Even worse, it meant entering a world where other, even greater, risks existed—the lure of cards and dice, the heady thrill of winning, the certainty that losing could be reversed with one more hand, one more roll of the dice.

Cards and gambling once took away everything she held dear. The road to ruin was only one bad hand of cards away.

But what choice did she have? How else was she to procure the money she needed?

She'd heard of this gaming hell at a recent musicale she'd attended and immediately thought it was a godsend. Two men had spoken of it within her earshot.

'Thing is, the ladies can attend. It is called the Masquerade Club and anyone may come in disguise,' one had said.

'They do not have to reveal themselves?' the other asked.

'Not at all. Any lady may gamble without fear of ruining her reputation.'

She could gamble for high stakes and no one would know! At last a way to earn the funds she so desperately needed.

'Your deal, my dear,' Sir Reginald said, bringing her back to the present.

She'd spied Sir Reginald at a few of the entertainments she'd attended, but they had never been introduced. There was little reason to suppose he would recognise her. The other two gentlemen, also unmasked, were unknown to her before this night.

She dealt the deck slowly and with deliberation.

'Nicely dealt.' The man on her left smiled condescendingly.

She inclined her head in acknowledgement.

Her father taught that gambling was part skill at cards and part skill with people. Let these gentlemen condescend. It was to her advantage if they underestimated her. They might become careless in their choice of cards to lay down.

When the serving girl came around offering spirits, the gentlemen accepted, but Celia nursed one glass of port. She needed all her wits about her.

She purposely played as if this were her first time at a green baize table, and, by so doing, the counters grew into a pretty little pile at her right elbow. These gentlemen were betting quite modestly and, she suspected, were sometimes letting her win.

She indulged their mistaken impression. Soon enough this room would know her skill and then the competition— and the risk—would intensify.

She glanced up. The establishment's proprietor, Mr Rhysdale, was watching her. Too often when she looked up he was watching her. It set her nerves on edge.

Her blood had raced with fear when he'd approached her after she'd entered the room. She'd thought she'd done something wrong, transgressed some secret code of behaviour that was known only to those who frequented gaming hells.

He was a magnificent man, tall and muscled and intense. His eyes assessed everything, but his expression remained inscrutable. What was he thinking as he meandered through the tables, when he turned his gaze towards her?

He raised a glass to her and she quickly looked away.

What earthly reason made him watch her so closely? There were other masked ladies playing cards in the room.

She took the last three tricks of the hand, winning the game.

'That is it for me,' one of the gentlemen said.

'And for me,' his partner added.

Sir Reginald straightened. 'Would you like to try your luck at *rouge et noir,* my dear?'

She shook her head. 'No, thank you, sir.'

She wanted to play more cards. Games of skill, not merely of chance. She was at a loss as to how to manage it. Certainly she would not seek out Mr Rhysdale to find her a new partner.

All three gentlemen bowed and excused themselves, leaving her alone. Celia rose. She busied herself with slipping her counters in her reticule. The night had been profitable. Not overwhelmingly so, but it was a good start.

'Was luck with you, madam?'

She startled and turned, knowing who she would find. 'Luck?' She smiled. 'Yes, luck was with me, Mr Rhysdale.'

'Do you cash in, then?' He stood so close it seemed he stole the air she needed to breathe.

She clutched her reticule, but tilted her head so as to look in his face. 'Frankly, sir, I would like to continue to play. Dare I presume on you to arrange another game for me?'

'My pleasure, madam.' His voice turned low.

Within a few minutes he had rounded up two gentlemen and a lady needing a fourth and Celia played several more games. The gentleman who became her partner was more skilled than Sir Reginald and her counters multiplied.

When the players left the table, Mr Rhysdale appeared again. 'More partners?'

Her heart fluttered. Why was that? 'I am done for the night.'

He took her arm and leaned close. 'Then share some refreshment with me.'

She did not know what to say. 'What time is it?'

He reached into a pocket and pulled out a fine gold watch. 'A quarter to three.'

Her carriage came at three-thirty.

She glanced around the room. There was not enough time to join another whist game, or even find someone willing to play piquet. 'Very well.' She was certain her tone sounded resigned. 'Some refreshment would be welcome.'

He escorted her out of the game room to the door of the supper room behind. His hand remained firmly on her elbow. Her heart raced. Was he about to tell her why he watched her so intently as she played?

If he discovered she was a card sharp, her plans could be ruined. If he presumed she was cheating, it would be even worse. Was not her father's fate proof of that?

She wished Mr Rhysdale would simply leave her alone.

When they crossed the threshold of the supper room, Celia gasped.

The room was lovely! It was decorated in the earlier style of Robert Adam. The pale-green ceiling with its white plasterwork mirrored the pattern and colour of the carpet and walls. The white furniture was adorned with delicate gilt. Servants attending the buffet or carrying trays were dressed in livery that belonged to that earlier time, bright brocades and white wigs.

Rather than appear old-fashioned, the room seemed a fantasy of the elegance of bygone days. With all its lightness, Celia felt conspicuous in her dark red gown and black mask. There were four or five tables occupied, some with men entertaining ladies, some with men in deep conversation. Several of them glanced up as she and Rhysdale passed by.

'Are you hungry?' Rhysdale asked as he led her to a table away from the other diners. 'We can select from the buffet or, if you prefer, order a meal.'

Her nerves still jangled alarmingly. 'The buffet will do nicely.'

'And some wine?' His dark brows rose with his question.

She nodded. 'Thank you.'

At least he displayed some expression. She otherwise could not read his face at all, even though it was the sort of face that set a woman's heart aflutter. His eyes were dark and unfathomable and his nose, strong. But his lips—oh, his lips! The top lip formed a perfect bow. The bottom was full and resolute, like the firm set of his jaw. In this early pre-dawn hour, the dark shadow of his beard tinged his face, lending him the appearance of a dangerous rogue.

It was his position as the proprietor of the Masquerade Club that posed the most peril to her, though. She did not want the attention of the proprietor. She wanted only to play cards and win as much money as she could.

He pulled out a chair and she lowered herself into it, smoothing her skirt. Her chair faced the curtained window, but she wanted to face the room, so she could see what he was doing behind her back.

When he walked to the buffet, she changed seats.

Even as he made his selections at the buffet, he looked completely in charge. There was no hesitation on his part to pick this or that tidbit. His choices were swiftly accomplished. When a servant came near, Rhysdale signalled the man and spoke briefly to him. A moment later, the servant brought two wine glasses and a bottle to the table. He poured wine in both glasses.

Celia sipped hers gratefully. The night's play had given her a thirst and the mellowing effect of the wine was a balm to her nerves.

When Rhysdale turned from the buffet, he paused slightly, noticing, she supposed, that she had moved from the seat in which he had placed her.

He walked towards the table and her nerves fired anew.

Setting a plate in front of her, he lowered himself into the chair directly across from her. She would be unable to avoid those dark eyes while they conversed.

'I hope my selections are to your liking.' His voice rumbled.

She glanced at her plate. 'Indeed.'

He'd provided some slices of cold ham and an assortment of cheeses, fruits and confections, all items she enjoyed, but she would have given her approval no matter what he had selected.

She pushed the food around with her fork.

'I am curious.' His tone was casual. 'Why did you come to the Masquerade Club tonight?'

She glanced up, her heart pounding. 'Why do you ask?'

The corner of his mouth twitched, ever so slightly. 'I am eager to make this place a success. I want to know what entices a woman to attend.' He paused. 'And what would entice you to return.'

Her brows rose. Was this all he wanted from her? She could not believe it.

She chose her words carefully. 'I heard that a woman might play cards here without revealing her identity.'

He nodded. 'I had hoped anonymity would be an appeal.' He took a sip of his wine. 'And where did you hear this of the place?'

Now it was she who must avoid the truth. To answer truthfully would reveal that she moved in society's finest circles and that she could not do.

What could she say that would avoid tipping her hand? 'At the theatre.'

Yes. That ought to suffice. Anyone might attend the theatre.

He stared at her for a moment too long for comfort.

Finally he tasted the food on his plate. 'And what do you think of my establishment now you have seen it?'

She relaxed a little. Perhaps he was being honest with her. It made sense that a proprietor would want to know if his place appealed or not.

'It meets my needs very well.'

He glanced up. 'And your needs are?'

She swallowed a piece of cheese. 'A place to play cards where a woman might feel secure.'

'Secure.' He held her gaze.

She struggled to explain. 'To feel safe from…the stories one hears about gaming establishments.'

He pinned her with his gaze again. 'You have felt safe here?'

'I have,' she admitted.

What she witnessed from behind her mask was not the worst of what she'd heard of gaming hells, where drinking and debauchery might share the night with charges of cheating and, worst of all, challenges to duels. It almost seemed as civilised as a Mayfair drawing room, except for the wild excitement in the eyes of those on a winning streak and the blanch of despair on the faces of losing players. Those highs and lows were part of gambling. Something she must guard against at all costs.

As well as guarding against this special notice from the proprietor. His watchful dark eyes made her tremble inside.

He turned again to his plate. 'And what about the gaming here appeals to you? You played whist. Would you also be interested in the hazard table? Faro?'

She shook her head. 'I do not trust so much in luck.'

Too often in her life luck had totally abandoned her.

His eyes bore into her again. 'You prefer to rely on skill?'

Her gaze faltered. 'One must have some control over one's fate.'

'I quite agree.' To her surprise he smiled and his handsome face turned into something wondrous.

She found it momentarily hard to breathe.

His smile turned wry. 'Although you might say opening a gaming hell cedes too much of one's fate to luck.'

She forced her voice to work. 'Chance favours you at the hazard and faro tables, which is why I do not play them. Nor *rouge et noir.*'

She finished her wine, aware that he continued to stare at her. She fingered her reticule, heavy with counters. 'May—may I ask the time, please?'

He pulled his watch out again. 'Three-twenty.'

She stood. 'I must go. My carriage arrives at three-thirty and I need time to cash out.'

He also rose and walked with her to the ground floor where the cashier sat in a room behind the hall. She felt a thrill watching the coins she'd won stack up in front of her. After scooping them into a leather pouch and placing it in her reticule, she collected her shawl from the dour-faced servant attending the hall.

And Rhysdale remained with her.

He walked her to the door and opened it. 'I trust you will return to us?'

She suddenly was very eager to return. So eager a part

of her wanted to re-enter the game room and deal another hand of whist.

She curbed her excitement. 'Perhaps.' Curtsying, she said, 'Thank you for your assistance, Mr Rhysdale. And for the refreshment.'

'You are very welcome.' His voice turned low and seemed to resonate inside her.

She crossed the threshold, relieved to take her leave of him, but he walked out into the dark night with her.

The rush lamp at the door must have revealed her surprise.

'I will see you into your carriage,' he explained.

Her coachman drove up immediately and she was grateful her carriage no longer had a crest on its side.

Rhysdale opened the coach door and pulled down the steps. He held out his hand to assist her. His touch was firm and set her nerves trembling anew.

He closed the door and leaned into the window. 'Goodnight, madam. It has been my pleasure to assist you.'

His pleasure? She took a breath.

'Goodnight,' she managed.

The coach pulled away, and she swivelled around to look out the back window.

He stood in the road, illuminated by the rush light.

Still watching her.

Rhys did not leave the road until her carriage disappeared into the darkness.

Who the devil was she?

He did not need to be captivated by a woman. A woman could become an inconvenient distraction and he needed to keep his wits about him. The gaming house must be his priority.

Rhys had known too many women who made their living by acting pleasing at first, then cutting the man's purse and dashing away. He expected that sort of woman to show up at the gaming hell—women who played at gambling, but who really merely wished to attach themselves to the evening's big winners.

This woman was not a cutpurse, however. Neither did she come to the gaming hell on a lark.

She came to win money.

He'd watched her play, had seen the concentration in her posture, the calculation in her selection of cards. She was here for the card play.

She was a kindred spirit, a gambler like himself.

Would she return? She must. He wanted her in every way a man wanted a woman.

He walked back into the house, nodding to Cummings as he passed him. When he reached the door to the game room, Xavier appeared, leaning against the wall in the hallway, his arms crossed over his chest.

'What was that all about?' his friend asked.

Rhys did not know how much he wished to say about the woman, even to Xavier. 'She intrigues me.' He gave his friend a warning look. 'If she returns, do not aspire to make her one of your conquests.'

Xavier, who attracted female company so easily he never needed to make a conquest, replied, 'I comprehend.'

They walked into the game room together.

'Do you know who she is?' Xavier asked.

Rhys grinned. 'Not yet.'

Chapter Three

Celia sat at the desk in her library in the rooms she'd taken for the Season, rooms she now had more hope she could afford. Her winnings were stacked in piles on the desk, one half set aside to stake her next venture to the Masquerade Club.

What would she have done had she not discovered the new gaming house? Her widow's portion had been stretched to the breaking point and the bills continued to pour in.

Now she could transfer some of the bills from one stack to another—ones to pay now, ones to pay later.

She rolled some of the coins in her hand, almost giddy at their cool texture and the clink of them rubbing against each other.

She stacked them again and leaned back, appalled at herself. To be giddy at winning was to travel a perilous path. She must never succumb to the mania that was gambling. Not like her father—and, by association, her mother. They both died of it.

If she played with her head and not her emotions, she should be able to resist. She planned to visit the place often enough to learn who the high-stakes players were. Think of the money she could win in games with such gamblers!

Stop! she warned herself. No emotions. Playing cards must merely be what she did to earn money, like any tradesman or skilled workman.

Celia turned her face to the window and gazed out into the small garden at the back of the house. At the moment she must depend on Rhysdale to find her partners, but soon she would become known to the regulars. Then she hoped to be sought after as a partner.

At least Rhysdale had set her up with partners skilled enough to bring her a tidy profit.

She riffled the stack of coins. She needed more. Her stepdaughter's Season cost money and her mother-in-law refused to stop spending recklessly.

Her late husband had been another whose gambling and debauchery ruled his life. Her husband had been excessive in everything. Gambling. Spending. Drinking. Mistresses.

He'd even been excessive in his disdain for his young wife.

Not that it mattered now. His death had freed her from a marriage she'd never wanted and from a husband she'd abhorred. It had left her with a stepdaughter nearly her own age and a mother-in-law who despised her.

'Celia!' Adele, her stepdaughter, called.

Celia's singular joy, the closest Celia would ever come to a daughter of her own. Adele. Bright and starry-eyed, and full of hope that her first Season in London would bring her the love match she pined for. Celia was determined Adele should achieve her dreams, dreams that might have been Celia's own.

If gambling had not robbed her of them.

'I'm in here, Adele,' she responded.

Dreams aside, it was pragmatic for Adele to make a good match. The girl deserved to be settled and happy with a husband wealthy and generous enough to support

Adele's grandmother, as well. Celia's modest widow's portion might be enough for her to live in some measure of comfort if she economised very carefully, but it definitely did not stretch so far as to support her stepdaughter and mother-in-law.

Besides, Celia had no wish to be shackled to her mother-in-law forever.

Adele bounced into the room and gave Celia a buss on the cheek. 'Grandmama and I went shopping. We went to the new Burlington Arcade. It was a positive delight!'

'Was it?' Celia would miss Adele. The girl was the delight of her life.

Adele danced in front of her. 'There must have been a hundred shops. We did not see half of them.' She sobered. 'But, I assure you, I did not purchase a thing.'

Celia smiled. 'I hope you enjoyed yourself, none the less.'

'I did. I cannot tell you of all the items I saw for sale.' Adele lowered herself onto a nearby chair. 'Do not tell me those are bills.'

'They are bills, but do not fret. I have funds to pay some of them.' Celia moved the stacks of bills to pay farther away from those that would have to wait. 'Including the modiste. So you may order a new gown or two.'

Adele shook her head. 'I do not need them. I can make do with my old ones.'

Celia rose from her chair and went over to the girl. 'Indeed you may not!' She took Adele's hands. 'It is very important for you to put in a good appearance! Your grandmother and I agree on that score. Besides I've—I've found some funds I did not know we had. We are not so poverty-stricken after all.'

Adele looked sceptical. 'I hope you are telling me the truth and not shielding me as if I were a child.'

Celia squeezed her hands and avoided the issue. 'Of course you are not a child. A child does not have a Season.' Adele was nineteen years old. Celia herself was only twenty-three, but she felt ancient in comparison.

'I am sending Tucker out with the payments today.' Tucker had been one of the footmen who had served the Gales for years. Without overstepping the boundaries between servant and master, he'd been loyal to Celia through her marriage and widowhood. He was now her faithful butler.

'Where did you find the money?' Adele asked.

Celia pointed to the coins. 'The silliest thing. I was looking for something else and I discovered a purse full of coin. Your father must have packed it away and forgotten about it.'

Adele's expression saddened. 'That was a fortunate thing. Had he found it he would have lost it gambling.'

What would Adele think if she knew where the money had really come from?

Only three people knew of Celia's trip to the Masquerade Club—Tucker, her housekeeper, Mrs Bell, and Younie, Celia's lady's maid. Younie was lady's maid to all three women since Lord Gale's death.

What would Adele think if she knew Celia planned to return to the gaming hell tonight?

An image of Rhysdale flew into her mind. Would he watch her again? Her heartbeat accelerated.

The Dowager Lady Gale, Celia's mother-in-law, entered the room. 'There you are, Adele.' She did not greet Celia. 'We must decide what you are to wear to the musicale tonight. It cannot be the blue gown again. Everyone has seen that gown twice already. It will be remembered.' She finally turned to Celia. 'She absolutely needs new dresses. You are excessively cruel to deny them to her.'

Celia pasted a smile on her face. 'Good afternoon, Lady Gale.'

Like Celia, Lady Gale wanted Adele to have a successful Season, ending in a betrothal. The difference was, Celia wanted Adele to find someone who could make her happy; Lady Gale cared only that Adele marry a man with a good title and good fortune.

Celia adopted a mollifying tone. 'You will be pleased to know Adele and I have been talking of dresses. I have payment for the modiste, so Adele may order two new gowns.'

Her mother-in-law, silver-haired and as slim-figured as she'd been in her own Season, narrowed her eyes. 'Only two? I cannot abide how tight-fisted you are!'

Celia forced herself to hold her tongue. Engaging in a shouting match with the dowager would serve no purpose. 'Only two for now, but I am confident our finances will soon improve and Adele may order more.'

Her conscience niggled. How many times had her father purchased something, saying he'd win enough to pay for it?

Lady Gale pursed her thin lips. 'And I am to wear my old rags, I suppose.'

Celia's smile froze. 'You may order two gowns for yourself, if you like.'

'Will you come with us tonight, Celia?' Adele looked hopeful. She was too kind to say she did not find her grandmother's company altogether pleasant at such gatherings.

Celia calculated what time the musicale would end. It would still give her time to attend the gaming house for a few hours of play. 'If you wish.'

'I do!' Adele's countenance brightened.

Her grandmother rolled her eyes. 'You will dress properly, I hope.'

'I will, indeed.' Celia always dressed properly. Her most daring gown was the one she'd worn to the Masquerade

Club the night before. Its neckline had always seemed too low. She'd only worn it because she thought no one would recognise her in it, as if anyone at these society events noticed what she wore. None the less, she would change into it to wear to the gaming house tonight, as well.

She turned to Adele. 'Why don't you see if Younie has any ideas of how to alter one of your old gowns for tonight? She is very clever at that sort of thing.'

Adele jumped to her feet. 'An excellent idea! I will do that right away.' She started for the door. 'I beg your leave, Grandmama.'

Lady Gale waved her away. 'Go.' She called after Adele. 'Younie is in my room, Adele. She is mending.'

Adele skipped away and Lady Gale turned to Celia. 'I do not see why my granddaughter and I must share your lady's maid.'

Celia kept her voice even. 'Because we do not have the funds to hire more servants.'

'Money!' the older woman huffed. 'That is all you ever talk of.'

Money had consumed her thoughts, Celia would be the first to admit. Except this day thoughts of money were mixed with combinations of hearts, spades, clubs and diamonds.

Would Rhysdale be pleased at her return? Celia wondered.

She gave herself a good shake. Why was she even thinking of the man? It was not a good thing that she had come to his notice, no matter how attractively masculine he was. She planned to win and win often.

What if he accused her of cheating?

Lady Devine's musicale was a sought-after event and Celia's mother-in-law said more than once how lucky they were to have received an invitation. Celia, Adele and Lady Gale were announced amidst Lady Gale's grumbling that they ought to have had a gentleman escorting them.

They strolled through the rooms where the pink of the *ton* were assembled. Celia recognised some of the men as having been at the gaming house the previous night and she wondered how many more of these people—ladies especially—had been there, as well, but wearing masks as she had done.

Some of the gentlemen's faces at this entertainment had been quite animated at the gaming house, impassioned by the cards or the dice. Here in this Mayfair town house their expressions were bland. It seemed as if the risks of winning or losing made them come alive.

She did not know their names. The *ton* were known to her only from newspaper articles or books on the peerage. When her parents had been alive she'd been too young for London society. By the time she was married, her husband chose to keep her in the country so as not to interfere with his other 'interests.' The arrangement had suited her well enough. She preferred him to be away.

If she had been with him in London, though, she might have had some warning of his profligacy and the condition of his finances. She would have seen in him the telltale signs of gambling lust. Her childhood had honed her for it.

Her mother-in-law ought to have known how debauched her son had become. Lady Gale had spent most of her time in London as part of the social scene. In fact, it was because of Celia's mother-in-law that they received as many invitations as they did. But her mother-in-law would never countenance anything negative being said about her only son.

Except his choice of a second wife.

One of the men who had been at the gaming hell passed

close by. Celia had an impulse to ask her mother-in-law who the gentleman was, but Lady Gale gestured to her dismissively before she could speak.

'Get me a glass of wine,' the older woman ordered. 'It is so tedious not to have a man about to perform such niceties.'

'I will get it for you, Grandmama,' Adele said. 'Do not trouble Celia.'

Before either lady could protest, Adele disappeared through the crowd.

Lady Gale pursed her lips at Celia, but something quickly caught her eye. 'Look. There is our cousin Luther.'

Luther was second cousin to Celia's husband. And he was the new Baron Gale.

Needless to say, Luther was none too pleased at the state of his inheritance, mortgaged to the hilt, all reserves depleted. He had not the least inclination to offer any financial assistance to the former baron's mother, daughter or wife, as a result.

'Yoo-hoo! Luther!' Lady Gale waved.

The man tried to ignore her but, with a resigned look upon his face, walked over to where they stood. 'Good evening, ladies.' He bowed. 'I trust you are well.'

'We are exceeding well,' Lady Gale chirped, suddenly as bright and cheerful as she'd previously been sullen. 'And you, sir?'

'Tolerable,' he muttered, his eyes straying to elsewhere in the room.

'My granddaughter is here, Luther, dear,' she went on. 'You will want to greet her, I am sure.'

Luther looked as if he'd desire anything but.

'It is her Season, do you recall?' Lady Gale fluttered her lashes as if she were the girl having her Season. 'We expect many suitors.'

'Do you?' Luther appeared to search for a means of escape.

'Her dowry is respectable, you know.' That was because her father, Celia's husband, had been unable to get his hands on it.

Luther's brows rose in interest. 'Is that so?'

Celia felt a sudden dread. Surely Lady Gale would not try to make a match between Adele and Luther? Luther had already proved to be excessively unkind. After all, he'd taken over Gale House as soon as Celia's year of mourning was completed, removing Celia, Adele and Lady Gale without an offer of another residence. Even now he was rattling around in the London town house by himself when he could very easily have hosted the three women for the Season. That simple act would have saved Celia plenty of money and would have given Adele more prestige.

'Gale!' some gentleman called. 'Are you coming?'

Luther did not hesitate. 'If you will pardon me.' He bowed again.

'But,' Lady Gale spoke to his retreating back, 'you have not yet greeted Adele!'

'He can see Adele another time,' Celia assured her. 'In fact, he could call upon us, which would be the civil thing for him to do.'

Lady Gale flicked her away as if she were an annoying fly. 'He is much too busy. He is a peer now, you know.'

A peer who cared nothing for his relations.

Adele returned, carrying two glasses of wine. 'I brought one for you, too, Celia.' She handed a glass to her grandmother and one to Celia.

Adele was always so considerate. Sometimes Celia wondered how the girl could share the same blood as her father and grandmother.

Lady Gale snapped, 'Adele, you missed our cousin,

Luther. He was here but a moment ago.' She made it sound as if Adele should have known to come back earlier.

'Oh?' Adele responded brightly. Did Adele simply ignore her grandmother's chiding or did she not hear it? 'I have wanted to meet him and ask how all the people are at Gale House. I do miss them!'

One of Lady Gale's friends found her and the two women were quickly engaged in a lively conversation.

Adele leaned close to Celia. 'The kindest gentleman assisted me. I—I do not know if I properly thanked him. I must do so if I see him again.'

Celia smiled at her. 'You will be meeting many gentlemen this Season.' She so wanted Adele to pick a steady, responsible, generous man.

Luther was certainly not generous.

'You grandmother will wish to select your suitors, you know,' Celia added.

Adele frowned. 'I do want her to be pleased with me.'

Celia sipped her wine. 'You must please yourself first of all.'

Adele would not be pushed into a marriage she did not want and should not have to endure—as Celia had been. Celia would make certain of it.

The start of the programme was announced and Lady Gale gestured impatiently for Celia and Adele to follow her while she continued in deep conversation with her friend. They took their chairs and soon the music began.

Lady Devine had hired musicians and singers to perform the one-act French opera, *Le Calife de Bagdad* by Boieldieu. The comic opera was ideal for an audience who were intent on marriage matches. In the opera, the mother of the ingenue Zétulbé, refuses to allow the girl to marry the Caliph of Baghdad, who meets her disguised as an ordinary man. When he tries to impress the family with extravagant gifts, the mother merely thinks he is a brigand.

It should be every family's fear—that the man marrying their daughter is not what he seems. It certainly was Celia's fear for Adele. If only Celia's experience had been more like Zétulbé's, discovering the generous and loving prince disguised as something less. Celia's husband had been the opposite. Presented by her guardians as a fine, upstanding man, but truly a cruel and thoughtless one in disguise.

As the music enveloped Celia she wondered if all men hid their true colours.

Of course, she disguised herself, too. She pretended to be a respectable lady, but she visited a gaming hell at night. Once there, she disguised herself again by wearing a mask and pretending to be a gambler, when gambling and gamblers were what she detested most in the world.

The tenor playing the Caliph's part stepped forwards to sing of his love for Zétulbé. Celia closed her eyes and tried to merely enjoy the music. An image of Rhysdale flashed through her mind. Like the tenor's, Rhysdale's voice had teemed with seduction.

Rhys watched the door from the moment he opened the gambling house. He watched for her—the woman in the black-and-gold mask.

'Who are you expecting?' Xavier asked him. 'Someone to make our fortunes or to take it all away?'

He shrugged. 'The woman I told you about last night.'

Xavier's brow furrowed. 'This is not the time for a conquest, Rhys. Your future depends upon making this place a success.'

Xavier was not saying anything Rhys had not said multiple times to himself. Still, he flushed with anger. 'I will not neglect my responsibilities.'

Xavier did not back down. 'Women are trouble.'

Rhys laughed. 'That is the pot calling the kettle black, is it not? You are rarely without a female on your arm.'

'Women attach themselves to me, that is true.' Xavier's blue eyes and poetic good looks drew women like magnets. 'But I've yet to meet one who could distract me from what I've set myself to do.'

'I did not say she was a distraction. Or a conquest.' Rhys tried to convince himself as well as his friend. 'I am curious about her. She is a gamester like me and that is what intrigues me.'

Xavier scoffed. 'Is that why you warned me away last night?'

Rhys frowned. 'That prohibition still stands. I do not wish to have *you* distract *her.*' He paused, knowing he was not being entirely truthful. 'I want to see what transpires with this woman gamester.'

Xavier gave him a sceptical look.

Truth was, Rhys did not know what to make of his attraction to the masked lady gamester. Xavier was correct. The woman did tempt him in ways that were more carnal than curious.

But not enough to ignore his commitment to the gaming hell, not when his main objective was to show the Westleighs he could succeed in precisely the same world in which his father failed.

The buzzing of voices hushed momentarily. Rhys glanced to the doorway as she walked in, dressed in the same gown and mask as the night before. Sound muffled and the lamps grew brighter.

His body indeed thought of her in a carnal way. 'There she is.'

He left Xavier and crossed the room to her. 'Madam, you have returned. I am flattered.'

She put a hand on her chest. 'I have indeed returned, Mr Rhysdale. Would you be so kind as to find a whist partner for me once again?'

Xavier appeared at his side. 'It would be my pleasure to partner you, madam.'

Rhys glared at him before turning back to the masked woman. 'May I present Mr Campion, madam. He is a friend and an excellent card player.'

She extended her gloved hand. 'Mr Campion.'

Xavier accepted with a bow. 'I am charmed.' He smiled his most seductive smile at her. 'Do me the honour of calling me Xavier. No one need stand on ceremony in a gaming hell.'

Rhys groaned inwardly.

'Xavier, then,' she responded.

He threaded her hand through his arm. 'Do you wish to play deep, madam?'

She did not answer right away. 'Not too deep, for the moment. But neither do I wish a tame game.'

Xavier nodded in approval. 'Excellent. Let us go in search of players.'

He looked back at Rhys and winked.

Rhys knew Xavier well enough to understand his intent was merely to annoy. Xavier would always honour his wishes in matters such as this. Rhys was less certain about the lady. Most women preferred Xavier to Rhys. Most women preferred Xavier to any man.

Rhys went back to patrolling the room, watching the play, speaking to the croupiers running the tables. He kept a keen eye out for cheating in those winning too conveniently and desperation in those losing. Gamblers could easily burst out in sudden violence when the cards or the dice did not go their way. Rhys's plan was to intervene before tempers grew hot.

His eyes always pulled back to the masked woman. She sat across from Xavier, posture alert, but not tense. Tonight her handling of the cards was smoother than the night before. She arranged her hand swiftly and never belaboured a decision of what card to play. She'd said she preferred games of skill and she was quite skilled at whist.

She was a gamester, for certain. Rhys could wager on that. He'd also bet that she remembered every card played and that she quickly perceived the unique patterns of play in her partners and her opponents.

He strolled over to the table to watch more closely.

'How is the game?' He stood behind the masked woman.

Xavier looked at him with amusement. 'We make good partners.'

Judging from the counters on the table, Xavier and the masked woman made very good partners indeed. Card partners, that was.

Rhys stood where he could see the woman's cards. If it bothered her, she gave no sign. He watched the play for several hands. She was clever. Deal her four trump and she was certain to win with three of them at least. Give her a hand with no trump and she took tricks with other cards when trump was not played.

She was a gamester all right.

He instantly looked on her with respect.

But, as fascinated as he was watching her play, he needed to move on. No gambler wanted such acute attention to his or her play, especially by the house's proprietor.

Rhys sauntered away.

An unmasked Ned Westleigh approached him. 'How are things faring?' Ned asked in a conspiratorial tone.

Rhys lifted his brows and raised his voice. 'Why, good evening, Lord Neddington. Good to see you back here.'

'Well?' Ned persisted.

'We are near to recouping the original investment,' Rhys replied. 'So all is as it should be.'

'Excellent.' Ned rubbed his hands together.

'There is more to our bargain, do not forget,' Rhys added.

He expected these Westleighs to try to renege on the earl's obligation to claim Rhys as a son. More than once Rhys wondered why he'd made that part of the bargain. Another man might wish for the connection to the aristocracy such an acknowledgement might bring, but Rhys cared nothing for that. Neither was the money he'd reap from this enterprise a motivation. He could always make money.

No, all Rhys really wanted was to force his father to do what he ought to have done when Rhys was a child—take responsibility for Rhys's existence. Once that was accomplished, Rhys was content to spurn him and his sons as they had once spurned him.

'Hugh and I do not forget,' Ned said in a low voice. 'Our father…requires some time.'

Rhys lifted a shoulder. 'I will not release the money until that part of the promise is assured.' The Westleighs, in their desperation, had ceded all the power in this matter to him.

Rhys glanced over to the masked woman and caught her looking back. She quickly attended to her cards.

Rhysdale was talking to the gentleman Celia had seen earlier at the musicale, she noticed. It was fortunate she had changed her gown, even though she doubted the gentleman would have noticed her. The widow of a dissolute baron who never brought his wife to town did not capture anyone's attention.

Rhysdale caught her watching and she quickly turned back to the cards and played her last trump. She guessed Xavier still had two trumps remaining. That should ensure they won this hand.

They'd won most of the games and each time Celia felt a surge of triumph. Their opponents, however, grew ever-deepening frowns. Xavier took the next trick and the next and the game was theirs.

Their opponents grumbled.

Celia shuffled the deck and the man on her right cut the cards. She dealt the hand and the play began, but this time Xavier did not play in the manner to which she'd accustomed herself. The opponents took tricks they ought to have lost. Xavier suddenly was playing very sloppily indeed. He was losing *her* money. She gave him a stern glance, but he seemed oblivious.

When the hand was done, the opponents won most of the tricks and won the game, to their great delight. Luckily that game's wagers had been modest, but Celia's blood boiled at losing so senselessly.

'That was capital!' the man on her right said. 'I'm done for now, however. Excellent play.' He stood, collected his small pile of counters and bowed to Celia. 'Well done, madam.' He turned to Xavier. 'You chose a capital partner, sir. We must play again.'

'I'm done, as well,' the other man said.

Both begged their leave and wandered over to the hazard table.

'They must wish to lose more,' Xavier remarked.

Celia gathered her counters. 'You let them win that last game.'

'You noticed?' Xavier laughed. 'Better they leave happy. Otherwise they might choose other opponents next time.'

Her eyes widened. 'You made certain they would be willing to play us again.'

He nodded. 'Precisely.'

He smiled and his incredibly handsome face grew even more handsome. He'd been an excellent partner, she had to admit. She now possessed even more money than she'd won the night before. Still, she sensed he'd had motives of his own for partnering her, something that had nothing to do with trying to win at cards.

Another man hiding something.

She stood and extended her hand to him. 'It was a pleasure, sir.'

His smile flashed again. 'The pleasure was mine.' He held her hand a moment too long for her liking. 'What's next for you? The hazard table?'

She shrugged. '*Vingt-et-un,* perhaps.'

'Ah, there is a *vingt-et-un* table. Let me take you to it and see if we can get you in that game.'

Vingt-et-un was another game where she could exercise her skill. All she need do was remember the cards played and bet accordingly.

Xavier led her to the large round table with a dealer at one end and players all around. Xavier facilitated her entry into the game and it soon occupied all her concentration.

When the croupier reshuffled the cards, she glanced up.

Mr Rhysdale was again watching her. He nodded, acknowledging that she'd again caught him watching. She nodded in return and refocused on the cards.

Time passed swiftly and Celia's excitement grew. She was winning even more than the night before. Her reticule was heavy with counters. She fished into it and pulled out her watch.

Quarter after three.

In only a few minutes her coach would arrive and she still must cash out.

Mr Rhysdale appeared at her elbow. 'Almost time for your coach, madam?'

Her senses flared with his nearness. 'Yes.'

He touched her elbow. 'I will escort you.'

'That is not necessary, sir.' His attention made it hard for her to think. And to breathe.

He touched her reticule. 'I cannot allow you to walk into the night alone. Especially with a full purse.'

As he had done the night before, he escorted her to the cashier and waited for her while the hall servant collected her wrap. He again walked her out the door and onto the pavement.

It had apparently rained. The street shone from the wet and reflected the rush lights as if in a mirror. From a distance, the rhythmic clopping of horses' hooves and the creaking of coach wheels echoed in the damp air. Celia's coach was not in sight.

Rhysdale stood next to her. 'How did you find the cards tonight, madam?'

She closed her hand around her reticule. 'Quite satisfying.' She glanced down the street again. 'Although I may not spend much time at *vingt-et-un* after this.' She feared he would catch on that she had been counting the cards.

'You did not lose.' He spoke this as a fact, not a question.

She smiled. 'I try not to lose.'

His voice turned low. 'I noticed.'

Her face warmed.

'You have an excellent memory for cards, do you not?' he went on.

Her stomach knotted. He knew. 'Is that a problem?'

'Not for me,' he responded. 'Not as yet.'

Her hands trembled. 'Are you warning me away?'

'Not at all.' His tone remained matter of fact. 'If I saw you make wagers that would jeopardise my establishment, I would certainly warn you away from my tables, but, as long as you play fair, it matters not to me how much you win off of any gentleman brave enough to challenge you.'

'Do you suspect me of cheating?' The very idea filled her with dread.

And reminded her of her father.

He shook his head. 'You are a skilled player.' He paused. 'I admire that.'

She relaxed for a moment, then glanced down the street, looking for Jonah, her coachman.

'Who taught you to play?' Rhysdale continued conversationally.

She averted her gaze, not willing to reveal the pain she knew would show in her face. 'My father.' Her throat grew dry. 'He once was also a skilled player.'

Before he died.

She faced Rhys again, wanting to take the focus off of her. 'And who taught you to play, sir?'

He made a disparaging sound. 'Certainly not *my* father.' He looked reluctant to tell her more. 'I learned in school, but I honed my craft later when it became necessary.'

'Why necessary?' she asked.

It was his turn to glance away, but he soon faced her again. 'I was living on the streets.'

She was shocked. 'On the streets?'

He shrugged. 'When I was fourteen, I had no one and nothing. I came to London and learned to support myself by playing cards.'

No one and nothing?

How well she remembered the desolation of no one and nothing.

She opened her mouth to ask why he'd been alone, what had happened to his parents, but her coach turned the corner and entered the street. She was silent as it pulled up to where they stood. As he had done the night before, he put down the steps for her and opened the door.

He took her hand and helped her inside, but did not immediately release it. 'Will you come play cards again, madam?' His voice seemed to fill the night.

She wanted to return. She wanted to win more.

And she wanted to see him again.

All seemed equally dangerous.

'I will return, sir.'

He squeezed her hand.

After he released her and closed the coach door, Celia could still feel the pressure of his fingers.

Chapter Four

Ned waited until almost noon for his father to rise and make his appearance in the breakfast room. He'd tried to confront his father on this issue before and knew he must catch him before he went out or he'd lose another day.

Hugh had waited with Ned most of the morning, but stormed out a few minutes ago, swearing about their father's decadent habits.

Not more than a minute later Ned heard his father's distinct footsteps approaching.

Wasn't it always the way? When Ned needed Hugh, his brother disappeared.

The earl entered the room, but paused for a moment, spying his oldest son there.

He gave Ned an annoyed look. 'I thought to have breakfast in peace.'

Ned stood. 'Good morning to you as well, Father.'

His father walked straight to the sideboard and filled his plate with food that had already been replaced three times. The earl detested cold eggs. 'Do you not have something of use to do? Itemising my bills? Recording my debt in a ledger?'

Ned bristled at his father's sarcastic tone. 'You ought to be grateful to me and to Hugh.'

His father sat down at the head of the table. A footman appeared to pour his tea. Ned signalled for the footman to leave.

His father waited until the door closed behind the man. 'I am anything but grateful that you treat me as a doddering fool. Makes me look bad in front of the servants.'

Ned sat adjacent to his father. 'You were the one to speak of bills and debts in front of Higgley.'

His father glared at him and stuffed his mouth full of ham.

Ned went on. 'But I do need to speak to you.'

His father rolled his eyes.

Ned did not waver. 'It has been a month since Rhysdale opened the gaming house and you have yet to fulfil your part of the bargain.'

'You truly do not expect me to speak to that fellow, do you?' He popped a cooked egg into his mouth.

'Speak to him?' Ned felt his face grow hot. 'You gave your word as a gentleman to do more than that. We need to include him socially. You need to acknowledge he is your son.'

His father waved a hand. 'I already did my part. I sent him to school. What more can he want?'

Ned gritted his teeth. 'You agreed to this, Father. Rhysdale has already amassed the amount we invested to get the place started. But he will not release the money until you do what you are honour-bound to do.'

'Honour?' His father's voice rose. 'Do you call it honourable that *he* is holding *my* money? It is more like extortion, I'd say.'

'I'd say it is more like sound business,' Ned countered.

'Rhysdale is no fool. The money is his leverage. You must do as he says.'

'I do not have to do anything I do not wish to do.'

Good God. The man sounded like a petulant schoolboy.

Ned would not put up with it. 'Father. You must do this. We are running out of time. No one will advance you more credit. The fields need tending. The livestock need feed. Our tenants need to eat—'

At that moment Hugh entered the room. 'Your voice is carrying, Ned.'

So much for keeping this private from the servants—not that one could keep anything secret from servants for long.

'Where were you?' he asked Hugh.

Hugh looked apologetic. 'I was going mad waiting for Father. I just took a quick walk outside.'

He sat across from Ned and poured a cup of tea.

'Father is reneging on his word.' Ned inclined his head towards their father.

Hugh took a sip. 'I presumed.' He slid his father a scathing look. 'Your bastard son has more honour than you, you know. He's kept his part of the bargain.'

Their father straightened in his seat. 'I'll brook no disrespect from you, you ungrateful cub.'

Hugh faced the earl directly, his face red with anger. 'Then be a man I can respect, sir! Do what you agreed to do. Introduce Rhys to society as your son. You gave your word.'

'Only to the two of you,' their father prevaricated. 'I never gave my word to him.'

Ned lowered his voice. 'Your word given to your sons means nothing, then?'

Hugh rose from his chair. 'Let him go, Ned! He is not thinking of us. Nor of the Westleigh estates. Nor the Westleigh people. Let him watch his creditors come ransack the house, carrying away our heritage and that of our own sons. He cares nothing for nobody. Only for himself.'

'See here, you cur!' the earl cried, jumping to his feet.

Ned stood and extended his arms, gesturing for them both to sit down. He had one more card to play. 'Let us bring Mother into this conversation.'

'You'll do no such thing!' his father cried.

'Ned's right.' Hugh seized on this idea immediately. 'Mother needs to know what a sorry excuse for a gentleman you've become.'

Ned suspected their mother already knew what a sorry creature her husband was. But she probably did not know the extent of his debt and the dire consequences that were imminent unless they could begin paying the creditors. This information would certainly shock her.

She, of course, knew of Rhys's existence and Ned did feel sorry that she must endure the humiliation of having him welcomed into the family.

'Very well,' the earl snapped. 'I'll go the gaming hell and make nice to Rhysdale. I'll do that much.'

'You'll have to do more,' Ned warned him.

The earl nodded. 'Yes. Yes.' His tone turned resigned. 'But first I want to see this place and ascertain for myself whether he is swindling us or not.'

'He is not swindling us!' Hugh said hotly.

Their father ignored him. 'If all is as it should be, then we may plan how to divulge the rest to your mother.'

Rhys wandered through the tables of the gaming house, watching the gamblers, perusing the croupiers at their work. He wished he had more eyes, more people he could trust to check on the tables. To make certain the croupiers stayed honest and the gamblers refrained from cheating. With so much money changing hands every night, it was a rare man or woman who would not at some time or another become tempted.

Cheating was the great danger of a gaming house. Gentlemen could accept losing huge amounts in honest games, but the whiff of a dishonest house might swiftly destroy everything.

He also had to admit to watching for the masked woman to arrive. She'd been attending almost every night. Whenever she came, Rhys contrived to spend a few minutes alone with her.

The mystery of her sometimes filled his thoughts.

Where had she come from? Who was she? Why had she chosen gambling to make money?

She had a life outside the gaming hell, a life she wished to protect, that much he understood. Was she married and hiding her gambling from her husband? He hoped not. Married women held no appeal for him.

He'd had some opportunity to attend the Royal Opera House and Drury Lane Theatre. He and Xavier had joined Xavier's parents in their theatre box. But Rhys had seen no one who resembled her. He knew he would recognise her without her mask. He'd memorised her eyes, her mouth, the way she moved.

He glanced up at the doorway, for the hundredth time. But it was not she who appeared.

He stiffened. 'Well, well,' he said to himself, looking around to see if Xavier noticed, but his friend was deep in play.

Earl Westleigh sauntered in with one of his cronies.

Rhys had spied the earl from time to time in the two years he'd been back from the war. He and the earl had sometimes gambled at the same establishments. At those times, though, Rhys doubted the earl noticed him. Even if he had, how would he recognise Rhys now from the scrawny fourteen-year-old he'd been when he'd begged the earl for help?

Rhys watched the earl survey the room in his self-important way. He leaned over to say something to his friend and both men laughed.

Rhys flexed his fingers into a fist, feeling as though the men were laughing at his youthful self, near-helpless and so desperately alone. He was not alone here. Not helpless. This was *his* place. Under his control. His to build into a success beyond any of the earl's expectations.

He straightened his spine.

'Where is the owner of this establishment?' Lord Westleigh asked in a booming voice. 'I should like to see him.'

Rhys turned to one of the croupiers and asked the man about the play at his faro table. It was the sort of surveillance he might do, but this time, of course, his motive was to avoid responding to the earl's beck and call.

Out of the corner of his eye he saw someone point him out to Lord Westleigh. He also saw Xavier looking up from his play, his gaze going from the earl to Rhys. Xavier appeared ready to vault out of his chair, daggers drawn.

Rhys did not need his friend's aid. He could handle the earl. He knew he was the better man.

He deliberately busied himself with checking the faro deck, but the hairs on the back of his neck rose when Westleigh came near.

'Rhysdale!' The earl made his name sound like an order.

Rhys did not respond right away, but finished replacing the faro deck in its apparatus.

Slowly he raised his eyes to the earl. 'Lord Westleigh,' he said in a flat voice.

'I've come to see what people are talking about. A gaming hell and a masquerade.' He made a somewhat disparaging laugh.

'What do you wish to play?' Rhys asked, treating him like any other gentleman—but with a bit more coldness.

'I fancy some faro,' the earl's companion said. 'Haven't tried my hand at faro in an age.'

It was a game going out of fashion, but still making enough here to satisfy Rhys.

'I do not know you, sir.' Rhys extended his hand to the man. 'I am Mr Rhysdale and, as the earl so loudly announced, I am the owner.'

The man clasped his hand. 'Sir Godfrey's the name.'

Rhys made room for Sir Godfrey at the faro table. 'I hope you enjoy yourself, sir.'

He turned to Lord Westleigh. 'And you, sir, what is your fancy?'

Lord Westleigh's attention had turned to the doorway where the masked woman for whom Rhys had been waiting all night entered.

'I'd fancy that,' the earl said under his breath.

Rhys's fingers curled into a fist again.

He stepped in front of the earl, blocking his view of the woman. 'This is an establishment for gambling and nothing more. Do you comprehend?' His voice was low and firm. 'The ladies who play here will be left in peace. Am I speaking clearly enough?'

Lord Westleigh pursed his lips. 'Meant no harm.'

Rhys narrowed his eyes.

Westleigh glanced away. 'My sons tell me this establishment is making money. Is that true?'

'It is true.' Rhys guessed the earl wanted his share. Not a damned chance until he met his part of the bargain.

'But you have not paid my sons a farthing.' Westleigh had the gall to look affronted.

Rhys levelled his gaze at the man. 'It is you who have held up payment, sir. I await you.'

'Yes. Well.' Westleigh looked everywhere but at Rhys. 'It is complicated.'

Rhys laughed dryly. 'And distasteful to you, I might imagine.' He shook his head. 'Matters not to me whether you do this or not. This place is making me rich.' He walked away.

Rhys had begged once from his father, but never again. Let his father beg from him this time.

As soon as she walked in the room, Celia's gaze went directly to Rhysdale. He stood with an older man, a gentleman, to judge by the fit and fabric of his coat. This man had not visited the gaming house before, at least not when she'd been here, and she had not seen him at the few society functions she attended with Adele and Lady Gale.

Whoever this man was, Rhysdale did not seem pleased at his presence. That piqued her curiosity even more.

She detested herself for looking for Rhysdale as soon as she walked through the door, for wondering about who he was with and how he felt about it.

As the days had gone on, she'd come to enjoy his attentions.

It felt almost like having a friend.

She turned away and made her way through the room, returning greetings from players to whom she was now a familiar figure. She no longer needed Rhysdale to find her a game of whist; plenty of men and some ladies were glad to play.

She passed by Xavier Campion. That man's eyes usually followed her, not with the interest of other gentlemen. She swore he watched her with suspicion. Tonight, however, Xavier watched Rhysdale and his brow was furrowed.

Who was that man?

Rhysdale turned away from the gentleman and walked away, his expression one of distaste and suppressed rage.

She lowered her gaze and set about finding a whist partner.

Not too long after, she was seated at a table and arranging a hand of cards into suits. Still, she was acutely aware of whenever Rhysdale passed near.

She no longer feared he was trying to catch her cheating. She liked his attention. It seemed as if the air crackled with energy when he was near, like it might before a summer storm. She liked him.

Even though he made his living from gambling.

To her distress, the cards did not favour her this night. Even when she had partnered with Xavier, she lost hand after hand. Counting in her head, she knew it was not a trifling amount. She kept playing, thinking the next hand would turn her luck around. When that did not happen, she counted on the hand after that.

As the night advanced, her pile of counters grew lower and lower. She'd lost over half the money she staked. Still, the urge was strong to keep playing, to bet more, to keep going so she could change it all back to the way it had been before.

But still she lost.

Celia stared at her counters and came to her senses. *Stop!* she told herself. *Before you return home with nothing.*

She stood up abruptly. 'I am done.'

Before the others at her table could protest, she hurried away and made her way to the cashier. She wanted the counters changed back to coin so she would not be tempted to return to the games.

It was only two in the morning, too early to wait outside

for her coachman. Instead, after cashing in her counters, she walked to the supper room, not hungry, but greatly desiring a glass of wine or two to quiet her nerves.

Several of the tables were occupied, but her gaze went instantly to the table where she'd sat before with Rhysdale.

He was there, staring into nothing, a glass in hand.

She approached him, needing at least the illusion of a friend. 'Hello, Rhysdale.'

He glanced at her with a look of surprise that turned into a smile. 'The lady with the mask.' He stood and pulled out a chair. 'Would you care to sit with me?'

She sat.

'What is your pleasure?' he asked. 'Shall I fix a plate for you?'

'Wine.' She sighed. 'Just wine.'

He signalled a servant to bring her wine.

Now that she'd so brazenly approached him, she did not know what to say.

'How was your night?' he asked finally.

'Not good,' she replied.

What more was there to say? Losing called into serious question her whole plan to finance Adele's come-out with winnings. Worse than that, it showed how easily she could slip into a gambling fever where nothing mattered but trying to win back her money.

The wine arrived and she quickly downed half of it.

His brows rose. 'Bring the bottle,' he told the servant and turned back to her. 'I take it you lost.'

Her fingers drummed the tabletop. 'I did.'

He reached across the table and quieted her busy hand. 'Do you need assistance? Are you in distress?'

She glanced into his eyes, which conveyed only concern and earnestness. His hand was warm against hers, even through the thin fabric of her glove.

She slipped her hand away, shaken at how comforting his touch felt and how much she needed comfort.

'I'll come to rights,' she said, although her voice lacked any semblance of confidence.

'I can lend you money,' he went on.

She shook her head. 'I know better than to borrow from moneylenders.'

His eyes flashed. 'I am not a moneylender. I offer as a friend.'

She took in a breath. 'But…you do not even know who I am.'

He traced the edge of her mask with a finger. 'Tell me, then. Who are you?'

She sat very still at his gentle touch while her heart fluttered in her chest.

'I am nobody,' she said, speaking with a truth that had been proved over and over. She had not mattered enough for anyone to care what the impact of their actions would be to her.

She raised her eyes to his.

His promise seemed so genuine, as if he was a man she could believe. Would he truly lend her money if she needed it? And then what? Without gambling she could not repay him. What would she do then? Turn to moneylenders?

She shivered as the memory of her father returned. He had to sell her pony, he'd told her. He had to pay the moneylenders. Life after that had been filled with more times of want than times of plenty.

Until the day her mother told her news even more horrible than losing a pony. Her father was dead. He'd been accused of cheating at cards and a man—an earl—had shot him dead in a duel.

'I do not need a loan,' she said absently, still caught in the memory of her father's senseless death.

At every society entertainment she feared she would encounter her father's killer. What would she do then?

Rhys spoke. 'But you need money.'

'I'll find another way.' Although she knew there was no other way.

She, Adele and Lady Gale would have to find a set of rooms that Celia's widow's pension could afford. She'd have to let the servants go and Adele's chances of making a good marriage would become extremely slim. At least Celia would not have to encounter the earl who killed her father.

She finished her glass of wine as the servant placed the bottle on the table. Rhysdale poured her another.

'Thank you.' She lifted the glass and decided to push the attention off herself. 'What of you, Rhysdale? When I came in you looked as if you were the one who had lost money.'

A corner of his mouth rose. 'The house never loses, you know. We are doing well.'

She smiled. 'I am glad of it. You seem to have more players each time I've come.'

'More women, as well.' Again he touched her mask. 'The Masquerade seems to be working.'

She put her fingers where his had touched. 'It has worked for me.'

He sat back. 'Until now.'

She shrugged. 'I shall have to consider whether to come again and try to recoup.'

He leaned forwards again. 'Do you mean to say you might not return?'

'I might not.' She paused. 'I should not.'

'Do not say so!'

Her heart started pounding faster again. She took another sip of wine. 'Does one gambler matter so much?'

His gaze seemed to pierce into her. He did not answer right away. Finally he said, 'I believe there are men who come merely in hopes of playing with you.'

She scoffed. 'Surely you are not serious.' She supposed the men who'd partnered with her and those who played against her recognised her skill. 'In any event, I doubt any man will want to partner with me after my losing streak tonight.'

She'd not only lost her own money, but her partners' money, as well.

'You place so little value on yourself?' He continued to pin her with his eyes.

No one else had valued her.

She glanced down. 'Who wants to partner with some-one who is losing?'

He drummed on the table like she had done earlier, while his steady gaze began to unnerve her.

'I have a proposition,' he said finally. 'Come work for me.'

Rhys did not know why he had not thought of this before.

Hire her.

'What do you mean, work for you?' She looked shocked. 'Doing what?'

'Gambling,' he rushed to assure her. 'Nothing more.' The idea grew in his head as he spoke. 'I would pay you to gamble. And to encourage others to gamble, as well.'

Her eyes through her mask grew wary. 'Am I to cheat?'

He waved a hand. 'Never! It is not cheating to pay you to gamble. You will receive no advantage.'

She glanced away, as if deliberating.

It gave him time to think, as well. Would he compro-mise the gambling house by paying her to gamble? He only knew he wanted her to come back. He needed her to come back.

She turned back to him. 'How much would you pay?'

He threw out the first number that occurred to him. 'Two pounds a night?'

'Two pounds?' She looked astonished.

Was that not enough? He paid his man only fifty pounds a year. 'That is more than generous, madam.'

She sat very still, but he fancied her mind was calculating.

Finally she spoke. 'I need money, sir, but if my task is to gamble, then, as generous as two pounds a night might be, it does not allow me to play for bigger stakes. What is more, I still stand a chance that I will lose as I have lost tonight. That I cannot risk.'

She had a point. In gambling there was always the possibility of losing it all.

He wanted her to agree, though. He wanted to see her again. If he did not offer enough to entice her, she might never return.

He tapped on the table again. 'Very well. I will stake you.' He thought for a minute. 'Say, for one hundred pounds. At the end of the night, you return my stake to me but keep your winnings. If you lose, you make an accounting to me of the loss.' If she lost too often, he'd reassess this plan, but his gamble was that she would bring in more money than she would lose.

Her eyes showed interest. 'Do I still receive the two pounds a night?'

He was not that big a fool. 'One pound. Plus your winnings.'

She calculated again, her eyes on his. What did she look like under her mask? He imagined lifting it off her face, discovering the treasure underneath.

In the back of his mind he could hear Xavier's voice, questioning his motives, accusing him of succumbing to the first pretty lightskirt who'd caught his eye in a long time.

She was not a lightskirt, but Rhys would wager she belonged on the fringes of society as did he. His money was still on her being an actress.

She opened her lovely mouth and, God help him, all he could think of was tasting her lips. She was about to agree—he could feel it.

Celia was so tempted. He'd handed her a way to gamble without losing her money. What could be better than that? What did it matter, then, if she succumbed to the excitement of the game? Losing would not imperil her.

It was as if he was handing her the future she so desired. To see Adele well settled. To retire to the country and live quietly within her means with no one directing her life but herself.

Rhysdale did not press her. He poured her another glass of wine and waited.

She accepted the glass gratefully and took a long sip, but even the wine did not loosen the knots of panic inside her.

He'd offered her this help as a friend. When had she last had a friend? For that matter, when had she last been able to trust a man? Even her beloved father broke promise after promise.

What if she refused Rhysdale's offer? Her mind spun with what she would have to do to economise. She'd have to try to pay back most of the creditors. She'd have to give up her coachman, her carriage, her servants. She'd have little left for rooms to let and food to eat. Adele did not deserve such a life. Even her mother-in-law did not deserve such a life.

Rhysdale's gaze was patient and, she fancied, sympathetic. 'You are not required to decide this minute. Come to me tomorrow, in the afternoon.' He glanced about the room. 'We can discuss it without anyone around.' His voice deepened. 'If you refuse employment, my offer of a loan still stands.'

She felt tears prick her eyes. 'You are kind, Rhysdale.'

A smile grew slowly across his face. 'Do not say so too loudly or you will ruin my reputation.'

She almost laughed.

Some gentlemen entered the room and she came to her senses. 'What time is it?' She fished into her reticule to check her timepiece. 'I must take my leave.'

He stood and offered his hand to assist her.

As they walked towards the door, they passed the older man she'd seen with Rhysdale when she'd arrived that night.

'Charming supper room!' the man remarked to his companion.

When he spied Rhysdale, his eyes hardened to ice. He walked past them without a word.

Even the air seemed chilled as he passed.

Celia inclined her head to Rhysdale. 'Who is that gentleman?'

Rhysdale's entire manner changed into something dark and bitter.

'No one you need know,' he answered.

It pained her to see him so disturbed. 'Does he come here often?'

'Never before.' Rhysdale's voice rumbled with suppressed emotion. 'But I suspect he will come again.'

He led her out into the hallway and down the stairs to collect her cloak. As had become his custom, he escorted her into the street to wait for her coachman.

Clouds hid the stars and made the night even darker than usual. Celia's own woes receded as she stood waiting with him for her carriage, an overwhelming desire to comfort him taking over.

She touched his arm. 'Rhysdale, it will not do for the both of us to be glum.'

He covered her hand with his and his typically unreadable face momentarily turned pained and vulnerable. 'Come this afternoon. Let us talk more about my offer.' His grip on her hand tightened. 'Do not leave me entirely.'

She blinked and her throat constricted. 'Very well. I'll come.'

He smiled and his gratitude was palpable. He leaned down, his eyes half closing.

Celia's heart thundered in her chest as the night itself wrapped around them and his head dipped lower and lower. She wrestled with an impulse to push him away and a desire to feel his arms around her.

The *clop-clop* of a horse team sounded in her ears and he stepped away. Her carriage approached from the end of the street. When the coach pulled up to where they stood, he put the steps down and reached for her hand to help her into the couch.

When she placed her hand in his, she suddenly turned to face him, her words bursting from her mouth. 'I will do it, Rhysdale. I will come work for you.'

His face broke out in pleasure. 'Indeed?'

She smiled, as well. 'Yes.'

For a moment he looked as if he would pull her into his arms and kiss her. Instead, he gently cupped her cheek. 'We will talk more this afternoon.'

'Until then,' she whispered.

She climbed into the coach and he closed the door.

As the carriage pulled away, her heart raced. Had she been afraid he would kiss her or had she yearned to feel his lips on hers?

Chapter Five

A gnarl of nerves amidst a flutter of excitement, Celia donned her hat and gloves. It was half-past twelve, barely afternoon, but she wished to be finished with her interview with Rhysdale before two, when no respectable woman dared walk near St James's Street.

She supposed she was not truly a respectable woman. Not when she spent her nights gambling in a gaming hell. But that did not mean she wished to suffer the taunts and catcalls of dandies who loitered on corners for that very purpose.

Her mother-in-law descended the staircase. 'And where are you going?'

Celia had hoped to slip out before her mother-in-law knew she was gone. 'I have an errand. I shall be back shortly.'

'Do you take Younie with you?' the older woman snapped. 'Because I have need of her.'

Celia kept her tone mild. 'She is at your disposal. My errand is not far. I have no need of company.'

'Hmmph!' her mother-in-law sniffed. 'I expect you will not tell me the nature of this errand of yours.'

'That is correct.' Celia smiled.

Lady Gale continued to talk as she descended the stairs. 'Most likely it is to pay a bill or beg for more credit from shopkeepers who ought to be glad to have our business. Needless to say you are not off to meet a man. My son always said you were frigid as well as barren.'

The barb stung.

The cruelty of this woman was rivalled only by that of her son. Ironic that Lady Gale was blind to her son's faults, but took great enjoyment in cataloguing Celia's.

Primary among Celia's shortcomings, of course, was her inability to conceive a child. Neither Gale nor his mother had forgiven her for not producing sons, but neither had they ever considered how crushing this was for Celia. A baby might have made her marriage bearable.

Knowing she could never have a child hurt more than her mother-in-law would ever know, but today her mother-in-law's abuse merely made her angry.

After all she'd sacrificed for the woman's comfort...

Celia faced her. 'You speak only to wound me, ma'am. It is badly done of you.'

Her mother-in-law stopped on the second stair. She flushed and avoided Celia's eye.

Celia maintained her composure. 'Recall, if you please, that your son left you in more precarious financial circumstances than he did me, but I have not abandoned you.' Much as she would like to. 'Nor have I abandoned Adele. I am doing the best I can for all of us.'

Lady Gale pursed her lips. 'You keep us both under your thumb with your tight-fisted ways. You control us with the purse strings.'

Celia tied the ribbons on her hat. 'Think the worst of me, if you wish, but at least have the good manners to refrain from speaking your thoughts aloud.' She opened the door. 'I should return in an hour or so.'

Younie had sewn a swirl of netting to the crown of Celia's hat. When she stepped onto the pavement, Celia pulled the netting over her face so no one would recognise her if they happened to spy her entering the Masquerade Club.

The afternoon was grey and chilly and Celia walked briskly, needing to work off her anger at the woman.

Lady Gale had well known of her son's debauchery, but still she preferred to blame all Gale's ills on Celia. In truth, the man had countless vices, many more than mere gambling. He'd treated Celia like a brood mare and then thrust her out to pasture when she didn't produce, all the while taunting her with his flagrant infidelities and profligate ways. As if that were not enough, he neglected his daughter.

And his mother.

Celia had known nothing of men when her aunt and uncle arranged her marriage to Gale. She'd still been reeling from her parents' deaths and barely old enough for a come-out. Her aunt and uncle simply wished to rid themselves of her. She'd never felt comfortable with Gale, but thought she had no choice but to marry him. She never imagined how bad marriage to him would be.

The only thing he'd wanted from Celia was a son and when she could not comply, he disdained her for it. Over and over and over. Life was only tolerable for her when he went off to London or anywhere else. Celia cared nothing about what he did in those places as long as he was gone.

Little did she know he'd squandered his fortune, leaving only what he could not touch: Celia's widow's portion and Adele's dowry.

She'd worn widow's black after Gale died, but she had never mourned him. His death had set her free.

And she would free herself of his mother, as well, when Adele was settled. As long as her husband would be gen-

erous enough to take on the responsibility of the Dowager Lady Gale.

It was not until Celia turned off St James's on to Park
Place that she remembered her destination. She was indeed
meeting a man. Would not Lady Gale suffer palpitations
if she knew? She was meeting a man who offered her the
best chance of escaping life with her mother-in-law. A man
who had almost kissed her.

The gaming hell was only a few short streets away from
her rooms. In daylight it looked like any other residence.

But it was an entirely different world.

As she reached for the knocker, her hand shook.

For the first time he would see her face. Was she ready
for that?

She sounded the knocker and the door opened almost
immediately. The burly man who attended the door at night
stood in the doorway.

Celia made herself smile. 'Good afternoon. I have an
appointment with Mr Rhysdale.'

The taciturn man nodded and stepped aside for her to
enter. He lifted a finger. A signal for her to wait, she supposed. He trudged up the stairs.

Celia took a breath and glanced around to try to calm
her nerves.

At night this hall looked somewhat exotic with its deep
green walls and chairs and gilded tables. At night the light
from a branch of candles made the gold gilt glitter and a
scent of brandy and men filled the air. To her right was a
drawing room, its door ajar. To anyone peeking in a window this house would appear as respectable as any Mayfair town house.

The doorman descended the dark mahogany stairs and
nodded again. Celia assumed that meant he'd announced

her to Mr Rhysdale. He then disappeared into the recesses of rooms behind the hall.

A moment later Rhysdale appeared on the stairs. 'Madam?'

She turned towards him and lifted the netting from her face, suddenly fearful he would not approve of her true appearance.

He paused, ever so slightly, but his expression gave away nothing of his thoughts.

He descended to the hall. 'Come. We will talk upstairs.'

Dismayed by his unreadable reaction, Celia followed him to the second floor where sounds of men hammering nails and sawing wood reached her ears.

'Forgive the noise,' he said. 'I'm having this floor re-modelled into rooms for my use.' He lifted the latch of a door to her right. 'We can talk in here.'

They entered a small drawing room. Its furnishings appeared fashionable, as well as comfortable. They were stylishly arranged.

He gestured for her to sit on a deep red sofa. He sat on an adjacent chair. 'I've ordered tea.'

She might have been calling upon one of her mother-in-law's society friends. Escorted into a pleasant drawing room. Served tea. The conventions might be identical, but this was no typical morning call.

In daylight Rhysdale was even more imposing. His dress and grooming were as impeccable as the most well-attired lord, even though he managed to wear the pieces as casually as if he'd just walked in from a morning ride. His eyes, dark as midnight in the game room, were a spell-binding mix of umber and amber when illuminated by the sun from the windows.

His gaze seemed to take in her total appearance, but his expression remained impassive. Did she disappoint? She was too tall to be fashionable. Her figure was unremark-able. Her neck was too long; her face too thin; her lips too full; her hair too plain a brown—she could almost hear her husband's voice listing her faults.

But what did Rhysdale think?

And why was it she cared so much for his approval?

He blinked, then averted his compelling eyes. 'I assume you have not changed your mind about my proposition?' His smooth voice made her quiver inside.

She swallowed. 'I would not have kept the appoint-ment otherwise.'

A smile grew across his face. 'Then, perhaps an intro-duction is in order?'

She was prepared for this, at least. He would be a fool to hire her without knowing her name.

And he was no fool.

She'd already decided to give him her true name. Her maiden name.

She extended her gloved hand. 'I am Celia Allen, sir.'

It pleased her to be Celia Allen again. The surname was common enough and her father minor enough that no one would connect the name to Lord Gale's widow.

He took her hand, but held it rather than shake it. 'Miss Allen or Mrs Allen?'

She pulled her hand away. 'Miss Allen.'

Rhys felt the loss of her hand as if something valuable had slipped through his fingers. With this first glimpse of her face, he wanted her more than ever.

She reminded him of a deer with her long regal neck and alert-but-wary eyes that were the colour of moss at twilight. She seemed wrong for the city. She was meant for the country, for brisk walks in fresh country air. The bloom in her cheeks, the hue of wild raspberry of her lips looked out of place in London.

But he was becoming distracted.

And much too poetic.

He could almost hear Xavier's voice in his head, admonishing him to keep his focus on the gaming house. He would tell his friend later about employing her—not of almost kissing her—both had been too impulsive to meet the approval of his friend.

Not that Rhys cared if his zealously protective friend approved of his employing Miss Allen. Or of wanting her in his bed.

He fixed his gaze on her again. To call her Miss Allen seemed wrong to him. He had no wish to be so formal with her.

'Will you object if I address you as Celia?' he asked. 'You may call me Rhys.'

She coloured.

Her discomfort made him wonder. A woman of the theatre would expect the presumption of intimacy of using given names.

She paused before answering. 'If you wish it.' She met his eyes. 'Not in the gaming house, though.'

Clever of her. 'Of course not. You are exactly right. No one must know you are in my employ. They will suspect us of manipulation.'

'Manipulation?' Her lovely brows knit in anxiety.

'I hire you because your presence in the gaming house encourages patrons—men—to gamble. You are not expected to do anything different from what you were doing before.'

She nodded.

He leaned closer and put his hand on her wrist. 'That is not my only reason for hiring you, however—'

A knock at the door interrupted. She slipped her hand away and Rhys straightened in his chair.

MacEvoy entered with the tea tray, managing to give her an un-servant-like look-over. Undoubtedly Rhys would hear Mac's assessment of the lady later.

'Shall I pour?' She looked rattled. 'How do you take your tea?'

'No milk, no sugar.' He'd accustomed himself to drinking tea that way from times when he could not afford milk and sugar. It pleased him that he did not need those inconsequential trappings of wealth.

He gestured to MacEvoy to leave.

MacEvoy closed the door behind him and Celia handed Rhys his cup of tea.

He lifted the cup and took a sip.

Perhaps it was for the best that Mac had interrupted him. His desire for her was making him move too quickly. When he got close, he sensed her alarm, another clue that his theory about her identity might be wrong.

He changed the subject. 'I should explain something else about your employment here.'

She gave him her attention.

'Some time ago, before I owned this gaming house, a woman came here in disguise to play cards. It is where I got the idea to set up the place as a masquerade.' He waved that tangent away. 'But no matter. About this woman. She created a stir. Men were taking wagers on who would be the first to unmask her.' He paused. 'And who would be first to seduce her. Men came and gambled merely for the chance to win the wager.'

She paled. 'You wish me to offer myself as some sort of prize?'

He shook his head. 'No. No, indeed. I am merely warning you. Some men who come to gamble may ask more of you than merely to partner them in a game of whist.'

Her eyes narrowed in calculation. 'Like that man who so distressed you last night?'

Westleigh, she meant.

His voice hardened. 'Yes. Men like him.' He looked directly into her eyes. 'I will be near if any men ill treat you. Do not hesitate to alert me or Xavier. We will protect you.'

She put her hand on her heart and glanced away.

He took another sip of tea. 'You are a good card player. And that is all that is required of you. None the less, your feminine allure will attract admirers.'

'Feminine allure?' She looked surprised.

How puzzling. Did she not know she was alluring?

'You are a beguiling mystery. A lovely young woman who knows how to play cards. You will—you *do*—attract men. Men will want to partner you, play against you, sit next to you.' He gave her another direct look. 'But they must not cross the line of proper behaviour. If they do, you must let me know.'

She became absorbed in stirring her tea. Finally she answered. 'If such a thing should happen, I will let you know.'

He became even more convinced he'd been wrong about her being an actress. If not someone connected to the theatre, who was she?

'May I know more of you, Celia Allen?'

She turned wary again, like a deer about to bound away. 'There is nothing else I can tell you.'

He must not push her further. He would learn about her in due time, he resolved. Even though he knew solving the mystery of her would not diminish his desire.

She placed her teacup on the table. 'The terms of payment are what we agreed upon last night?'

He nodded, regretting the conversation turning businesslike. The desire to taste her lovely lips grew more difficult to resist. 'One pound per night, plus all your winnings. I stake you one hundred pounds, which you will return if you win. I will forfeit if you lose.'

She stood. 'I will try not to lose.'

'I know you will try not to lose. You are a true gamester.' He rose with her. 'Chance sometimes does not favour us, though, Celia. You will lose. At hazard or faro, at least, but those losses will come directly to me, so I do not credit them. Play all the hazard and faro you like. At whist or *vingt-et-un* I suspect you are skilled enough to win most of the time.'

'I hope I do not disappoint.' Her lips formed a tremulous smile. 'For both our sakes.'

That was another thing. Why did she need money so urgently?

She pulled on her gloves. 'I will try to come to the gaming house as many nights as I am able.'

What might keep her away? She was one mystery after another, even without her mask.

'Good.' He adopted her businesslike tone. 'When you arrive, stop at the cashier. He will be instructed to provide you your stake.'

'Is there anything else?' she asked. 'I must leave now.'

'One thing more.' He extended his hand. 'We must shake on our agreement.'

Slowly she placed her hand in his. He liked the feel of her long graceful fingers and strong grasp.

He drew her closer to him, just short of an embrace. 'I am glad of our partnership, Celia Allen,' he murmured, his lips inches from hers.

Her eyes widened. The deer wished to bolt, he feared.

He released her and she started towards the door.

'Will I see you tonight?' he asked.

She reached the door and turned. 'If I can manage it.'

He let her walk out on her own, but when he heard the front door close, he stepped to the window and held the curtain aside to watch her.

She paused for a moment on the pavement, as if getting her bearings. Seeming to collect herself suddenly, she walked down the street with purpose.

He watched until he could see her no more.

'I'll solve the mystery of you, Miss Celia Allen,' he said aloud. 'And I will see you in my bed.' He dropped the curtain. 'Soon.'

Celia gulped in air and tried to quiet her jangling nerves. Taking one more quick breath, she hurried away.

God help her, being with Rhysdale excited her even more than the prospect of gambling without losing her own money. What was wrong with her?

She'd had no experience with men—other than Gale, that is. Rhysdale looked as if he wanted to try to kiss her again, but she could not be sure. He'd called her *alluring,* but had he meant it?

Gale had poured on pretty compliments at first, when he'd been courting her. He'd obviously not meant them. How was she to know if Rhysdale spoke the truth?

She paused.

Why was she even *thinking* this way?

Her task was not to become enthralled with the handsome owner of the gaming house. He was blowing her off course, robbing her of the power to think straight. She must never allow another man any power over her. Not emotionally. Certainly not legally. Never would she marry again and become the property of a man, legally bound to his every whim.

Once had been enough.

Rhys represented a different sort of bondage, one that captured her thoughts and senses. She had no idea how to cope with the temptation to allow his kiss, to allow what was simmering below the surface to burst forth and consume her.

All Celia needed to do was return to the gaming house and play cards, but that presented another temptation. Rhys's offer encouraged precisely what she should battle. She should eschew the cards and games, not throw herself into playing them. How did she know she would be able to escape when Rhys's employment ended? Would she be able to stop gambling then, or would she become like her father, compelled to return to the tables against all good sense? Gambling might not be content to have merely killed her father and mother and ruined her young life; it could destroy her future, as well.

She started walking again, though her vision was blurred by the storm of thoughts inside her.

There would be no future at all for Adele unless Celia accepted this risk.

Adele was everything to her. The daughter she could never have, even though only a few years younger.

Rhysdale had given Celia this chance to secure Adele's future and Celia must embrace it.

She quickened her pace.

All she needed to do was remain resolute. Resist temptation. Play cards and nothing else. What did she care what Rhys or any man thought?

He'd suggested that men might become attracted to her while she played cards with them. What utter nonsense. If anything, it was the mask and nothing more. The novelty of a disguised woman who liked to play cards.

Rhysdale, though, had seen her face. He'd still thought her alluring.

A frisson of pleasure raced through her. She closed her eyes and again stopped walking.

She was back to Rhysdale. He could so easily invade her thoughts.

How pitiful she was. The first time a man showed her any kindness she turned as giddy as a girl fancying herself in love with Lord Byron after reading *Childe Harold's Pilgrimage*.

Had Rhysdale been the reason she agreed to his proposition? Was he, not money, the reason she agreed to face the gambling demons again?

Chapter Six

That evening William Westleigh, Viscount Neddington, searched Lady Cowdlin's ballroom as he had done every other entertainment he'd attended this Season.

He'd thought she was a vision when he first gazed upon her. Pale skin flushed with youth. Hair a shimmer of gold, its curls looking as artless as if she'd just stepped in from a breezy day. Lips moist and pink as a summer blossom.

She'd turned him into a romantic in an instant. He'd felt both exhilarated and weak when she'd allowed him to assist her in selecting wine at the musicale, but he'd lost her in the crowd afterwards.

He needed an introduction to her. If she appeared tonight—if he found her again—he'd beg someone to do the honours. He'd try his damnedest to dance with her and share supper with her.

Thinking of her was a welcome respite from worry over the finances, the estates, the welfare of his sister and mother. Those matters were largely out of his hands and under the control of his father at the moment.

Unless his father fulfilled the bargain they'd made with Rhysdale, they were about two weeks from disaster.

He walked the rooms of this ball three times without

finding her, but it was early yet and guests continued to arrive.

'The Lord Westleigh and Lady Westleigh,' the butler announced.

Ned twisted away. He was too angry at his father to witness his joviality, as if he had not caused his family the extreme stress that currently plagued them. How his mother could walk at his father's side foxed Ned.

Of course, she did not yet know how severely her husband had squandered their fortune.

If only the beauty he encountered at the musicale would walk in, Ned could momentarily free himself from thoughts of their troubles. He glanced around the room once again, looking everywhere but in the direction of his father.

The butler's voice rang out again. 'Lady Gale, Dowager Lady Gale and Miss Gale.'

Ned turned to the door.

It was she!

She stood a little behind two other ladies, one tall and as young as herself and the other certainly the dowager. This family was unknown to him, but the name *Miss Gale* now pressed into his mind like a hot iron brand.

She was as lovely as he remembered, this night donned in a pale pink gown that had some sort of sheer skirt over it that floated about her as she moved. Her lovely blonde hair was a mass of curls on top of her head and was crowned with pink roses.

As she and the other two ladies made their way to greet the host and hostess, she paused to scan the ballroom and caught him staring at her. He bowed to her and she smiled, ever so slightly, but enough for his hopes to soar.

Hope that he could find someone to present him to her. Hope that she was unattached. Hope that her smile meant she felt the same strong attraction to him that he felt towards her.

Ned kept her in view and occasionally he caught her eye again. But he'd seen no one of his acquaintance talking or dancing with her. The time neared for the supper dance and he was determined to partner her.

He marched over to the hostess. 'Lady Cowdlin, may I beg a favour?'

'A favour?' She patted his hand. 'Tell me what I might do for you.'

'There is a young lady here…' He paused. 'I need an introduction.'

'Who is it, my dear?' She smiled.

'I believe she is Miss Gale.' He inclined his head in her direction.

'Ah, I knew her mother. A lovely lady.' Lady Cowdlin gave him a knowing look. 'I understand, Neddington, that Miss Gale is worth five thousand at least—'

As if he cared a fig about that.

'But she is not very grand. Her father was only a baron, you know. This is her first time in town and Edna—her grandmother—wants her to marry her cousin who inherited the title.'

That was not welcome news. 'Who is her cousin? Do I know him?'

'Luther Parminter. He is the son of her father's cousin. I am certain you have seen him around London. Of course, now he is the new Baron Gale. He inherited, you see.'

Ned knew who the man was, but could not even count him an acquaintance. Now must he think of him as a rival?

Lady Cowdlin took his arm. 'Come with me. Let us make this introduction forthwith.'

She brought him directly to where Miss Gale stood next to her grandmother's chair. Lady Gale stood nearby.

Lady Cowdlin spoke to the dowager. 'Ma'am, may I present this young man to you and the other ladies.'

The dowager looked up.

'This is Lord Neddington.' She turned to the younger Lady Gale, who looked upon him with a quizzical expression. 'Lady Gale and Miss Gale.' She nodded towards Ned. 'Lord Neddington.'

Ned bowed. 'Madams.' He looked into the eyes he'd longed to see up close again. 'Miss Gale.'

She lowered her long thick lashes and curtsied. 'Lord Neddington.'

'May I perform any service for you ladies?' He glanced at Miss Gale. 'Bring you some wine, perhaps?'

She coloured and looked even more lovely.

'That is kind of you, young man.' The Dowager Lady Gale smiled.

'None for me, thank you,' the younger Lady Gale said.

'I will return directly.' He hated to leave Miss Gale's presence.

Ned quickly found a servant toting a tray of wine glasses. He took two and returned to the ladies.

When he handed a glass to Miss Gale, their fingers touched and his senses heightened.

'Thank you, sir,' she murmured.

He took a breath. 'Are you engaged for the supper dance, Miss Gale?'

She lowered her lashes. 'I am not.'

'Adele,' the Dowager Lady Gale broke in. 'I have asked your cousin to claim you for that dance.'

'But, Grandmama…' she murmured.

The younger Lady Gale spoke up. 'He did not ask Adele, though, Lady Gale. Let her decide.' She turned to Miss Gale. 'You do not want to sit out at a ball when you could dance, do you?'

Miss Gale smiled. 'Indeed not.'

Lady Gale faced him. 'Then it is settled.'

Ned peered at this woman who had just helped him engage the dance. He had the oddest notion that he'd seen her before.

Ned bowed. 'I will return for the pleasure of dancing with you, Miss Gale.' He walked away, hoping the supper dance would be announced very soon.

Celia noticed the change in Adele as she danced with Lord Neddington. The girl gave evidence of enjoying every dance and every partner, but never had such a dreamy look crossed her face as when she glanced at this man.

'He is likely a fortune hunter,' Celia's mother-in-law commented.

'Her dowry is respectable, nothing more,' Celia responded. 'Perhaps he just fancies her.' That he visited gaming hells was Celia's prime worry. She'd recognised him immediately.

'Hmmph.' The dowager frowned. 'You ought not to have encouraged that young man, in any event. You know I am determined she should marry her cousin.'

Celia probably should not have encouraged Neddington. She'd done so only to oppose her mother-in-law. And because she'd seen the look in Adele's eye, how much she wanted to dance with the man.

'Luther shows very little interest in Adele, Lady Gale,' Celia said.

Luther was the more likely fortune hunter.

Celia would not see Adele forced into a marriage, but could she allow Adele to marry a gambler? She had seen Lord Neddington at the gaming hell more than once. She could never recall seeing him play more than once or twice at hazard. He spoke to Rhysdale on occasion.

Rhysdale.

Rhys, he'd asked her to call him, although could she really think of him in such intimate terms? Her heart skipped at the mere thought of speaking his name aloud. Her name on his lips came back to her, as well as his smile and the way those lips touched the edge of his teacup.

And had almost touched hers.

She placed her hand over her heart.

She would see him tonight after the ball. And once again yield to the temptations of the gambling den, with no need to wager her own money. She felt a dangerous excitement at the prospect of playing cards with a hundred pounds to wager. Think how much she could win!

The Dowager Lady Gale's voice broke through Celia's thoughts. 'You should have refused Neddington the supper dance. Now he will spend supper with her. That is entirely too much time.'

Her mother-in-law had a point.

Celia gazed in Adele's direction. Adele was glowing with pleasure each time the figures joined her with Neddington. His face was filled with admiration.

Was this how young love appeared?

Celia had been given no chance to experience a youthful romance. She could not bear to take such joy away from Adele.

She turned to her mother-in-law. 'Do not interfere, Lady Gale. Allow your granddaughter the pleasure of supper with an admirer.'

Lady Gale's nostrils flared. 'I've half a mind to fetch her to me for supper.'

Celia seized her arm with just enough pressure to make her point. 'You will do no such thing. Do you hear me clearly?'

Lady Gale shrugged. 'You are indeed a wretch, are you not?'

'Interfere with Adele's life and you will see what a wretch I can be.'

Celia's conflicting wishes for Adele waged inside her. Let the girl choose her suitors. Let her fall in love with whom she wished. But not a man who would be cruel or thoughtless or more enamoured of gaming than of a wife and children. Celia had endured all of those.

Later that night Celia's lady's maid helped her get out of her ballgown and prepare to dress for the Masquerade Club. Celia sat at her dressing table, pulling pins from her hair so that they could fix it to fit under the new turban Younie had fashioned, to go with a new mask of white silk adorned with tiny seed pearls taken from one of her mother-in-law's discarded gowns.

There was a knock on the door and Adele entered. 'Celia, I saw the light under your door.'

Celia grabbed the new mask and hid it under her table. 'I am still awake.'

Younie, new gown in hand, quickly retreated to the dressing room.

Adele flopped onto Celia's bed. 'I cannot sleep!'

Celia brushed out her hair. 'What is the matter?'

Adele stretched and sighed. 'Nothing is the matter! Everything is wonderful!'

'What is so wonderful that you cannot sleep?' Celia asked, although she was certain she knew.

'I had such a lovely time at the ball. The best ever!' Adele sat cross-legged. In her nightdress with her hair in a plait, she looked as young as when Celia first met her six years ago.

Celia smiled. 'And to what do you attribute this pleasure?'

Adele wrapped her arms around herself. 'I—I think I met someone I really like.'

Celia turned back to the mirror. 'Lord Neddington?'

Adele's reflection showed surprise. 'How did you know?'

Celia kept brushing her hair. 'A lucky guess, I suppose.'

'He is so wonderful!' She flopped back onto the bed. 'And so handsome.' She sat up again. 'Do you not think he is handsome?'

'I do,' Celia agreed. 'Very handsome.'

'And very gentlemanly,' Adele continued. 'It was he who helped me procure the wine for you and Grandmama at the musicale. And tonight he fixed me the nicest plate at supper and gave me the choice of sitting with my friends. He was so agreeable, do you not think?'

'Indeed.' Celia had watched Neddington carefully and had seen nothing to object to in his manner towards Adele. It was his activity after the society events that concerned her.

Adele bounded off the bed and paced. 'I do not know how I can sleep. Do you think he will call? I hope he will call. But I'm afraid Grandmama does not like him. Do you think she will send him away if he calls?'

Celia rose and hugged the girl. 'She would not be so impolite.' Celia would see to it.

Adele clung to her. 'But she wants me to marry Cousin Luther and I do not even know him!'

'Leave your grandmother to me. She will not interfere in your wishes.' She loosened her hold on Adele and made the girl look into her eyes. 'But know that neither your grandmother nor I would let you marry a man who was unsuitable.'

'Lord Neddington is very suitable!' Adele cried.

Celia hugged her again. 'Indeed he seems to be, but you must not put your hopes beyond tomorrow. Merely hope he calls and, if he does, see if you still like him so well.'

'I will like him tomorrow and the next day and the next,' Adele cried. 'But will he like me?'

Celia kissed her on the cheek. 'Any man would be a fool not to fall heels over ears in love with you. But you should go to sleep now so you will not have dark shadows under your eyes tomorrow.'

Adele's hands went to her cheeks. 'Oh, my goodness, yes! I must look my very best.' She kissed Celia and hugged her tightly. 'Goodnight, Celia. I hope you sleep well.'

'Sweet dreams,' Celia murmured as Adele rushed out of the room.

Celia breathed a relieved sigh and looked towards her dressing room door. 'It is safe to come out, Younie.'

Her maid appeared in the doorway. 'That was a near go, wasn't it?'

'Indeed.' Celia retrieved the mask from beneath her dressing table. 'We'd best wait until we are certain she is sleeping.'

Celia arrived at the Masquerade Club later than she'd ever done before. Would Rhysdale—Rhys—be angry at her for being late?

She rushed inside, undeterred by the doorman, who seemed to recognise her even with the new gown and mask.

Rhys stood in the hall, as if waiting for her. Her breath caught. He wore an impeccably tailored but conservative black coat and trousers. With his dark hair and glowering expression he looked as dangerous as a highwayman.

'You are late,' he said.

'I had difficulty getting away.' She handed her shawl to the footman and tried not to sound defensive.

Rhys walked her out of the hall and she prepared to hear him ring a peal over her head as soon as they were out of earshot.

But he said nothing. When they stepped up to the cashier's desk, Rhys withdrew. The cashier was the same man who had served the tea in Rhys's drawing room and the only other person connected to the gaming house who had seen her face. He obviously knew precisely who she was, even masked, because he counted out the exact number of counters Rhys had promised her.

As she turned to make her way to the game room, she caught Rhys still standing in the doorway. She forced herself to lift her chin and meet his gaze head-on.

His eyes shone with admiration, much like Neddington's had done when looking upon Adele. 'The new gown is effective.'

Celia felt an unfamiliar rush of feminine pleasure and immediately forced herself to sober. She would not melt at mere compliments.

Her smile was stiff as she clutched her reticule, the counters safe inside. He stepped back for her to pass, but he followed her into the game room.

The room was crowded and she recognised many gentlemen who a couple of hours before had been dancing in Lady Cowdlin's ballroom.

Xavier Campion approached her with his disarming smile. She sensed something unpleasant beneath it.

'Madam.' He bowed. 'Do you fancy a game of whist?'

She glanced at Rhys, who frowned.

'I came to play,' she answered, unsure if she should accept Xavier's invitation or not.

'I will partner you if you wish,' he said.

She glanced back to Rhys, but his back was to her and he was conversing with a group of gentlemen.

'Yes, Mr Campion. Do you have some opponents in mind?'

He smiled again as he took her arm. 'It is Xavier, remember. Let us go in search of some worthy opponents.' His grip was firmer than was necessary. He leaned towards her and murmured in a tone that seemed falsely convivial. 'I understand you are in Rhys's employ. How did you manage that, I wonder?'

She did not miss a beat. 'He made me the offer and I accepted. How else might it have been accomplished?'

'He is my friend,' Xavier said through gritted teeth. 'I will not have him trifled with.'

Celia lifted her chin. 'Rhysdale seems capable of selecting his own employees. Ought I to tell him you think otherwise?' His concern was ridiculous. 'Or perhaps he has asked you to protect him from me?'

Xavier's eyes flashed. 'He does not need to ask. I protect all my friends. Do you tell tales on all of yours?'

'I do not.' Celia paused. 'But, then, you are not my friend, are you?' She shrugged from his grip. 'I have changed my mind, *Mr Campion*. I believe I will try my luck at hazard.'

She left him and did not look back.

It made her feel wonderfully strong. A man had tried to intimidate her and she'd held her own against him.

The hazard table was crowded with mostly men. Celia faltered a bit, then remembered Rhys said she was equally as alluring as his mysterious masked woman who had played here before.

She'd just stood up to a man; perhaps she could also be a little bit alluring.

'Pardon me.' She made herself smile in what she hoped was a flirtatious manner. 'Might a lady play?'

The gentlemen parted. One was the man who had so disturbed Rhys the previous night. Her skin turned to gooseflesh. He, too, had been at Lady Cowdlin's ball.

What did such a gentlemen say to his wife to explain going out again after a ball? Did the wife pace with worry as Celia's mother had done?

'You are welcome to play, my dear.' The gentleman flicked his eyes quickly over her person. 'Have you played before?'

Disgust roiled through her. She remembered Rhys's warning.

She dropped any flirtatious affectations. 'I am accustomed to card games like whist and piquet and *vingt-et-un*. I've not tried a game of dice before.' But tonight she had money she could afford to lose.

The croupier at the hazard table was a pretty young woman with curly red hair. 'Do you play, miss?'

The gentleman rose on his heels in self-importance. 'I will assist the lady, if she so desires.' He scooped up the dice. 'I will stake you for this first round.' He put a pound counter on the table and placed the dice in her hand. 'Call a number between five and nine.'

'Nine,' she called, the date her father died.

'Nine,' he repeated.

Around the table there was a flurry of side-betting accompanying her call.

'They are betting on your chances to win,' he explained. 'If you roll a nine, you will win. If you throw a two or a three, or an eleven or a twelve, you will lose. Now shake the dice in your hand and roll them on the table.'

She shook the dice and threw them down. They landed

in the middle of the green baize, one landing on three, the other, on five.'

'Eight!' the croupier called.

'That is a called a *chance,*' the gentleman explained. 'You did not win, but neither did you lose.' The croupier handed him the dice. 'Roll again.'

He dropped the dice into her palm.

'I want a nine, correct?' She shook the dice in her hand.

'No, this time you want a two or a three to win. Or anything but the *main*—your nine—to continue to roll.'

She dropped the dice onto the table, this time rolling one pip on one die and two on the other.

'Three!' called the croupier. 'A winner.'

Westleigh handed the winnings to her.

A man next to her pushed the dice back to Celia. 'Let the lady keep playing. She has the luck.'

Celia continued to play and to win. The rules of winning and losing changed depending upon what number she chose as chance and she quickly calculated that choosing the numbers five or nine reduced the odds of winning. The crowd around the hazard table grew, most betting with her.

Each time she won she jumped for joy and could not wait to throw the dice again. Her heart was beating fast and her breath as rapid as if she'd run all the way to Oxford Street. Even knowing this gentleman was having a grand time as her host did not dampen her excitement. The impact of his presence faded with each roll of the dice, each possibility that her pile of counters would increase.

As the gentlemen betting with her gathered their winnings, she caught sight of Rhys. He stood at the edge of the crowd, his face a dark cloud.

No wonder he was upset. Every time she—and those who bet with her—won, Rhysdale lost. It woke her from her reverie.

When the dice were again handed to her, she held up her hands. 'I am done, gentlemen.' She made herself smile. 'I wish to keep all these lovely counters.' She'd won at least forty-five pounds.

She gathered her counters and backed away from the table, shocked at herself. She'd lost all sense of time, all reason.

Rationally she should continue to play until losing again and lead her followers to do the same.

She blinked.

Like a swarm of bees around a hive, the other players filled her space at the table and resumed the play.

To her dismay the gentleman who had assisted her was not among them. Instead he remained at her side.

'Allow me to introduce myself.' He bowed. 'I am Lord Westleigh.'

She felt the blood drain from her face. 'Lord Westleigh.'

Lord Westleigh was the man who'd accused her father of cheating at cards, who'd accepted her father's challenge of a duel, who'd fired the pistol ball that pierced her father's heart.

Because he was an earl with friends and influence, he'd walked away from killing her father with impunity, broke her mother's heart, destroyed her health and, in effect, killed her, as well.

Celia tried to remain upright, even though her legs trembled. She tried to keep her face expressionless.

Westleigh waited, as if expecting she would reveal her name.

He finally smiled. 'You will not tell me who you are?'

She took a breath. 'I have chosen to wear a mask. That means I do not wish to reveal myself.'

He laughed. 'I thought you might make me an exception.'

Never for him.

Undaunted by her obvious reserve, he glanced around the room. 'Shall we find some partners for whist?'

'No!' she snapped.

She scanned the crowd for Rhys, needing him. He'd said she should find him if this man bothered her. He was bothering her greatly. He was making her ill.

She caught herself and moderated her tone of alarm. 'I—I am looking for someone.'

Rhys stood some distance away and he did not glance her way.

She found another familiar face. Sir Reginald. 'There he is. I must speak with him.' She inclined her head. 'Thank you for teaching me hazard.'

Before he could protest, she started to cross the room to where Sir Reginald stood, but someone stepped in her way.

Rhys.

Tears of relief pricked her eyes.

He touched her arm. 'I saw you with Westleigh. Was he uncivil to you?'

'Yes,' she blurted out. 'No. Not really. He wanted me to play cards with him.' She took a deep breath. 'I did not know that man was Westleigh. It—it surprised me.'

His brows lowered. 'What do you know of Westleigh?'

'I cannot tell you here.' Her knees weakened.

He must have noticed because he offered her his arm. 'Come with me.'

He walked them to a back staircase, one used by the servants, perhaps. They climbed to the second floor. They passed dark rooms that smelled of sawed wood and linseed and entered the drawing room where he had received her earlier.

He led her directly to the sofa. 'Sit here.'

She removed her mask and rubbed her eyes, trying to

calm herself from the shock of learning she'd spent the greater part of her night in the company of her father's killer.

Rhys handed her a glass. 'Have some brandy.'

She took the glass gratefully and drank, the liquid warming her chest. She sipped more. And finished it.

Rhys sat in an adjacent chair and poured her some more. He asked nothing. Just sat with her.

She finally calmed enough to look up at him. 'Thank you, Rhys.' The brandy was helping. 'I am afraid it was a shock to learn that gentleman was Westleigh.'

He did not press her to tell him more.

Since her mother's death she had spoken to no one about Westleigh, but suddenly it seem too great a burden to carry alone. 'You must wonder why I became so upset.'

He shrugged. 'With Westleigh, nothing would surprise me.'

She stared into his eyes. 'Would it surprise you to learn he killed my father?'

His brows rose, but his gaze did not waver.

She glanced away. 'My father enjoyed gambling…too much. He sometimes played unwisely. He played cards with Lord Westleigh and apparently was winning when Westleigh accused him of cheating.' She looked back to see his reaction to that information. Would he think her father a cheat? 'My father would never cheat. He was outraged and challenged Westleigh to a duel.' She blinked away tears. 'The duel was fought and Westleigh killed my father.' She choked on her words and quickly took another sip of brandy. 'He walked away with impunity.'

The sound of her mother's voice telling her of her father's death returned to her and the horror and grief struck her anew. Dear God, she was about to lose control of her emotions.

He moved from the chair to the sofa and took her into his arms.

Celia collapsed against his chest, heaving with sobs, and he held her and murmured to her. She could not even tell what he said, she just felt his voice, low and rumbling.

It had been so long since she'd been held, so long since anyone had comforted her. The years of loneliness and loss overwhelmed her and his arms were so warm and strong.

She had to pull herself together, though. She could not do this.

Rhys held her close, relishing the feel of her in his arms, but, even more, feeling her pain and wanting to do anything he could to ease it.

Damned Westleigh! The man had killed her father? It was more than even Rhys would have suspected. Fighting a duel over a game of cards was foolish beyond belief. Killing a man over cards was a million times worse.

'There, there,' he murmured, realising he sounded like his mother. His own throat tightened with the memory of her loss. Another deed he could throw at Westleigh's feet. His mother might have lived a long happy life if not for that cursed man.

She pulled away, wiping her eyes with her fingers. 'I am so sorry.'

He handed her his handkerchief. 'Do not say so.'

'It is the surprise of seeing him.' She blew her nose. 'I wondered how it would be. I did not know I would turn into a watering pot.'

He suspected that weeping was not something she often allowed of herself. 'What would you like me to do about Westleigh?'

She gaped at him in surprise. '*Do* about him?'

'It cannot be comfortable for you that he comes here.

I can prevent him, if you like.' Rhys disliked seeing the man here anyway.

She finished her second glass of brandy. 'I do not know what to say. I do not know what to think. I do not want him to know who I am.'

Rhys did not know who she was.

Her face hardened. 'I would like to make him pay in some way.'

'Revenge?' He well knew the need for revenge.

'Yes!' She covered her mouth with her hand. 'I suppose that is wrong of me.'

A corner of his mouth turned up. 'Quite natural, I would say. You are probably one of many who would like revenge on Lord Westleigh.'

She peered into his eyes. 'You detest him, as well.'

He could explain to her that Westleigh was his father, but, at the moment, the idea that the blood of such a man flowed in his veins filled him with disgust. He did not wish to take the chance she would feel the same.

They could each keep their secrets from the other, could they not?

He held her gaze. 'I detest him. It will give me pleasure to throw him out for you.'

She stared for a moment, as if thinking, then shook her head. 'It would not do to ban an earl from your gaming house, would it? Especially one who likes to gamble. I would never ask this of you.'

'Nonetheless,' he responded. 'It would be my pleasure to do so, if it will ease your mind.'

She reached over and touched his hand. 'It is enough to know I have an ally.' She withdrew her hand almost as quickly and turned away. When she turned back, she smiled the ghost of a smile. 'Perhaps there is some restitution I can force on him. Engage him in a card game and win all his money…'

As if he had any sum of money to lose, Rhys thought.

She straightened. 'At least that would be something, would it not?'

He would have preferred an excuse to toss Westleigh out on his ear, although her course was undoubtedly the wiser for both of them. He preferred a more subtle revenge, one that would cause Westleigh even greater pain.

'It will be as you wish.'

She dabbed at her face again and folded his handkerchief. 'I will launder and return this.'

He waved that away. 'It is of no consequence.'

She picked up her mask. 'I have taken up enough of your time. We should return to the game room, do you not think?'

Leaving her was the last thing on his mind, but she was correct. He should get back. 'You may stay here, if you wish. Stay until it is time for your coachman.'

She shook her head. 'I think it is like falling from one's pony. One must remount immediately.'

She'd ridden a pony? Riding a pony seemed unlikely for an actress.

He'd pursue that thought another time. 'Then I will go down first. You may follow a moment later. It will not seem as if we have been together.'

She gave him a grateful smile.

They both rose. She lifted the mask to her face and fussed with its ribbons. He stepped behind her and tied the mask in place.

She stood very still as he did so.

When he finished, his hands hovered over her shoulders, wanting to explore more of her.

Instead, he stepped away and walked out of the room.

* * *

Down in the game room, he found Westleigh almost immediately, laughing at something his companion had said. Westleigh caught his gaze and froze for a moment, an icy expression on his face. Rhys returned the unfriendly glare and resumed his patrol of the room.

In a few moments Celia appeared, searching the room, her reaction to finding Rhys as warm as Westleigh's had been cold. She appeared perfectly composed, strolling to where Sir Reginald stood.

Sir Reginald greeted her like a long-lost friend. This man was a member of the aristocracy who Rhys could like. Sir Reginald was kind and friendly to everyone.

Westleigh also noticed Celia's entrance. Rhys watched him leave his friend and make a beeline to where Celia stood.

Xavier appeared beside Rhys. 'Would you mind telling me what all this is about?'

'All what?' Rhys countered.

Xavier inclined his head towards Celia and Westleigh.

Rhys waved a dismissive hand. 'Nothing of consequence, I am certain.'

Xavier frowned. 'Between Westleigh and the woman who captivates you? Do not take me for a fool.'

Celia watched Westleigh make his way across the room and knew he was coming after her. She cast a glance towards Rhys. He stood close by.

She turned to Sir Reginald. 'Do you need a whist partner tonight, sir?'

Sir Reginald smiled in a jolly way. 'Is that an invitation, madam? If so, I would be honoured.'

Westleigh came up to her side. 'There you are, my dear. I feared I had lost you forever.'

She inclined her head slightly and spoke without expression. 'Lord Westleigh.'

He bowed. 'Are you ready for our game of whist?'

He presumed she would play cards with him? 'I fear you are too late.' She managed to sound civil. 'Sir Reginald and I will be playing.'

That did not daunt him. 'Whist? You will need partners, certainly. Allow me and my companion to challenge you to a game.'

Whist had been the game that Westleigh had played with her father that fateful night.

Her eyes narrowed.

Sir Reginald broke in. 'Madam, I am completely at your disposal. We do need partners, but I leave it to you to say who that should be.'

She glanced over to Rhys, who had stepped away from his friend, but looked her way.

He was still near.

It emboldened her. 'Very well. Sir Reginald and I will play whist with you.'

Westleigh fetched his companion. Celia wondered if his companion had been his partner when Westleigh engaged her father in play. If so, why had the man not intervened? Someone should have stopped such folly.

They took their places at a card table and the cards were dealt.

Soon Celia focused on the play instead of the detested player who sat at her right, too often brushing his arm against hers or fussing over her counters as if it were his job to tend to her.

The play was tame. Westleigh and his partner were particularly predictable in which cards they put down and when. Even Sir Reginald's limited skills more than outmatched them. Westleigh could not have been a challenge to her father, who was very good at whist. Her father would have had no reason to cheat.

That knowledge was like a burden lifted from her shoulders. She now had no doubts that the charge of cheating against her father had been unfounded.

It also made Westleigh's actions that night all the more reprehensible.

Perhaps the revenge she could enact against him was to play cards with him as often as she could. To take as much of his money as she could. It would probably not put a dent in an earl's fortune, but it would be some restitution—the sort of restitution her father might admire.

While Sir Reginald shuffled the cards for the next hand, Celia glanced around the room, as she often did, looking for Rhys. Instead, her gaze caught upon Lord Neddington.

It did not please her that this young man was so frequent a visitor to this place. She had no wish for Adele to be enamoured of a gambler.

Celia watched Neddington walk through the room aimlessly. He turned towards her table and she quickly averted her eyes, but Neddington was not concerned with her. He was scowling at Lord Westleigh.

At least that was in the young man's favour.

Between hands Celia kept tabs on Neddington who walked around, but never seemed to gamble. How odd. It did make her a bit less concerned about his character, though.

After several games Westleigh's partner threw up his hands. 'No more!' He turned to Celia. 'You have emptied my pockets, madam.'

He was even worse a player than Westleigh.

She smiled good-naturedly. 'Perhaps you would like a rematch another night, sir.'

He laughed. 'A night when luck is with me.' He winked. 'At least I won when you played hazard. We must coax you back to the hazard table, must we not, Westleigh?' He turned to the earl.

'It would be my pleasure to play whatever game the lady wishes.' Westleigh eyed her in the same manner her husband had done before they were married.

It made her cheeks burn.

Sir Reginald, so harmless and friendly, said, 'Well, madam, you may count on me to partner you any time.'

'You are an excellent partner, Sir Reginald.' She dropped her counters into her reticule and stole a glance at her watch. It was nearly time for her coach to arrive.

She stood.

Westleigh took her elbow. 'Shall we play more hazard, my dear?'

'Thank you, no.' She drew her arm away. 'I bid you gentlemen goodnight.'

She looked for Rhys, but he was not in the game room, so she made her way to the cashier and repaid the hundred pounds she'd not touched in her play. At the end, she carried away over seventy pounds. The huge sum filled her with guilt. Winning at hazard would cost Rhys directly. It was a poor way to repay his generosity.

Celia wanted to see Rhys before she left. After cashing out, she glanced in the supper room, but he was not there. She asked the hall servant where Rhys was.

'Drawing room,' the man told her.

Celia climbed the stairs. As she neared the doorway to the drawing room, she heard Rhys's voice and held back.

'Your concern is unfounded, Xavier,' Rhys said. 'And insulting, as well.'

'Insulting?' His friend's voice rose.

'I am well able to make my own decisions about business and about women.' Rhys spoke with heat. 'I do not caution you against dallying with any of the several women who vie for your attention, you know.'

'There would be no need.' Xavier's tone was just as angry. 'I know how to handle women.'

'And I do not?' Rhys countered.

'Come now.' Xavier turned placating. 'This infatuation with the masked woman is something else. You do not know who she is. Or what she wants.'

'She wants what I want. Money,' Rhys answered. 'And she has given me her name. That is enough for me.'

'Rhys—' Xavier began.

'Enough,' Rhysdale broke in. 'I need you as a friend, not a nursemaid. Do not press me further on this matter.'

Celia stepped away from the doorway as Xavier strode out of the room. Seeing her, he hesitated only briefly, long enough to look half-apologetic, half-provoked. He continued on his way down the stairs.

She knocked on the door.

Chapter Seven

'May I speak to you, Rhys?'

Rhys turned in surprise at the sound of her voice. 'Celia! Come in. Close the door.'

She looked wounded, as well she might. He'd been about to pour himself some brandy. Now he needed it even more.

He lifted the decanter. 'Would you like a glass?'

She nodded.

'How much of that did you hear?' he asked as he poured.

She took the glass from his hand. 'Enough to know that Mr Campion does not like that you hired me.'

He'd been afraid of that.

'It is none of his affair,' he assured her. 'He thinks he is acting out of friendship.'

'If my employment causes you a problem—' she began.

'You cause me no problem.' He reached over and gently removed her mask. 'That is better.' He brushed a lock of hair off her face and gestured to the sofa. 'Please sit, Celia.'

By God, she looked lovely this night. The white of her gown was embroidered with a cascade of flowers created from shimmering silver thread. In the game room amongst the sea of black-coated men, she'd glowed like moonlight.

She lowered herself onto the sofa where she'd sat before. Where he'd held her before.

'I did not mean to overhear,' she said. 'I only came upstairs to thank you again. And to let you know that I managed being in Westleigh's company without too much distress.'

'I was watching.' He sat in the nearby chair. 'I also noticed that you won.'

'I did.' She shook her head. 'He is a terrible player.'

Their conversation was stilted and devoid of the intimacy they had so recently shared in this room. That she'd overheard Xavier did not help.

'Terrible?' That knowledge pleased him. Rhys was a master of cards. He took a sip of brandy. 'A competent card player would have no need to cheat against him, then.'

Her face shone with pleasure. 'You have guessed my thoughts.'

She looked even more lovely.

He took another sip. 'How much did you win?'

'From Westleigh and his partner? About twenty-five pounds.'

His brows rose. 'So much?'

She waved a hand. 'They were reckless in their betting, as well. I decided to play him as much as I can. Take as much of his money as I can.' Her voice cracked. 'For my father.'

He understood her need for revenge, but it puzzled him. How did Westleigh have that much to lose? He was supposed to be on a tight leash regarding his spending.

She lowered her gaze. 'I must confess that I won much more than the twenty-five pounds from Westleigh. I won even more from hazard.'

He'd noticed. 'You had a winning streak. How much did you win finally?'

She looked apologetic. 'Fifty pounds.' She quickly added. 'I know it was not well done of me. It is a great deal of money out of your pocket.' She opened her reticule. 'I wanted to see you so I could pay it back. I only regret I cannot repay all that the patrons betting with me must have won.'

He pushed the reticule away. 'I'll not take your winnings. And do not concern yourself about the gentlemen betting with you. Those who stayed at the hazard table will have lost it all again. Or will another night.' He gazed at her. 'Not everyone is so wise as to stop when ahead.'

'I was not wise....' She made a nervous gesture with her hand. 'To own the truth, I was terrified. The excitement made me lose all sense.'

'Not all sense, or you would have played until your reticule was empty.' He finished his brandy. 'That excitement is all part of the game. I have been a gambler too long not to have felt that same exhilaration.'

'It makes a person foolish,' she rasped. 'I cannot afford to be foolish. It will hurt me, but tonight my foolishness hurt you.'

'Gambling is always a risk, but remember that this was a risk I agreed to take. This night you won and I lost. Tomorrow it may be different. We will keep an eye on it.' He reached over again and touched her cheek. 'Do not fear. I will not let you be harmed by it.'

Her eyes grew wider and her fair skin glowed like an angel's.

Xavier was right when accusing him of wanting to make her a conquest. He wanted her as intensely as a man could desire a woman. But Rhys also genuinely liked her. He felt a kinship with her.

It was rare for him to feel kinship with anyone. He'd long ago accepted that he was alone in the world. He even expected to lose Xavier's friendship eventually, when the man finally found a woman he wished to marry. Xavier's allegiance would shift, as it should, to a wife and family of his own making.

Or perhaps his friendship with Xavier was ending over Celia.

Rhys dared not hope for anything more than temporary with Celia. No doubt her secrets would eventually separate them.

As his secrets might from her.

But for the moment he relished her company. When had a woman ever made him feel such sympathy as he felt towards her? He wished he could make Westleigh pay for killing her father, for bringing her such pain.

He wanted to enfold her in his arms and take all her pain away.

He looked into her eyes. 'I like you, Celia Allen.'

Her eyes darted around the room. He'd frightened her.

She smiled nervously at him. 'You have been…like a friend. I cannot tell you how grateful I am to you for paying me to gamble. For enduring my fit of tears over Westleigh.'

He held up a hand.

She twisted the laces of her reticule. 'I should go. My coachman will be here soon.'

He stood and offered her his hand. She hesitated a moment before placing her hand in his. He pulled her to her feet, but did not stop there. He pulled her into an embrace.

He could not tell if she was alarmed or pleased.

'I suspect we are two of a kind, Celia,' he said. 'I am glad you are in my employ. I am glad I will see you night after night.'

Her eyes grew huge and her voice trembled. 'You are holding me. Are—are you going to kiss me?'

'Is it what you wish?' He could feel the rise and fall of her breast against his chest.

It fired his senses, but he waited. She must want this, too.

She rose, no more than an inch, but it was all the invitation he needed.

He lowered his mouth to hers.

Her lips were warm, soft and tasting of brandy and he wanted more, much more. She melted into him and her lips pressed upon his, as if she, too, could not get enough. He lost himself in the pleasure of her, his hands eager to explore her, undress her, pleasure her—

She broke away. 'This is not wise, Rhys,' she cried.

His body was still humming with need, but he forced himself to give her the space she needed.

'You are sounding like Xavier.' He smiled. 'It probably was not wise to hire you in the afternoon and kiss you in the night, but I do not feel like being wise with you, Celia. I want more from you.'

Her eyes grew big. 'More from me?'

Did she not understand?

He would be clear. 'I want you in my bed.'

She stepped away. 'I—I do not know.'

He honoured her distance. 'It is your choice, Celia. No matter what you decide, our employment agreement still stands.'

Her expression turned puzzled. 'My choice,' she said to herself.

The clock on his mantel chimed four bells, causing them both to jump.

She rubbed her forehead. 'I must go. I am already late. My driver will be concerned.'

He reached out and took her hand. 'Tomorrow, give your driver a later time.'

She looked like a frightened deer.

He did not wish her to bolt. 'Do not distress yourself,' he spoke in a soothing voice. 'You know what I want, but do not let that keep you from coming back and gambling. You need not answer me now. I am a patient man.'

She stared at him, but finally said, 'I will think about it.'

It was not the answer he had hoped for, but he contented himself that it was not a definite no.

'Do not think.' He touched her cheek. 'Feel.'

She made a sound deep in her throat, before turning away from him and hurrying towards the door.

'Celia,' he called to her.

She stopped and looked over her shoulder at him.

'You forgot your mask.' He picked up the piece of white silk and crossed the room to her. 'Stay still. I will put it on you,' he said.

Her breath accelerated as he affixed the mask to her face and tied the ribbons that held it in place.

'There you go,' he murmured.

She stepped away, but turned and gave him a long glance.

He opened the door. 'I will walk you to your coach.'

As they left the room he kept his distance, but walked at her side down the stairs to the hall where Cummings quickly retrieved her shawl. She put it on herself carelessly, but as soon as they were out the door, he wrapped her in it to protect her from the misty night's chill. Almost immediately the sound of her coach reached their ears even before it became visible.

She stepped forwards so her coachman could see her. He stopped the horses and Rhys lowered the steps. He squeezed her hand as he helped her into the coach.

He watched her face in the window as the coach started off, disappearing into the mist as if only a dream.

* * *

The next day Rhys sounded the knocker at the West-leigh town house. It was time to confront Westleigh. He'd had enough of the man, especially after what he'd learned from Celia.

He was ready to drop the whole bargain with the West-leighs, but Celia wished her revenge and Rhys would not deny her it. He would, however, push along his own dealings with the Westleighs and be done with them.

A footman opened the door.

'Mr Rhysdale to see Lord Westleigh.' Rhys handed the footman his card.

The footman stepped aside and gestured for him to enter the hall. 'Wait here a moment.'

The last time Rhys called at this house, he'd been escorted into the drawing room. Why not now?

Likely Westleigh had left instructions to treat him like a tradesman.

The footman disappeared towards the back of the house.

Rhys gazed at the marble-tiled floors and swirling staircase. Such grandeur in contrast to the set of rooms in which he and his mother had lived. Or how he had lived after her death.

Gazing at it all, Rhys realised this was not what he wanted in life. Yes, he wanted comfort, but comfort would be enough. More than anything, he wanted to build something. A business. A factory. Something useful. He wanted not to be like his father, who had wasted his life and squandered his fortune.

He did not give a fig about being acknowledged as Westleigh's bastard son. In fact, he'd just as soon not be known to have the connection. He'd go through with it, though, only because it was *his* revenge against Westleigh. He would make the man do what he would detest the most, what he ought to have done when Rhys was born—to declare openly that Rhys was his son.

This bargain with the Westleighs had become like a game of cards. Westleigh behaved as if he held all the trumps, but he was bluffing. It was time to up the ante and win the hand.

It was a gamble. Everything in life was a gamble. Westleigh could choose poverty over admitting Rhys was his son, but how likely was that? Rhys knew a good bet when he saw one.

A servant who could only have been the butler entered the hall. He lifted his nose at Rhys. 'Do you have an appointment with his lordship?'

Rhys glared at the man and used the voice he'd once used to command men in his regiment. 'I do not need an appointment. Announce me to Lord Westleigh.'

The butler shrank back and quickly ascended the stairs. Rhys's eyes followed him. Westleigh would show himself promptly or Rhys would go in search of him.

A huge allegorical painting hung in the hall. Rhys turned to examine it. The painting depicted Minerva, representing wisdom, pushing Mars, the god of war, away from the goddess of peace. He chuckled to himself. Would Minerva prevail with Westleigh? Or would he and Westleigh engage in battle?

A woman's voice said, 'Ned! I thought you had gone.'

He turned to see a finely dressed woman descending the stairs.

She looked startled. 'I beg your pardon. I thought you were my son.'

He recognised her from the times he'd glimpsed her in his old village, an older but still beautiful Lady Westleigh.

He bowed. 'Allow me to present myself, my lady. I am Mr Rhysdale, here to speak with your husband.'

Her eyes flickered at the mention of his name. Did she know of him? Did she remember that poor woman who'd once been in her service so many years ago?

'Mr Rhysdale.' Her voice tightened. 'Perhaps you can tell me why you call upon my husband.'

'I have no objection to doing so, ma'am, although perhaps Lord Westleigh ought to be present.' He inclined his head. 'As a courtesy.'

She swept across the hall. 'Come into the drawing room. I will ring for tea.'

It was the same room where he had spoken to Ned and Hugh. She pulled a bell cord and the butler appeared.

'Some tea, Mason,' Lady Westleigh ordered. 'Do sit, Mr Rhysdale.'

He waited for her to lower herself into a chair and chose one a distance from her that she might consider comfortable.

She could not look at him.

Rhys took pity on her. She was merely one more person who had been ill-used by Lord Westleigh. 'I surmise you know who I am, my lady.'

She glanced at him and gathered some pluck. 'Why would you show your face here, after all this time?'

He spoke gently. 'Your sons involved me...' he paused, trying to think how to say it '...in a business matter.'

Her mouth opened in surprise. 'Ned and Hugh?'

'Yes.'

Lord Westleigh thundered in. 'See here, Rhysdale. You were told to wait in the hall.' He came to a sudden halt. 'Honoria!'

'Charles.' Her lips thinned.

Rhys rose. 'Lady Westleigh happened upon me and was gracious enough to invite me into the drawing room.'

'Yes, well.' Westleigh wiped his brow. 'Thank you, Honoria. You may leave. This does not concern you.'

She remained in her seat. 'Mr Rhysdale has no objection to my presence.'

Westleigh tossed him a scathing look. 'It is a matter of business, Honoria. You would find it tedious.'

She smiled at him. 'Oh, since it also involves Ned and Hugh, as I understand, I doubt I should find it tedious. You know that nothing about my sons is trivial to me.'

'Did you think you could conceal the whole from Lady Westleigh?' Rhys asked him. 'I do not see how, unless you decided to go back on your word. Which is why I am here. To determine once and for all if you intend to keep to the bargain your sons made on your behalf.'

The butler brought in the tea tray, halting the conversation at that point. He placed the tray on the table in front of Lady Westleigh. 'Thank you, Mason,' she said.

The butler bowed and turned to leave, but she called him back. 'Mason? If Hugh is about, tell him to join us, please.'

The man bowed again. 'As you wish, my lady.'

When he left the room and closed the door behind him, Lord Westleigh spoke again. 'We do not need Hugh here.'

'I would not talk behind his back,' his wife countered. 'I would invite Ned, as well, but he went out a little while ago.'

Rhys realised his revenge upon his father was certainly going to hurt his wife, which suddenly gave Rhys no pleasure. Still, it was better than the complete financial ruin of the family.

'Shall we wait for Hugh?' Rhys asked the lady.

'I would prefer it,' she said. 'Do sit, Mr Rhysdale. How do you take your tea?'

'No cream. No sugar.'

* * *

Ned was surprised at the modest accommodations Miss Gale had on Half Moon Street. He'd expected something grander—not that it mattered to him. She just looked as if she belonged in luxury, protected from any discomfort or stress.

Not that he could provide her such a setting at the moment. He really had no business courting her, except that he could not bear it if her heart went to another.

He sounded the knocker and was admitted by the butler who announced him.

He entered the drawing room where Miss Gale sat with her stepmother and grandmother.

Also present was Luther Parminter, the new Baron Gale.

He bowed to the ladies.

The grandmother frowned in an unwelcoming manner, but Lady Gale extended her hand. 'How nice of you to call, Neddington.'

He glanced to where Miss Gale was seated with the baron. 'Am I interrupting a family visit? Do forgive me.'

'Nonsense,' the young Lady Gale said. 'You are welcome here. Join us.' She gestured to a chair near Miss Gale. 'Shall I pour you some tea?'

'I'll not trouble you.' He bowed to Miss Gale.

She sat in a pool of sunlight from the window, her hair shining like spun gold. Her skin was flawless and her eyes sparkling and clear as a cloudless sky.

She robbed him of speech.

He glanced from her to Luther, whom he'd known in school. 'Gale.'

'Neddington,' Luther said without expression.

Ned was distressed to see him here. Was he courting Miss Gale? Most people liked to keep their wealth and property in the family. Lady Cowdlin said Miss Gale's dowry was a generous one. Was that why Luther was here?

Still, if she had a large dowry, why did she live in such economy?

'I hope you are well today, sir,' she murmured to him.

'Very well, miss,' he responded.

'Hmmph,' the Dowager Lady Gale broke in. 'Our cousin Luther was telling us about Gale House and its people. And the news from the village. We have always made it a point to concern ourselves with the needs of the people, you know.'

Ned turned to Gale. 'I hope you found the people at Gale House in a good situation.'

'Of course,' Luther snapped.

The man was as happy to see Ned here as Ned was to see him. It depressed Ned that he might have a rival. Ned had so little to offer, how could he compete?

His family's partnership with Rhysdale must reap its hoped-for benefits. It all depended upon his father.

Ned could hardly abide the presence of his father these days; he was so angry with the man. His father was being stubborn about Rhysdale and could ruin everything. They'd be worse off than before.

Then there would be no use in pursuing Miss Gale at all.

They chatted about the ball the night before. At one point Luther pulled out his timepiece and examined it.

A few minutes later, Luther stood. 'I must take my leave.' He bowed to Miss Gale, her stepmother and grand-mother. 'Ladies, it has been a pleasure.' He tossed an un-happy glare at Ned.

After he left, Miss Gale asked Ned about the weather.

It gave him courage. 'I wonder if you would like to take a turn in the park this afternoon, Miss Gale. I would consider it an honour to drive you in my curricle.' He turned to her stepmother. 'With your permission, ma'am.'

Lady Gale smiled. 'If Adele wishes.'

'Oh, I do!' she cried. 'I mean, I would like that very much, my lord.'

Miss Gale's grandmother frowned.

He rose. 'Then I shall return at four.' A good three hours. How would he be able to pass that much time knowing he would have her company all to himself?

And with everyone else crowding Hyde Park during the fashionable hour.

Ned took his leave, his heart soaring.

'What is this?' Hugh entered the Westleigh town house drawing room. 'Rhysdale, what are you doing here?'

Rhys was accustomed to Hugh's brashness. He had always been so.

Rhys straightened and glanced at each of them. 'I will not prevaricate. I came to get what is due me. I fulfilled my part of our bargain and—' he turned to Lord Westleigh '—you, sir, have not fulfilled yours. I am done being trifled with.'

'See here, Rhysdale—' Lord Westleigh snapped.

'What bargain?' Lady Westleigh asked.

Rhys gestured to Westleigh and Hugh to explain.

Hugh glared at his father. 'You explain it to her, Father.'

Lord Westleigh, still standing, wrung his hands.

'Well.' He looked at his wife. 'Your sons made the plan. Just because finances have become a little strained these days—'

'A little strained!' Hugh broke in. 'It is more serious than that.' He turned to his mother. 'We are a hair's breadth from complete ruin. We owe everybody and Father has not kept up with payments to the bank, for money he borrowed to cover his gambling debts.'

Her gaze flew to her husband, who did not deny this. 'What has this to do with Mr Rhysdale?'

Hugh answered her. 'Ned and I went to him with a proposition.' He explained the scheme to run a gaming house. 'But Father will not do what he gave his word he would do.'

'What is that?' Lady Westleigh asked.

Her husband made a sound of disgust.

Rhys spoke up. 'My lady, I fear what I've asked may cause you some distress. For that, I am sorry.' He riveted his gaze on his father and spoke only to him. 'I once came to you with one request—to support me after my mother died until I had a means of supporting myself. You refused. Now I have no need of your money, so I ask more.' He turned back to Lady Westleigh. 'Your husband must acknowledge me publicly as his natural son. It must seem to society that I am welcomed into the family. I do not ask for a true welcome,' he assured her. 'This is more a matter of recompense. But I insist upon a plan for this to be done and done soon. If it is not accomplished in a reasonable length of time, I will not release any of the money from the gaming hell to your sons.'

Hugh swung around to his mother. 'We need the money, Mother. We need it *now*. Matters are desperate.' His eyes shot daggers at his father. 'If you had behaved with any decency, with any thought to our mother and sister, you would have done the right thing in the first place and you certainly would not have gambled and caroused until money for their food and clothing would be in jeopardy!'

Lady Westleigh's eyes grew huge. 'Is it as bad as that?'

'It is desperate, Mother. Desperate.' Hugh dropped into a chair.

The lady closed her eyes and pressed her fingers to her

temples as she took in all this information. Finally she spoke. 'We shall give a ball and introduce you, Mr Rhysdale. I'll arrange the date with you, but it might take a few weeks. The social calendar is full. You will, I presume, wish to have good attendance.' She lifted her chin. 'I will give you my word that it will happen. Will that be enough to release some of the money?'

Rhys stood. '*Your* word will be enough, my lady. I will release the money to Ned today. Have him call upon me this afternoon.' He turned to Lord Westleigh. 'If you prevent this ball in any way, no further profits will be forthcoming.'

'I have no other choice, do I?' Westleigh said.

'As my mother had no choice when you forced her into your bed. As I had no choice but to survive on my own when I was fourteen.' He bowed to Lady Westleigh. 'I will act in a manner that will not embarrass you, my lady. It will suffice that the truth become known.'

She nodded.

'Hugh.' He nodded to his half-brother. 'I'll bid you all good day.'

As he left the house and walked out to the street, he lacked the feeling of triumph that he'd expected. Instead he thought of Lady Westleigh. Her pained expression. Her evident distress.

He'd succeeded in putting his father in a helpless position, but in so doing he'd hurt someone even more helpless. Lady Westleigh.

Another casualty of his father's selfish behaviour.

But it was done.

Rhys would make arrangements with his bank and get the money to Ned this day.

Sun peeked through the buildings and Rhys was reminded of his youth in the village. It had not all been unhappy. He remembered running over hills, fishing in the river, climbing the highest tree he could find to look down on a world where he ordinarily felt quite small. The seeds of his ambition were sowed in that childhood—to succeed. To build something lasting.

The world was changing. The gaming hell belonged to a past where a few had so much money they could throw it away on dice and cards. The future belonged to men with brains and courage, no matter who parented them. Rhys had brains and courage and, with the help of the gaming hell, he'd soon have enough capital to build anything he liked.

His thoughts turned to Celia Allen as the sun warmed the air and lit the buildings in a golden light. Which world did she belong to? He no longer knew. He only knew that in the gaming hell, they were one of a kind.

Would she share his bed this night?

Would she approve of his actions this day?

Not that he would ever tell her, but, somehow his visit to the Westleighs, the family to which he would never truly belong, had left him feeling abandoned.

He wanted the comfort of her arms, her kiss.

He looked up to cross the street and saw Ned approaching from the other side. He stopped and waited. He might as well inform Ned about the afternoon's events.

Ned walked right past him, not pointedly cutting him, as was typical of him, but apparently utterly oblivious.

Rhys called after him, 'Ned!'

Ned stopped then and shook his head as if in a daze. He finally turned around. 'Oh, Rhys. I did not see you there.'

He must be dazed. He called him Rhys, not Rhysdale.

He peered at Ned. 'Are you unwell?'

Ned laughed. 'Not at all. Merely thinking.'

The man looked like a sapskull. 'What is so engrossing?'

Ned grinned. 'Nothing.'

Oh. A woman.

A man only acted in such a manner when he was a besotted fool. 'May I pull your head from the clouds?'

Ned sobered. 'What is it?'

'I've come from your father.' Their father, he meant. 'I have forced the issue with him and I am satisfied that my introduction to society will happen soon. I am prepared to transfer the money back to you. Your original investment and some modest profits.'

Ned brightened. 'My father came through? I feared he would not.' He grasped Rhys's arm. 'This means... This means... We may retrench. We may actually pull out of this!'

Rhys recoiled from this unexpected camaraderie. 'Do not be so hasty. It is not all song and celebration. I am afraid this matter has caused your mother some distress. For that, I am regretful.'

'My mother?' Ned's demeanour blackened. 'Did Father tell her?'

'I did,' Rhys said. 'Although not by design. She encountered me in the hall.'

Ned lowered his head, his euphoria gone.

Rhys felt badly for him. 'Think, Ned. She would have to know of this.'

'I realise that,' Ned responded. 'I just hate what this does to her.'

Rhys actually felt sympathetic to Ned. 'If it is any consolation, she knew who I was as soon as I told her my name.'

Ned nodded. 'That does not surprise me. I am certain, though, that she did not know the state of our finances.'

'Yes, I do think that shocked her,' Rhys admitted. 'I admired her. She handled the whole situation with exceptional grace.'

Ned glanced up at him. 'She is an exceptional woman.'

Rhys clapped Ned on the soldier, surprising himself that their conversation was devoid of hostility. 'Come with me to Coutts Bank. I'll transfer the money to you right now.'

'Excellent!' Ned's mood improved. 'But I must be done by four o'clock.'

'We'll be done,' Rhys assured him.

Celia excused herself after two of her mother-in-law's friends came to call. Adele had already begged to be excused so that she might ready herself for her ride in Hyde Park.

It was endearing to see Adele so excited and happy. This past year of mourning had been so difficult. First the shock of their financial situation, then what amounted to an eviction from the only home Adele had ever known.

And now Luther thought he could court Adele?

Not if Celia could help it.

Although Celia was unsure about Neddington, as well.

But she was getting ahead of herself. Adele was engaged only for a ride in Hyde Park, not marriage.

Celia retreated to her bedchamber.

Her lady's maid emerged from her dressing room. 'Good afternoon, ma'am.' She lifted a gown she carried in her arms. 'I came in for this. Needs some mending.'

'Thank you, Younie.' Celia smiled. 'I am surprised to see you here, though. I thought Adele would be running you in circles to get ready for Hyde Park.'

'Oh, I am to go to her in one half hour,' Younie said. 'After she has rested so the dark circles under her eyes disappear.'

'What dark circles?' Adele looked as fresh-faced as ever.

Younie chuckled. 'The ones in her imagination, I expect. It is best to go along with these notions, though. You cannot convince a girl that age of anything.'

'I am certain you are right.' Celia had never had an opportunity to be so young and infatuated. She'd been married two years by the time she was Adele's age. Love seemed impossible.

An image of Rhys flew into her mind.

'And what of you, ma'am?' Younie asked. 'Do you go out tonight?'

Celia knew what she meant. 'After the theatre? Yes.'

Her insides fluttered.

She could hardly think of anything else but going to the Masquerade Club tonight. Or that Rhys wanted to bed her.

Her body roused as if he'd again been near. Could Younie tell? she wondered.

'Which gown do you wear tonight?' Younie asked, appearing not to notice anything amiss.

Celia wished she had something new and even more fashionable to wear tonight. She wanted him to look on her with admiration.

Which made her not much unlike Adele, she supposed.

Celia sat at the dressing table and peered at her reflection. 'Do you think I have dark circles?'

Her maid clucked. 'You ought to have, with the amount of sleep you are getting.'

She looked closer, pulling the skin under her eye taut to examine it better. 'Oh, dear, is it taking a toll?'

Younie put her fists on her waist. 'Does it look like you only sleep four or five hours? No. No one would know.'

'That is good,' Celia murmured.

Younie picked up the dress again and walked over to her. 'You ought to rest, ma'am. You need it more than the young miss.'

'Excellent advice.' Celia touched the woman's hand.

'Perhaps I will lie down a little. Will you make certain I am up before Adele leaves?'

'That I can do! Shall I untie your laces?' Younie asked.

'Yes. I'll take off the dress only, though. I can lie down in my shift and corset.'

After Younie helped her from her gown, the maid left. Celia climbed into the bed.

And thought about Rhys.

His invitation was scandalous.

And exciting.

He *liked* her, he'd said. And he had been kind to her. And protective, all of which was extremely novel to her. Besides, he was young and vital and strong. What would it be like to lie with such a man?

She was inexperienced, but not naive. One could not be naive having been married to a wastrel like Gale. She well knew that men and women engaged in affairs without being married.

What would she discover if she allowed herself to accept Rhys's proposition? Would she feel pleasure?

His kiss had promised pleasure. It made her yearn for more.

That was what shocked her.

She hugged herself and imagined his arms around her again.

Would there be any harm in having an affair with him? Plenty of widows had affairs and society turned their eyes away from it. She would never marry again, so this might be her only chance to see what the sexual act would feel like with a man other than her husband.

It might even erase the memory of what it had been like with her husband.

That was something she very much desired.

Her time with Rhys was limited. As soon as Adele was

settled, Celia would move away and live the quiet, independent life she craved.

She was in no danger of losing her heart to Rhys. He was a gambler. Her mother had shown her that loving a gambler was a very bad risk. The only person she intended to place her bets on was herself. She could trust herself to pay the bills, to live within her means, to do whatever she chose to do.

She sat up and climbed off the bed.

There was the one thing she wished most to do that she could not choose. She could not choose to have a baby.

She paced the room, finally coming to the window. She gazed into the street below, but saw nothing of the carriages passing by or people walking to and fro. Her arms still ached to hold a child of her own, and nothing would replace that void in her life—not even the babies Adele would have.

Those babies would never be hers.

She swung away from the window and sat at her dressing table, staring at her reflection.

Rhys had said she was alluring.

She could not see it, but his words did thrill her.

He admired her, liked her, comforted her, protected her. Why not let him make love to her, as well?

Why not accept what Rhys offered her?

Chapter Eight

Rhys strolled through the game room, keeping his eye on what he'd laboured to create. The hazard and faro tables were the most crowded, but several patrons also played *vingt-et-un* and *rouge et noir*. The occasional gentleman wore a mask, but all of the women came disguised. More and more of them came each night.

Xavier glanced up at him from a game of whist and gave him a look that showed Xavier was still at outs with him. Rhys could forgive it. Xavier's concerns came from friendship, a friendship Rhys valued. Xavier, and perhaps MacEvoy, were the only people in the world who cared a fig about whether Rhys lived or died.

Rhys nodded to Xavier and continued his rounds.

He turned towards the doorway and saw Celia enter.

She wore the same gown and mask as the night before, but her hair was simply dressed with only a ribbon threaded through it. She paused just inside the room and turned in his direction.

Their gazes caught and held.

He smiled. Her mouth moved ever so slightly.

Was that a yes?

It surprised him how much his spirits were heightened.

He'd not quite allowed himself to think about whether she would come this night. And whether she would agree to his invitation.

Some gentlemen approached her and, amidst her protests, led her to the hazard table. She finally nodded her head and took the dice in her hand.

'Rhys?' A voice at his elbow caused him to turn away from the sight of her.

Both Hugh and Ned stood there. They rarely came to the Masquerade Club on the same night.

'Gentlemen.' He nodded to them. 'Did you make your appointment in time?' he asked Ned.

'My appointment?' Ned looked puzzled.

'At four?'

Ned coloured. 'Ah, that appointment. I did indeed.'

Hugh's brows rose.

Rhys asked, 'How is your mother?'

Hugh glowered. 'Quite upset.'

Rhys said, 'I regret that.'

Hugh turned away.

Ned broke in, 'We came to say again how grateful we are that you paid the money today.'

'Your mother gave her word,' he responded. 'It was enough for me.'

Hugh glanced back at him, his expression quizzical.

Ned surveyed the room. 'It looks like a good crowd.'

Rhys agreed. 'The numbers grow every day.'

Ned paused, but finally said, 'We will not stay long. We came only to thank you again.'

If their situation were different, Rhys might find Ned a comfortable acquaintance. He was sober and earnest, a decent sort. Rhys had known boys like him at school. They'd always treated him fairly. Hugh, though, was a different story. Rhys suspected they were too much alike to ever co-exist without battling each other.

The same blood flowed in their veins, so it should be no surprise that their personalities were similar. Of course, Rhys had learned to hide his emotions. Hugh's emotions were always on display.

'I bid you goodnight, then,' Rhys said, extending his hand.

Ned shook hands with him. Hugh did not.

Rhys turned back to the hazard table. Westleigh had joined the crowd and handed Celia the dice.

'Pass them on, sir,' Rhys heard her say. 'I've lost enough.'

'One more roll,' Westleigh urged. 'Your luck could change.'

She hesitated, but finally accepted the dice and threw them on the table. 'Six!' she called out.

She nicked the roll with a twelve.

A cheer went up from the men crowding around the table. At their urging the young woman croupier scooped up the dice and handed them back to Celia.

She called out a seven this time, but rolled a four and a two. The croupier handed her the dice again and she won this toss with another roll of six.

Another cheer rose from the table.

It looked like she was on another winning streak tonight. Last night's tally showed they had indeed lost at the hazard table, but nothing alarming. The profits at faro and *rouge et noir* more than made up for it. Rhys liked that her winning drew a bigger crowd to the hazard table. In the long run hazard would turn a profit.

Rhys moved through the room again, still keeping an eye on the hazard table. Celia won a third time, and, egged on by the patrons betting with her, she more eagerly accepted the dice from the croupier to try again.

He'd seen winning streaks like this before. He did not mind if she had some big wins, since money was important to her. Better she win than lose.

He wanted her to be happy.

He also wanted her to come to him this night. He felt the twinges of arousal merely thinking of it.

When Celia had entered the game room, she'd immediately caught of glimpse of Rhys. She'd also seen Neddington and another young man approach him, so she avoided speaking to him right away. Before his conversation ended, two gentlemen whisked her over to the hazard table.

'Come give us the luck, madam,' they'd said to her.

'As you wish,' she responded.

She played hazard again because she expected to lose. If she could encourage men to bet with her like the night before, they would also lose and maybe she could return to Rhys some of the money she'd cost him.

It worked, too. An occasional roll was successful, but most were not. She'd set her limit at fifty pounds, which she would then try to recoup by playing card games that gave her better odds.

As she tossed the dice on to the green baize table, a man's hand touched her back.

Westleigh.

Her skin shuddered where he touched.

'Greetings, my dear. Allow me to assist you.' He scooped up the dice, put his closed hand up to his lips and blew. 'For luck.' He smiled.

It made her sick.

She tossed the dice and won. And won again. And again.

Soon she'd lost all sense of time. All she knew was the feel of the dice in her hand, the sound of dice hitting the table, the cheers when the right numbers turned up. Her heart pumped wildly and she became dizzy with excitement. The fever had returned.

This night she woke from her reverie at the sight of Xavier Campion scowling at her.

She came to her senses and threw up her hands. 'I am done!'

She hurried away from the table. Pausing to check the timepiece in her reticule, she realised she'd not even thought about Rhys while in the fever. The dice had been too important.

It was two-fifteen! She'd spent all her time at the hazard table.

Someone touched her back again.

'Would you care for some supper, my dear?' Westleigh had followed her.

She'd even forgotten he'd stood next to her all that time. 'No. Not at all. Forgive me. I must speak with Mr Rhysdale.'

'Rhysdale?' Westleigh sniffed with contempt.

'Yes.' She could not be bothered with this man.

She searched instead for Rhys and found him leaning against the door jamb, his arms folded across his chest.

He saw her, nodded and walked out of the room.

Surely he knew of her new winning streak.

'I must go,' she said to Westleigh.

As she made her way to the door, she suddenly felt unable to breathe. She'd not decided about his proposition, but now she feared he would withdraw it. She walked briskly through the room.

A gentleman stopped her. 'Some whist, Madame Fortune?'

'Madame Fortune?' She did not comprehend.

The man smiled. 'That is what we call you now.'

She groaned inwardly. Her good fortune was Rhys's loss. 'I see.'

'It would honour me if you would partner me in whist,' he persisted.

She glanced toward the door. 'I—I cannot tonight, but perhaps next time?'

He bowed. 'I shall count on it.'

She hurried to the door and made her way to the room where the cashier sat.

'Cashing in early, ma'am?' he asked.

She nodded.

When her accounts were settled she thanked him and made as if she were leaving, but instead of entering the hall, she turned towards the servants' stairway and climbed those stairs to Rhys's private rooms, not knowing what reception she would find.

The drawing-room door was ajar and she could see him in the centre of the room. He'd removed his coat and waistcoat and stood only in his shirtsleeves, his back towards her. Her hands flew to her suddenly flaming cheeks.

She took a breath. 'Rhys?'

He turned, but his expression was impassive. 'I was uncertain you would come.'

'Of course I would come.' She spoke the words without thought. 'I needed to.'

His brows rose.

She entered the room and closed the door behind her, her heart pounding. 'I—I mean I must speak with you.'

He did not move, but she felt him withdraw as she came closer.

'I must explain.' A wave of guilt washed through her. 'I won tonight, Rhys.' Had this been how her father had felt when he lost? Ironic she should feel it for winning. 'I must have cost you over a hundred pounds between my winning and those who bet with me.'

The experience was now a blur of dice hitting the table, people cheering and the intoxication of win after win.

She took a breath. 'Surely you noticed.'

'Is that why you are here?' His posture was stiff and his shirt so white it seemed to light the room.

She gripped her reticule to keep her hands from shaking. 'I expected you to be angry.' Her husband had become angry at so much less.

He stared at her. 'I told you it is of no consequence. You and the others will lose eventually.'

His tone was still so stiff she feared he'd meant the opposite of what he said.

He gestured to her. 'At least take off your mask, Celia.'

Her hand flew to her face. She'd even forgotten her mask. She wearily lowered herself onto the sofa, setting her reticule down beside her. She untied her mask and dropped it next to the reticule.

He crossed his arms over his chest. 'You have not answered my question.'

She searched back, but could not remember what it was. 'I've forgotten it.'

He remained standing, but sipped his drink. 'Did you come here merely to tell me you won tonight?'

She gazed at him, so tall, so taut in his stance that it felt he was coiled like a spring. A flutter of nerves—or excitement—made her press her hand against her stomach. It did not help that his shirtsleeves accentuated his broad shoulders and narrow waist. She was robbed of breath.

'Not only for that,' she answered. No matter her fear or her nerves, her decision was made.

He met her gaze, but remained grim. 'For what, then?'

She blinked. 'Are you going to make me say it?'

One corner of his mouth turned up. 'Indeed.'

Courage was failing her. 'What you asked of me—I might say yes.'

He tilted his head. '*Might* say yes?'

She gathered her resolve and stood. 'Will say yes.'

He took her hand and raised it to his lips, which were warm and firm and sent a thrill deep within her.

'When does your driver return?' he asked.

'Five-thirty,' she said. Three hours away.

Her coachman had raised his brows at the request for a later hour. She herself was surprised she'd asked for it.

Perhaps she'd always known what she would decide.

He raised a hand and touched her cheek. 'You are certain?'

No. She was not certain at all. But she could not make herself refuse.

She did not *want* to refuse.

'Come.' He took her by the hand. 'I will show you my bedchamber.'

He led her to another room on that floor. Candle flames fluttered when they entered, illuminating a chest of drawers, a table, side chairs…and a bed. He'd prepared for her.

She had not thought beyond her impulsive yes. Once inside the bedchamber, she was as unsure as a new bride.

He led her to a table where two glasses of wine stood. 'A toast to you.' He handed her one of the glasses and lifted the other. 'And to pleasure.'

'To pleasure,' she whispered in return, her heart racing in her chest.

The wine was a strong and sweet sack. She drank it quickly and he poured her another. When she finished that glass she felt as if she were floating.

'Come to the bed,' he said.

Acting precisely like an experienced lady's maid, he unbuttoned the row of buttons decorating the back of her gown. She let it fall to the floor. Next he untied the laces of her corset. Each motion of his fingers made her tremble, more and more unsure of herself. Still, she slipped off her corset, leaving only her shift.

His eyes raked over her, dark as the night and full of desire.

He made quick work of removing his shirt, tossing it aside in a flash of white that tumbled to the floor. Dark hair peppered his chest and his muscles were as defined as those of a Greek statue. He moved slightly and the lamplight caught a webwork of scars on his side.

Her hand reached out to touch them, but he picked her up by her waist and sat her upon the bed. 'Next your shoes and stockings.'

She could not move. Never had a man touched her feet, nor slipped his hands up her legs to remove her stockings. An ache grew inside her, an ache of want.

Her legs still tingled when he stepped back, removed his trousers and stood before her naked.

She stared transfixed. No mere Greek statue could appear as magnificent.

He climbed on the bed, cupped her face and kissed her.

At first his kiss was gentle, a mere touch, but he pressed harder, moving his lips as if needing to devour her. Such a kiss was not one to be endured, but one that made her want to return such ardour. She kissed him back, daring even to touch her tongue to his. His lips parted and the kiss became something wondrous.

Sensation shot through her and his hands moved to explore her body through the thin fabric of her shift. She could do no more than rest her hands on his shoulders, but even that contact gave a thrill. His skin was warm and slightly damp to the touch.

Not cold. Not clammy.

He bunched the fabric of her shift in his hands, pulled it over her head and tossed it aside. Leaning back, he gazed at her, his eyes darkening, his breathing deepening.

Her husband's gaze always made her wish to cover herself. Rhys's felt like a caress.

'You please me,' he said.

Filled with a delight she'd never known before, she lay back on the pillows.

And he rose over her.

All at once it seemed as if the room grew dark.

Her heart raced so hard that it hurt. Her limbs trembled.

He covered her with his body and she gasped for air.

His male member pressed against her skin—

Panic engulfed her. She cried out and flailed at him, struggling to free herself.

He lifted himself off her immediately, shock on his face. 'What?'

She was still trapped by his body. She pushed at his chest, but he seized her arms and held her down.

'What is it?' he demanded. 'Have I hurt you?'

'Get off!' she begged. 'Please get off!'

He released her and moved off her. She scooted away from him, curling up into a ball, trying to hide from her panic and her shame.

'Celia!' He sounded as if he'd run a great distance. 'Tell me. What. Happened.'

She sat up, hugging her knees to her chest. 'I—I remembered.'

'Remembered what?'

For the second time that night she expected anger from

him. Not anger. Rage. Her husband always raged at her if she'd dared push him away.

Rhysdale merely sat up. She braced herself for a blow.

But he did not strike her. He tucked her in front of him, wrapped his arms around her and held her close like her mother used to do when she woke from a nightmare.

'What did you remember, Celia, that frightened you so?' His voice was low. Soothing. Comforting.

It calmed her. 'I—I remembered. The only other man I was with…' She paused, searching for the right words. 'He was not gentle.'

The muscles of his arms bunched. 'He hurt you?'

She nodded. 'It came back. I thought it was happening again.'

'Who is this man?' His voice turned hard. 'I will pay him a call.'

She did not even think of inventing a story. 'My husband,' she answered.

He tensed. 'You have a husband, *Miss* Allen?'

She'd misled him on purpose. Now she regretted it. 'I once had a husband. Not any more. He is dead.'

'How fortunate for him. And me.' He laughed as if in relief. 'Tell me of this husband of yours.'

She owed him an explanation. 'I was very young when I married him. Younger than—' She stopped herself. She'd almost said she was younger than Adele, but giving him a clue to who her husband was—who she was—still felt too exposing. She took a breath. 'It all came back. I am sorry.'

He nuzzled her and rocked her. 'Do not be distressed, Celia. Lovemaking is not supposed to bring pain. It is supposed to bring pleasure. I will not hurt you, I promise.' He paused. 'I will stop now, if you wish it.'

She twisted around to face him. 'No. I—I want to know what it is like without me being so—so afraid.'

She rose to her knees, as did he. He pulled the pins from her hair and released the ribbon threaded through. When her hair fell about her shoulders, he combed it with his fingers.

'I will be gentle, Celia.'

Slowly her panic dissolved. He stroked her, like one might pet a cat. Like a cat, she relaxed under his fingers. She lay down again and urged him down beside her. 'Your touch is gentle.'

He kissed her neck and murmured, 'Say my name, Celia.'

'Rhys.' It was a name to be whispered beneath sheets.

'See? I am not the man who hurt you,' he soothed. 'I will never hurt you.'

He remained beside her, keeping his promise so well her limbs turned to warm butter under his touch. His fingers traced around her nipples and she writhed at the pleasure of it. His hand slipped down her body and rested on her belly.

Aching with need, she pushed it further and still his touch was excruciatingly gentle as he explored her most private of places. Her hips rose to meet his hand, urging him to take greater access.

'You must tell me when you want me,' he whispered.

She wanted him at that very moment, but she held back. The fear hovered near, ready to flood her again. He waited and eventually his touch pushed away the fear and replaced it with more need.

'Now,' she rasped.

He rose over her again and she opened her legs to him even as she braced herself for the event that inevitably brought her pain.

To her surprise his entry was as tender as his touch. He eased inside her and new, unimaginable sensations flooded her. He moved softly as if she might break beneath him.

The rhythm lulled her and slowly a sensation akin to bliss arose inside her, growing more urgent with each thrust.

Suddenly his restraint became torture, albeit an exquisite one. Her hands grasped his backside and a frustrated sound escaped her lips.

He moved faster and she gladly kept up with him. This wonderful new sensation grew. The stronger it became, the more she wanted to rush towards it.

Suddenly pleasure exploded within her. She cried out and, at the same time, he convulsed inside her, spilling his seed, slaking his desire a moment after fulfilling hers.

He did not collapse atop her, as her husband had done, crushing her with his weight. He eased himself off her, settling at her side again. She could feel the rise and fall of his chest against her bare skin.

'Rhys,' she managed to whisper as tears formed in her eyes. She blinked them away.

'We have made love, Celia,' he murmured, his voice rumbling. 'Whatever your husband did to you, it was not making love.'

She curled up against him. 'I did not know of that—that pleasure. It was a surprise. I thought the pleasure was going to be only in how you touched me.'

'You are built for such pleasure, Celia. Settle for nothing less.' He cradled her under his arm.

She placed her hand on his chest, relishing the feel of him.

'Tell me about why you married this husband of yours.' He placed his hand over hers.

At this moment she wanted to pretend Gale had never existed, but she acquiesced. 'I was only seventeen.'

'Seventeen?' He rose on an elbow to look down on her.

'My guardians demanded I marry him,' she explained. 'I had no other choice. To be fair to them, they thought it a good thing for me. He was quite a bit older and—and of good reputation, at least of what they knew. He wanted a young wife.'

He frowned. 'How old are you now?'

'Three and twenty.'

'And he is dead?' His voice turned gruff.

'Over a year,' she said. 'He left me little money. That is why I must gamble. So that I have enough to support… myself.' She'd almost said *us*. 'I want to take care of myself, so that I do not have to do what any one else wants me to do. I do not require much. Not a large fortune. Just enough for comfort and security.' It was not the whole truth, but enough of it.

He kissed her temple. 'I am glad you came here.'

She looked into his eyes. 'I am glad of it, too.' And for more than just the chance to win at cards.

He grinned. 'It seems to me that you may need many lessons in lovemaking, though. To catch up.'

She smiled in return. 'I expect I do.' She feigned innocence. 'I do not suppose you know of a man who might be willing to teach me?'

'Only one.' He lowered his lips to hers for a long, lingering, arousing kiss. 'It would be my pleasure to teach you.'

He made love to her again, every bit as tenderly. The pleasure of her climax was equally as intense and she was left wanting more.

When they were finished he asked, 'Do you need to take care of yourself?'

'Take care of myself?' Her brows knitted.

'Do what women do after. To prevent a baby,' he explained.

Her eyes widened. Women could *prevent* a baby? She'd had no idea.

'I do not need to do anything.' That familiar empty feeling returned. 'I am barren.'

He peered at her, saying nothing, but gathered her in his arms again and kissed her. 'We should check the time.'

He climbed off the bed and searched the clothing on the floor. 'Drat. I left my coat in the drawing room.' He pulled on his trousers.

She wrapped herself in the bed linens. 'There is a timepiece in my reticule.' She scrambled from the bed. 'Oh, my goodness! I left my reticule in the drawing room. It has all my money.'

He lifted a hand. 'I will bring it to you.'

He put on his shirt and walked from the room in his bare feet.

By the time he returned she'd donned her shift.

He lifted the reticule before placing it on a table. 'It feels like you did win a great deal tonight.'

She picked up her corset. 'What time is it?'

'Ten minutes after five.'

'I must hurry.' She turned her back to him. 'Would you help me with my corset?'

She held it in place while he tightened the laces.

In a reverse of the more sensual undressing, they quickly put on all their clothes.

She felt the floor for her hairpins and quickly twisted her hair into some sort of order. She stuffed the ribbon in her reticule.

As they rushed down the stairs, she covered her face with her hand. 'My mask.'

'I'll get it.' He bounded back up the stairs.

She waited on the stairs, covering her face.

Xavier Compier entered the hall. He did not speak to her, merely leaned against the wall and watched her. When

Rhys's footfall sounded on the steps, Xavier retreated into the shadows.

'Here it is.'

She turned away and held the mask in place while he tied its ribbons.

They made it outside and he blew out a breath. 'I think we made it.'

There was the faintest glimmer of dawn peeking through the darkness. She smiled at him. 'Thank you for a lovely time, Rhys.'

He put an arm around her. 'Come to me again tonight.'

She looked up at him. 'For more lessons?'

His eyes darkened. 'Yes indeed.'

After Celia's coach turned the corner, Rhys re-entered the house and saw Xavier standing in the hall.

'You are still here?' He was not particularly pleased. No doubt his friend had known he'd been with Celia.

'I waited for you,' Xavier said.

Rhys gestured for Xavier to come up the stairs with him. 'Well, come upstairs. You might as well have a brandy with me.'

They sat together in the drawing room, a bottle of brandy between them on the table.

'Do you want to stay?' Rhys asked. 'You can use one of the beds upstairs.'

Some of the rooms remained unchanged from when the house's girls once entertained gentlemen in them.

Xavier shook his head. 'I'll go back to the hotel.' He'd kept his rooms at Stephen's.

'Any problems in the game room after I left?' Rhys asked.

Xavier frowned. 'We lost at hazard again.'

Here it comes, Rhys thought. Xavier would have noticed Celia's winning streak. 'I heard about it. We didn't recoup later?'

'Not enough.' Xavier inclined his head towards the cashier's room. 'I asked MacEvoy to count the money right away.'

Rhys tapped his fingers on his brandy glass. 'It happens sometimes. Luck occasionally turns bad, even for the house. You know that.'

Xavier gave him a direct look. 'The only time we lost at hazard was when she was winning.'

Rhys met his eye. 'I know. I watched her, too.'

'I have a bad feeling about this,' Xavier persisted. 'You do not know who she is. What she is about. You don't know what she wants from coming here.'

'We've been through this already, Xavier,' Rhys shot back. 'She wants to win money, like everyone else.'

Xavier's voice rose. 'I know you've taken her to your bed. Your judgement is clouded.'

Rhys levelled a gaze at him. 'Stay out of it, Xavier. I mean this.'

But Xavier went on. 'All I'm saying is, do not close your mind too tightly. Watch her.'

Rhys glared at him. 'Enough. Say no more.'

Xavier opened his mouth, but wisely closed it again. He stood. 'I ought to be going.' He glanced towards the windows where slivers of light appeared through the gaps in the curtains. 'It's morning already.'

Rhys stood, too, and clapped him on the shoulder. 'Do not worry over me, Xavier. You are like a mother hen sometimes.'

Xavier merely nodded. 'I'll see you tonight.'

Xavier would not let this go, Rhys feared. He'd consider it his duty to look out for Rhys, even if Rhys demanded he stop. It was ingrained in Xavier's character.

Rhys knew precisely what he was doing and had no need of Xavier's caution. Rhys intended to enjoy this affair with Celia for as long as it lasted, and if Xavier did not like it, it would stand like a wall between them.

Chapter Nine

Celia hugged herself during her short ride back to her rooms. Her body felt languorous, at peace with itself for the first time in her memory.

How could she have ever guessed lovemaking could be like this?

The carriage turned a corner.

She'd turned a corner, too. She felt free of her husband at last. There was no reason ever again to think of what it had been like being married to him. That part of her life was over and nothing like it would ever again happen to her.

A new door had opened. A door to new experiences and new delights. Celia planned to enjoy every minute of them.

Her heart was as light as gossamer when the carriage stopped. She gathered her mask and her reticule, opened the door and climbed out.

'Thank you, Jonah,' she called to her coachman. 'Get some rest.'

He touched his hat in acknowledgement and flicked the reins. The coach pulled away.

Celia walked to the door and turned the latch. Tucker

knew what time to unlock the door for her. He would have risen from his bed and be waiting to attend her in the hall.

How good her servants were to her.

She opened the door and stepped inside. Her butler indeed stood before her, but with an anxious expression and wringing hands.

She tensed. 'What is it, Tucker?'

He inclined his head towards the staircase. 'The dowager.'

Was Lady Gale ill? 'What about her?'

His face turned grim. 'She awaits you in your bedchamber.'

Celia froze. She was discovered.

She lifted her chin, though. This would change nothing. Her mother-in-law had no control over her life. The woman was dependent upon Celia, not the other way around.

She gave Tucker a rueful, but reassuring smile. 'Well, this will be unpleasant, will it not?'

'Quite, ma'am.' He relaxed a bit at her calm manner.

Celia climbed the stairs, feeling weary and in a great need of sleep.

Her maid stood outside her bedchamber door. 'She's in there,' Younie whispered. 'Fit to be tied.'

'So I would expect.' Celia opened the door.

Lady Gale had positioned one of Celia's chairs to face the door. She sat on the chair as if it were a throne and wore an outraged expression.

Celia did not give her mother-in-law time to speak. 'You have not been invited into my private room, Lady Gale. Nor were you given permission to rearrange my chairs.' When holding a weak hand, it was always best to make a bold move. Celia's father had taught her that. 'Leave now and never trespass here again.'

The dowager's mouth dropped open and it took time for

her to find her voice. She rose out of the chair. 'How dare you speak to me like that, you little wretch! Especially when you have been out all night. Where have you been?'

'I do not owe you an explanation, Lady Gale.' Celia stood at the open door.

The dowager grabbed her cane and pounded it across the floor. She stopped inches from Celia. 'You have been with a man. I'd wager a fortune on it. Who did you find willing to bed you? Surely someone you had to pay.'

Celia recoiled from the insult and fought the impulse to strike her mother-in-law across the cheek.

Instead she leaned down into her face. 'Remember your place, ma'am.' Her voice trembled. 'It is only because of my affection for Adele that you are here.'

The older woman shook a finger at Celia. 'You need me, girl! You are known to nobody. Without my connections, you would be invited nowhere.'

'I care nothing for your connections, ma'am.' Celia wanted nothing to do with society. 'The invitations are for Adele's sake, not mine.'

'You have obviously found some opportunity through my connections or you would not be out all night.' Lady Gale sneered. 'Unless you merely walk the streets like a common strumpet.'

Adele appeared in the doorway, rubbing her eyes. 'I heard shouting. You said my name. Are you arguing about me? Because I do not want you to argue about me.'

Lady Gale jabbed her finger at Celia. 'This woman is trying to ruin your reputation. She is gallivanting on the streets of London all night. If anyone discovers this, we'll all be ruined. Even your cousin will not wish to court you.'

She was still pushing Luther on poor Adele.

'That would be a good thing,' Celia snapped.

Adele clapped her hands over her ears. 'Stop! Stop!'

Celia caught herself and lowered her voice. 'Lady Gale, please leave now. Say no more.'

Younie stepped forwards. 'Come along, ma'am.' The maid spoke soothingly. 'Let me have Cook fix you a nice posset, so you can have a rest. All this fuss does you no good.'

Lady Gale allowed Younie to put her arm around her and coax her out of the room. 'She has given me palpitations!' she wailed.

'There, there, my lady,' Younie murmured. 'Let me fix you up.'

The maid got her into the hall and halfway to her own bedchamber before Lady Gale turned around. 'Ask her whose bed she's been warming, Adele. She's trying to ruin us all!'

When Lady Gale disappeared into her bedchamber with Younie, Adele turned to Celia, with her lip trembling. 'Is it true?'

'Come in my room.' Celia took the girl's hand and led her to the chair her grandmother had so recently vacated.

She moved another chair closer and sat. 'I will tell you the truth.' Or rather part of the truth, Celia thought. Enough of it, she hoped. 'It is true that I have been out all night, but I have not been walking the streets as your grandmother suggests.'

'Have you been with a man, though?' Adele asked, her voice wobbling.

Celia sidestepped that question. 'I have been at a place called the Masquerade Club.' That was truth enough. She lifted her arm where her mask dangled. 'It is a place where ladies may dress in disguise and gamble.'

Adele's eyes widened. 'Gamble?'

Celia nodded. 'Play cards. Hazard. Faro. It is where I go almost every night.'

'You go to a gambling house?' Adele's voice rose in alarm.

'That is how I have funded your new gowns and paid our bills.' Celia opened her reticule and removed the leather purse, heavy with coin. 'See? These are my winnings. They will pay the servants' wages. And pay for another ballgown for you. And more.'

'You pay for my gowns with money from *gambling?*' Adele looked horrified.

'Adele.' It was time to acquaint her stepdaughter with the realities of their situation. 'I have never had enough money to fund this Season for you. I had to do something.'

'But to *gamble?*' She said the words with disgust. 'Is not gambling what ruined my father?'

Not merely gambling. Debauchery, gluttony and carousing greatly contributed.

'Your father gambled rashly.' As did Celia's own father when he was on a losing streak. 'I am not rash.' At least she would not be rash again. She lifted the purse. 'This is proof.'

Adele jumped to her feet. 'Oh, Celia! What if you are found out? What if Lord Neddington learns you *gamble?*'

Celia did not have the heart to tell the girl that her dear Neddington was a frequent visitor at the same gambling house. 'No one will find out. That is the beauty of this establishment. Because ladies may come in disguise, no one knows who they are.'

'You do not understand, Celia,' Adele cried. 'He comes from an *important* family. He will never look at me again if it is discovered you gamble every night.'

Before Celia could respond, Adele ran out of the room. Her sobs could be heard in the hallway.

Celia rubbed her eyes. Wearily she rose and sat down

at her dressing table, taking her hair down and putting it in a plait.

Younie entered. 'Her ladyship has settled a bit.'

'Thank goodness.' She stood and Younie undid her buttons. 'I fear I handled that badly.'

Younie did not disagree. 'No sense in weeping over shed milk.'

'I am so tired I feel like weeping. I need to sleep. Perhaps I can think better when I am rested.'

She slipped out of her dress and Younie helped her off with her corset. She climbed into her bed in just her shift.

Once under the bed linens she closed her eyes.

She pushed her mother-in-law and Adele out of her thoughts and let her mind wander. It went immediately to Rhys. How it felt lying next to him. How his arms had comforted her and his touch had thrilled her.

Did she not deserve some happiness after all she'd been through? All she needed was to avoid the intoxication of the hazard game and confine herself to whist. She wanted to gamble at the Masquerade Club and share Rhys's bed for as long as she wished, for as long as she needed to stay in London.

When the Season was over, when Adele was settled, it would be over.

That afternoon Ned again called upon Adele for a drive in the park. While he waited for her in the drawing room, he could not even sit, he was so filled with excitement. Rhys had opened the door to restoring his future. Ned could dare to anticipate better fortune from now on.

She walked in and he knew immediately that something was amiss.

'Miss Gale.' He moved towards her.

'I am so sorry to keep you waiting, sir.' She glanced at him and her eyes looked red as if she'd been weeping.

What had upset her? Ned vowed to fix whatever it was, if it was at all in his power.

He did not press her to speak until he turned his curricle in to the park. It was early for the heaviest traffic and he was able to keep some distance from other carriages.

'What is distressing you, Miss Gale?' he began. 'I dislike seeing you so unhappy.'

'Oh.' She sighed. 'Nothing.' She tried to paste on a smile, but he could see it was false.

'Do not say it is nothing,' he pressed. 'I am your friend. Whatever troubles you, I will help.'

She looked away and wiped her eyes with her fingers. 'I ought not to be such a watering pot.'

He wanted to gather her in his arms, but he settled with covering her hand with his. 'Let me share your burden.'

She glanced up into his eyes and it took his breath away. 'It will seem nonsensical to you.'

He squeezed her hand, trying his hardest not to kiss her. 'Nothing you do or say will ever seem nonsensical to me.'

She blinked and one tear slid down her flawless cheek. 'It is just…just that my grandmother and my stepmother are quarrelling and there is nothing I can do about it.'

'What are they quarrelling about?' he asked.

She glanced away. 'I cannot tell you!'

He felt his face grow hot. 'Forgive me. I do not want to pry into your family's business. I only wish to help if I can.'

She sighed. 'Oh, you did not pry. I—I just cannot tell you.'

'I know what it means to keep family matters private.' His whole family situation was a carefully guarded secret. No one—except Rhys, that is—knew how near they were to financial ruin. 'But I want to help you in any way possible. All you need do is ask.'

She gazed at him again, her blue eyes glittering like sapphires through her tears. 'You are the kindest of men.'

He took a deep breath. 'There is…perhaps…something I wish to ask of you. If you feel able to listen to it.'

Her expression softened. 'You may ask anything of me. I am your friend as you are mine.'

He made himself attend to the horses and the path. 'It is an impertinence, I know, but I cannot resist.' He dared glance back to her. 'May I have permission to court you? I desire it above all things.'

She gasped and covered her mouth with her hand. 'Oh, my! Oh, yes. Yes!' She laughed, but quickly sobered. 'You should speak with my stepmother. She will tell you about my dowry and about—about my family. You should know our situation before committing yourself so.'

'If you wish it, I shall do so,' he said. 'This afternoon, if possible. But you must know that your dowry, your family, will make no difference to me. I want you to be my wife.'

'Oh, Neddington,' she whispered.

He glanced around quickly. They did not seem to be in view of any other carriage. Holding the reins in one hand, he cupped her cheek with the other and touched his lips to hers.

Celia did not wish to receive callers. All she wanted was to remain in her bedchamber and sleep.

And avoid her mother-in-law.

And wait for night and time to return to Rhys.

But Adele knocked on her door. 'Lord Neddington is in the drawing room. Will you see him, Celia?'

At least she was dressed. 'Of course I will.'

Adele walked with her down the stairs, whispering instructions the whole way. 'Please listen to him, Celia. Do not tell him about Grandmama's plan for me to marry Cousin Luther. Tell him the truth about my dowry and about Father. I do not wish to hold anything back from him.' She paused for a moment. 'But, do, please, refrain from telling him about your gambling. I fear he will disapprove greatly and I so want him to like me. And you. And Grandmama, too.'

Adele walked with her all the way to the drawing-room door. 'I cannot go in with you, but do treat him well, Celia. My entire life and happiness depends upon it!'

'I will treat him well, I promise.' Celia reached for the latch.

Adele seized her arm and pulled her back. 'Come find me as soon as you are finished. Will you?'

Celia suppressed a smile. 'I will. The moment I am finished.'

She opened the door and walked in the room.

Lord Neddington stood at the window. He turned quickly and bowed. 'Lady Gale.'

She hated being called that. In her mind her mother-in-law was Lady Gale and she was Celia Allen.

'Good afternoon.' He gestured to the window. 'I was just checking my curricle. Your man was good enough to hold the horses for me.'

She walked over and peeked out. 'A lovely pair of horses.'

'Thank you, ma'am.'

She gestured to the sofa. 'Do sit, sir, and tell me why you wished to speak to me.' She might be standing in the role of Adele's father, but, ironically, Neddington was probably older than she. She guessed him to be at least thirty.

He waited for her to sit first. 'I will speak plainly. I wish to court your daughter—your stepdaughter, I mean.

She wished me to seek your permission. I know you are not her guardian, but she said you were the one I should speak to first.'

Adele's guardian was an old friend of her husband's, a man who was in ill health and had retired to Bath. He did not care enough about Adele to oppose anything Celia decided.

'I am very inclined to comply with Adele's wishes.' Celia wanted Adele to be free to make her own choices. 'Whatever makes her happy.'

He frowned. 'I, too, desire her happiness.'

'You have only just met each other.' Adele should not make too hasty a decision. More importantly, she should not marry a gambler.

'I realise this,' Neddington said. 'That is why I request a courtship. Adele must be sure of me. To be frank, there is one matter that may cause you to decide against me.'

Celia's brows rose. 'Oh?'

He rubbed his face. 'I have tried to behave as a gentleman ought, but, at the moment my family finances are strained. I have taken steps to resolve the problem and in a matter of a year, I expect to be on solid ground again.' He paused. 'But it is not a given. It is…a sort of gamble.'

'A gamble?' She tapped on the arm of her chair with a finger. 'Are you fond of gambling, sir?'

He looked surprised. 'Me? Not at all.' Comprehension dawned. 'I do not gamble at cards and such, if that is what you mean.'

As she had noticed at the gaming house. She longed to ask him why he showed up there.

He went on. 'In any event, my family's finances are not yet quite what they ought to be, so I need time before I can in good conscience commit to marriage. I wanted you both to know that.'

She narrowed her eyes. 'Do you know of Adele's dowry?'

He waved a hand. 'I care nothing for her dowry. Whatever the amount, it will satisfy me.'

He certainly sounded genuinely like he was not in pursuit of her fortune. 'It is ten thousand pounds,' she told him.

His brows rose, but he turned thoughtful. 'It will be designated for any children we might have, of course. I'll not touch a penny.'

'Adele also wishes you to know that her father was a gambler and carouser, which was why I asked about your gambling habits. Besides her dowry, she inherits nothing. Her grandmother has only a pittance, as well.'

'And you?' he asked.

'I have enough.' She bit her lip, but decided to speak further. 'It would be desirable for Adele's husband to support her grandmother. It would be, shall we say, a great deal for her grandmother to bear to live with me.'

He bowed. 'It shall be my honour to do whatever is required of me.' His expression turned imploring. 'I would not have presumed to ask permission to court Miss Gale but for my fear of another suitor.'

Cousin Luther, he meant.

'I see,' Celia responded. 'I can assure you that no other man has secured Adele's affections.'

Neddington expelled a relieved breath, but he turned earnest again. 'Miss Gale does, of course, have every right to cry off.' His expression turned miserable. 'If she should ever prefer another gentleman to me.'

She reached over to touch his hand. 'As I said, Adele's happiness is of great importance to me. I think you prudent to request a courtship. Take your time to become acquainted, to see if marriage is truly what you desire.

Perhaps by the time your finances are in order, you will know for certain if you are suited.'

And Celia would have time to find out why Neddington regularly attended the Masquerade Club.

He clasped her hand. 'I am grateful, my lady. Truly grateful.'

She stood. 'Shall I send Adele in so you might apprise her of our conversation?'

He rose, looking as if the sun had come out after a month of rain. 'Yes. Yes. I would greatly desire to tell her.'

Celia walked to the door and called for Adele, who, she suspected, was waiting in the hall. Adele came running. Celia gestured for Adele to enter and the girl rushed in. Instead of joining them, Celia retreated to allow the besotted young couple some privacy.

Celia had already decided not to attend the evening's social event with Adele and her grandmother. It was to be another musicale, and this time the attendees would be providing the entertainment. She did not think she had the patience to sit through such an event.

She'd been able to remain in the background at the few other parties she'd attended. That suited her very well. The less she was noticed, the less chance anyone would guess who she was when she wore her masks.

She rather hoped Neddington's finances would be quickly restored; that is, assuming he told the truth about not gambling. If that were the case, though, she would have no reason to continue her double life and she was suddenly in no hurry to leave London, to leave Rhys.

She would see him tonight.

Avoiding the musicale also meant she could go to the Masquerade Club early…and avoid her mother-in-law's company a little longer.

* * *

Celia had pleaded a headache and confined herself to her room, asking that her dinner be brought to her. It would be assumed she was asleep when Adele and her grandmother returned from the musicale.

There was a knock on her door—Adele, probably, needing her opinion on her gown. 'Come in.'

Her mother-in-law appeared in the doorway. 'Did I behave properly this time?'

It was not worth keeping up the feud, not if it upset Adele so much.

Celia returned a civil smile. 'I do appreciate your knocking. It is very courteous.'

Lady Gale did not look in a conciliatory mood. 'I have something to discuss with you.'

Celia kept her tone mild. 'Certainly.'

The older woman took a deep breath before glaring at Celia. 'Did you allow Adele to make an arrangement with that Lord Neddington?'

Celia stiffened. 'I gave her permission to decide for herself.'

Lady Gale stood with elbows akimbo. 'How dare you! You knew I meant her for Cousin Luther. You must undo this hasty decision.'

Celia met the woman's eye. 'If you can present me with some reason to object to Adele's choice, I will discuss the matter with her. But it is her decision.'

'What can she know of it?' Lady Gale snapped. 'She is but nineteen.'

'She has time to decide,' Celia assured her. 'Neddington is not pressuring her.'

'What do you know of his family? I have heard gossip about his father—'

Celia put up a hand. 'I am certain there was plenty of

gossip about Adele's father, as well. If there is anything to cause undue concern, we will discuss it with Adele. She is a sensible young woman.'

'She is too young—' Lady Gale began again.

Celia levelled a gaze at her mother-in-law. 'Lady Gale, I was younger than Adele and I assure you I knew my own mind.'

The woman's eyes flashed. 'Hmmph! My son should never have married you.'

'Indeed.' Celia did not miss a beat. 'He was a great deal older than Adele's nineteen years and look what an unwise choice he made.'

'That was your fault,' Lady Gale countered. 'You bewitched him.'

Celia stared at her. 'Do not be absurd. I was seventeen. I did not choose him. I was not even given a choice. Adele will have a choice. Do not interfere or you will have to answer to me.'

Lady Gale spun around and made her way to the door. Before she crossed the threshold she turned back in a dramatic flourish. 'You have not heard the last of this from me.'

After she stormed out and closed the door behind her, Celia whispered, 'I agree. I have not heard the last, because you will never leave it alone.'

Chapter Ten

The next three weeks settled into a predictable routine for Celia, encompassing her greatest happiness, but also her greatest risk. Each night she entered the gaming house she risked losing control over her gambling, but when her night was finished she found unspeakable pleasure in Rhys's arms.

She stayed away from the hazard table as often as she could, but sometimes the gentlemen gambling there, Lord Westleigh especially, insisted she play.

'Madame Fortune,' they implored. 'We need you at hazard. We need your magic touch.'

She continued to win more than she lost, but she thought this was because she forced herself to stop as soon as the euphoria of the game bubbled inside her. It was always a struggle, but the other gamblers began to respect her skill at card playing as well as her luck at the dice, and their pressure to play hazard eased somewhat.

They also quickly learned that Madame Fortune had become Rhysdale's lover, preventing any attempts at flirtation. None wanted to offend the gaming-house owner. It suited Celia very well that she did not become an object of seduction like the woman Rhys had told her about, the one who inspired his idea for the Masquerade Club.

Neddington often came to the Masquerade Club, but Celia never saw him play. He talked to other patrons and watched others gamble, but never did so himself. She was relieved for Adele's sake, especially because the two were becoming more and more attached.

Life was splendid at the moment, even if the Season demanded ever more expenditures and the coach required an expensive repair. Other bills were paid. Adele was in raptures over Neddington and even Lady Gale's taunting could not spoil Celia's optimism.

Celia indulged Lady Gale in as many new gowns as she wished, as she did Adele and even herself, although at times she reminded herself too much of her father on a spending binge. She rationalised that looking prosperous for society was still an investment in Adele's future. Celia herself wanted to look presentable to society, but even more she wanted the gowns designed specifically for the night to look alluring. For Rhys. She delighted in night-time costumes in fabrics of vibrant red, blue or green, with matching masks that grew more elaborate as Younie came up with new ideas for how to make them.

It pleased her when her appearance caused Rhys's eyes to darken with desire as it had this night, when she'd walked in wearing a midnight-blue silk dress embroidered at the hem and bodice with pink roses. Her mask matched the pink and was bordered with tiny green embroidered leaves. It thrilled Celia when Rhys later removed her dress and gazed upon her with reverence.

He constantly surprised her in his ability to delight her and be delighted by her. Celia's old fears about lovemaking had vanished completely. Rhys would never hurt her. Never.

This night brought on yet another new experience.

He was not gentle.

And she did not care.

Their lovemaking took on an urgency, a frenzy that had been entirely new to her. It was she who pushed him, almost violent in her need. She rushed them towards their release as if time was running out, even though the night was young. The pleasure that burst forth from her came with a new intensity. No sooner had they finished than she wanted more.

It felt to Celia that her body had changed into one that always wanted more, more, more.

This night her lovemaking with Rhys was wild with sensuality. The violence of it all was evident in the tangled bed linens and the aching of her womanly parts. She did not feel pain, precisely—nothing like it had been with Gale. But it seemed as if Rhys could not make love to her fast enough or hard enough or often enough.

She'd just propelled them towards another frenzied release when he collapsed atop her and slid to her side. 'I never thought I would say it, but I am worn out.'

She lay back, still throbbing, still needing. 'I do not know what has happened. It feels different. More—more intense. I cannot explain it.' It reminded her disturbingly of when she lost control of her gambling.

He rolled towards her and caressed her face. 'I do not complain of it. You are magnificent.'

She smiled. 'You have heard me say this before. I never imagined lovemaking could feel like this.'

He kissed her lips. 'You have mentioned it. Almost every night.'

She pushed on his chest. 'But this is different.'

He kissed her again. 'It certainly is different.'

If he continued she would start all over again.

The clock struck four. She sat up and the room swam. 'I must go.'

He pulled on his trousers. 'Will you come this night?' he asked.

She nodded.

Unexpectedly her stomach roiled.

Oh, no, please! She did not wish to be ill. She pressed her hand on her abdomen, hoping he did not notice.

'Although I may be later than usual,' she answered aloud.

She never explained why and he never asked.

He kissed her. 'I will wait for you.'

She dressed with his help, always an intimate experience. He tied her mask on last. It came off only when she was in his private rooms.

When he walked her down the stairs, she gripped the rail to keep herself steady.

He noticed. 'Are you feeling unwell?'

'Just tired, I expect.' She smiled. 'Worn out.'

He grinned. 'I know precisely how you feel.'

When they reached the hall Xavier was just leaving with Belinda, the croupier at the hazard table. Celia still felt tension from Xavier, but at least he'd stopped watching her so closely.

When Rhys walked her out into the night air, Celia felt much better. Her carriage came quickly and her kiss goodbye was hurried.

The carriage ride did nothing to help her stomach feel any better, though. She could not be ill! Tonight was a ball Neddington's family was giving and Adele would simply perish if Celia were unable to attend.

That evening Ned invited himself to dine with Adele and her family. He'd hinted very strongly to Adele that it would be a good idea for him to dine with her and her family before the ball.

He wanted plenty of time to talk with them.

At the dinner table, the subject of the ball that night inevitably came up.

He took it as his opening. 'I need to warn you about something.'

Adele's grandmother rolled her eyes. 'I knew all was not well,' she said not quietly enough to prevent his hearing.

He swallowed. 'I—I told you my father was not the best of men—'

'Indeed,' commented Adele's grandmother.

It pained Ned that the Dowager Lady Gale still did not like him, although Ned had tried every way he knew to get in her good graces. What he was about to tell them was not going to help.

He took a breath. Might as well come out and say it straight off. 'I must inform you that my father had a natural child.'

The dowager shrugged. 'He is a reprobate. Everyone knows this.'

'Grandmama!' Adele cried. 'Do not speak so!'

'Neddington is our guest,' warned Adele's stepmother.

Ned turned to Adele's grandmother. 'I must agree with you, ma'am. My father is a reprobate. I do not blame you for holding it against me. I can only say that I am not like him.'

'I am sure great numbers of gentlemen have natural children,' Adele said.

He faced Adele. 'You may meet my father's natural son tonight.' There. He had said it. 'He is to be introduced. At the ball.'

Adele's grandmother pursed her lips in disapproval. 'Hmmph!'

He turned back to her. 'I will not present him to you if you do not wish it, ma'am.'

'I certainly do not wish it!'

'I do not mind,' Adele piped up. 'If you wish to present him to me, I do not object. And neither does Celia. Is that not correct, Celia?'

'Whatever you wish, Adele,' Adele's stepmother responded.

She looked ill to Ned, although she denied it. She merely picked at her food.

'I, for one, am eager to meet your family at last.' Adele gazed at him with eyes full of affection.

How was he to wait to wed her? Perhaps he could ask Rhys if the profits of the gaming house would increase soon. Perhaps it would be enough.

'I am particularly eager to meet your sister,' Adele added.

'You have a sister?' her stepmother asked.

'Phillipa,' Ned responded. 'She is not much in society, but my mother wishes her to attend the ball.'

'I suppose something is wrong with her,' Adele's grandmother said sarcastically.

Ned was determined to tell them all. 'She suffered a terrible...accident when she was a child.' It had been an attack, a mysterious one. His family never spoke of it. 'She has a scar that disfigures her face.'

'Oh, how terribly sad!' exclaimed Adele. 'I am sure I will love her all the same.'

When she said things like this, Ned could only adore Adele more.

He disliked that this shameful family event—introducing Rhys—had to take place the same night he was to present Adele to his parents. He was sorry he had to tell her grandmother all about Rhys and his sister, not that Phillipa was to blame for what happened to her. The grandmother would certainly use this information to try to influence Adele to marry her cousin instead of him. Ned could not bear that.

Worse, even her cousin was invited to the ball. So, Luther, too, would learn that the proprietor of the new gaming house was Ned's illegitimate brother.

At least the women would not know about the gaming house. Unless they were among the masked women who attended the club to gamble.

He chuckled inwardly at that impossibility.

Rhys and Xavier waited in the drawing room, which had been transformed into a ballroom. The folding doors between it and the formal dining room had been opened, creating a space double the size. The carpets had been rolled up and removed, as had the larger pieces of furniture. All the small tables, chairs and sofas had been pushed to the walls.

Standing in the space, at the moment empty, made their presence stand out all the more.

'I hope you know what you are doing with this,' Xavier remarked. 'You've always disdained society.'

Xavier, whose pedigree entitled him to be included in the highest of social circles, had not mixed much in society since the war. He attended this event only because of Rhys.

'Acceptance in society is not the objective, as you know.' At this point, the event was merely something to get through, the next step in a road he'd set upon the evening Ned and Hugh asked him to run the gaming house.

Xavier shook his head. 'Reaching an objective can sometimes involve unintended consequences.'

Rhys was losing patience with his friend. 'Xavier, I need you as a friend, not a nursemaid.'

'I am not so certain,' Xavier muttered, turning away and pretending to look at some inconsequential piece of chinoiserie.

Someone approached the door and both men turned to see who it was.

A young woman in a ballgown of pale blue silk. Her presence was lovely, but for a crooked scar that started below her eye and ended near her mouth. Rhys knew immediately who this was.

'Oh!' she exclaimed, taking a step back and staring directly at Xavier. 'I thought my parents were already here.'

'Phillipa.' His half-sister.

She glanced at Rhys and her eyes widened. 'You must be—'

He stepped forwards. 'I am Rhys.' He surveyed her. 'But I remember you as a little girl I sometimes saw in the village.'

'I do not remember you at all.' Her gaze slipped to Xavier. 'But I know who you are now.'

Xavier returned her gaze and became unusually silent.

Rhys spoke to her again. 'I hope my presence does not cause you undue discomfort, Phillipa. If so, I am sorry for it.'

She lifted one shoulder. 'It is I who usually cause discomfort. That is why I rarely attend events such as this.'

He extended his arm towards Xavier. 'Allow me to present my friend, Mr Campion.'

'We are acquainted,' Xavier said, stepping forwards. He'd never mentioned that fact to Rhys. 'Miss Westleigh. It is a pleasure.'

Her eyes narrowed. 'How do you do, Mr Campion.'

It was not the sort of reception Xavier usually received from ladies.

'You are known to each other?' Rhys gave Xavier a glance. 'How interesting.'

'Since we were children,' Xavier explained. 'Our families often summered at Brighton at the same time.'

'And most recently in 1814,' Phillipa added. 'Perhaps you do not recall, though.'

Xavier met her gaze. 'I recall. I was briefly in London.'

Rhys looked from one to the other. This was fascinating. Would Xavier tell him what happened between these two? It was obvious something had. To Rhys's surprise he felt a protective brotherly impulse. Had Xavier ill-used her? He'd certainly done something to cause this chilly treatment.

At that moment, Hugh entered the room and after him the Westleigh butler and several musicians.

Hugh walked directly to his sister. 'I did not know you were here, Phillipa.'

'I thought I was late, but no one was here…except…'

Hugh turned to Rhys and inclined his head. 'Rhys.'

Rhys returned the gesture.

Hugh looked discomfited. Once Rhys would have relished putting Hugh out of ease, in repayment for all the fights Hugh had picked with him when they were boys. But Hugh had restrained himself lately.

Hugh shook hands with Xavier. 'Campion. Good of you to come.' He looked back at his sister. 'Papa is stalling and Mama is dealing with him.'

'Ned?' she asked.

'He rushed in a little while ago. I expect he is getting dressed.'

The musicians set up their instruments and began tuning them. Other servants came in, carrying trays of wine glasses.

Hugh stopped one of them. 'We might as well have a glass while we wait.'

Xavier handed a glass to Phillipa, but she waved it away. Rhys welcomed the refreshment. He was not plagued by nerves, but seemed to be catching the discomfort of all three of his companions. Frankly, Xavier had been more correct than Rhys wanted to admit. This had been a foolish idea.

Lady Westleigh swept in, followed by a dour-looking Lord Westleigh.

He bowed to his hostess. 'Ma'am.'

She extended her hand to him. 'Rhys. Your night has come. I hope it is to your satisfaction.'

He clasped her hand. 'Thank you, my lady.'

Xavier stepped forwards to greet her.

'I expect your parents to attend tonight,' Lady Westleigh told Xavier.

'As they told me, ma'am,' Xavier responded.

Rhys and Xavier had dined with them only a week ago.

She turned to her daughter. 'Phillipa, you forgot your headpiece. After the milliner worked so carefully on it.'

'The feather irritated my face,' Phillipa retorted, her hand touching her scar. 'Besides, everyone knows of my scar. Why should I hide it?'

Rhys looked at his half-sister with new admiration. The young woman had pluck.

Lord Westleigh, Rhys noticed, did not greet him, but instead contented himself with glowering.

Lady Westleigh turned away from her daughter. 'Rhys, I thought we would have you stand in the receiving line with the rest of us. We will greet our guests as a family and Charles will introduce you to each guest in turn. Will that do?'

He preferred that to a general announcement. For one thing, it forced his father to do the right thing over and over and over. 'It seems an excellent idea, ma'am.'

Of all the Westleighs, it was Lady Westleigh who seemed the least affected by this uncomfortable situation. Rhys liked her, he realised. She faced the occasion like a soldier.

'Where is Ned?' She glanced around impatiently. 'I can hear the carriages pulling up to the door.'

'I am here, Mama.' Ned rushed in, still pulling at his sleeves and straightening his coat.

Xavier gave Rhys one more sceptical glance before wandering away from the family.

Lady Westleigh positioned them all in order. She stood first, then her husband. She placed Rhys next to Lord Westleigh, then Ned, even though etiquette would have put Rhys lowest. After Ned came Hugh and Phillipa.

As the guests arrived, Lady Westleigh made certain her husband did not skip a single introduction, although he tried. Some of the gentlemen and a few of the ladies reacted with recognition. A few even said, 'Ah, the proprietor of the Masquerade Club!'

The entire process became tedious as it went on. Ned, for one, fidgeted and spent a great deal of the time leaning over to see who next approached the door.

'Lord and Lady Piermont,' the butler announced.

Xavier's parents.

When they were introduced to Rhys, they reacted with pleasure.

'But we know Rhys!' Lady Piermont exclaimed. 'He is like one of our own.'

Lord Piermont pumped Rhys's hand. 'Good to see you here, my boy.' He looked around to anyone who was in earshot. 'This man saved our son's life on the battlefield.'

'Good to see you both.' He bowed to Lady Piermont. 'Ma'am. Your son is here. He is about somewhere.'

'Is he?' She immediately began scouring the room. 'Oh, do let us find him straight away.'

They quickly moved through the rest of the receiving line and hurried off in search of their son. Xavier was fortunate in his parents, Rhys had always thought.

More names began to blur as other guests arrived. Suddenly Ned seized Rhys's arm. 'She is here!'

'Who?' he asked.

But Ned leaned across him to speak to his parents. 'She is here. The young lady I told you about.'

Lady Westleigh looked interested. Lord Westleigh looked as bored as Rhys felt.

'Lady Gale. The Dowager Lady Gale. Miss Gale,' the butler announced.

'She looks like an angel,' Ned murmured.

Rhys glanced over and froze.

The first woman approaching the reception line stopped suddenly. She was not looking at Rhys, but at Lord Westleigh. Shock and dismay filled her expression.

He glanced at Westleigh, who showed not the slightest sign of recognition.

Lady Gale greeted Lady Westleigh cordially. She moved on to Westleigh, who appeared as uninterested as she was cold.

Westleigh gave his desultory introduction. 'May I present my natural son, Mr Rhysdale.'

She turned to him.

'Rhys,' she mouthed.

Rhys took her hand and applied more pressure than would have been polite. 'Lady Gale.'

She fixed her gaze somewhere in the vicinity of his neckcloth. 'Mr Rhysdale.'

'Hurry up, Celia,' the older woman with her snapped. 'You are blocking everyone.'

The older woman passed by Rhys without a word, as she did Ned and his brother and sister. Ned had already left the line to go directly to the young woman announced as Miss Gale. She was already speaking to Lady Westleigh.

'Mama. Papa,' Ned said. 'May I present Miss Gale to you. You have heard me speak of her, I am sure—'

While they spoke with Miss Gale, Rhys turned back to Celia. She met his glance, but there was no pleasure on her face. She, instead, looked horrified.

His attention was called back to Miss Gale, as Ned presented him to the young lady. Her attention to the family, including to Rhys, was more pointed than any other person going through the line.

Once the young woman had finished exuding her pleasure at meeting Phillipa and moved away from the line, Ned said to none of them in particular, 'There is the lady I wish to marry.'

Who was she to Celia? A stepdaughter? A sister-in-law?

A few minutes later a Lord Gale went through the line. Celia's husband? Had she lied to him?

As the man offered Rhys a limp hand, Rhys said, 'Your family precedes you. They went through the line a few minutes ago.'

Lord Gale did not look him in the eye. 'My cousins?' he said. 'Yes, they would be here, would they not?' He shot a scathing glance towards Ned, who was too happy to notice.

Rhys was relieved.

One thing was for certain. As soon as this receiving line was finished, he would speak to *Lady Gale*.

Celia pressed her hand against her stomach. It felt as if someone had knocked the wind out of her. Twice. She could not even think about Rhys at the moment.

She stopped her mother-in-law. 'Lady Gale, did you know that Neddington was Lord Westleigh's son?'

'Certainly.' Lady Gale sniffed. 'Everyone knows that.'

Everyone except Celia, of course. She'd merely accepted the young man's title without thinking what title his father carried.

She was never meant for London. In that her husband had been entirely correct.

Adele caught up with them. 'I hope they liked me. Do you think they liked me, Celia?'

'I think they liked you,' Celia answered by rote.

'The natural brother seemed respectable enough, did he not?' Adele went on.

Rhys had looked incredibly handsome in his formal clothes. Pristine white breeches and linen. Impeccably tailored coat. How she'd missed seeing him as soon as she was in the doorway was a mystery. Except she'd caught sight of Westleigh and could see no one else.

They were all connected. Adele. Westleigh. Rhys.

'And I adored Phillipa.' Adele was oblivious to Celia's distress. 'I thought her scar was not very evident at all.'

Goodness. Celia had not even noticed.

Lady Gale ignored Celia completely and latched on to one of her cronies. Adele begged to join her friends, obviously eager to pour over each minute detail of her introduction to Ned's family. Celia retreated to the wall. At least her malaise had left her, but now her stomach ached with a different sort of pain.

She glanced back to Rhys at the same moment his eyes found her. Her skin heated and she could feel the tension that fairly raced across the room between them. Matters had changed between them.

Xavier Campion crossed in front of her. She held her

breath. He paused for a moment and his eyes widened ever so slightly.

He bowed and walked on.

Her heart pounded. Had he recognised her? He had never seen her without her mask, but she would wager his had been a look of recognition.

Finally the reception line broke up. Ned made immediately for Adele.

And Rhys came directly to her.

'Lady Gale.' His eyes seemed to bore into her.

'Rhys.'

The music started and Lady Westleigh announced the first dance, taking Lord Westleigh as her partner.

Celia could not even look at Westleigh. It was difficult enough to disguise her abhorrence of him beneath her mask at the gaming house—how was she to do so as a possible family connection? How could she bear being around any of them, knowing he was behind them in the shadows?

How could she again be with Rhys, knowing Westleigh was his father?

'You never told me Westleigh was your father,' she said in a low voice. 'You knew what he did to my father.'

'You never told me you were Lady Gale.' He gazed out to the dance floor as if engrossed in the couples forming for the dance. 'I did warn you about Westleigh.'

She smiled as if they were merely passing pleasantries. 'You acted as if you disdained Westleigh. That does not fit with this family camaraderie.'

He turned to her. In spite of herself her breath caught at how handsome he looked. 'You make an excellent point and I agree with you. I do disdain Westleigh, but I cannot explain here and now why his bastard is suddenly introduced as a son.' He extended his hand. 'Would you do me the honour of this dance? I suspect these people think me deficient in all the social graces.'

'I usually do not dance,' she said.

He held his hand in place. 'Help me, Celia.'

She glanced into his eyes and put her hand in his.

They joined the line and faced each other.

The music began—'Miss Moore's Rant,' a country dance.

Rhys and the other gentlemen bowed to the ladies, who curtsied in return. Then they joined right hands, forming a star with the couple next to them and turning. They completed the figures, changing sides and moving one place down the line.

When she'd been a mere spectator to this dance, Celia appreciated the symmetry. The dancing couples moved like petals falling from a flower.

Inside the dance was an entirely different experience. She was aware only of Rhys. How he turned. How effortlessly he moved. How he gazed at her when the figures brought them together again. He did not look as if he gave any of the steps a single thought, but performed them as if it were as natural as walking down a country path.

His lovemaking was like that, she realised. Confident, natural and so very excellently done. Her senses came alive at the memory of it. When their hands touched, even gloved, she could feel his bare fingers on her flesh. When his gaze caught hers, she remembered how his eyes darkened at the height of their passion.

They reached the bottom of the set and had to stand out one sequence. Celia's body still felt alive to him. She fanned herself with her hand. It was too bizarre to feel so aroused by him after learning who he was, whose blood flowed through his veins.

She glanced away from him.

To her surprise she glimpsed Xavier dancing with Lady Phillipa. Adele, of course, was Neddington's partner and looked the very picture of delight. How could Celia spoil that for the girl even though it now connected Adele to Westleigh?

Lord Westleigh also danced, but she turned cold at the sight of him.

Rhys leaned towards her. 'Do not allow him to dampen your enjoyment.'

It was time for them to move up the line.

Any further pleasure she might feel from dancing with Rhys was spoiled by glimpsing Westleigh, who was like mould spreading through a bowl of fruit, spoiling everything she loved.

The dance moved her apart from Rhys.

When they came together again, he said, 'Is Miss Gale your sister-in-law?'

It was the sort of question a dance partner might ask to further an acquaintance, but everything they said to each other was now replete with hidden meaning and more questions. 'She is my stepdaughter.'

The dance ended and the couples scattered off the floor.

Rhys escorted her back to where they had been standing. He bowed to her. 'There is much more to say, is there not? You will come to the gaming house later?'

Before she could answer, Hugh Westleigh, whom she had so briefly met in the receiving line, approached them.

'Lady Gale.' He bowed perfunctorily to Celia before turning to Rhys. 'Father wants you in the card room. Apparently several gentlemen are eager to have you play.'

Celia recognised Hugh as another frequent visitor to Rhys's gaming house. The family certainly supported Rhys's enterprise, did they not? At least the family connection explained why Neddington attended the gaming house even though he did not gamble.

Rhys nodded and turned to Celia. 'Thank you again, Lady Gale.'

Rhys followed Hugh through the dancers gathering for the next set. They walked out of the ballroom.

Hugh turned to him. 'Smart of you to dance.'

'Was it?'

Hugh was probably surprised he knew the steps.

'And to ask Lady Gale,' Hugh added as they walked back to the hallway.

'Oh?' Rhys had been certain asking Celia had been unwise. 'And why is that?'

'Surely you noticed Ned is besotted with her stepdaughter.' Hugh spoke with sarcasm. 'Lady Gale would certainly not want to offend the family by refusing you.'

Rhys took hold of Hugh's arm and pulled Hugh back to face him. 'I am accustomed to your insults, Hugh, but Lady Gale does not deserve them.'

He expected Hugh to flare up in anger. Hugh's face turned red, but he averted his gaze. 'By God. I did not realise...' He looked back to Rhys. 'Accept my apology, Rhys. You behaved decently.'

Rhys could not help but smile. 'Almost like a gentleman, I suppose?'

Hugh's mouth twitched as if he'd contemplated smiling. 'Precisely like a gentleman.'

'Did you think I meant to embarrass all of you?' Rhys asked.

Hugh faced him. 'That is exactly what I thought.'

'Then you do not know me.' Rhys released him.

'None of us know you, do we?' Hugh responded in a low voice.

* * *

Rhys did not see Celia again until the night grew late. Half the gentlemen at the ball were frequent patrons of the Masquerade Club and were eager to engage its proprietor in play.

The aristocracy foxed him. Ned and Hugh were certain they would be ruined if the *ton* knew they owned a gaming hell, but he, their bastard brother, somehow earned cachet for the role.

Although he'd bet none of these gentlemen would want him to marry their daughters.

As if a gambler should marry at all.

He returned to the ballroom and immediately found Celia. She stood against the wall near her mother-in-law who was chatting to another lady. He watched her.

He'd never guessed that she belonged to the world he scorned, the world he wanted to join merely so he could turn away from it.

Xavier came to stand beside him. 'Did you win?'

'Enough to impress.' He had learned long ago the benefits of not winning every hand. 'I want them to come back to the gaming house.'

'Wise man.'

'How have you been occupying yourself while I was in the card room?' Rhys asked.

Xavier shrugged. 'Dancing, of course.'

'Careful,' Rhys warned. 'These young ladies will think you are looking for a wife.'

Xavier looked completely serious. 'Perhaps I am.'

Rhys was taken aback. 'Are you serious?'

He shrugged. 'I am merely humouring my parents, who would so like to see me settled.'

Rhys said, 'They were more than gracious to me, as they always are.'

Xavier nodded. 'They are excellent parents, I would say.' Which made it all the more mysterious to Rhys why Xavier rarely saw them and rarely attended events that would include him in their circle. Xavier had come to this ball at Rhys's request, not his parents'.

Xavier glanced around the room. 'It has been a much more interesting ball than I had imagined, has it not?'

Rhys's eyes narrowed. 'What is your meaning?'

Xavier gave him an intent look. 'I recognise her, Rhys.'

Xavier knew? Had any others recognised her?

A waltz was announced.

Xavier cocked his head. 'I am engaged for this dance.'

He walked quickly away to where Lady Phillipa stood alone.

Rhys hesitated only a moment more before striding directly to Celia.

He bowed to her. 'Another set, Lady Gale?'

She hesitated and her mother-in-law's face flushed with disapproval.

She suddenly said, 'I'd be delighted, sir.'

He took her by the hand and together they joined the circle of couples forming for the dance. The music began and, facing each other, Rhys bowed and Celia curtsied.

Rhys put his hands on her waist and Celia rested hers on his shoulders. He remembered their first lovemaking when she'd rested her hands in just this way. Their gazes caught and he swirled her into the dance.

No wonder many thought this dance scandalous. The intimacy of moving as one, touching with hands and eyes, left the illusion of being alone on the dance floor, even as the circle of dancers rotated like a wheel.

He was reminded of their lovemaking, of watching her face as pleasure built inside her, her skin flushing, her lips parting. He wished they were this moment in his bed rather than in this ballroom. He did not know how a respectable widow justified an affair with the proprietor of a gaming hell. The secrecy enabled it, he suspected.

They did not speak during the dance; nor did they change position, even though there were several different holds that could be used in the waltz. Rhys saw only Celia. At the same time he fancied he was losing her, that this was their goodbye.

He wanted to hold her tighter, closer, and never release her.

But the music concluded and he blinked as if waking from sleep.

He reluctantly released her. 'Come to me tonight.'

She stepped back. 'I—I do not know.'

He stiffened. Perhaps he'd been correct about the goodbye. 'We need to talk…about who you are, who I am. Will you come?'

She averted her gaze. 'Yes.'

He walked her back to where her mother-in-law stood. 'I bid you goodnight, then.' He leaned to her ear and whispered. 'Until later.'

Chapter Eleven

When Celia walked in to the game room that night, Rhys caught Xavier. 'Watch the room, will you?'

Xavier, for once, did not lecture. He merely nodded.

Celia had transformed herself from the very proper aristocratic widow to the slightly scandalous, mysterious and masked Madame Fortune. Not only by her costume, its deep red more theatrical than the pale green gown she wore to the ball, but by the way she carried herself with a seductive confidence. At the ball she made herself fade into the background, unnoticed apparently, although to him, there had been no other women present.

It was like that in the gaming house, as well. Other women attended, some masked, some not, and he was not blind to the fact that some left with gentlemen patrons. For Rhys, though, Celia was the only one worth a second glance.

He moved through the game room to where she was chatting with other gamblers. Her gaze flicked to him and back to the others.

He touched her arm. 'Madame? May I have a moment of your time?'

She stiffened. 'Certainly.'

He escorted her out of the game room and together they climbed the servants' stairs to his private drawing room.

He closed the door behind them.

She pulled off mask, no longer looking like Madame Fortune or the Lady Gale of the ballroom, but a woman ready to fend off an attack. 'It is good you approached me. Better we discuss this right away. Do we start with who you are or who I am?'

'I think it more to the purpose to talk of who you are.' He lifted a decanter. 'Some port?'

'Please,' she responded.

He poured them each a glass.

She took the glass of port and he noticed her hand trembled. 'Why is it more to the purpose to discuss who I am? Why is that more important than discovering that my lover is Westleigh's natural son and my stepdaughter is being courted by his heir?'

He took a gulp of his drink and set down his glass. 'Because it makes your being here more of a risk.' He moved closer to her and grasped her arms. 'Xavier recognised you. What if others do, too? Your reputation—'

Her eyes widened, but she quickly recovered. 'If your friend wishes to expose me, there is little I can do now, is there?'

He tightened his grip on her. 'He will not expose you, Celia. But if anyone else guesses who you are...it is already known we are lovers. A lady cannot take the owner of a gaming hell as a lover without tarnishing her reputation.'

Her eyes gleamed like the coldest emeralds, but behind them he could see her pain. 'My reputation? I assure you, no one cares enough about Lady Gale to even think she has a reputation.' Beneath her bravado he could see her pain. 'Except you, perhaps. You clearly would prefer not to be a lady's lover.'

'Of course I would not.' Could she not see? 'I would not put a respectable woman in such a position. And I certainly would never have offered you employment, had I known you were Lady Gale.'

She lifted her chin. 'You regret bedding me.'

'Never.' He released her. 'You regret bedding me.'

She turned away and walked towards the window. 'Because of Westleigh. I cannot bear your connection to him and this change of heart towards him—'

'There has been no change of heart,' he broke in. 'I detest Westleigh.'

Now more than ever. Once again Westleigh stood in the way of something Rhys wanted. Needed. He could lose Celia.

In this moment Rhys knew, as strongly as he had ever known anything, that he did not want his affair with Celia to end.

She gave him a sceptical glance. 'Do not take me for a fool, Rhys. You just attended a ball which, for all I could see, had the purpose of welcoming you into Westleigh's family.'

'It was not how it appeared.' Rhys could almost hear Xavier's voice: *I warned you*...

'Then why did you do it?' she asked.

He averted his gaze. 'For restitution.'

'Restitution?' She shook her head. 'Your restitution was to *join* his family? I wish to escape him.' She walked towards the door. 'I need to return to the game room.' She turned. 'That is, if I am still in your employ.'

He frowned. 'Celia, it is not worth the risk.'

She straightened her spine. 'My situation is unchanged. I need the money. Does our bargain still hold?'

* * *

Celia kept her posture stiff as she waited for his answer. Inside she felt as bleak as she'd ever felt.

Rhys looked ashen. 'If you wish it, our bargain remains.'

'Thank you.' She donned her mask and walked out, deliberately not looking back at him.

Nothing was settled between them. They'd said nothing to any purpose at all. And nothing made sense.

Her emotions were raw, as raw as if she'd just heard that Westleigh had killed her father. As if she'd just witnessed her mother's last laboured breath. As if she once again heard her own voice speak the marriage vows shackling her to Gale.

She wanted to forget it all, to escape this new pain.

Instead she adjusted her mask and descended the stairs to the game room.

'There she is!' cried one gentleman when she entered.

'Come play hazard, Madame Fortune,' said another. 'We need your luck.'

She straightened and made herself smile. If ever there was a night to lose herself in a game, this was it. 'I hope to be lucky tonight.'

She played hazard, losing more than she won, but still recklessly playing on. The men still cheered her on and bet with her, but one by one they left the table. When she realised they had stopped betting, she woke from the reverie and rid herself of the game quickly.

'Enough,' she said to the croupier.

'Surely one more game will not hurt.'

She looked to see who had spoken. It was Lord Westleigh. She felt a wave of nausea, but forced herself to greet him congenially. 'You are later than usual, are you not?'

He bowed. 'I am flattered you noticed, madam.' His

words were slurred as if he'd imbibed too much wine. He picked up the dice. 'One more roll?'

She waved him away. 'No more hazard.'

He placed the dice back on the table. 'How about *vingt-et-un?*'

She glanced around the room, but did not see any likely partners for whist. At least at *vingt-et-un* she would not have to face him across a table. 'Very well. *Vingt-et-un.*'

She allowed him to escort her to the *vingt-et-un* table. He walked unsteadily. Another gentleman and a masked lady were playing against the dealer. Celia and Lord Westleigh joined them.

Celia ignored Westleigh as best she could and concentrated on each turn of the cards, remembering which had been played and calculating the odds of her being dealt what she needed. It worked. She recouped some of her losses and almost forgot her pain.

Then she would glance up and her eyes would inevitably turn to wherever Rhys stood. Her pain would return.

At least she won as often as Westleigh lost. She suspected his vanity was wounded that a mere woman was more skilled than he.

The dealer dealt them each one card down, one up. Westleigh peeked at his hidden card and tapped the table. The dealer placed another card on his pile and his face fell. Celia requested another card and won.

Westleigh glanced around the room as if looking for someone. 'I fear I must leave you, my dear. Unless you desire more of my company?'

She did not look at him. 'I'm winning. I want to play.'

He grunted and staggered off, unsteady on his feet. She had no time to feel relief at his absence.

Xavier joined the table.

'It seems your luck holds here, as well, Madame Fortune,' he remarked.

'Indeed!' she said with false cheer.

He distrusted her, she knew. And now he was a threat.

He was also as skilled as she at the game, and, ironically, she suspected it was her skill that made Xavier distrust her.

Could he not accept that she was good at cards? And now, after nearly a month of playing several nights a week, she was even better than before. She made money nearly every night, and, so far, she'd been able to stay mostly in control.

She suspected Xavier had noticed every single time the gaming fever overtook her. He watched her that closely.

The dealer reshuffled for a new game and Xavier leaned towards her, speaking low. 'So we meet twice in one night, do we not, my lady?'

She nodded. 'You recognised me.'

'Yes.'

She glanced around. 'Please say no more.'

He merely smiled his charming smile at her.

The dealer asked Celia to cut the cards and she tried to turn her attention to the game, but her concentration failed her.

After losing three hands in a row, she gathered her smaller pile of counters and told the dealer, 'That is all for me.'

Xavier left the table at the same time. Without being too obvious she followed him to a corner of the room where a servant served wine and other spirits.

When she was certain no one else could hear, she said to him, 'I beg you, sir. Tell no one who I am.'

He did not smile this time. 'I will not.'

She nodded. 'Thank you.'

The scent of the wine made her stomach feel queasy and she was so exhausted she could not stand on her feet. She excused herself to Xavier and made her way to the supper room. Westleigh was there, sitting with a group of gentlemen. She stayed clear of him and made her way to the sideboard where she chose the blandest food she could find.

She chose a table alone and one far from Westleigh, but, to her dismay, he left his table and joined her. 'Would you like some company, madam?'

She did not feel friendly. 'No. I will not stay long. I just needed something in my stomach.'

He lifted his wine glass. 'As did I.'

She glanced down at her plate, thinking he would leave, but he lowered himself into the chair adjacent to hers.

He took a big gulp from the wine glass in his hand. 'Perhaps you wonder why I mostly play only the table games.'

She bit into her biscuit and swallowed lest she retch in front of him. 'I had not.'

She had noticed that he played whist infrequently; thus she'd had few opportunities to revenge her father by winning Westleigh's money.

He leaned towards her. 'It is a secret.' His breath smelled of the wine.

She waved her hand in front of her nose. 'I see.'

He wagged a finger at her. 'You must tell no one.'

She broke off another piece of biscuit. 'Do not tell me.' She did not want to share confidences with this man.

'I am certain I can trust you,' he slurred.

He steadied himself by gripping the back of her chair. It was nearly an embrace. Or a trap within his arms.

He again leaned towards her ear. 'I mostly play games where the losses go directly to the house, not to the other players. Do you wonder why?'

She shrank back, but could not escape him. 'No, I do not.'

He leaned away and gestured expansively. 'I own this place. It is mine.'

Ridiculous. 'Rhysdale owns this place.'

He lifted a finger. 'Rhysdale is my natural son, you see. Everything is in his name, but only to protect my reputation. It was my money that bought this place.'

She did not want to believe him. She did not want to believe that Rhys kept this information from her. She did not want to believe that Rhys was merely Westleigh's figurehead.

She swallowed her piece of biscuit.

Westleigh went on. 'So, you see, if I lose at the tables, the money goes right back into my pockets.'

She pressed her fingers to her now-aching head. 'How very clever of you, my lord.'

He seized her hand. 'I can be clever at other things, if you will allow me to show you. There are rooms upstairs, you know.'

She gaped at him, horrified, and pulled her hand away. 'How dare you speak to me in that manner! Surely you know, as well as everyone else here, my attachment is to your son.'

He did not even have the grace to look contrite. 'My dear, the son is nothing to the father.'

A wave of nausea washed through her. She clamped her hand against her mouth.

One of the gentlemen from the table where Westleigh had previously sat called to him. 'Wes, we are leaving. Are you coming with us?'

He looked at Celia with regret. 'I might as well.' He seized her hand again and kissed it. 'I will say goodnight, madam. You must let me know if you change your mind. I can make it quite worth your while.'

Worth her while? He would pay her as if she were a common prostitute?

'Leave me, sir,' she said in a clipped tone.

As soon as the men left the supper room, Celia rose and went up another flight to Rhys's private rooms. She glanced to the floor above. Were those rooms for Lord Westleigh's use? The idea sickened her.

Rhys noticed when Celia left the game room, but could not follow her at that moment. It was late before he could get away, so late, in fact, the patrons were leaving. Even Xavier bid him goodnight.

Cummings manned the door and would know if she had left.

Rhys made his way to the hall. 'Did Madame Fortune leave yet?' Rhys asked.

'I didn't see her,' Cummings said.

She must be waiting upstairs. Rhys had not expected her to stay. His tension eased and he took the stairs two at a time. He checked the drawing room, but she was not there. He hurried to his bedchamber and opened the door.

She was seated on a chair, resting her head against her hand, her eyes closed.

He crossed the room to her. 'What is it, Celia? Are you ill?'

She raised her head and it seemed that all colour had left her face. 'I waited for you.'

'I am glad.'

Her eyes narrowed. 'Do not mistake this. I waited to tell you what Lord Westleigh said.'

His spirits fell. 'What did he say?'

She stiffened. 'He said you are working for him. That this gaming house is his, not yours.'

Rhys clenched his fist.

Her voice turned raw. 'I will not be back, Rhys. I will not work for Westleigh. I cannot. I detest him!'

Rhys walked over to the side table and poured himself a brandy. 'He lies, Celia. I own this place. It is mine.' He gripped the brandy glass so hard he thought it might shatter. 'And I detest him, as well. Even more for lying to you. For speaking to you!'

'How do I know what is true, Rhys? I do not know who to believe.' Her hand trembled.

He sat across from her.

'This is the truth, Celia.' He ought to have told her this long ago. 'Westleigh brought the family to near ruin with his gambling and excessive spending. Ned and Hugh came to me, needing a great deal of money quickly. They asked me to run a gaming hell for them. They scraped together the initial investment. In exchange, they receive half of the profits. The property is in my name. I paid back the original investment, but I paid it to Ned. None of it goes to Westleigh. I own the gaming house. I am fully in charge of it. Those were my conditions in agreeing to do this for them.' He paused. 'My other requirement was that Westleigh publicly acknowledge me as his son, something he should have done when I was a child.' He glanced away. 'Or when my mother died.' He faced her again. 'That was why I was introduced at the ball.'

She shook her head. 'It mattered that much to you? To be known as *his* son?' She spat out the words.

He did not answer right away. 'There was more to it. There were many people who were kind to my mother when I was a boy. If the Westleigh estate failed, they would suffer. That was why I agreed to run the gaming house. No other reason.' Except his own desire to make his father beholden to him for something.

'But you wanted him to acknowledge you. You wanted to be known as his son.' Her voice was scathing.

He glanced away. 'I thought it the one thing he would most object to.'

She made a disparaging sound. 'That was your restitution?'

It was time he faced the truth. 'The restitution was for my mother. My birth was the ruin of her life. She might have lived a respectable life if it had not been for me. She might have married, borne legitimate children. She might not have died so young.' His throat tightened.

She leaned towards him and placed her hand on his. 'Oh, Rhys. I am so sorry.'

He'd not told her how Westleigh had left him penniless and alone. He was not trying to win her sympathy. He merely wanted her to understand the truth.

She stood and began to pace. 'I cannot be *connected* to him. I cannot. If I am with you, I will be connected to him. And if Adele marries Ned, I will be connected to him.' She turned back to him. 'I will lose her like I lost… everyone else. Because of him.'

He rose and walked over to her, putting his arms around her. 'He can't make you lose your stepdaughter.'

She took a deep, shuddering breath. 'She will become a part of that family. I would not blame her for it—it is the natural course of things. But I want no part of that family. Or of him.'

'Celia.'

Eventually she melted against him. He wanted to kiss away her pain. He wanted to make love to her and show her that now she was not alone. He would not leave her.

But he had connected himself to the one man she could not abide.

Rhys wished he could open a vein and rid himself of

any Westleigh blood flowing through him. 'Do not let him come between us, Celia.'

She held her head between her hands. 'I cannot think any more. I am so weary. I just want to go home. This night has brought too much back.'

'It is almost time for your carriage,' he said, releasing her. 'I'll walk you out.'

Like so many nights before this, Rhys escorted her outside and waited with her until she was safely in her coach, although this time it felt as if everything had changed between them.

Because of Westleigh.

Chapter Twelve

The next day Adele insisted upon calling on Lady Westleigh, to pay her respects to the hostess of the ball and Ned's mother. Celia's mother-in-law refused to go with her to *that house,* so the task fell to Celia.

She wanted to refuse. She did not want to be in surroundings that reminded her of Westleigh, where there was a chance she might see him and have to pretend to be cordial.

She and Adele were announced to Lady Westleigh and entered the drawing room, which had been transformed into a ballroom only the night before.

Immediately Celia noticed the portrait of Lord Westleigh that dominated the room. She had to see him after all.

'How good of you to call.' Lady Westleigh extended her hand to them and the ladies exchanged greetings.

There were no other callers at the moment, although Lady Westleigh was with her daughter. Lady Phillipa wore her hair pulled back into a simple knot. It made her scar even more prominent.

'Come sit with me, Miss Gale.' Lady Westleigh patted the space next to her on the sofa for Adele. 'Let me become better acquainted with you. Last night I did not have a chance to really converse with the young miss who has so captivated my son.'

'Oh, my lady, I would be delighted.' Adele was in raptures.

'I will pour tea,' Phillipa said. 'How do you take it?'

At first the conversation was general enough to include all of them. Compliments from Adele and Celia about the ball. Comments about the weather and the next society event, an opera that night.

Lady Westleigh was a puzzle to Celia. Such a gracious lady to be married to a man who did not care about taking a life and leaving a family in tatters.

The lady took Adele's hand. 'I should tell you, my dear Miss Gale, that I knew your mother.'

'You knew my mother?' Adele's eyes grew wide with excitement. 'Oh, please tell me something about her. I miss her so terribly!'

Celia turned to Phillipa, allowing Adele to have her private conversation with Lady Westleigh. 'Did you enjoy the ball, Lady Phillipa?'

The young woman picked up a piece of needlework. 'It went well, I suppose. I do not attend many balls, but my mother seemed satisfied.'

She did not answer the question.

Phillipa pushed her needle through the fabric. 'You danced with our—our natural brother, I noticed. It was kind of you.'

'Kind?' He'd been a wonderful dancer.

'No one else danced with him.'

Celia had not seen him ask anyone else to dance. She felt compelled to defend him. 'I found nothing to object to in him.' Except his connection to this family.

Phillipa frowned. 'I did not know of him until lately.'

Celia did not want to make Rhys the topic of conversation. She took a sip of tea and felt the eyes of Lord Westleigh's portrait upon her. 'You danced with Mr Campion, I noticed.'

Phillipa shrugged. 'I suspect his mother or mine put him up to it. Our families have known each other a long time.'

Celia did not know what to say in response to that.

'To own the truth,' Phillipa went on, 'I do not like to attend balls or any of the London events.'

'Will you not come to the opera tonight?' It was the event everyone was attending.

'I think not,' Phillipa said.

At that moment Neddington entered the room. 'Forgive me for intruding, Mother,' he said. 'I merely wished to say hello to Miss Gale and Lady Gale.' He bowed to Celia. 'How do you do, my lady?'

'Very well, Ned. Thank you,' she responded, thinking now that he looked like a younger version of his father. Why had she not seen it before?

He turned to Adele and his voice softened. 'And you, Miss Gale?'

She glowed. 'I am very well, sir.'

Celia felt like weeping. She would surely lose Adele when she married this man.

She would lose Rhys, as well.

She glanced at the clock on the mantel. 'We ought to be on our way, Adele.' They'd been there longer than the typical fifteen minutes.

'Will you allow me to see you to your carriage?' Ned asked.

'Oh, we walked. It is such a fine day,' Adele said.

Ned smiled. 'Then might I escort you both back home?'

Adele gave Celia a pleading look.

'That would be kind of you,' Celia said.

* * *

Rhys prowled around the gaming house like a bear in a cage. He'd felt like a caged beast since the night before, the night of the ball, the event that had changed everything with Celia. How could he have guessed that Celia would be present at that ball? At any ball?

She was nothing like the aristocracy.

He should have told her his connection with Westleigh right from the beginning—especially after she confessed that Westleigh had killed her father.

He'd used that fact as an excuse not to tell her.

Would she come tonight?

He wanted another chance to make her understand.

To ask her to forgive him.

He wandered to the cashier's office and stood in the doorway. MacEvoy was busy with a patron, but Rhys did not need to speak aloud. He merely raised his brows.

MacEvoy shook his head.

She had not arrived.

Rhys spun around, his frustration growing.

Xavier stood there, leaning against the wall, arms folded over his chest. 'Let me guess. Mac told you matters were unchanged since the last time you checked with him. Twenty minutes ago.'

Rhys scowled at him. 'Were you counting the time on your pocket watch?'

'I probably could have set my watch by you.' Xavier straightened. 'Care to tell me why you are pacing the rooms?'

He was in no mood to go into this with his friend and hear again Xavier's cautions. 'I'm merely making certain all is well.'

He pushed past Xavier and re-entered the game room.

A few minutes later, Rhys spied Xavier at the hazard table watching the play.

Rhys wandered over to him. 'It seems slow tonight.'

'Everyone is at the opera,' Xavier answered in a good-natured tone, somewhat easing Rhys's guilt for having snapped at him.

A patron threw the dice on the table.

'Nine!' Belinda called.

'I'm out,' the man cried.

'How do you know everyone is at the opera?' Rhys asked Xavier.

'I called upon my parents today,' his friend replied. 'They were bound for the opera and said that was the entertainment for the evening.'

Rhys nodded. 'Your parents looked in good health last night.'

'As always.'

Xavier's parents were, in Rhys's eyes, a rarity—members of the *ton* who were selfless and generous, and not at all concerned with the status of one's birth. Xavier's brothers and sisters had each found their places in society. Xavier had not.

Rhys noticed Xavier's attention shift and his brows rise.

Lord Westleigh had entered the game room. Celia was at his side, but looked as if she were trying to remove a leech.

'Now what?' Xavier commented.

'Now what indeed,' growled Rhys who crossed the room to get his father away from her.

'Westleigh,' he said in a sharp voice.

His father gave him a contemptuous look. 'Well, well. If it isn't my *son*.'

Through her mask, Rhys saw Celia's eyes reflecting distress. She took advantage of the situation and turned to greet other gamblers who walked in behind them.

'Some whist, Madame Fortune?' Rhys heard one of them ask.

He faced his father. 'What are you about, Westleigh?'

Westleigh made a helpless gesture. 'Whatever do you mean, my *son?*' He smirked. 'Are you fearing I will steal your paramour from you?'

Rhys leaned threateningly into his face. 'Do not plague her. Do you hear me?'

They were attracting some attention, so Rhys walked away from him. He searched for Celia, but she was seated at a whist table with Sir Reginald and another masked couple he strongly suspected were Lord and Lady Ashstone. Ashstone's pockets were deep and Rhys hoped Celia would win a good sum from him.

She raised her eyes and caught Rhys's gaze, but her opponents gestured to the cards and she looked away.

Rhys wandered back towards the hazard table where Xavier was now in conversation with Belinda, the table's croupier, whose complexion had brightened at his attention.

Rhys approached Xavier from behind and heard him say, 'Let me know if anything seems amiss. Especially if Madame Fortune plays.'

Rhys stepped back quickly, but caught sight of Westleigh intently watching the exchange.

Had Westleigh heard Xavier, as well?

Celia should have skipped the gaming house this night. She was so weary. She supposed the constant late hours were taking a toll. She'd come, she told herself, to win more money, but truly, she had come to see Rhys. Except she doubted she could last long enough to see him. All she could think about was sleep.

She struggled to make it through the whist game. Her

play was so badly off that quitting was the only decent thing to do.

'Another game?' Sir Reginald asked eagerly. 'We need a chance to recoup.'

The masked couple playing them were eager to continue.

'By all means,' the lady said with a smile.

Celia scooped up the few counters she had left. 'I must beg off. I fear I am so fatigued that I cannot think straight.'

Her gentleman opponent chuckled. 'All the more reason we wish to play you another game.'

She smiled at him. 'I am no challenge tonight. You both would be bored by me.'

'I suppose you are correct, madam,' the man responded.

She dropped her counters in her reticule and stood. 'Another time, perhaps.'

Her feet felt leaden as she walked to the cashier's room.

She poured out her counters. 'I am done for the night, Mr MacEvoy.'

He looked surprised. 'Early for you, is it not, madam?'

She tried to smile. 'It is, indeed. If—if you think Mr Rhysdale would not wish to pay me, just cash in what is left.'

'You may pay her, MacEvoy,' came a voice from behind her.

Celia turned. Rhys stood there, filling the doorway, his expression indiscernible.

'Forgive me, Rhys. I am so very tired. I cannot stay.' She took four crowns from MacEvoy's hand and placed them in the leather purse inside her reticule.

When she stepped towards the door again, he did not move. She raised her eyes to his and he gave way for her.

But he walked with her to the hall.

'You are fatigued?' He made it sound as if she were making an excuse.

'I am, Rhys. Truly. There is no other reason.'

He touched her arm, an expression of concern on his face. 'How do you plan to summon your carriage?'

She placed the back of her hand against her forehead. 'I had not thought that far ahead.'

He took her arm. 'Come. I'll sort it out for you.'

She was too tired to protest.

They reached the hall.

Rhys said, 'Tell me where your coachman waits for you and I'll send for him.'

She shook her head. 'I do not know where he waits. I think he goes back to the stable.'

'Then I will send for a hackney coach and alert your coachman when he calls for you.'

He'd have to send someone to Piccadilly to a coach stand. It seemed a foolish fuss. 'Rhys, I do not live far from here. Would you have someone walk me home?'

'I will walk you home.' He turned to Cummings and asked for Celia's shawl and his hat and gloves.

When they stepped outside, he asked, 'You do not mind me knowing your address?'

She shrugged. 'You know who I am. It would be a simple matter for you to discover where I live.'

He offered his arm. 'Which way?'

She held on to him, grateful for his strength. 'To Half Moon Street.'

As they walked to St James's Street and turned towards Piccadilly, Celia removed her mask and carried it by its ribbons.

The night air felt cool on her face, reviving her. 'I feel better in the fresh air.'

'Are you ill?' he asked.

'Not ill, I do not think. Tired.' Her limbs felt heavy. 'All I wish is to go to bed.'

Her gaze flashed to him. She realised what she'd said. He simply kept walking.

Finally he spoke. 'The late nights are too taxing for you.'

They hadn't been. She'd been energised by the success of her gambling—and the pleasures of her affair with him. The fatigue came on all of a sudden.

'I just need a little rest, I expect,' she told him.

In spite of herself she relished the feel of his strong arm under her fingers. It reminded her of how it felt to be held by him.

Her body flared merely at the memory and the intensity of her desire momentarily drove away fatigue. She wanted him so desperately she thought of asking him to take her back to the Masquerade and put her to bed in his room.

And remain there with her.

But an image of Rhys standing next to Westleigh, greeting guests in the ballroom, also flashed through her mind. She tried to shake it away.

She broke the silence between them. 'One could almost like London if it always felt like this.'

'Like what?' His voice matched the night.

'Quiet and still.' A carriage sounded in a nearby street, the horses' hooves and the wheels loud even at a distance. She smiled. 'At least, mostly quiet and still.'

He reached over and touched her hand, but released it and kept walking.

They reached Piccadilly and he gestured down the length of the street. 'It is an impressive sight.'

Gas lamps bathed the street in gold and the busy traffic of the day was reduced to a carriage or two. All the dirt of the day was obscured by the night.

'It is lovely,' she admitted.

They crossed Piccadilly.

'But you plan to leave.' He said this as a statement.

'I am not meant for London,' she said.

They fell silent again.

This time he spoke first. 'I want you to stay.'

She stopped and turned to him, but she could not speak. Instead she reached up and touched his cheek.

He clasped her hand and pressed it to his lips. 'I do not want what we've had to end.'

Neither did she. 'Oh, Rhys.'

He pulled her into an embrace and she could not help but melt against him. Encircled in his arms she did not feel alone.

She rested her head against his heart and was comforted by its steady beat. 'I am not leaving yet, Rhys.'

She felt his voice rumble in his chest. 'Then come to me as often as you can, Celia.'

She pulled away, only to nod her head.

She'd endure the contact with Westleigh and risk the intoxication of gambling to be with him a little longer.

They walked arm in arm along Piccadilly, the night wrapping them in an illusion that there was no one else in the world except the two of them. For the first time since the ball, Celia felt at peace.

They approached Half Moon Street. 'My street,' she said.

They turned on to the street and she wished her rooms were at the far end instead of so close to Piccadilly.

'Here.' She stopped, already bereft at parting from him.

He gathered her in his arms again and lowered his head, touching his lips to hers. 'Come to me tomorrow,' he whispered. 'If you feel well enough.'

He kissed her again and desire flamed through her, its

intensity taking more of a toll on her body than her fatigue. All she wanted was to share a bed with him and re-experience the delight of joining her body with his.

She threw her arms around him and hugged him close. 'I will if I can, Rhys,' she cried.

It would be impossible for her to stay away.

Celia knocked lightly on the door to her rooms and listened through it until she heard footsteps approach. 'Tucker?' she called through the door. 'It is Lady Gale.'

The lock turned and the door opened.

Her butler looked surprised.

'Do not be concerned, Tucker.' She walked inside. 'I merely decided to leave early.'

He leaned outside. 'The carriage, ma'am?'

She turned around and glimpsed Rhys walking away, a mere shadow in the darkness. 'No carriage, but I was escorted home. Someone must tell Jonah.'

'I will see to it, ma'am.' He closed the door and turned the lock again.

'You can go to bed early.' She gave a wan smile. 'I am indebted to you for the long hours I force you to keep. Please know how grateful I am.'

He bowed his head. 'I can only admire you, my lady.'

She started up the stairs. Her flesh ached from missing Rhys and her fatigue returned. Suddenly it was like scaling the Alps to reach the first floor.

She opened her bedchamber door and startled her maid.

'Oh!' The woman popped up from a chair. 'I must have dozed. What time is it? Forgive me, ma'am.'

'I do not mind if you doze, Younie.' Celia yawned. 'I am home early. It must only be half-past two. I became so fatigued.'

Younie hurried over to her. 'Are you ill, ma'am? Let me

feel your forehead.' She put the back of her hand against Celia's forehead.

'I do not feel feverish,' Celia responded. 'Merely tired.'

Her maid took her shawl from her shoulders and Celia dropped her reticule and mask on a table.

As soon as she was all dressed and ready to crawl into bed, the door opened. 'Another night of gallivanting, I see.' Her mother-in-law strode in.

Celia turned to her maid. 'You may go, Younie. Goodnight and thank you.'

Younie ducked her head down and walked out of the room.

Celia turned away from her mother-in-law. 'I did not hear you knock, Lady Gale.'

'Well, I didn't knock,' the woman answered without apology. 'Was that the man whose bed you are warming? I saw you with him outside.'

Celia rubbed her temples. 'What were you doing at the window at this hour?'

The older woman pursed her lips. 'Why, waiting to see you, of course. Otherwise I'd be asleep.'

Celia swung around. 'Why? Is something amiss? With Adele?'

Lady Gale put her fists on her hips. 'Nothing is amiss with Adele except having a stepmother who is a strumpet.'

Celia's fingers pressed into her temples. 'So you have merely come to lash me with your tongue. I have no patience for it. Leave me, Lady Gale. I will not discuss my private affairs with you. I cannot tolerate you any longer.'

Lady Gale lifted her chin. 'What will you do? Toss me out?'

Celia speared her with her gaze. 'Do not tempt me, ma'am.'

Her tone must have penetrated, because her mother-in-law turned around and left the room. Celia climbed into bed, but now was so agitated by her mother-in-law that sleep evaded her.

By morning Celia was convinced she was ill. When she woke she felt so nauseated she feared she could not reach the chamberpot in time to vomit. She remained in bed the whole day and begged off from attending the social event of the evening.

She also had Tucker deliver a message to Rhys to tell him she could not come to the gaming house that night.

When she felt equally unwell the next day, as well, she sent a message to Rhys saying she would return when she was recovered.

She missed him. And not only for the lovemaking. She missed watching him walk through the game room watching everything with an experienced eye. She missed sharing supper with him and sharing the trivialities of each night together. She missed being held by him.

Days passed. Sometimes by afternoon, Celia would feel the malaise leave her, but by evening all she wished was to retire early and sleep.

She had apologised to Younie and the housekeeper more than once for not being able to hold down her food and causing them such unpleasantness.

One morning Younie brought her dry toast and tea in bed.

'I do not know why I am not recovering,' she said to her maid. 'I am never ill. Adele thinks I should call the physician, but I keep thinking tomorrow I will feel better.'

Younie put her hands on her hips and frowned. 'You

are fatigued. You have nausea. Do you have any aches or pains?'

Celia coloured. 'It might be shameful to say, but my breasts are sore. I've had aches with ague before, but never in such a part of me.'

Younie cocked her head. 'When are your courses due?'

When were her courses due? She could not remember the last time she had bled. It must have been…several weeks ago. About the time she and Rhys—

She blanched. 'Younie, you do not think?'

'That you are increasing?' Her maid lifted her brows.

Celia covered her mouth with her hand. 'It is not possible!'

In all the time her husband tried to make her conceive a child, she'd failed. Failed. She was barren. Gale had called her barren. Even his physician had called her barren.

She hugged her abdomen. Could it be? Could she have a baby inside her? Rhys's baby?

What a miracle! A blessing.

'Younie! Could it be true? Could it really be true?' Was she truly carrying Rhys's child?

'Time will tell, ma'am, but it is my guess.'

For a moment Celia felt like dancing, but only for a moment. Then the reality of her situation descended upon her.

She was a respectable baron's widow and she was pregnant with her lover's child.

'Oh, Younie,' she cried, 'then what am I to do?'

Chapter Thirteen

Celia was too restless to remain in bed. She rose and dressed. The idea of a baby had firmly taken route and her head spun with wonder and fear.

Fear, because it could very well be that she merely suffered from some sort of stomach malady and her bleeding would start any day. She could so easily suffer a crushing disappointment.

But if it were true? She hugged herself in delight.

She would move to a place where no one knew her, a place where she could present the child as legitimate and no one would question it. Mentally she calculated how much money it would cost to give her child a trouble-free life—

She caught herself making plans and stopped herself. Patience, she cautioned herself. As Younie said, time will tell.

To keep her mind busy, she came downstairs to the small parlour where she kept her desk and papers. Her mother-in-law and Adele were out, so it was a good time to go through the bills that had arrived in the last few days. She counted what she owed and tallied her funds.

Being away from the Masquerade Club had hurt her finances. How could bills mount so swiftly?

She had reworked the figures for the third time when her butler knocked on the door.

'A gentleman to see you,' he announced.

She looked up in surprise. 'To see me?' Callers came to see her mother-in-law or Adele, but never Celia. 'Who is it?'

'Mr Rhysdale, ma'am,' Tucker said.

Her face heated. 'Is he waiting in the drawing room?'

'Yes, ma'am.'

Her heart beat faster. 'I'll go there directly. Bring some tea, though, will you?'

'Immediately, ma'am.' He bowed.

She took a breath and pressed her hands to her abdomen before rising from her chair.

As she approached the open door of the drawing room, he turned and her heart leapt in her chest.

She'd never seen him in daylight.

'Celia.' He crossed the room to her and he took her into his arms.

At the same instant, she closed the door behind her. 'I have been worried over you.' He let go to examine her. 'You look pale. You are still ill. What can I do?'

He could hold her again. She'd desperately missed the comfort of his arms, the warmth of his concern.

Instead she smiled up at him. 'I am better. Truly. It is an odd illness that comes and goes, but I think I am over the worst.'

His strong forehead creased. 'What does the physician say?'

She glanced aside. 'I did not consult a physician. It did not seem so serious.'

He surprised her by wrapping his arms around her

and holding her close. The sheer glory of it made her want to weep.

A knock sounded and she pulled away. 'Tea.'

Tucker entered and set the tea tray on the table.

When he left, Celia said, 'Would you sit, Rhys? I'll pour you tea.'

He hesitated, but lowered himself onto the sofa adjacent to her chair.

A glance at the biscuits Cook had provided and the scent of the tea made Celia queasy again, but she managed to pour for him and for herself.

She quickly took a bite of a biscuit and swallowed it. 'You should not have come, Rhys.'

He frowned. 'Do not say that. I had to see how you went on. There was no way I could ask anyone.' He lifted the teacup, but set it down again without drinking. 'I chose a time when you were unlikely to have other callers.'

She opened her mouth to ask him what he would have done if she'd been abed? Or if Adele had spoken to him? Or, worse, her mother-in-law? But she bit her tongue.

She was too glad to see him. 'I am truly much better. I—I might even come to the club tonight.' She needed to play cards. She needed money. 'How are things there?'

'The same.' He shook his head. 'Not the same. You are missed.' He took her hand in his. 'I have missed you.'

She warmed to his touch.

And thought of the baby inside her.

But it likely was not a baby inside her, but merely a fanciful dream.

His gaze seemed to caress her face and his hand warmed hers.

He stood again. 'I should not stay long, I know.'

She rose, as well, and he reached out and touched her

hair. 'I needed to see you for myself and now that I have—'
He pulled her into an embrace and kissed her.

Passion rushed through her, demanding release. She hungrily kissed him back, wanting him inside her, wanting to be joined with him and together climb the heights of pleasure. He pressed her against him and she felt his male member from beneath his clothes.

Most of all, she wanted to be carrying his child inside her.

He broke off and leaned his forehead against hers. 'Come tonight, but only if you are well enough.'

She nodded.

He stepped away and straightened his clothes. With a grin and another quick kiss, he walked out of the room. She ran to the window to watch him leave and catch the last glimpse of him.

To her horror, she saw her mother-in-law and Adele approaching.

The front door opened and Rhys walked out just as they reached the door. He tipped his hat to Adele and Lady Gale before turning in the other direction and striding away.

A moment later Celia heard her mother-in-law's strident voice quizzing Tucker.

Celia walked to the drawing-room door. 'Leave Tucker in peace, Lady Gale. If you have questions, ask me.'

Her mother-in-law marched directly to the drawing room. Celia retreated to the middle of the room and awaited the assault.

Her mother-in-law slammed the door behind her. 'Was that Westleigh's bastard son leaving our rooms?'

How detestable her mother-in-law was!

Celia straightened. 'It was Mr Rhysdale.'

'He had the gall to call upon us?' Lady Gale looked completely affronted. 'How dare he?'

Celia glared at her. 'He did not call upon you. He called upon me.'

The older lady peered at her. Her mouth worked, but no words emerged. She jabbed her finger at Celia. 'I see what it is,' she finally managed. '*He* is the one.'

Celia lifted her chin.

Adele's voice came from the doorway. 'What do you mean, he is the one?'

Celia flashed her mother-in-law a warning look. Adele did not need to know this.

But Lady Gale swung around to her granddaughter. 'He is the one she has been bedding! Imagine it, Adele. He is not only a bastard but a gambler, as well.'

'Lady Gale!' Celia cried. 'You will not speak that way in my presence. Leave the room this instant!'

The old woman tossed her head and in her outrage swirled around as nimble as a nymph. 'That suits me perfectly. I cannot abide the sight of you.' When she reached Adele, she said, 'Come with me, Adele.'

Adele shook her head, instead entering the room. 'What is she talking about, Celia? Is it true? Are you having a—a—liaison with Ned's half-brother?'

Celia put her hand to her abdomen. 'Listen to me, Adele—'

Lady Gale re-entered the room. 'And this illness of yours. This vomiting and fatigue. I know what it is about!'

Celia raised a hand to halt her.

Her mother-in-law took no heed. 'You are pretending to be with child, are you not? What a convincing act. What do you hope to accomplish from that, I wonder?' She marched off again.

Adele stared at Celia, eyes wide, mouth agape. 'Celia! Are you—?'

Celia turned to the girl. 'I do not know why I am ill.'

'You are *increasing?*' Adele was not listening to her. She tried again. 'It is impossible—'

Adele covered her mouth with her hand. 'You lied to me! You said you were gambling. But you were—were—engaging in lewd behaviour. Or were you doing both? Ned told me his half-brother runs a gambling place.' She tore at her hair. 'Oh! Ned! What will he think of me when he finds out? He will despise me. You have ruined everything! You have ruined my whole life!'

'Adele!' Celia raised her voice. 'Stop this nonsense at once.'

Adele covered her ears. 'I will not listen to you ever again!' She ran out the door and her footsteps pounded up the stairs, accompanied by loud sobs.

Celia collapsed into a chair, clutching her stomach, trying to quiet the waves of nausea, rage and fear that swept through her.

When Ned pulled up to Adele's rooms in his curricle, the door opened and she ran out to him. She climbed into the curricle before he could do more than extend his hand to assist her.

'What is it, my darling?' he asked her.

'Oh, Ned!' Tears poured from her beautiful eyes. 'Please just drive. I wish to be away from here. Is there somewhere we might be alone? I do not wish to see another person.'

As a gentleman, he ought not be alone with her, but he could not resist indulging her every request.

'We should walk, then.' They could be more private on foot. 'I can take the horses back to the stable if you wish.'

She threaded her arm through his and leaned against his shoulder.

When something troubled her, Ned wanted only to ease

it, but he did not press her to tell him what distressed her. Better wait until they could be alone.

His horses were stabled at Brook's Mews behind Brook Street. If the stablemen were surprised to see him return so soon, and in the company of a young lady, they gave no indication.

'I will not need them the rest of the day,' he told the men.

He jumped down and reached up to help Adele by placing his hands at her tiny waist and lifting her down. It was so close to an embrace that he felt the blood rush through his veins.

From the mews they walked to the park and found a path leading to a secluded bench overlooking the Serpentine.

'No one will disturb us here, my love,' Ned told her.

She flew into his arms and sobbed against his chest.

'Tell me what is the matter?' he begged, unable to bear this helpless feeling.

'Oh, Ned!' she cried. 'It is all too wretched. I must tell you, because I would not hold back anything from you, not for the world. You must know all, even though—even though—' She shuddered. 'You will despise me and I know you will never want to marry me.'

He became very alarmed. 'Come. Sit with me and tell me what it is.'

He led her to the bench. When they sat, he kept hold of both of her hands.

She took a deep breath. 'I come from a wretched family.'

Was that all? No family member of hers could be more wretched than his father.

'Today I discovered that my stepmother—although I never call her that—she is Celia to me. More like a sister, really, than a mother—' She waved a hand in front of her mouth and was too overcome to speak.

He used a soothing voice. 'I am sure it cannot be as bad as all that.'

She gulped. 'It is worse. I discovered—I discovered today that dear Celia—although she cannot be dear to me now—not after this…' She paused and held her hand against her chest. 'Celia is having an affair with your brother.'

'My brother!' He gaped at her. 'Hugh?'

'Not Hugh,' she snapped. 'Rhysdale.'

'Rhysdale?' He could not wrap his mind around it. 'But did they not just meet at the ball?' Comprehension immediately dawned. 'Oh, my God. She is…' He could not say it.

'She is gambling, as well. She goes out to gamble at night. I think that is how she met him.' Her tone was so disdainful that he dared not tell her why he knew precisely how her stepmother knew Rhysdale.

He collected his wits. 'Adele, this is not so dreadful. Surely Lady Gale has been discreet. And she is a widow. Widows are allowed some licence.'

She gazed at him with wonder. 'Do you mean you will not despise me for this?'

He put his arm around her and held her close. 'I could never despise you. It has nothing to do with you.'

'Oh, you are too wonderful.' She sighed against him and he revelled in the feel of her in his arms.

It almost made him forget the complications Rhys and her stepmother created.

'Oh…' She suddenly sounded more despairing. 'But you have not heard the worst of it.'

It could get worse?

She pulled away. 'Celia is going to have a baby.'

* * *

Celia returned to the Masquerade Club that night, but in turmoil, not anticipation. She felt more agitated than she'd been that night of the ball.

Adele refused to speak with her and Celia had been unable to explain to the girl that she could not be increasing. It was impossible. Wasn't it?

Celia had absolutely no idea how to tell any of this to Rhys. How could she say anything until her fears were confirmed once more—that she did not and could never have a child growing inside her?

'Good to see you, madam,' Cummings greeted her as he took her wrap. It was the most he'd ever spoken to her.

'I am pleased to be back.' She hoped it was wise to have returned. Her spirits were extremely low and she was still very tired.

MacEvoy grinned when she entered the cashier room. 'There she is at last. We've missed you, Madame Fortune.'

It touched her that her absence had been noticed, even in this devil's den.

MacEvoy handed her the counters with a friendly wink. 'I'll expect more from you later.'

'I will endeavour to please you, then.' She smiled and dropped the counters in her reticule.

As she approached the door to the game room, she adjusted her mask. She was dressed as she'd been the very first night she'd come here. Only then she'd not known that her heart would leap for joy to catch sight of the man who ran the establishment and that sharing his bed had taught her more about pleasure than she'd ever dared imagine. How unfair of fate to pair him with all that was dark and painful in her life.

But, then, fate had never been kind to her.

She pressed her hand against her stomach and stepped across the threshold.

The noise in the room swirled around her. She scanned the room looking for Rhys, but all she saw were men with red faces and bulging eyes playing at the gaming tables, a few women, masked and otherwise, hanging on to them with every throw of the dice or play of a card. At the card tables players kept emotion out of their faces, but their postures were tense and she knew nerves were exploding inside them.

There was nothing pleasant in view, nothing happy or peaceful. But as much as the scene revolted her sensitive stomach, another part of her was impatient to play.

A man broke away from the hazard table and approached her.

Lord Westleigh.

'Madame Fortune!' He seized her hand and kissed it. 'You have returned! I've despaired of ever being in your company again. Come, play hazard with me.'

She was due for losing at this game; she just knew it. But there was little chance she could avoid it. Others joined him in begging her to roll the dice.

'Very well,' she said, feigning enjoyment.

Another man cried, 'Madame Fortune is back! Quick. To the hazard table.'

The crowd around the hazard table grew larger as she walked closer.

'Shall we allow Madame Fortune to roll next?' Westleigh said loudly.

'I'll give it up.' The man in possession of the dice dropped them into Westleigh's hand.

Westleigh immediately gave the dice to Celia. 'Roll and make us all rich, Madame.'

She rolled, calling out, 'Six,' but made seven. She rolled

the second time and made seven again and won. The men and women around her cheered and a thrill rushed through her.

She continued to roll and to win more times than she lost. The betting was high and the winners feverish with excitement. Celia forgot she was tired, forgot that she loathed the sight and sound of gambling, forgot that she'd been looking for Rhys.

But soon it was as if a London fog parted and she suddenly saw him, watching her through the crowd like he'd watched her that first night.

She rolled a losing number.

Amidst the groans of defeat, she lifted her hands. 'That is enough for me, gentlemen!'

Westleigh scooped up the dice. 'One more roll, Madame. Have pity on us.'

She stepped away. 'My luck is turned. It is time to stop.' And time to see Rhys.

The players closed ranks around the hazard table and play continued without her. She backed away and felt a hand on her shoulder.

'Celia.' It was Rhys.

She turned to face him.

His expression was all concern. 'Are you feeling well enough to be here?'

She wanted to say her illness was merely the effect of carrying his child inside her, but that was no more than a foolish dream, one she'd dreamed before and been disappointed. She could say nothing to him about a mere foolish dream.

A week. If another week went by and she did not have her menses, she would dare to believe in it. She would tell him then.

'I am still tired.' And queasy. 'But I think it is a little better today. I need to be here. I need to play.'

He turned impassive. 'Then I will leave you to play. You no longer require my assistance gaining partners.' He stepped away.

She placed a hand on his arm to halt him. 'May I see you later?'

His eyes darkened and she felt the air between them grow alive with desire. 'Come to my room when you are ready.'

Rhys walked away from her, but turned to watch her. She remained where they'd stood together for a moment, before strolling through the room, greeting others and stopping for brief chats. Finally she joined three others for whist and he was satisfied that she was well settled.

Xavier came up to him and turned to look in the same direction as Rhys. 'She has returned, I see.'

The two friends had achieved a sort of truce while she'd been ill, but now Rhys heard something in Xavier's voice that put him on guard.

'Her illness is improved,' Rhys said in as matter of fact a tone as he could muster.

'She won at hazard again.' Xavier's voice was mild, but Rhys knew his message. 'Quite a winning streak. Unlike any we've seen these last few days.'

Rhys faced him. 'Your meaning?'

Xavier backed away. 'No meaning. A mere observation.'

In spite of himself, Rhys's suspicions were aroused and he played a version of Xavier's discourse in his head. There was still much Rhys did not know about her. How many more secrets had she kept from him? She needed money. Maybe her need was so great she was driven to cheating.

She was skilled enough to know how. Her father had been accused of it.

He stopped himself.

Her father had been killed because of cheating. Certainly that alone would serve as a caution to her. Besides, he did know her. In an intimate way, where secrets were harder to keep.

He glanced towards the doorway and saw Ned and Hugh advancing directly on him.

He met them halfway.

'We would speak with you,' Ned demanded.

Hugh looked as if he were ten years old again and ready to throw the first punch.

Rhys nodded. 'Let us go somewhere private.'

He led them up to his drawing room on the floor above.

Once inside the room, he closed the door. 'Now what is it?'

'How could you do this?' Hugh spat. 'It is abominable even coming from the likes of you.'

Rhys's brows rose. 'Perhaps you might tell me what it is I have done.'

Ned faced him squarely. 'Lady Gale is with child and you are the father.'

It was like a blow direct to his gut.

For a second Rhys could not even breathe. But he knew better than to give away his utter shock. He kept his face still, his expression bland. They obviously held all the aces and he had nothing.

'Who told you this?' He kept any emotion from his voice.

'Miss Gale,' Ned responded. 'And her distress over the matter is sufficient reason for me to call you out.'

Rhys merely raised his eyes to him. 'Are you calling me out, Neddington?'

Ned backed off. 'No. Of course not. But this is badly done of you, Rhys.'

Hugh's hands curled into fists. 'Haven't you done enough to our family?'

Rhys turned his steely gaze on him. 'You are forgetting who you came to when the family needed rescuing.'

'See here—' Hugh shot back.

'Stop it, Hugh,' Ned snapped. He faced Rhys again. 'Do you deny this? That you have been engaging in an affair with Lady Gale, who we now know must be Madame Fortune? That you have got her with child? A respectable woman from a respectable family. Think what this will mean to her stepdaughter.'

'To her stepdaughter?' Rhys laughed. 'You malign both Lady Gale and Madame Fortune and your concern is solely for the stepdaughter?'

Ned's eyes flashed. 'Miss Gale is my sole concern. Do you deny what we say?'

Hugh broke in. 'What are you going to do about it?'

Rhys made himself look blandly from one brother to the other, while inside he was furious with their implication that he was not worthy of a respectable woman. He was furious that they would criticise Celia as if her behaviour would somehow soil her stepdaughter's virginal mind. Mostly he was wounded to the depths of his soul that Celia had not told him herself that she carried his child.

Finally he spoke. 'If any of this were true, I fail to see how it is your concern. Do not come here and shout insults at me and to ladies who are not present to defend themselves. And stop spreading gossip like a set of garrulous hags.'

'Everyone knows you are having an affair with Madame Fortune!' Hugh cried.

Rhys countered, 'They suspect. They do not know.'

Hugh sprang at Rhys.

Ned held his brother back. 'Are you denying this, Rhys?'

'I am not crediting any of it with more comment,' Rhys replied in a firm voice. 'One thing I will tell you. Do not speak with Madame Fortune about this. I will not have you throwing out accusations and speculations against patrons who have chosen to be masked and anonymous. You will keep silent on this manner or you will answer to me. And, do not forget, you need the money I provide to you.'

'It is our money,' Hugh cried. 'We invested everything we had left in this.'

'And I have paid back that investment,' Rhys responded. 'We are even now.'

'You still owe us!' Hugh leaned into Rhys's face.

Rhys pushed him away. 'If I hear one more word of this from anyone else, I'm holding you responsible and these doors will be closed to you.'

'But this is our gaming house!' Hugh cried.

Rhys swung so close his face was inches from Hugh's. 'This is my gaming house. That was the bargain. I decide who may enter and who will be banned.'

Ned pulled Hugh away. 'We've said our piece. Let us go now.'

Rhys drove them towards the door. 'Remember my warning. Keep silent on this or answer to me!'

They left the room and he slammed the door shut behind them.

Chapter Fourteen

With Ned and Hugh gone, Rhys had no need to hold in his rage. He prowled through the room, wishing he were in some seedy tavern in the East End so he could pick a fight and break some furniture, smash some glass.

Why had she not told him?

With a growl he pulled the door open and ran down the stairs, slowing only when reaching the last step. Cummings glanced up at him in surprise.

'Cummings, ask Madame Fortune to come upstairs as soon as she is able,' he ordered.

Cummings gave him a queer look, but nodded.

Rhys returned to the drawing room to pace and contemplate what in the room he might smash against the wall.

She said she was barren.

Had she lied to him about that? To what purpose? Having a child would shame her and, in his station of life, make no difference to him.

Except it did make a difference to him.

He gripped the back of a chair.

No child of his would come into the world in shame. No child of his would bear the burden of being called bastard.

It seemed a long time until he heard her footsteps on the stairs. He waited in the doorway.

She climbed the stairs wearily and a wave of worry washed over him. She was still ill.

She glanced up and saw him waiting for her. 'Rhys?'

He turned and re-entered the drawing room.

She followed, pulling off her mask. 'What is it, Rhys?'

He supposed he looked like thunder. He composed his face. 'Neddington and Hugh just called upon me.'

She gave him a wary look. 'And?'

He stepped close to her and leaned even closer. 'They said you are carrying my child.'

She blanched. 'I—'

He seized her arms for a moment, but immediately released her. 'Were you planning on informing me of this fact?'

'It—it cannot be a fact,' she countered. 'I was told by a physician that I am barren, that I would never conceive.'

He seethed. 'Then why say so to Miss Gale?'

'Adele,' she whispered in an exasperated tone. She raised her head to Rhys. 'I told her it could not be true, but she would not listen.'

He held her arms again and looked down into her eyes. 'But it is true, is it not? Tell me now.'

She glanced away. 'I can only say that—that I am late in bleeding.'

'Then it might be true,' he persisted.

She bit her lips and pain contorted her features. 'It might be,' she said in the tiniest voice.

He made an angry sound and released her again, swinging away and putting some distance between them.

Celia reeled under the force of his anger, so unexpected. So crushingly disappointing.

She blinked away sudden tears and straightened her spine. 'Do not concern yourself, Rhys. If it is true, I ask nothing of you. I have enough money to care for a child.' Or she would after a few more weeks of gambling.

He swivelled back, fire shooting from his eyes. 'Do you think I am trying to shirk responsibility? Is that the sort of man you think I am?'

She was taken aback. 'Why else be angry about my possible condition?'

He seized her wrists and pulled her close. 'I am angry you did not tell me. You might have done so this morning when I called and we were private. I am angry that you excluded me from this.'

She tried to pull away. 'How could I say a word of it when everything I know speaks against it?' Her throat grew tight. 'I cannot hope it is a child.'

He released her, his expression full of pain. 'You do not want it to be true.'

The grief of many years' duration enveloped her once again. 'I want it to be true with all my heart.'

He reached out to her again, this time tenderly touching her arm. 'Then we have no conflict, no scandal. We can marry. You and our child will want for nothing.'

'Marry?' No. Never. Marriage was misery, a prison.

But this was Rhys. She might wake every morning in his arms, see his smile when sunshine filled the room. She might walk with him to the shops, sit next to him at the opera, share every meal with him across the table from her.

A knock sounded at the door and Cummings's voice carried into the room, 'Mr Rhysdale. Come. There is trouble in the game room.'

He looked at her with regret. 'We'll continue this.'

He left with Cummings, leaving the door ajar. Sounds

of raised voices reached her ears. She tied her mask in place and followed him.

From the game room door the scene unfolded.

One man lunging after another, Xavier and another man holding him back. 'You took my money! All of it! I am ruined! It is out of all fairness!'

The other man leaned threateningly towards him. 'Are you calling me a cheat? I play a fair game!'

Rhys stood between the two. 'We'll have none of this. No fighting.' He turned to Xavier. 'Take him away.' To the other man, Rhys said, 'Calm yourself, sir. I suggest you cash out and leave. Tempers are too high at the moment.'

'I won't be accused of cheating!' the man cried. 'I demand satisfaction.'

'I will have you banned if you do not calm down.' Rhys pushed him away. 'He is upset at losing, nothing more.'

Xavier and the other man dragged their charge out of the game room. As they passed by Celia, the man continued to wail, 'I am ruined! What am I to do? I am ruined.'

Rhys meanwhile stuck with the other man, waiting for him to pick up his counters and a vowel written by the loser. He walked with the man past Celia, out the door, presumably to the cashier.

The other patrons turned back to their games and soon the sounds of wins and losses returned in its familiar cadence. Celia grew cold as she watched their faces. At the hazard table all eyes were riveted on the roll of the dice. At *vingt-et-un,* the players were spellbound by each turn of a card, at faro, the dealing box. Yet one man's life was ruined and another man was willing to risk death for some dubious code of honour.

The room held perhaps seventy players and it seemed to Celia that each of the men wore her father's face. She closed her eyes only to see him again returning home with smiles and gifts, swinging her mother around and swearing that life would be easy from then on. She blinked and he was now weeping into her mother's lap, begging for forgiveness for losing money for rent, for clothing, for food.

Lord Westleigh sidled over to her. 'Might I interest Madame in some more hazard? A little luck is in order, do you not think?'

She gaped at him. The scenario played out before her eyes a moment ago might have been the way it had occurred with her father. Did not Westleigh remember that night? Should she ask him if her father won? Was that why Westleigh accused him of cheating? Was that why her father had challenged him to a duel? Should she ask how it felt for Westleigh to shoot the pistol and see her father fall? Or how he lived with himself for merely running away? He'd hid behind some gentleman's code of silence and had never been held accountable for the crime.

'No hazard, sir,' she managed.

'Then let us have some supper.' He took her arm.

She recoiled. 'No!'

He gripped her harder. 'Come now, madam, you must know I have developed a regard for you. You would do very well to take advantage of that fact.'

'Take advantage!' The very sight of him sickened her.

'I would pay handsomely for some…private time with you. You would not regret the money or the experience.' He leered at her.

'Release me, sir,' she demanded. 'I'll not bear your insults.'

He pulled her closer. 'Do not say you prefer that bastard Rhysdale? He is nothing compared to me, I assure you. A mere hireling. You cannot prefer him to me.'

She lowered her voice, so angry at him it trembled. 'How dare you call him a hireling! And I do prefer him

to you. I prefer any man to you. Do not ever approach me
again. For any reason.' She wrenched out of his grasp and
walked out of the game room.

He caught her in the hall and pinned her against the
wall, leaning down into her masked face. 'You will regret rebuffing me, madam. I have ways of retaliating
against such insults.' His mouth stretched into a malevolent grin. 'Perhaps I will unmask you. You would dislike
that, wouldn't you.'

When he let go of her to reach for her mask, she pushed
hard on his chest, knocking him off balance.

She hurried to get away from him. As she neared the
cashier's office. Rhys had entered the hallway, escorting
the winning gentleman out. He gave her an apologetic
glance, but she could not meet his eyes, nor tell him what
just happened to her at the hands of Westleigh. She walked
into the cashier's room.

MacEvoy looked up at her. 'Cashing out, Madame?'

'Yes.' She could hardly speak.

When she made her way to the hall, Westleigh was nowhere to be seen.

Xavier emerged from Cummings's coat room.

'Is Rhys in there?' she asked.

'He is. He is calming the fellow down,' Xavier responded. 'Do you wish me to get him for you?'

She shook her head. 'But I must beg a favour from you.'

'Of course.' He inclined his head graciously.

'Walk me home.'

It took all of an hour to calm Mr Poole enough to release him to go home without the intention to kill himself
on the way. It also took a loan from Rhys of one hundred
pounds, money Rhys suspected he would never see again.

But he did not want the pall of suicide hanging over his

gaming house. Besides, the man had a wife and children. They should not have to pay for the man's sins.

Poole had to endure a strong lecture from Rhys regarding the duty a man owed to his children. It was a lecture that had special meaning to Rhys now and he was eager to settle matters between him and Celia.

As soon as Poole walked out of the house, Rhys ran upstairs to the drawing room, but Celia was not there. He checked the bedchamber. She was not there, either.

He returned to the hall.

Cummings stood in his usual place.

'Did you see Madame Fortune?' he asked.

Cummings shook his head.

Rhys checked the game room, the supper room and the cashier. MacEvoy told him she'd cashed out.

He returned to the hall just as Xavier opened the front door and entered.

Xavier held up a hand. 'She asked me to walk her home.'

'Did she say why?' Was she ill again?

Xavier walked over to him. 'She barely said a word. Something upset her. That was evident.'

He waited for Xavier to say more or to indicate that her leaving was somehow proof that her intentions were nefarious, but Xavier said nothing.

Rhys's impulse was to rush out and run to her rooms to demand to speak with her, but it was nearly three o'clock in the morning.

He would see her when it was day and a civil time to call. He'd not wait a moment longer to discover why, after he had proposed marriage to her, she fled from him.

Chapter Fifteen

Ned spent the morning poring over his father's accounts with his father's secretary, attempting to decide which bills to pay and which to defer. Thanks to Rhys, the task was now tedious rather than desperate.

It was a task his father ought to be performing, but, ever since Ned and Hugh had discovered the dismal state of their financial affairs and confronted their father with it, their father had washed his hands of his responsibility, as if the bearers of the bad news were responsible for the problems.

Now, though, Ned had even more to worry over. Rhys had not confirmed or denied an affair with the younger Lady Gale, nor even if Lady Gale was Madame Fortune, which Ned strongly suspected. It agonised Ned that he and Hugh had managed merely to muddle matters rather than rescue Adele from this vexing problem.

Ned tallied a list of numbers for the third time, getting yet another total, when the butler knocked on the door.

'What is it, Mason?' Ned asked.

Mason bowed. 'Your mother requests your presence in her sitting room.'

What now? Ever since Rhys called that day and made

certain his mother was informed of the crisis, she'd demanded to know every detail of every decision he and Hugh made. And every problem they encountered.

He did not wish his mother to know this new scandal Rhys had created, not when it so involved and affected Adele.

He handed the ledger to the secretary and left the library to climb the stairs to his mother's private sitting room.

To his astonishment, when he opened the door to enter, she was there, his Adele, sitting next to his mother on her chaise longue.

'Adele!' He went straight to her, clasping her hands in his and looking into her beautiful eyes.

'Do sit, Ned,' his mother said impatiently. 'Miss Gale has been telling me an extraordinary tale. We wish to know what you have done about it.'

Adele's lip trembled. 'I have told your dear mother *everything*. I simply had to talk to someone and I could think of no one but her.'

'I see,' he said non-committally. He'd wanted to handle it without his mother's intervention.

'Did you speak to Rhysdale about it?' his mother asked. 'He must marry Lady Gale, of course. I hope you told him so.'

He frowned. 'Rhysdale would not speak to us of it. He called it gossip and all but tossed us out.'

'It is not gossip!' Adele cried. 'It is my life! I know that Celia is going to have a baby. Our maid verifies that it is so…' She paused as if reconsidering her words. 'Or, rather, she admits it is *possible*. Celia has all the signs, Younie said. You can ask her yourself. She came with me.'

Ned's brow knit in confusion. 'Lady Gale is with you?'

'Not Lady Gale!' Adele rolled her eyes. 'Younie. Our ladies' maid.'

His mother waved a dismissive hand. 'Rhysdale denies it?'

Ned shrugged. 'He did not confirm or deny it.'

'Then it must be true.' His mother nodded with certainty.

That logic escaped him.

'What I cannot understand...' Adele put a finger to her flawless cheek '...is how it could be true? How can Celia be carrying a baby when she was barren all those years with my father?'

'Maybe it was your father who could not...' how to put it delicately? he wondered '...father a child.'

Her eyes grew wide. 'But...but there is me! I am proof there was nothing wrong with my father.'

'Not necessarily so,' interjected his mother.

'What do you mean?' Adele turned to her.

His mother did not answer right away. 'I told you that I knew your mother, did I not?' she finally said.

Adele nodded her head.

His mother went on. 'She confided in me.' She gave Adele a very sympathetic look. 'Your mother was unhappy in her marriage to your father.'

Adele's expression darkened. 'I know that. My father was not a nice man. I remember him shouting at her when I was a little girl.' She glanced away in thought. 'He shouted at Celia, too.'

Ned's mother patted her hand. 'He was a cruel and thoughtless husband.' She grasped Adele's hand. 'You mother sought comfort elsewhere.'

Adele looked appalled. Ned wished his mother would stop. Surely this was no comfort to the poor young woman.

His mother went on. 'One Season, here in Mayfair, she fell in love with a fine gentleman, an army officer of good family, but nothing else to offer anyone. They had several months of happiness before he was sent to the Continent to fight the French.' She continued to hold Adele's hand. 'When news came to her that he'd died fighting the French in Holland, you were already growing inside her.'

Adele's eyes widened. 'Do not tell me!'

His mother turned very sympathetic. 'I am sorry to tell you, my dear.'

Ned reached over and took Adele's other hand. How difficult this must be for her. Had she not had enough to bear?

Adele squeezed his hand and broke out into smiles. She looked from his mother to him and back to his mother again. 'Oh, this is marvellous news. I disliked my father very much. I am glad I am not his daughter. I only wish I could have known my real father—' Her voice cracked and tears fell from her eyes.

'I will tell you all I know of him, but this is enough for one day,' his mother said to her.

Adele hugged his mother and all Ned could wish was that he could feel her arms around him, as well, but that, of course, would not be proper.

Perhaps if he could contrive to see her alone?

She glanced at him and concern filled her lovely face. 'Do you object very much, Neddington? I mean, I am not really the daughter of a baron. Does this change your opinion of me?'

He seized her hand again and pressed it to his lips. 'Nothing could change my opinion of you.'

His mother clapped her hands as if summoning re-calcitrant children. 'We are still left with the problem of Adele's stepmother and Rhysdale. Perhaps I should call upon Lady Gale and speak to her about this.' She turned to Adele. 'As your future mother-in-law, it might be seen as my duty.'

Celia sat in her bedchamber nibbling on toasted bread and sipping tea. The events of the night before returned to her mind, even though she wanted to banish them. Rhys's offer of marriage. The nightmare that was the gaming house. Its winners and losers.

Lord Westleigh.

Her stomach heaved and she quickly bit down on another piece of toast. The queasiness was manageable as long as she could keep some food down.

Her butler knocked on the door. 'A word with you, ma'am?' he asked.

'Come in, Tucker,' she responded. 'What is it?'

'Ma'am, I thought you should know that the new Lord Gale is at this moment in the drawing room. I am of the impression that the Dowager Lady Gale summoned him. They are in deep conversation about something.'

Celia pressed her fingers against her temple.

'What is she up to now?' she said below her breath. She looked up at Tucker. 'Is Adele with them?' Had Lady Gale not given up the scheme to marry Adele off to her cousin?

'No, ma'am,' replied Tucker. 'Miss Gale went out with Younie a while ago.'

Where would Adele have gone with Younie? That was a worry. Adele had been so upset with Celia the previous day she would neither speak to nor listen to Celia. Who knew what she was thinking today?

Celia stood. 'Thank you, Tucker. I will attend to it.'

Tucker left and Celia sat at her dressing table and hurriedly twisted her hair into a chignon. She pinched her cheeks to put some colour into her face and rushed out the door, not caring if her morning dress was presentable enough for Cousin Luther.

When she approached the drawing-room door, she slowed her pace, strolling in as if by accident rather than design. 'Why, Lady Gale. Luther. What a surprise.'

Lady Gale looked lightning bolts at her.

Luther rose and did not look any more pleased to see her. 'Good morning, Celia. We have been talking about you.'

Her gaze darted to her mother-in-law. 'I dare say you have.'

Luther pointed to a chair. 'Sit down. Now you are here, I wish to talk to you.'

She advanced to the seating area, but stopped some distance from their chairs. 'I prefer to stand.' There was nothing that would entice her to sit and be scolded as if a child.

His lips pursed. 'As you wish.'

Besides, if she stood, he also had to stand. That would make it easier for him to leave.

He shifted on his feet. 'Lady Gale informs me that you have been very indiscreet and that you are attempting to entrap the owner of a gaming hell into marrying you.'

Celia glanced at her mother-in-law. How cruel and heartless could that woman be? First to tell this tale to Adele and now Luther.

Celia put on a bold face. 'Lady Gale has been busy telling stories.'

Luther baulked. 'What? Do you say it is not true?'

She straightened. 'I do not feel compelled to say anything.'

He raised his nose at her. 'As the head of the family, I believe you owe me an explanation for this scandalous behaviour.' He shook his head in dismay. 'Imagine *trying* to marry a gamester. It is the outside of enough.'

A shaft of pain impaled her at the thought that Rhys wanted to marry her. She'd been unable to face him the previous night, but tonight, she must.

Not that Luther had any say in what she did.

'Head of the family?' She shook her head. 'You are not the head of *my* family. I owe you nothing.'

'See here, Celia!' His cheeks puffed out.

Her temper was lost. She went on. 'And if you were any *decent* head of the family, you would take responsibility for those who need your protection. Adele and her grand-mother should have been allowed to stay at Gale House, at least until you bring a wife there. Or you should have given them the dower house. What's more, you should have financed Adele's come-out and seen that her future was well settled. Adele and Lady Gale should have been your guests at the town house, not forced into rented rooms.' Her arm swept across the room.

'Celia!' her mother-in-law snapped. 'I will not have you speak to Cousin Luther in that manner.'

She turned her glare onto Lady Gale. 'Do not you speak to me at all.'

Lady Gale drew back as if struck.

Luther pounded the air with his fist. 'Your husband left his property and finances in such a sorry state that I am strained to the limit. You expect me to dole out more money?'

She shot back, 'A baron takes care of those in his charge. Or he should. The title comes with responsibility, not just property.'

Luther fussed at his collar. 'I do not need to stay here and listen to these insults.' He turned to Celia's mother-in-law. 'I planned to make an offer of marriage to your grand-daughter, ma'am, but you may rest assured that will never happen now. I wash my hands of the lot of you.'

'Spoken like a true gentleman,' Celia said sarcastically.

For a moment he looked exactly like her husband. He looked as if he might strike her, which Gale had done. Once.

Instead, Luther started for the door.

Celia's mother-in-law rushed after him. 'Luther! You cannot credit anything she says. I beg you to reconsider.'

He threw up his hands. 'I said I wash my hands of you.'

As soon as the two of them had left the room, Celia collapsed in a chair. Her legs trembled, her stomach heaved and she could taste vomit in her mouth. She fought to keep her food down.

She rested both hands on her abdomen. If only this were indeed a baby, then at least she would not be alone.

It would be some comfort.

Celia did not know how long she sat there, but the sounds of her mother-in-law pleading with Luther faded and she heard the front door close. Soon after, the sounds of the mantel clock ticking and an occasional carriage passing by were the only sounds she heard.

The knocker sounded and Tucker's voice reached her ears.

Another caller.

She ought to have retreated to her bedchamber when she'd had the chance, so she might have avoided anyone.

Tucker rapped at the door, still slightly ajar from Luther and Lady Gale's hasty departure. 'A gentleman to see you, ma'am.'

She turned, knowing instantly who she would see.

He stepped into the room. 'Hello, Celia.'

'Rhys.' She rose. 'Do come in.'

He walked towards her and the air changed around her. Her body came alive to him with a yearning she knew could never be satisfied. Why should this man capture her heart, of all men?

'I will skip the niceties, Celia.' His face was serious. 'Why did you leave last night? What happened?'

She turned away. 'I do not know how to explain.'

He took her arm and turned her back. 'I suggest you

try.' His eyes flickered with pain. 'Explain why you left me moments after I told you I will marry you.'

She opened her mouth in an attempt to explain what settled like a pit of fear inside her, but voices from the hall distracted her.

A moment later the door opened and Adele walked in. Behind her were Lady Westleigh and Ned.

'Celia, Tucker said you were in here—' Adele stopped cold when she caught sight of Rhys. 'Oh.'

A wave of nausea hit Celia, but she had to ignore it. She curtsied, instead.

'Lady Westleigh.' She and Rhys spoke at the same time.

'Lady Gale,' the woman responded. 'Rhys. It is just as well you are here. We ought to get this sorted out.'

Tucker stood at the door, looking apologetic.

'Some tea, if you please, Tucker,' Celia said.

From behind him she saw her mother-in-law approaching. 'I heard voices. Who is here?'

Tucker gave her a sympathetic look before turning away.

Her mother-in-law strode in.

Adele stopped her. 'Grandmama, you must be civil.'

Her grandmother gave the girl a scathing look.

Rhys nodded to her and she turned her head away, instead greeting Lady Westleigh. Ned said a stiff hello to Rhys.

'Shall we sit?' invited Lady Westleigh as if she were the hostess.

Adele and Ned sat together on the sofa. Lady Gale settled in one chair and Lady Westleigh in another.

Both Rhys and Celia remained standing.

'To what do we owe the pleasure of your visit?' Celia asked Lady Westleigh.

'Adele told me about this situation of yours,' the lady answered. 'I will help devise a plan that will minimise any scandal to the family.' She turned to Rhys. 'Rhysdale, you are crucial in how we must manage it.'

Celia felt him stiffen as her ladyship spoke.

'Adele has been busy,' he remarked in a low voice only Celia might have heard.

Lady Westleigh went on. 'Now, the only thing to do, of course, is for you to marry—'

'Do not be ridiculous,' Celia's mother-in-law piped up. 'This is all a sham. She is not increasing. It is impossible. She is unable to conceive. It is a proven fact.'

Rhys put his hand on Celia's arm, a steadying gesture that surprised her as much as her mother-in-law's unrelenting abuse.

Lady Westleigh immediately swung to the dowager. 'Why do you say that, ma'am?'

The older woman straightened. 'Because my son told me so. A physician confirmed the diagnosis.' She inclined her head towards Celia. 'She was a great disappointment to him.'

Lady Westleigh shook her head. 'I dare say the problem was not your daughter-in-law's, but your son's.'

Celia's mother-in-law huffed, 'Of course it was not my son's problem. He already sired a daughter.'

'Grandmama,' Adele broke in. 'Papa was not my real father. My mother gave birth to me after a love affair with an officer.'

Her grandmother clasped her heart. 'It isn't so—' She protested in every way manageable.

But her words did not penetrate through the blood pounding in Celia's ears. She touched her abdomen. She'd been so afraid to hope, but now hope turned to possibility and possibility to certainty. The magic and wonder of it made her want to throw herself in Rhys's arms. He'd given her this life growing inside her. There was no other man she would rather be the father of her child.

Her mother-in-law's words finally penetrated. 'My son was a virile man. Her womb was as dry as an old woman's!'

'Ma'am!' Rhys gave Celia's mother-in-law a fierce look. 'I demand you apologise to her. Do you hear me? I will not tolerate it.'

'*You* will not tolerate it?' her mother-in-law went on. 'You dare speak to me that way when you are nothing but a—'

'Bastard?' He said it for her. 'Madam, none of us choose our birth, but we do choose our behaviour. I've known women forced to live on the streets who have more grace and kindness than you.'

Lady Gale gave a disparaging laugh. 'I wager you would know countless women who live on the streets—'

'Lady Gale!' Celia cried. 'Leave this room now or I will have Younie pack your trunk and I will personally escort you out of the house.'

Adele shrieked and covered her mouth with her fist.

Her mother-in-law rose and, grumbling outrage and insults, flounced out of the room.

As soon as the door closed behind her, Lady Westleigh again spoke. 'Well, that was unpleasant. But perhaps now we can address the problem at hand.'

Rhys put up a hand. 'No, Lady Westleigh.'

Celia quickly added, 'I appreciate your concern, my lady, but I have no intention of discussing anything.'

'Lady Gale—' Ned sounded outraged '—this affects Adele and that reason alone gives me the right to speak with you about this. My mother, as well.'

Celia turned to him. 'I am not going to discuss it with you or your mother. Adele should have come to me first.'

She turned to her stepdaughter. 'I tried to speak with you yesterday, you recall.'

Adele crossed her arms over her chest. 'I did not wish to speak with you.'

'No, you preferred the ravings of your grandmother to anything I might say.' Celia gave her a penetrating look. 'And then you carried tales about me.'

'See here, Lady Gale,' Ned cried. 'She came to me and to my mother. There is nothing to object to in that.'

They were Westleighs and Celia wanted nothing to do with any of them. If it made Adele happy to join that family, so be it, but Celia was not obligated.

'Your family is not my family,' Celia said to Ned. 'Adele should have respected that.'

'You are maligning my dear Ned,' wailed Adele.

'She is not maligning Ned,' Rhys broke in. 'Stop acting like a child.'

'See here, Rhys!' Ned pressed his hands into fists and leapt from his chair.

Celia faced him. 'Ned, if you had an ounce of sense in your head, you would marry Adele now. You'd get a special licence and marry without delay. I dare say even with your financial difficulties, you have more resources to care for her than I have. You do not even have the courage to officially declare yourselves betrothed. It is wrong to leave her in such a precarious position.'

Ned fumed. 'I have good reasons! Besides, you cannot tell me when Adele and I should marry. That is for us to decide.'

Celia nodded. 'And you cannot tell me what I should do. That is for me to decide.'

Lady Westleigh stood. 'Your point is well taken, Lady Gale. We have been unforgivingly presumptive. Do forgive us.' She turned to her son. 'Ned, we should take our leave.'

He gave his mother a pleading look. 'I would like some time to speak with Adele.'

Celia turned to Rhys. 'Would you escort Lady Westleigh home?'

He gave her a questioning glance.

She spoke more quietly. 'I will see you later. We can talk then.'

Celia needed time. Time to think of her child, time to think of what was best to do.

Rhys bowed to Lady Westleigh. 'Ma'am, I would be honoured to escort you.'

Lady Westleigh nodded to Rhys. 'I accept. That is very kind of you.'

'I'll walk you both out,' Celia said.

As they stepped out of the room, Tucker approached with the tea tray.

Celia shook her head. 'We do not need tea now, Tucker. Lady Westleigh and Mr Rhysdale are just leaving.'

He nodded and carried the tray back to the hall and placed it on a nearby table. He went to retrieve Lady Westleigh's wrap and Rhys's hat and gloves.

Rhys took Celia aside. 'Come tonight, Celia. We must talk this out.'

She nodded, but did not know what she would say to him when the time came.

Chapter Sixteen

That night Rhys told Cummings to send Celia up to the drawing room as soon as she arrived and to summon him immediately.

She arrived at her usual time and Rhys left the game room to go to her.

When he entered the drawing room, she was standing in the centre of the room, waiting for him. In the candle-light her white shimmering gown made her look as if she were a vision created from his dreams.

She smiled tentatively. 'Do you think we will be disturbed this time?'

He frowned. 'Not for anything.'

He walked over to her as if under a spell, his body craving her almost as much as his soul. He did not wish to need her so much. He prided himself on not needing anyone. If one was alone, one had nothing to lose. Suddenly he risked losing this woman.

And their child.

He would never do what his father did. He would never abandon her or their child.

Rhys tried to pour all those emotions into an embrace.

She sighed and melted against him and, as their bodies entwined, the need to join with her grew to an even greater intensity.

He bent his head and placed his lips upon hers in a hunger that shocked him.

But her returning kiss felt like regret.

He broke away from the intense contact and held only her arms. 'I have missed you, Celia.'

Her lips trembled. 'I have missed you, too.'

So why had she left after he'd proposed marriage to her?

He released her and walked over to the decanter on the table. 'Brandy or port?'

She pressed her stomach. 'Neither. Just the thought of spirits makes me feel out of sorts.'

He turned back to her. 'You are still ill?'

'I am now thinking it might be because of a baby,' she said. 'My ills are expected, I am told.'

'Do you now believe you are increasing?' He poured himself some brandy.

'Yes.' She walked over to the table where his stood and fingered the wood. 'Lady Westleigh made me dare hope.'

'Hope?' He was more confused than ever.

Her eyes filled with tears. 'It is a miracle for me.'

He gulped his brandy and stared directly into her eyes. 'Then finish what we started this afternoon. Explain why things are not right between us.'

She turned away.

He drained the contents of his glass and pressed on. 'Explain why you will not simply say you will marry me and give our baby my name. Is it because of my birth?'

She turned in surprise. 'Not at all. I never even thought such a thing.'

'Then why?'

She averted her gaze again. 'I do not know how to say it.'

His insides twisted in pain, but he kept his expression blank. 'Celia. Just say it.'

She took a breath. 'I went down to the game room. And the men there—the ones you were sent to deal with—it was so much like what happened to my father and Westleigh.'

He could see that. 'You must know, though, that what happened had nothing to do with you or me.'

She held up a hand to stop him from interrupting. 'After you took the men out of the room, everyone went back to gambling as if nothing had happened. One man ruined. Another wanting a duel. And they all went back to the games. And then Westleigh came up to me and wanted to play hazard…' She stopped.

Westleigh.

What was she not telling him? What had Westleigh done?

'What did Westleigh do?' His voice deepened to a growl.

She made a nervous gesture. 'Nothing.'

He did not believe her.

She paced in front of him. 'It is merely that—that this is your world. It connects you to Westleigh, but I cannot be connected to it.'

He burned inside. 'You connected yourself to it.'

'Yes,' she admitted, 'but before I knew of him. And out of necessity. I needed—still need—the money. I loathe this—*him*—I loathe all this represents.'

'I am here out of necessity, as well.' Did she think he was given a choice? It was gamble or starve. 'But you are being less than truthful. You enjoy the play.'

'That is it,' she agreed. 'That is the seduction. The fever. It robs everyone of their senses. It is what killed my father.'

'I am not your father, Celia.' Rhys never played cards with emotion. 'Cards are nothing more than a tool to me.

A means to an end.' Survival once; now something more. 'I know when to play on and I know when to cash out.'

She shook her head. 'You cannot control luck, Rhys. No one can. All it takes is a turn of luck. I've lived this all during my childhood. I'll not subject my child to such a life.'

'And if I said I would give it all up?' He'd always intended to give it up. He had figured three years would do the trick. By then the Westleighs' fortunes would be solid and he would be wealthy enough to buy a factory or a ship or something.

She gave him a direct look. 'Do you know how many times my father promised to give it up?'

He stepped towards her, seized her arms and held her gaze. 'There is a difference between those men like your father and those like me. I am a gambler because when I had nothing, it was an honest way to get food to eat. When I won, I ate; when I lost, I didn't. I learned how to win. I learned how to survive and eventually I learned how to thrive. I will not go backwards. So do not hold up my gambling as a reason not to give your child a father.'

She averted her face. 'There is another reason.'

'And that is?'

She met his eye again. 'Westleigh. You are connected to Westleigh.'

He let go and swung away. 'He should not be considered at all!'

She would refuse to marry him because he was fathered by Westleigh? How ironic. When a boy he'd hoped his father would once call him son. Now that he accomplished it out of spite, doing so meant losing the woman he loved and a child he could call his own.

Rhys felt the pain of it as if a thousand sabres cut into his flesh. 'Westleigh keeps you from me? Am I again to be punished because of my birth?'

She reached out to him with sympathy on her face. 'Not because of your birth. Because you chose to entangle your life with his.'

He turned away, too angry at her—at himself—to trust what he would say or do next. 'Then we are done here.' He looked back with a sardonic smile. 'I must return to my gaming hell.'

She picked up her mask. 'Do you object to me playing tonight?'

That she would gamble after that speech of hers, after rejecting him for his gambling life, a life that was providing her needed funds, was a final sabre thrust.

'You are still in my employ, Celia.'

He walked out.

She'd hurt him and it agonised her. Almost as much as having to turn away from him for the sake of her child.

Rhys was a good man, a man to love. She'd never know his like again and her heart shattered at the thought that she had rejected him when she wanted him more than she could bear.

It was the gambling she did not want, *could* not want around her child. She could not bring a child into the sort of childhood she'd endured.

Gambling, its seductions and its perils, was the real villain. Now it had dealt her another blow. It had robbed her of the man she loved.

Celia tied the mask to her face and peeked in the mirror above the mantel to see if it concealed her identity well enough. The bone-weariness she felt tonight had little to do with her condition. She was exhausted from the battle she'd waged inside herself, the battle her heart had lost.

She walked down to the cashier's office and picked up her counters. She made her way to the game room, paus-

ing in the doorway while its sounds and sights enveloped
her. Lifting her chin, she walked through the room, looking around.

Looking for Rhys.

She found him conversing with a masked woman and
her partner at whist. He lifted his gaze to her as she moved
past him and her heart ached inside her chest.

'Madame Fortune!' a gentleman cried. 'Come! Play
some hazard. I'm in need of a little luck.'

Some others joined his plea.

A man came up to her from behind and leaned into her
ear. 'Do play hazard, my dear. See if your luck still holds.'

It was Lord Westleigh.

She straightened her spine and took another man's arm.
'If you insist. I will play hazard.'

Her first roll was a loss and the dice passed to another
player. When it came around to her again and she reached
down to scoop up the dice, Westleigh beat her to it.

He took the dice in one hand and grasped her hand in
the other, dropping the dice into her palm.

'Best of luck, Madame Fortune.' He smirked.

She expected to lose again, but she won the toss.

A shout rang out from the crowd, 'Madame Fortune
has found her luck!'

The next bets placed were overwhelmingly with her
next roll. Westleigh bet with her, as well.

With the crowd's enthusiastic encouragement, she rolled
again and again, not always winning, but more often than
not. More often than seemed likely. In spite of herself, it
roused her excitement and she was eager for the next roll.
Even Xavier's intent scrutiny did not deter her. The counters piled up and more and more players pushed their way
to place their bets.

Rhys appeared next to Xavier, watching her play. She

froze, dice in hand. She might be winning, but she was losing him a great deal of money. Bets were already placed and her next roll called. She had no choice but to roll, telling herself she'd stop after this.

She'd called seven and the dice fell into a three and a four. A cheer went up and the wagerers collected their counters.

Westleigh picked up the dice from the table and bounced them in his palm. 'They are weighted!' he said in a loud voice. 'I declare. The dice are weighted.'

She stared at him.

'Watch,' he said pointedly to Rhys and Xavier.

He placed one die on its corner and tried to make it spin. It fell immediately to the number four. He tried to spin the other die. It, too, failed and fell to a two.

Loud rumblings went up from the crowd.

'Weighted dice,' Westleigh intoned.

The voices grew more outraged.

'But, I never—' Celia tried to protest.

Rhys broke in. 'The hazard table is closed.' He walked around the table and seized Celia's arm. 'Come with me, madam.' He inclined his head to Westleigh. 'You, too, sir.' He turned to Belinda. 'Pay the winners, then you and Xavier come find us.'

'Rhys, I did not cheat,' Celia tried to tell him. He nearly dragged her through the room. 'I know nothing of fixing dice.'

But she did instantly understand her part in it. She'd chosen favourite numbers, not realising that the dice themselves were training her which numbers were more likely winners. She also knew that Westleigh had somehow planted the dice.

But why would he do such a thing? It lost money for the house and his family if he planted weighted dice.

Xavier had suspected her all along, though. He often watched her at hazard and she'd even admitted to him that she counted cards at *vingt-et-un*. Counting cards was not cheating, precisely, but it did put her in a class beyond the typical player.

As they reached the door, Ned and Hugh were walking in. 'What is this?' Hugh asked.

His father looked triumphant. 'She was caught cheating.'

Ned gaped at her. 'Cheating!'

Rhys led Celia to the hall. Westleigh and his sons followed.

Cummings became very alert when they all strode in.

Rhys said to him, 'We will be in my private drawing room. Tell Xavier and Belinda to come to us there.'

'Yes, sir,' Cummings responded.

Rhys practically dragged her to the room where he had just embraced her and kissed her and where she had spurned him.

Once inside the drawing room with the door closed, Ned blurted out, 'My lady, what more scandal are you going to bring to your family?'

His father's brows rose. 'My lady? Who is she?'

Celia did not want Westleigh, of all people, to know her identity, but, even more, she did not wish for someone other than herself to reveal it.

She pulled off her mask.

He looked at her blankly.

'Do you not recognise her?' Ned looked aghast. 'She is Lady Gale.'

Westleigh still appeared mystified.

'Miss Gale's stepmother,' Ned tried. 'You met them both at the ball.'

'He still doesn't know!' groaned Hugh.

Westleigh protested, 'I cannot be expected to recall every person ever introduced to me.'

Celia broke in. 'Perhaps he would know me better as Mr Cecil Allen's daughter.'

Westleigh's eyes flickered with comprehension.

'Yes,' she said in a low voice. 'I hoped you would remember him.'

Xavier and Belinda walked in the room.

'Sit, everyone,' Rhys said.

Westleigh shot him a withering glance, but did as he was asked. He turned to Ned and Hugh. 'She was using weighted dice at hazard. I dare say the house had some big losses.'

'If the dice were weighted, I knew nothing of it,' Celia retorted.

'I didn't know.' Belinda turned to Rhys. 'I put out new dice each night, as you ordered.'

Westleigh pointed to Xavier. 'You suspected Madame-whoever-she-is, did you not? You've watched her play.'

Xavier nodded. 'I did suspect her.'

Celia looked from him to Rhys. 'I do not cheat. It was not me.'

Rhys and Xavier both remained standing and Rhys gave nothing away in his expression.

He had every reason not to believe her. He knew she needed money, knew she was the daughter of a gamester, knew her father had been accused of cheating.

She also had hurt him.

'Who, then?' Hugh asked.

Rhys's brows rose.

Celia turned to Belinda. 'Have I always won at hazard?' she asked.

Belinda's forehead furrowed. 'Mostly.'

'But always?' Celia persisted. 'Was there not a time I did not win so much?'

The young woman seemed to be thinking hard. 'Only for a little while once.'

'What was different about that time?' she asked.

Belinda shrugged. 'I can't think of anything.'

Celia leaned forwards. 'Was Lord Westleigh with me that time?'

'When you lost?'

Celia nodded. 'When I lost.'

Belinda glanced away. When she turned back, she said, 'I can't remember him there that time.'

Rhys picked this up. 'When Westleigh was there, did he touch the dice?'

'What is this?' Westleigh sounded outraged. 'Do not accuse me. I am the one who showed you it was she who played the bad dice.'

Rhys turned to him. 'Where would she procure the dice?'

Westleigh's eyes shifted as if he was composing the answer. 'Why, from her father, of course. He was a cheat.'

Xavier looked pensive. 'Westleigh was always with her. He was always asking her to play hazard. And he always touched the dice.'

'You cannot remember all that!' Westleigh raised supplicating hands. 'Besides, what reason would I have to cheat? The profits come to me anyway. I have no motive to steal from myself.' He laughed, but his laugh rang false.

Belinda looked puzzled.

Hugh glared at his father. 'Except that the profits are under Ned's control, not yours. You have no money except what Ned gives you. You are cheating to have more money to gamble with!'

'You cannot prove that.' Westleigh pointed to Rhys.

'You just want to blame me. You sleep with her. Everyone knows that. You are behind this. So you can keep her in your bed.'

Rhys appeared to ignore him. 'It should be easy to discover proof,' Rhys said to the others. 'Whoever has the original set of dice is the culprit.'

Celia stood up and stretched her hands out to her sides. 'Search me.'

Rhys walked over to her, and, as he did so, she removed her gloves and handed them to him. There were no dice in her gloves. She had no sleeves in which to hide the dice.

Westleigh harrumphed. 'She would not put dice in her gloves. She dropped them down her dress.'

Rhys signalled to Belinda. 'Would you step out of the room and check her dress?'

When the two women walked out, Westleigh continued his barrage. 'Who is to say she did not drop the dice on the floor or conceal them in the table? You want to refute what I say, but I saw her rolling the weighted dice. I called your attention to it. Why would I do so for any other reason than an abhorrence of cheating? She is cheating our gaming house, after all.'

Rhys let him go on, but only with difficulty.

Celia would not cheat. It went against everything he knew of her, everything he'd countered when Xavier suggested she was not to be trusted. She was being set up and he knew precisely who was behind it.

He caught Xavier's eye. Xavier was perhaps the only one who could tell how near Rhys was to murderous rage. He would control it. He'd spent a lifetime perfecting control of his emotions.

He'd settle his accounts with this man once and for all.

This man had made a fatal mistake. He'd involved Celia in his dealings, and in the most hurtful way possible.

Hugh looked over at his father. 'Would you stubble it, Father? Your accusation of this woman does you no credit at all. What do you have against her?'

'She prefers the son over the father,' Xavier said.

That was it, Rhys thought. Westleigh had decided to make Madame Fortune a conquest, because Rhys had warned him off. Westleigh had moved from complete indifference towards his bastard son to resentment and rivalry.

The two women returned.

'I could not find anything,' Belinda said.

Celia did not appear steady on her feet. Rhys crossed the room to her and gave her his arm for support.

'This is too taxing for you,' he murmured.

She gave a dismissive wave of her hand. 'I am managing.'

He helped her back to her chair.

'Touching display,' Westleigh said sarcastically.

Rhys swung around to him, losing his composure momentarily.

Ned spoke first. 'This is enough, Father.'

'Stand up, Father,' Hugh ordered. 'It is time to search you.'

Westleigh's eyes bugged out in alarm. 'Me? Why me? This is an outrage. I will tolerate no such thing. You forget who I am.'

Hugh released an exasperated breath. 'We know precisely who you are. Stand up.'

'I will not!' Westleigh gripped the arms of his chair.

Hugh commenced to search his father's sleeves while the man sat in the chair and tried to wave him away. Westleigh gave up the fight as Hugh searched though the pockets in his father's coat and waistcoat and patted him to see if he could feel the dice underneath his clothing.

He moved away, his hands empty.

Celia spoke in a weary voice, 'Check around his chair.'

Ned crouched down and felt the carpet under Westleigh's chair. He looked up and shook his head. Hugh reached behind his father, who tried to prevent access. 'This is a humiliation!' Westleigh cried.

But Hugh pulled his arm out from behind his father and lifted the dice in the air for all to see.

'Oh!' exclaimed Belinda. 'The dice.'

'You are an abomination,' Ned said to his father.

'Which is worse?' Rhys asked Ned. 'What you lately accused this lady of, or your father cheating his own sons and attempting to put the blame on an innocent person?'

Ned glanced away, chastened.

Xavier inclined his head towards Westleigh. 'What will you do with him?'

'I am not certain.' Rhys knew what he would like to do with him, but that punishment belonged to the Middle Ages. 'Would you and Belinda return to the game room? You can reopen the hazard table with new dice.'

'What shall we say to the patrons?' Xavier asked.

'Say only that we do not tolerate cheating and that we have stopped it.' He was not certain what other action he wished to take.

After Xavier and Belinda left the room, Rhys turned to Ned and Hugh. 'Are you able to keep your father in your custody and return him here tomorrow?'

'You are not going to accuse me of cheating! I will be ruined,' Westleigh ranted. 'I will ruin you first. I will take this gaming hell to the devil and all of you with it. I have powerful friends.'

Rhys had no doubt that Earl Westleigh did indeed have

powerful friends, but the code of honour for gambling was sacred among the highest reaches of the *ton*. Would they tolerate even a friend who cheated his own sons at hazard and tried to place the blame on a woman?

'You have contrived to make me look guilty,' Westleigh went on, 'because of *her*. You do not want it known that you were duped by a common cheat.'

Rhys leaned into the man's face and his rage turned his voice low and treacherous. 'Do not say another word about her.'

Westleigh flinched, but quickly recovered. He waved a finger at his two legitimate sons. 'Do not believe this man! You traitorous pups. I am your father. You owe your allegiance to me!'

Hugh wheeled on him. 'You were cheating *us,* Father. You knew the profits went to us.'

'And to him!' Westleigh pointed to Rhys. 'Besides, I needed more money than you provided me.' He glared at Ned, but quickly caught himself. 'But I did not cheat. The weighted dice are not mine.'

'Rise, Father,' Hugh ordered. 'We are taking you home.'

Westleigh's two sons pulled him out of his chair and each held one of his arms.

Rhys turned to Celia. 'I will see them out.'

But he would return to her afterwards to assure himself that these stressful events had not done an injury to her health.

As he followed the three Westleighs down the stairs, he had to admit that Celia had the right of it. Gaming houses were ugly places where greed and desperation drove men to unseemly acts. Rhys might be able to control himself and his emotions around gaming and gamblers, but he could not control others. The veneer might be pretty, but a gaming house was not so different than the desperate streets he'd been thrown into at age fourteen.

When they reached the hall, Westleigh demanded, 'I want to cash out. I need to cash out.'

'Let us just give the cashier the whole lot,' Hugh said to his brother.

On their way to the cashier's office, the game-room door opened. Westleigh seized that moment to break free.

He ran into the game room and shouted, 'Rhysdale is making an unjust accusation. He says he will accuse me of cheating. But you all saw it! It was Madame Fortune!'

Rhys dashed into the room after him.

Westleigh swung around to him. 'I will not be unjustly accused! I demand satisfaction!'

'Here! Here!' some of his cronies shouted. 'Cannot have this!'

One gentleman stepped forwards and said, 'I will be your second, if you wish, Westleigh. It is an outrage. We saw her cheating with our own eyes. Now we know why she always won. How many other cheats are here, I wonder?'

The patrons started to glance at each other in sudden suspicion.

'Lord Westleigh planted the weighted dice on Madame Fortune,' Rhys shouted above the din. 'There is no false accusation here.'

Westleigh smiled a malevolent smile. 'Let us settle this with a duel.'

'A duel! A duel!' others shouted.

'What say you?' Westleigh challenged Rhys. 'We can settle this like gentlemen—'

Chapter Seventeen

Celia heard the shouting from below and feared something had gone wrong. She hurried out of the drawing room and down the stairs, tying her mask to her face as she went.

She reached the doorway of the game room in time to hear Westleigh say, 'Pistols at dawn, Rhysdale?'

'No!' Her voice pierced through the room.

She ran to Rhys's side and grasped his arm. 'No, Rhys! You mustn't do this.'

He pulled her fingers away. 'I will manage it. Trust me.'

Westleigh laughed. 'Madame Fortune, have you come to admit to cheating at hazard?'

Celia's heart pounded. She could stop this! All she had to do was admit to cheating.

She stepped forwards, but Rhys held her back.

'You, Westleigh, are still trying to blame her,' Rhys said. 'Even your sons saw proof of your lies.'

'You set me up!' Westleigh cried. 'You and—and your lover here.'

'Nonsense,' Rhys countered. 'What gaming-house proprietor conspires to lose money?'

Several men nodded their heads.

'You have not answered my challenge, sir.' Westleigh re-turned to that horrible question. Would Rhys accept a duel?

Because of her.

Rhys glanced around. 'Forgive me, gentlemen. You may know this better than I, but is a gentleman allowed to issue a challenge to one such as me? I am certainly his social inferior.'

'You are his natural son,' one man blurted out.

The murmurs of the crowd grew louder.

'And I am older than you,' Westleigh said. 'That more than cancels out the inferior blood of your mother.'

Celia's gaze darted to Rhys. Surely he would react to such an insult.

But if he felt the blow, as she had, he did not show it. His face was as composed as if he were strolling through the room watching the gamblers.

'What say you, gentlemen?' Westleigh asked the crowd.

'I say pistols at dawn,' one man shouted.

Others cheered.

Ned walked up to his father and seized his arm. Hugh hurried over and grabbed the other one.

'We are leaving now!' Ned said.

As they pulled him past where Celia and Rhys stood, she heard Ned say, 'Are you mad? We could have kept this quiet and now all London will know of it. A duel, Father? With your son?'

'He's naught but a bastard, Ned,' Westleigh said.

She knew Rhys heard, as well.

Xavier walked up to him. 'That was unfortunate. What will you do?'

'Meet him,' Rhys said.

She grasped his arm. 'No, Rhys! I will not let you!'

He took her chin in his fingers and lifted her face to

his. 'I must, Celia. But trust me in this. I know what I am about.'

It was akin to what her father had said to her mother— *It is something I must do.*

'Please, Rhys!' she begged.

He walked her into the hall. 'Celia, you were barely able to stand on your feet a while ago. You must be exhausted. When does your coachman come?'

'Not for an hour.'

He touched her cheek. 'Go upstairs. Lie down. Rest. I need to be visible in the game room. I cannot be seen as hiding from what just occurred.'

She nodded. 'But promise me you will not fight a duel.'

'I cannot promise that.'

Celia was too tired to argue. She walked up to his bed-chamber and took off her mask and let down her hair. She kicked off her slippers, climbed onto his bed and fell asleep immediately.

She woke to his arms around her and rolled over to face him. All the candles had been extinguished and the only light came from the glow of the coals in the fireplace. He was shirtless and his face was shadowed with beard. He was warm and comfortable.

And comforting.

His eyes opened for a moment and he gathered her closer, so that her head rested against his heart, lulling her with its rhythmic beat. She wanted to stay in his arms for ever.

But she pulled away. 'What time is it? My carriage.'

He gathered her close again. 'I sent your coachman away. I told him to leave word you were staying here to-night.'

She ought to protest. Her mother-in-law and Adele would have fits of apoplexy.

But she could not care. Not when he held her, when the scent of his skin filled her nostrils, and the even sound of his breathing lulled her into an illusion that everything was as it should be. Everything was wonderful.

She fancied she could feel his baby inside her and she thrilled anew with the wonder of it. She imagined them as a family, saw herself rocking their baby to sleep while she and Rhys quietly conversed about the day.

But it would never be that way. Because she refused to listen to tales of men and women winning and losing, elated and despairing. She could not live in fear of bad luck or challenges to duels.

She did not want him to face Westleigh with pistols. Rhys could die as her father died. It was the greatest cruelty that he would not refuse for her sake, if for no other reason.

And even if he did not die, what would happen to him? An earl might escape arrest, but the proprietor of a gaming hell would certainly be hanged.

He purported to know how to play the odds, but in this case the odds were stacked solidly against him.

She clung to him tighter as tears rolled down her cheeks.

She must discover where the duel was to be held. She would stop it. Somehow, she would stop it.

She might not be able to live with Rhys and his gambling ways, but life would be unbearable if he did not live at all.

If it was wonderful to fall asleep in Rhys's arms it was glorious to waken in them. When Celia opened her eyes he was already gazing at her. They each lay drinking in the sight of the other for several long moments before he closed the space between them and kissed her.

Silently, he helped her out of her clothing and made

love to her. Quietly. Gently. So gently that she thought she would shatter under the sheer beauty of it. He stroked her body as if worshipping it, and every sensation inside her lit up like the illuminations at Vauxhall Gardens. She'd missed him so terribly that her desire burned white-hot for him.

She would have taken him fast and hard. Her body urged her to do that very thing, but his pace remained lazy and leisurely, as if they had all the time in the world.

As if this would not be their last time.

As if he were not intending to engage in a duel at the next sunrise.

When he entered her, she moaned in relief. He'd already driven her to a fevered state with his hands and lips. Now her body could take over, meet his thrusts and urge him to go faster.

But, still, he built the passion slowly and she finally surrendered to his pace, savouring every moment, every sensation.

Even her climax built slowly, like a stack of wood meant to last most of the day instead of the flash of brush she'd initially craved. Once released, it seemed as if the culmination of their lovemaking would have no end. Inside her she felt him spill his seed while she still convulsed with unbelievable pleasure.

An act like this had resulted in a new life, a baby for Celia to love. She said a prayer of thanks that her child had been created out of love. That in itself was a miracle.

He collapsed beside her, holding her as if she would disappear if he let go.

That was not too distant from the truth.

'How are you this morning, my love?' he asked.

He'd never before used such an endearment. 'I feel very

well,' she responded. 'I think you have found a cure for the morning sickness.'

He stared into her eyes. 'Then let me treat you every morning.'

He kissed her again.

Later they sat across from each other at the small table in his bedchamber. She was wrapped in a banyan he'd lent her to wear. He was in shirtsleeves and trousers.

Over a cup of hot tea, he continued what he'd begun after lovemaking. 'We could make a marriage work for us, Celia,' he insisted. 'The gaming house is temporary. No more than three years or so and I'll be done with it.'

He thought he was telling the truth, she knew, but she'd heard her father promise to quit gambling over and over. *Tomorrow I'll quit. Just one more game. A chance to re-coup.* If he won he could not interrupt his winning streak. If he lost, he still needed one more game. Then it would start all over again.

But even that would be preferable to his death.

She lifted her chin. 'Give up the duel with Westleigh and I will marry you, Rhys.'

He frowned at her. 'I cannot.'

'You could! You could admit to him and the world that Madame Fortune was cheating. She could vanish, then. All who know I am Madame Fortune would have good reason not to tell anyone.' She gave him a pleading look. 'I do not mind giving up being Madame Fortune. It could work.'

He shook his head. 'I am going to stop Westleigh once and for all. He has had this coming for a very long time.'

Did he mean to kill Westleigh? She shuddered. 'I burn to have my father's death avenged, but not at the risk to your life.'

He did not waver. 'I said before, you must trust me on

this matter.' He rose. 'And do not use marriage as a bargaining chip. Either you wish to marry me or you don't. But you know marriage would be best for the child.'

'I am not so certain.' She raised her eyes to his. 'I lived that life, Rhys.'

He reached across the table and took her hands. 'You need to trust me, Celia. If I tell you I will give up the gaming house in three years, I will.'

It was not that simple, Celia thought.

He went on. 'If I say I will come out of the duel without a scratch, I will.'

Celia pulled her hands away. 'How can you promise that? You cannot.' Her voice broke. 'My father promised the same thing.'

'Trust me.'

'Tell me how you will do it,' she countered.

He shrugged. 'My plan is not yet in place, but it will be. This duel will solve everything.'

Celia wanted to believe him. She supposed her mother wanted to believe her father, too.

'No. I will not listen.' She waved his words away. 'A duel is too big a risk.'

'Everything in life involves risk, Celia.' He spoke in a low, firm voice. 'The best we can ever do is stack the odds in our favour. Trust me to do that.' His gaze was intense. 'I am not your father. I've never trusted my life to fate. I've made my own luck against all the odds. That is what I will do and can do again.'

She wanted to believe him.

One thing she knew. She'd always been a victim of fate. No more.

If he could make his own luck, so could she. She had no intention of leaving his life to fate. Somehow, she would stop this duel.

* * *

It was about noon when he sent her home in a hackney coach. She walked slowly into her set of rooms, passing Tucker in the hall.

'Good morning, ma'am,' he said in a concerned tone.

'Do not worry,' she responded to his implicit question. 'I am well.'

She walked straight to her bedchamber, but Adele appeared before she made it inside.

'Celia, I must tell you something.' Adele's voice was still cold.

'Very well,' Celia said. 'Come into my room. You can help me change my clothes.'

Adele followed her inside. 'Younie is here somewhere. I'll get her to help. I only need a minute of your time.'

Adele would not even help her with her laces?

Celia stepped into her dressing room and managed to remove her dress by herself. She put on one of her morning dresses. 'What is it you wished to tell me?' she asked, walking back out to the bedchamber.

'Ned and I are getting married. As soon as he can procure a special licence. I need you to secure my guardian's permission.'

So they were following her advice. 'I will send a letter today.'

'Good.' Adele started towards the door, but stopped before opening it. 'After my wedding, I will be moving in with Lord and Lady Westleigh until Ned and I can find rooms of our own.'

'And your grandmother?'

Adele lifted her chin. 'She does not wish to live with you or with me. We are not relations, she says. She wishes to retire to Bath. Ned will pay for her.'

They both would be free of the woman.

And Celia would be free to leave London in perhaps a matter of days.

Unless she agreed to Rhys's proposal.

Assuming he lived.

Anxiety clenched her insides. 'Will you see Ned today, Adele?'

'No,' the girl answered mournfully. 'He sent word that he has business to attend to. He will not see me tomorrow, either.' She narrowed her eyes. 'I do hope his absence is not due to some trouble you or your lover have caused.'

Adele's barb hurt.

Celia spoke quietly. 'That was not well said of you, Adele. Nothing I have done was meant to hurt you, but you deliberately wound me.'

Adele looked chastened for a moment, but she cried, 'You are going to have a baby out of wedlock!'

Celia put a hand on her abdomen. 'I am going to have a baby. What greater happiness could there be for me?'

Adele's expression remained obstinate. 'Why did you ask about Ned?'

She certainly was not going to confide in Adele. 'No reason. I merely wanted to know your schedule for the day.'

Adele opened the door. 'I am calling upon some of my friends. Younie will accompany me.' She walked out.

Celia went in search of Younie. She had decided to make a call of her own and needed Younie to help her dress again.

Younie helped Celia into a walking dress and she soon was off again, walking through Mayfair to the Westleigh town house. She knocked upon the door and was admitted by the butler.

A few minutes later she was escorted to the second floor

and announced to Lady Westleigh. Fortunately the lady was alone. Even her daughter was not present.

Lady Westleigh remained on her chaise longue when Celia was admitted into a small parlour. The lady's private sitting room, Celia suspected. It was a very feminine room, with upholstered chairs in blue brocade and gilded tables with white marble tops. Celia immediately felt comfortable. She could not imagine Lord Westleigh setting foot in such a room.

'Ma'am, thank you for receiving me.' Celia curtsied.

Lady Westleigh nodded. 'I confess I am surprised to see you.' She gestured for Celia to sit.

'May I enquire whether your sons or your husband are at home?' Celia asked.

Lady Westleigh raised her brows. 'They are not. They all went out. I confess they sounded as if in a quarrel.'

Celia could believe it. 'I am guessing you do not know of any of this, but your husband has challenged Mr Rhysdale to a duel.'

'A duel?' Lady Westleigh sat up straight. 'Whatever for?'

Celia explained the circumstances. 'I must stop this.'

'Certainly we must,' the lady agreed.

A footman served tea.

Lady Westleigh said to him, 'Tell Mason I wish to see him.'

The butler presented himself shortly. 'You asked for me, my lady?'

Lady Westleigh spoke in an officious tone. 'It has come to my attention that my husband is fighting a duel at dawn. I want you to tell me where it will be held.'

The man blanched. 'I am certain I do not know such a thing, my lady.'

Lady Westleigh did not back down. 'And I am certain

you do. One of the valets will have heard of it and I am certain it was mentioned in the servants' quarters. It is imperative you tell me.'

Chapter Eighteen

At first morning's light the next day, Rhys and Xavier stood on Hampstead Heath, fog swirling around their ankles.

'I wonder how many duels have been fought here?' Rhys mused.

'It is popular with those of us with no imagination.' Xavier, as Rhys's second, had had to attend to all the details of the duel. 'It is not too late to get out of this.'

Xavier had suggested the same thing as Celia. Blame Madame Fortune and have her disappear. But Xavier lacked the imagination to use this duel as an opportunity.

'Westleigh will pay this day. Madame Fortune did nothing wrong.' He walked the spot where they would take their positions.

'You don't truly plan to shoot him?' Xavier asked. 'He is your father, after all.'

Rhys turned as he would turn to fire. 'I intend to finish it here.'

They heard a carriage approaching.

'They are here.' Xavier shivered. 'Blast. It is as cold as winter this morning.'

Rhys turned at the sound. 'The coldest summer anyone recalls,' he remarked.

A curricle emerged through the mist and a moment later two men climbed down. It was not Westleigh who had arrived, but Ned and Hugh.

Rhys nodded to them. 'You came after all.'

Ned shivered. 'We said we would.'

Ned and Hugh had called upon Rhys the day before and discussed the duel and its likely aftermath. They had parted in agreement, which surprised Rhys.

It also surprised him that he'd come to a grudging respect for these two men with whom he shared a father. Ned might make a cake of himself over Miss Gale, but he took his responsibilities to his family and his people very seriously. Hugh, as volatile as Rhys was controlled, none the less did not suffer fools gladly. Neither of them exhibited the self-conceit of their father.

'Our father is not here yet?' Hugh asked, his tone contemptuous. 'Perhaps he will not show.'

Rhys was probably the only one who knew that their father had fought a duel at least once before. 'He will show.'

Sure enough, the sound of a carriage reached their ears. It, too, came through the mist and stopped nearby. Westleigh and his second climbed out of the carriage, the surgeon after them.

Rhys looked back to where he would stand in a few minutes. The sky was lightening by the minute.

Time to deal the cards and play the game.

Rhys and Xavier walked towards the new arrivals, followed by Ned and Hugh.

His second drew Xavier aside for the final task. Loading the pistols.

'What are you doing here?' Westleigh gave his sons scathing glances.

Hugh smiled. 'We would not miss this.'

Westleigh waved a hand at him as if he were an annoying fly. He turned to Rhys. 'Do you have anything to say to me?'

'Only that you are a fool.' Rhys spoke calmly. 'Did you not recall that I spent almost a decade in the army? I am very used to killing.'

Westleigh's brows knit.

'And I am steadier and thinner than you.' He looked Westleigh up and down. 'You'll make a bigger target.' He let Westleigh contemplate that for a moment before adding, 'And since you made the challenge, the weapons are mine. I will be firing a pistol I've fired many times before.'

Westleigh wiped his forehead with his sleeve. 'All that is to no purpose.'

'Suit yourself.' Rhys folded his arms across his chest and waited for Xavier and the other man.

Westleigh tossed the two seconds worried glances. As Rhys had suspected, Westleigh had hoped he would back out. He underestimated Rhys's resolve.

Ironically, only Celia and his brothers believed he would truly go through with it.

The two seconds approached them.

'We agreed the duel will allow for one shot each at thirty paces. No shooting into the air,' Westleigh's second said.

Xavier opened the case containing the duelling pistols. 'Choose first, Westleigh.'

Westleigh tossed Rhys one nervous glance and his hand shook as he selected a pistol. Rhys remained impassive.

'Take your positions,' Xavier said.

Rhys walked at a brisk pace to the spot he had chosen. Westleigh breathed hard to keep up. They stood back to back and Westleigh's second counted the paces. '…nine. Ten. Eleven—'

Ned and Hugh sprinted to Rhys's side and paced with him.

Westleigh's second paused, but Xavier gestured for him to continue.

'Twelve. Thirteen. Fourteen. Fifteen. Turn and fire!'

Rhys, Ned and Hugh turned quickly, as if they were one unit.

Westleigh turned, as well, but his arm faltered when he faced, not only Rhys, but his heir and his spare, as well. 'See here! This is not how it is done.'

Rhys's arm was raised and his aim steady. 'You would know precisely how it is done, would you not, Westleigh?'

Westleigh gestured with his free hand. 'Get them away.'

'Fire, Father,' Hugh said. 'We are not moving.'

'We chose to watch from here,' Ned added.

'Do not fire,' his second cried. 'What if you hit one of your sons?'

'That is the point, is it not, Westleigh?' Rhys held his aim. 'To shoot a son? You are bound to succeed, are you not? Who knows? With luck you might even hit me.'

'You are traitors,' Westleigh cried. 'Siding with him.'

'Should we side with you, Father?' Hugh asked. 'A liar and a cheat? A man who hides his guilt behind a skirt?'

'You cannot shoot your own sons,' his second cried. 'The scandal will ruin you.'

'Shoot, Westleigh,' Rhys called again. 'Or shall I fire first? I am an excellent shot.'

Westleigh's arm trembled.

'Do not do it!' his second begged.

His legs began to shake, as well.

Rhys's arm did not waver. 'You can end this another way.'

Westleigh's face contorted. As the sun lightened the sky it showed a sheen of perspiration on his brow.

Rhys was unshaken. 'Apologise. Confess that it was you who cheated, then leave the country and never return.' He wanted Westleigh far away. Out of his family. Far from Celia. He wanted her to never see the man again. 'Or fire so I can kill you.'

Westleigh fired the pistol into the air and collapsed to his knees. 'Very well. I did it. I planted the dice and blamed Madame Fortune or whoever she is.'

Rhys, Ned and Hugh strode over to him.

From the mist came a cry, 'No!'

The men turned to the sound.

A woman appeared, running towards them. 'Rhys!' she cried.

'Celia,' Rhys whispered. He stepped in her path.

She came to a halt, then vaulted into his arms. 'I thought he'd shot you.'

'No one is shot.' He held on to her. 'Celia, what are you doing here?'

'I came to stop you,' she cried.

He touched her stomach. 'You should not have exerted yourself. I told you to trust me. It is all over. All over. I have fixed it.'

Ned and Hugh pulled their father to his feet and another woman appeared.

Ned peered at her. 'Mother?'

'She would meddle,' Westleigh mumbled.

'You sorry creature,' she spat.

Rhys released Celia and faced Lord Westleigh. 'Here is what you will do. You will leave today for the Continent. You will stay there. You'll have an allowance large enough for comfort, but if you gamble it away or waste it on carousing, there will be no other money. You will leave your family alone, with Ned in charge and empowered to act on your behalf in all matters. What say you?'

'You had better agree,' Lady Westleigh demanded.

Westleigh nodded. 'Yes. I agree. I'll do as you say.'

'Your word as a gentleman?' Rhys persisted.

'I give you my word,' Westleigh said.

'Louder,' Rhys said.

'I give my word as a gentleman!' he shouted.

Ned and Hugh walked him past his second. The man made a sound of disgust and signalled to the surgeon to come with him. They left in the carriage.

Xavier walked up to Rhys and Celia. 'Lady Gale, I am not surprised to see you.' He bowed. 'I would have expected no less from you.' He turned to Rhys. 'Well done. Quite clever, actually.'

Rhys grinned. 'I suppose it violated some part of the gentleman's code, but, as we all know, I am no gentleman.'

'Rhys,' Ned called to him. 'We'll take charge of Father. Hugh and I will take him directly to our solicitor in the curricle. We'll be on our way to Dover by noon and to Calais on the morrow.'

'Take him in the carriage with me,' Lady Westleigh said. 'Rhys can take the curricle back to the stables.'

'I'll take our horses back,' Xavier said.

Before Rhys knew it, everyone had left them, except Ned's tiger. He helped Celia into the curricle and the tiger hopped on the back.

'Where do I take you, Celia?' he asked.

'To your house.' She caressed his cheek. 'I believe I can trust you at the Masquerade Club.'

He peered at her. 'Are you saying you have reconsidered?'

She nodded and put her arms around him. 'I trust you will do as you say.'

Epilogue

London—April 1820

Rhys walked through the game room watching the play. The Masquerade Club was as popular as ever—and as profitable. It was hard to believe that so much had happened in under a year.

Change had come to the monarchy in this year, with the mad king's death and George IV inheriting the throne.

But there were even more important changes in Rhys's life. His friend Xavier was still at his side, but also were his brothers. Ironically, he was now accepted as a Westleigh, after all, but only because his father was gone, still banished to the Continent and keeping his word to leave his family in peace.

Best of all, Rhys had married Celia.

At Ned's insistence, they'd been married by special licence in the drawing room of the Westleigh town house on the same day and place as Ned and Adele's wedding, very shortly after he'd almost lost Celia because of the duel.

But he'd managed to rid them all of Westleigh, save the Westleigh estates, and convince Celia that he was a man of his word. In return he'd been given happiness greater than he ever thought possible.

He glanced towards the game-room door. To his surprise Celia stood there. She never came downstairs during the night's play, not since she'd grown so large.

A memory flashed of his first glimpse of her in her mask and deep red gown that now would never contain her full breasts and rounded abdomen.

She braced herself against the door jamb and signalled for him to come to her. He was already heading there.

He touched her arm. 'What are you doing down here?'

She smiled. 'I don't want to alarm you, but I think it is time.'

'Time for what?' he asked.

She looked him in the eye. 'Time for our baby to be born.'

He blanched. 'Indeed?'

She nodded. 'I had Xavier send for Lady Westleigh and the physician.'

'You should not have risked the stairs.' He took her by the arm. 'We must get you back upstairs.'

They'd prepared one of the rooms upstairs for the birth, with a comfortable bed, a tiny cradle and a window for fresh air.

He helped her up the stairs and stayed with her, letting her grip his hand when the contractions came, wishing he could ensure that nothing went wrong.

Lady Westleigh arrived and immediately took charge, telling even the physician what he should do.

'You must leave, Rhys,' she told him.

'Do not waste your breath arguing with me over it,' he told her. 'I am staying with her.'

'I want him to stay,' Celia managed as yet another contraction came.

He endured twelve hours of witnessing Celia in more pain than he could ever imagine, even after being in battle.

Finally Lady Westleigh, not the physician, declared that it was time for the birth. Rhys let Celia grip his hand as hard as she wished as she bore down, trying to push the baby from her body.

Finally, after yet another of her agonised cries, another sound erupted. The cry of a newborn baby.

'You have a son,' Lady Westleigh announced.

'A son,' he rasped.

Celia laughed in relief and reached out for her baby.

Later when she, the baby and the room were cleaned up and she put the baby to her breast, Rhys sat back and just gazed at his lusty-lunged son and his beautiful wife.

He made a wager. He wagered this baby would never be hungry or alone, not if Rhys could help it. He would always be loved. Rhys also wagered that Celia, too, would always be loved and that he'd give her the security she had lacked as a child.

He knew the odds of winning these wagers were extremely high.

'Is he not the most handsome baby you have ever seen?' Celia said. 'And so clever to learn how to nurse right away.'

'He is as wonderful as his mother,' Rhys replied. He leaned down and kissed the baby on top of his head. He kissed Celia, too, a kiss of thanksgiving that she and their son had come through the ordeal so well.

'I love my family,' he murmured, kissing her again.

* * * * *

A LADY OF
NOTORIETY

To Catherine, a beautiful friend in all ways.

Chapter One

Ramsgate, Kent—April 1821

'My lady! My lady! Wake up! Fire!'

Daphne, Lady Faville, jolted awake at her maid's cries. Smoke filled her nostrils and stung her eyes. Shouts and pounding on doors sounded in the hallway of the Ramsgate inn.

'Fire! Get out,' a man's voice boomed.

Fire. Her biggest fear.

Daphne leaped out of bed and shoved her feet into slippers. Her maid began gathering their belongings, stuffing them into a portmanteau.

'Leave them, Monette.' Daphne seized her coin purse and threw her cloak around her shoulders. Her heart raced. 'We must go now!'

She reached for the door latch, but her maid pulled her arm away.

'Wait! The hall may be on fire.' The maid pressed her hand against the door. 'It is not hot. It is safe.' She opened the door.

It was not safe.

The hallway was filled with smoke, and tongues of

flame licked the walls here and there, as if sneaking up from below. In a moment the wallpaper would curl and burn. The fire would grow. It could engulf them.

Daphne saw a vision of another time, another fire. Her heart pounded. Was she to die in flames after all?

'Keep your skirts away from the fire,' she cried to Monette.

They moved blindly ahead, down the long hallway, through its fiery gauntlet.

'Hurry, Monette.' She took the maid's hand and lamented asking the innkeeper for rooms that were as private as possible.

Their rooms were far from the stairway.

'Someone is in the hallway. At the end,' a man's voice cried.

Through the grey smoke he emerged, an apparition rushing towards them. He grabbed them both and half-carried them through the hallway past other men who were knocking on doors, and other residents emerging in night-clothes.

They reached the stairway and he pushed Monette forwards. The girl ran down the stairs. Daphne shrank back. The flames below were larger, more dangerous.

'I'll get you through.' The man gathered her up in his arms and carried her down the three flights of stairs. She buried her face in his chest, too afraid to see the fire so close.

Suddenly the air cooled and she could breathe again. They were outside. He set her down and her maid ran to her, hugging her in relief. They were alive! Daphne swung back to thank the man who rescued them.

He was already running back into the fire.

Her footman appeared. 'You are safe, m'lady. Come away from the building.'

He brought them to where a group of people in various stages of undress huddled together.

'I must go back to the buckets.' He looked apologetic.

'Yes, Carter. Yes,' Daphne agreed. 'Help all you can.'

He ran to the brigade passing buckets of water to the fire. Other men led horses out of the stables and rolled coaches away from the burning building.

Daphne's eyes riveted on the doorway, willing their rescuer to reappear. Other men carried people out, but she did not see him. She'd not seen his face, but she knew she would recognise him. Tall, dark haired and strong. He wore the dark coat and fawn pantaloons of a gentleman.

Finally he appeared, two children tucked under his arms and a frantic mother following behind.

Daphne took a step forwards, eager to speak to him, to thank him. To her shock, he ran towards the door again. One of the other men seized his arm, apparently trying to stop him, but the man shrugged him off and rushed back inside.

Daphne's hand flew over her mouth. *Please, God, let him come out again.*

An older gentleman approached her. 'Lady Faville?'

She wanted to watch for her rescuer, not engage in conversation.

'Do you remember me?' he asked.

She presumed he was someone she'd met in London. 'I am sorry. I do not—'

He looked disappointed. 'I am Lord Sanvers. We met several times at the Masquerade Club.'

The Masquerade Club?

It was a place she wanted to forget, the London gambling house where players could gamble in masks to protect their identity. It was also the place she almost destroyed.

By fire.

'It is two years since I attended there,' she answered him. 'There were so many gentlemen I met.'

It was inadequate as an apology. Surely he—and everyone—knew that she'd been obsessed by only one man, a man who would never love her. She'd fled to the Continent and eventually to Switzerland and Fahr Abbey. The abbey had become her retreat and her salvation, chosen by whim because its name was similar to her husband's title name and the name of the village where she'd once felt secure. At Fahr Abbey, though, she'd come face-to-face with her failings.

But could she change?

Could she be as selfless as her brave rescuer?

Minutes seemed like hours, but he finally emerged again, leading two more people to safety. The fire intensified, roaring now like a wild beast. Were there more people inside? Would he risk his life again?

He ran back to the fire and was silhouetted inside the doorway when a huge rush of glowing embers fell from the ceiling. The building groaned, as if in the throes of death. Timbers fell from the roof and the man's arms rose in front of his face. Daphne watched in horror as one large flaming timber knocked him to the floor.

'No!' Without thinking, she ran towards him.

Other men reached him first, pulling him by his clothing until he was in the yard. The building collapsed entirely.

Daphne knelt down next to him as they brushed away glowing cinders from his coat and patted out smoking cloth.

'Is he alive?' she cried.

They rolled him on his back, and one man put a finger to the pulse in his neck. 'He's alive for now.'

Daphne gasped. 'I know him!'

Though his face was dark with soot and pink with burns, she recognised him. He was Hugh Westleigh, younger brother of the new Earl of Westleigh. He was also the brother of the lady she'd so terribly wronged at the Masquerade Club.

Had he arrived on the packet from Calais, as she had? Or was he bound there? Either way, she suspected he would not have liked seeing her after all the trouble she'd caused.

He was not conscious, and that alarmed her.

'We'd better carry him to the surgeon,' one of the men said.

They lifted him. Daphne followed them.

Her maid and footman caught up to her. Monette's eyes were wide. 'My lady?'

'I know this man,' she explained. 'I must see he receives care. Wait for me here.'

They carried him to what looked like a nearby shop-front. Inside several people sat on benches while one man, the surgeon apparently, bandaged burns.

'We have a bad one here, Mr Trask.'

The surgeon waved a man off the chair where he'd been tending to him and gestured for the men to sit Westleigh in it. He was still limp.

Daphne wrung her hands. 'Will he live?'

'I do not know, ma'am,' the surgeon said.

'He was hit on the head,' she said. 'I saw it.'

The man checked Westleigh's head. 'Appears to be so.'

Westleigh groaned and Daphne released a pent-up breath.

The surgeon lifted his head. 'Wake up, sir.' He turned to Daphne. 'What is his name?'

'Mr Westleigh,' she said. 'He is the younger brother of the Earl of Westleigh.'

'Is he?' One of the men who had carried him in raised

his brows. 'Who would have expected it of the Quality? The man has pluck.'

'Westleigh!' The surgeon raised his voice. 'Wake up.'

He groaned again.

'Open your eyes.'

Westleigh tried to comply, straining. He winced and tried to rub his eyes. 'I cannot…'

Thank God he could speak.

The surgeon pulled his hands away. 'Do not do that. Let me look.' He examined Westleigh's eyes and turned to Daphne. 'His eyes are cloudy. Damaged from the fire.' He tilted Westleigh's head back and rinsed his eyes with clear water from a nearby pitcher. 'His eyes must stay bandaged for two weeks or he will lose his sight.' He shrugged. 'He may lose his sight no matter what, but sometimes the eyes heal remarkably well. I'm more concerned about his head. He is certainly concussed. He needs to be cared for.'

'In what way?' Daphne asked.

'He needs rest and quiet. No excitement at all. For at least a week.' He looked into Westleigh's mouth and in his nose. 'No bleeding. That is good.'

'Head hurts,' Westleigh mumbled.

The surgeon folded bandages over Westleigh's eyes and wrapped his head to keep them in place. No sooner had he finished than another victim of the fire was brought in, covered with burns. The surgeon's attention immediately went to his new patient. 'I must see this man.' He waved Daphne away. 'Keep his eyes bandaged and keep him quiet. No travelling. He must stay quiet.'

Daphne dropped some coins from her purse on the table. The surgeon deserved payment.

The man who had carried Westleigh to the surgeon got him to his feet. 'Come along, sir.' He turned to Daphne. 'Follow me.'

He must think she was in Westleigh's party.

They walked out of the building into a day just beginning to turn light.

Carter, her footman, ran up to her. 'M'lady, John Coachman found a stable for the horses. He and your maid are waiting with the carriage, which was left near the inn.'

The man assisting Westleigh strained with the effort to keep him upright. 'Give us a hand, would you?' he asked her footman. Carter rushed to help him, but the man handed off his burden entirely. 'I must see to my own family, ma'am.' He pulled on his forelock and hurried away.

Westleigh moaned.

'What do I do with him?' Carter shifted to get a better hold on Westleigh.

Daphne's mind was spinning. 'Take him to the carriage, I suppose. We must find someone to care for him.'

Men were still busy at the inn, extinguishing embers, salvaging undamaged items, of which there were very few. Daphne's and her maid's trunks had been with the carriage, so they had lost only what had been in their portmanteaux.

Carter and John Coachman helped Westleigh into the carriage.

'Is he coming with us?' Monette asked.

'Oh, no,' Daphne replied. 'He would detest that. He must have been travelling with someone. We should find out who.' She turned to Carter. 'Can you ask, please? His name is Hugh Westleigh, Lord Westleigh's brother.'

Westleigh stirred and tried to pull at the bandages covering his eyes.

'No, Westleigh!' Daphne climbed inside the carriage and pulled his hands away. 'You must not touch your bandages.' She arranged the pillows and rugs to make him more comfortable.

'Thirsty,' Westleigh mumbled.

How thoughtless of her. He must have a raging thirst after all his exertion.

'Monette, find him some ale and something nourishing.' What ought an injured man eat? She had no idea, but dug into her purse again and handed both her maid and footman some coins. 'Both of you buy something for yourselves to eat and drink and bring something back for John Coachman, as well.'

Monette returned within a quarter-hour with food and drink from a nearby alehouse for Westleigh and the coachman.

'They have a room where we might change clothes,' she told Daphne. 'I paid for it and for a meal, so that we can eat privately.'

It was better than eating in the carriage on the street with the smell of ashes still in the air.

'I'll tend to the gentleman, m'lady,' John Coachman said. 'I must watch the carriage in any event. He'll be comfortable enough inside, with your pillows and all.'

Monette climbed on top of the carriage and retrieved clothing from the trunks, rolling them into a bundle. She led Daphne to the alehouse, about two streets away.

The place was crowded with people in various stages of dress and from various walks of life, who had all apparently escaped the fire. Daphne followed Monette through the throng. The smell of sweat, smoke and ale made Daphne's empty stomach roil.

Surely a lady of her stature should not be required to endure this sort of place.

She placed her hand over her mouth.

The words of the abbess at Fahr came back to her. *You must practise compassion for all people, my lady. We are all God's children.*

The dear abbess. The nuns at Fahr had told her the abbess was very old, but to Daphne she'd seemed ageless. For some unfathomable reason the abbess had bestowed her love and attention on Daphne.

Her eyes filled with tears. The woman's death had been a terrible blow, worse than her own mother's death, worse than her husband's. She could not bear to stay at Fahr after such a loss.

At least the abbess's words remained with her. Sometimes, when Daphne needed her words, it was almost as if the woman were at her side, whispering in her ear.

Daphne glanced around once more and tried to see the people in the alehouse through the abbess's eyes. Most looked exhausted. Some appeared close to despair. Others wore bandages on their arms or hands.

Daphne ached for them.

More truthfully, a part of her felt sorrow for their suffering; another part was very grateful to have been spared their troubles.

As they reached the door to the private room, a gentleman rose from a booth where he'd sat alone. He was the gentleman who had spoken to her before, who remembered her from the Masquerade Club. What was his name?

Lord Sanvers.

'My good lady. There you are. I was concerned about you.' His silver hair was neatly combed and he appeared to have changed into fresh linen. Compared to the others he was pristine.

'I am unharmed, sir.'

He blocked her way. 'May I assist you in any way? I am at your disposal.'

He could take charge of Westleigh! Would that not be a better situation for everyone?

She glanced at the booth Lord Sanvers had all to himself and to the numbers of people who did not even have a chair.

Would he have extended his offer of help if she had not been the beautiful, wealthy widow of a viscount?

She curtsied to him. 'My servants have seen to everything, sir, but I thank you.'

She walked past him and through the open door where Monette waited.

Once inside the room, Daphne collapsed onto a chair in relief.

And guilt.

Why should she have this private room and so many others so much less? Was she just as selfish as Lord Sanvers?

She hurriedly changed out of her nightclothes and into the dress Monette had pulled from her trunk. Monette did the same. After quickly eating a breakfast, she handed the innkeeper money and asked him to give the room and some food to those most in need. She and Monette did not stay to see if he honoured her request.

They left the alehouse and returned to the carriage.

Carter waited there with the coachman.

'Did you find Mr Westleigh's travelling companions?' Daphne peeked in the carriage, but saw Westleigh lying against the pillows.

'I found the innkeeper, m'lady,' Carter told her. 'He said that Mr Westleigh travelled alone. Not even with a manservant.'

Who would care for him, then?

'How is he?' she asked her coachman.

'Sleeping,' he answered. 'Talking a bit and restless, but sleeping. He did drink the ale, though.'

Daphne glanced around. 'We must find someone to care for him.'

Carter shook his head. 'I believe that cannot be done. There were many people injured in the fire and many others displaced. It would be difficult to even find him a room. Or rooms for ourselves.'

'We should leave today, then, m'lady,' John Coachman said. 'If we start soon we can find lodgings on the road and still reach Faville the day after tomorrow.'

It would take three days for them to reach her property in Vadley near Basingstoke. Her husband had left her the unentailed country house and estate instead of consigning her to the dower house in Faville. She'd spent very little time in Vadley, though, only a few weeks past her days of mourning. Now she planned to return and live a retired life. Whether by doing so she could atone for her days of vanity and thoughtlessness, she was not certain.

'We cannot take him with us,' she said.

But she could hear the abbess, clucking her tongue. *You must find grace to help in time of need.*

'The surgeon said he cannot travel,' she protested.

'We don't have a choice, m'lady,' Carter said in a low voice.

'I say we start out and ask at every posting inn until we find someone to care for him,' her coachman added. 'It will be a more practicable task once we are out of Ramsgate.'

'We cannot leave him.' Monette's eyes pleaded.

These servants were prepared to take care of a stranger, but she was merely trying to think of a way to abandon him, just because she knew he would hate being cared for by a lady who'd wronged his sister.

Or was she merely thinking of her own discomfort? *You must find grace to help in time of need.*

'Very well.' She nodded decisively. 'But let us head towards London. I am certain his family will be in town. When we find a place for his recuperation, we can send for them and they will not have far to travel. Or if we fail to find him care, we will take him the whole way.' It would mean not even two full days of travel.

By late afternoon they'd not found any suitable place for Westleigh, nor had they found anyone willing to take responsibility for his care. Worse, it became clear he could not travel another day to reach London.

The ride had been a nightmare. The coach jostled him and he cried out in pain. He woke often, but was feverish and disoriented and difficult to calm.

They managed to reach Thurnfield, a small village on the road to Maidstone. Its one inn could not accommodate them, but the innkeeper knew of a cottage to let nearby. Daphne signed the papers and paid the rent. Before they set out the short distance to the cottage, she spoke to Carter, John Coachman and Monette.

'I told the leasing agent that I am Mrs Asher, not Lady Faville. I think Mr Westleigh will be more comfortable if he does not know it is me seeing to his care. He only knows me as Lady Faville, you see, and—and his family has reason to dislike me. He would be quite displeased if he knew Lady Faville was caring for him.' She took a breath and rubbed her forehead. 'Asher was my maiden name, so we would not really be lying to anyone....'

Who was she fooling? She was lying to herself as well as lying about her true identity.

Had not the abbess said she must break herself of telling falsehoods as a means of avoiding unpleasantness? Even if the lies were little ones.

She would do so, she vowed.

Next time.

She swallowed more guilt. 'Try to remember to call me Mrs Asher and don't call me m'lady, if you can help it.'

The three servants nodded agreeably.

Was she wrong to make them go along with her lie? Of course she was.

'It will be as you wish it, m'lady,' Carter said. 'I mean, ma'am.'

'Let us go, then.' She allowed Carter to assist her into the carriage. Monette climbed in after her and Carter sat with John Coachman.

They drove the short distance to a white stucco cottage with well-tended shrubbery and a small stable for the horses.

Carter opened the carriage door and put down the step. Daphne and Monette climbed out as the housekeeper and caretaker walked out to greet them.

'We are Mr and Mrs Pitts, ma'am,' the caretaker said. 'At your service.'

'I am Mrs Asher,' Daphne shook their hands, feeling only a twinge of guilt. She introduced the others. 'We have an injured man with us. Mr Westleigh. He will need to be taken to a bedchamber as quickly as possible.'

The housekeeper gestured to the door. 'Come in, then, Mrs Asher, and tell us which room shall be the gentleman's.'

Leaving Monette to watch over Westleigh, and Carter and Mr Pitts to unload the trunks, Daphne followed the housekeeper inside. The decor was modest, but luxurious if she compared it to Fahr Abbey. They should do very nicely there. It would only be for a day or two, until Westleigh's family could come.

'Let us look at the bedchambers.' Mrs Pitts started up the stairs. 'You may pick which one should go to the gentleman.'

Carter and Mr Pitts entered.

'We have Mr Westleigh's trunk,' Carter said.

'Follow us.' Daphne walked up the stairs.

She chose the nicest of the bedchambers for Westleigh. It was a corner room with windows on both sides to let in lots of light and fresh air.

'Does the bed have fresh linens?' she asked.

'Indeed,' responded Mrs Pitts. 'We readied the rooms when the agent sent a message that you were to arrive right away.'

That was what a good housekeeper should do, Daphne thought. She'd learned, though, that even servants liked to be thanked.

'How very good of you.' She smiled at Mrs Pitts and turned towards Carter. 'Bring him here.'

He and Mr Pitts set down the trunk and left the room.

'Do you wish to see the rest of the house now?' Mrs Pitts asked Daphne.

'I will see the gentleman settled first,' she replied.

'Let me see to the meal, then, ma'am.'

Mrs Pitts left and a few moments later, the men helped Westleigh to the bed.

'Where am I?' Westleigh asked, tense and confused. 'Where have you taken me?'

Daphne came to his side and touched his hand. 'You are in a cottage on the road to Maidstone.' She used her most soothing voice.

'Not going to Maidstone. Going to London.' He tried to stand.

Daphne put a hand on his shoulder and he sat again. 'You are too ill to travel to London.' She had been making explanations like this for the past two hours—every time he woke and did not know where he was. 'You were in a fire and you injured your eyes and your head. You need to rest in this bed here and we will care for you until you are better. Then you will go to London.'

'Rest?' He relaxed. 'Then London.'

Carter spoke. 'You should leave the room, m'l—Mrs Asher, while I undress him.'

She turned to the housekeeper's husband. 'Would you bring him water? Soap and towels, too, if possible, so Carter can bathe him a little? I am certain he will be more comfortable when clean again. Be gentle with his face, though.'

'Water, soap and towels are already here, ma'am.' The man pointed to a chest of drawers upon which sat a pitcher and basin and folded towels. He left the room.

Carter spoke. 'I'll clean him up, ma'am. Leave him to me.'

Daphne moved her hand, planning to step away, but Westleigh groped for it and seized it, pulling her back. 'Do not leave,' he rasped. 'Do not leave me alone.'

His firm grip and his intensity shook her. She did not know how to calm him.

She stroked his hair—what little hair was not covered by bandages. 'Shh, now,' she said, trying to sound like the abbess who'd soothed her when she'd become overwrought. 'You are not alone. Carter is here.'

'I am here, sir,' Carter said.

Daphne continued. 'Now remain still and Carter will take off your boots. Will that not feel more comfortable?'

'I'll give you a little wash and put you in clean bedclothes,' Carter added.

Daphne felt Westleigh's muscles relax.

'Do not wear bedclothes,' he murmured.

Chapter Two

~~~~~~~~~~~~⁂~~~~~~~~~~~~

The dragon pursued him, its fiery breath scorching his skin. Stinging his eyes.

Hugh pushed himself to run faster, to escape.

The way out was ahead, a pinpoint of light that seemed to become more distant the harder he pumped his legs to reach it. The flames roared, as if the dragon laughed at him. The blaze encircled him, bound him. Devoured him.

He jolted awake.

To darkness.

He sat up and his hands groped for his eyes. 'I can't see! Why can't I see?' His eyes were covered in cloth.

Then he remembered. The fire had not been a dream. It had burned his eyes, all brightness and pain. Was he blind?

'The bandages. Take them off!' He pulled at them.

There was a rustle of fabric and the scent of roses filled his nostrils. Cool hands clasped his.

'Your eyes are injured.' The voice was feminine and soothing, but not familiar. 'The bandages need to stay on for you to heal.'

'Who are you?' He swallowed. His throat hurt when he spoke.

'I—I am Mrs Asher. You carried me out of the fire—'

He remembered only one woman he'd carried out of the fire, down the flame-filled stairway, all the way to the cool night outside.

'Where am I?' he rasped.

'You—you are in my cottage in—in Thurnfield.'

Thurnfield?

The village on the road to London? He'd passed through it many times.

She went on. 'You cannot travel, so we brought you here.'

That made no sense. 'I was in Ramsgate. If I cannot travel, how is it I came to Thurnfield?'

Her voice turned cautious. 'We could not find a place for you in Ramsgate. Not one where you could receive care.'

She was caring for him? Who was this woman? He wanted to see her. Look her in the eye. Figure out the reason for the uneasiness in her voice.

But that was impossible.

He cleared his throat. 'You said *we*.'

'My maid and footman and me.'

She had a maid and a footman. A woman of some means, then. Of wealth? Were there more servants, perhaps? 'A maid and footman. Who else is here?'

'A housekeeper and her husband.' She paused. 'That is all.'

Modest means, then, but she was holding back something, he would bet on it. 'Where is Mr Asher?'

'I am a widow.' Her voice turned low, and that provoked a whole new set of emotions.

He suddenly recalled that the woman he'd carried had weighed hardly more than a whisper. She'd curled trustingly against his chest, hiding her face from the fire.

He cursed the bandages covering his eyes. He wanted to see her. Face her like a man.

'My name is Westleigh.' He extended his hand, which seemed to float in empty space.

She grasped it.

Her hand felt soft, like the hand of a gently bred woman.

'I know who you are,' she said, her voice turning tight again. 'We learned at the inn that you are Mr Hugh Westleigh. We have your trunk. Like ours, it was with the carriages and spared from the fire.'

Had she also learned he was the younger brother of the Earl of Westleigh? Was this a factor in bringing him here?

If only he could look into her eyes—he could read her character.

If only he could see.

He pressed the bandages covering his eyes. The pain grew sharper.

A soft, cool hand drew his fingers away as it had done before. 'Please do not disturb your bandages. The surgeon said your eyes are to remain bandaged for two weeks. That is how long they will take to heal.'

'Will they heal, then?' he demanded. 'Or am I to be blind?'

She did not answer right away. 'The surgeon said they must stay bandaged or they will not heal. That much is certain. He said they could heal, though.'

Hugh laughed drily. '*Could* heal. That is not very reassuring.'

Her voice turned low again. 'I am only repeating what he told me.'

He caught himself. She obviously had taken on the task of caring for him. He need not be churlish in return.

He lifted his throbbing head again and turned in the direction of her voice. 'Forgive me. I do not customarily succumb to self-pity.'

'Of course you do not.' Now she sounded like his old governess. 'Are you thirsty?'

Good of her to change the subject.

He was thirsty, by God. Parched.

He nodded.

He heard a swirl of her skirts again and the sound of pouring liquid. She lifted his hand and placed a glass in it. He took a sip.

It was water, flavoured with a touch of mint. Who took such trouble for a stranger?

He gulped it down. 'Is there more?'

He held out the empty glass, again into nothingness. He waited for her to grasp it.

She took it and poured more, then again put it in his hand.

He drank and handed the glass back to her. 'I detest feeling so helpless.'

'Certainly you do,' the *governess* responded. 'But you must rest. You not only burned your eyes, you also suffered a blow to the head. The surgeon said you need rest to recover.'

He lay back against some pillows. The mere exertion of waking in strange surroundings and drinking two glasses of water had fatigued him. How annoying. How weak. He hated weakness.

'Shall I bring you breakfast?' she asked. 'Or would you like to sleep some more?'

His stomach clenched at the mention of food.

He forced his raspy voice to remain calm. 'Breakfast, if you would be so good.'

Again her skirts rustled. 'I will be right back.'

Without his eyes, he must depend on this woman for food, for everything. How much more helpless could he be?

Her footsteps receded and a door opened. When he

heard it close again, it was as if the room turned cold and menacing.

He'd never been afraid of darkness as a child. He'd never been afraid of anything, but this was a living nightmare. Had he traded the fiery dragon of his dream for darkness?

Blindness?

Carefully he felt his bandages. They were thick over his eyes and wound firmly around his head. He tried to open his eyelids, but they hardly moved, the bandages were so snug. The effort shot daggers through his eyeballs and he dared not try again lest he injure them even more.

Was his fate to be blind and helpless?

He pounded a fist on the mattress, but wished he could put his hands on something he could smash into a thousand pieces.

He didn't fear darkness. He didn't fear danger, but the idea of being helpless was too abhorrent for words. And he was, indeed, helpless. Helpless and confined.

He patted his arms and legs and torso—someone had put him in a shirt and drawers, he realised. He lifted the fabric of the shirt to his nose. Clean clothes. Not a hint of smoke. Someone had bathed and clothed him.

Had she undressed him and clad him in a clean shirt? In drawers?

He strained to remember. He recalled leading people out of the fire. Of fire blasting his face. He vaguely remembered being jostled in a carriage, but those memories were mere flashes, with no coherence at all.

His head throbbed and he pressed his temples. How injured was he? He stretched his arms, flexed his legs. The rest of him seemed in one piece. He felt the sting of burns here and there on his skin, but nothing of significance.

He could still walk, could he not? If so, he'd be damned if he remained bedridden.

He slipped off the bed. His legs held him, so he felt his way around the bed's edge before stepping away. He hated not knowing what lay in his path. Waving his hands in front of him, he took tentative steps. Was this life without sight? Caught in emptiness? Unsure of every step?

A door opened.

'Mr Westleigh!' It was Mrs Asher's voice. 'You should not be out of bed!'

He heard the clatter of dishes—and smelled porridge. He felt her come near. Caught the scent of roses.

She took his arm. 'Let me help you back to bed.'

He pulled away. 'I will not be an invalid.'

She tugged at him. 'No, but you must rest or you risk being that very thing.'

He still did not wish to comply. 'Did you bring food?'

'Yes,' she replied. 'And a tray. See? You will be able to eat nicely in bed.'

He jerked away. 'I cannot see.'

She stepped back and left him in the emptiness again.

Let her abandon him! He'd find his own way back, if necessary.

He turned to where he thought she stood. 'Is there a table and chair in this room?'

She did not answer right away. 'Yes.'

'Then I will sit and eat like a man.'

'Very well.' She sighed. 'Stay where you are.' He heard furniture being moved. She took his arm again. 'Come here.'

She led him to a chair. He sat and heard the table being moved towards him. A moment later he smelled the food and heard the sound of a tray being placed in front of him.

She took his hand and placed a spoon in it, and showed him the bowl. 'It is porridge. And tea.'

He was suddenly famished, but he paused, trying again to face her, wherever she might be. 'Mrs Asher?'

'Yes?' Her voice was petulant, as it should be after his abominable behaviour.

'Do forgive me.' He'd behaved badly towards her again. 'I should be thanking you, nothing else.'

It took several seconds for her to speak. 'Your apology is accepted, Mr Westleigh.' Her voice softened. 'But do eat. You need to eat to gain strength.'

'I am grateful for the food. I am quite hungry.' He dipped the spoon, but missed the bowl. 'Blast.' He'd forgotten where the bowl was located.

She directed him on his next try. This time he scooped up a spoonful of porridge and lifted it. He missed and hit the corner of his mouth.

She wiped it with a napkin. 'Let me help you.' Putting her hand on his, she guided the spoon to his mouth.

The first taste made him ravenous, but he could not bear being fed like a helpless infant. 'I think I can manage it.' He groped for the bowl and picked it up in one hand and held it close to his mouth. With his other hand he scooped the porridge with the spoon and shovelled it into his mouth.

No doubt his manners were appalling.

He scraped the bowl clean and felt for a space on the table to put it down. With his fingers, he carefully explored what else was there.

A tea cup, warm to the touch. How was he to manage lifting a tea cup without spilling it?

'How do you take your tea?' she asked. 'I will fix it for you.'

'Milk and one lump of sugar.' He listened to the clink of the spoon as she stirred.

When the clinking stopped, she again guided his hand to the cup. He grasped it in both hands and carefully brought it to his mouth, aware of the aroma before attempting to take a sip. He sipped slowly, not because he savoured the taste, but because he did not wish to spill it.

When he finished, he managed to place the cup into its saucer. 'Thank you, Mrs Asher. You have been very kind.'

'You should rest now,' she responded. 'The surgeon said—'

'I will give you no further argument.' He felt for the napkin and wiped his mouth.

She came close again and touched his arm.

'I want to try to manage by myself.' He pushed the chair back and stood, getting reoriented to where the bed was. He groped his way back to it and climbed under the covers, aware that she must be watching his every awkward move. In his underclothes.

'Shall I write to your family and tell them where you are and what has happened to you?' she asked.

His family? Good God, no.

After this trip he intended to throw off the shackles of family responsibility for a time. He'd been at the family's beck and call ever since leaving the army.

'Do not write to my family.' He raised his voice. 'They must know nothing about this.'

She did not speak.

He shook his head, realising how he must have sounded. 'I apologise again.' He spoke in a milder tone. 'My family would be the very worst of caretakers.' They were not expecting him, so they would not worry. He'd not written that he'd left Brussels. Better to not give them any time to find a new task he might perform for them. 'I beg you would find another solution. I realise I am imposing, but I can well pay for my care. I must not be put in the hands of my family. On that I must insist.'

'Very well. I will not contact your family.' He heard the

sounds of her picking up the tray from the table. 'But you must rest now. Someone will check on you later.' He heard her footsteps walking towards the door. It opened and she spoke once more. 'Mr Westleigh?'

'Yes?' He stiffened, expecting a rebuke.

'You are not imposing.'

The door closed.

He was alone again. In the dark.

Mrs Asher's presence was a comfort, an anchor. Alone it was as if he floated in a void. He listened and thought he heard a bird singing outside, a dog's bark at some distance, footsteps outside the room.

He stilled, waiting to hear if the door would open.

The footsteps faded.

His head ached, his throat ached, his eyes ached, but he was determined to remain awake. If he remained awake, he was not totally helpless.

To keep awake, he recalled the details of the fire.

He'd been leaving the inn's tavern, returning to his room, when shouts of 'fire!' reached his ears. He'd jumped into action, knocking on doors, getting people out. The fire had started in a room on the ground floor. He and others had cleared that floor and worked their way up to the higher floors while the fire kept growing and the task grew more dangerous.

The excitement of it had spurred him on. People had needed saving and someone had to brave the threat to save them, a perfect role for Hugh. He always did what needed to be done. If there was risk involved, so much the better.

He'd fought in the war because England needed him and, if truth be told, he'd loved the adventure of it, the risk to one's life, the chance to test his mettle. The army in peacetime was not for him, though. He'd sold his commission and prepared to discover his next adventure. He'd travel, he thought. To Africa. Or the Colonies. Or Chile—no, not Chile. With his luck he'd get embroiled in their War of Independence. It was one thing to risk one's life for one's own country, quite another to act as a mercenary. Besides, it was his own independence he yearned to indulge.

Instead, a family crisis had snared him. First his father had nearly impoverished the family by gambling and philandering away its fortunes, then he had tried to cheat the man who'd come to their rescue, his own natural son, John Rhysdale.

After that, Hugh, his brother Ned and Rhysdale had forced their father to move to Brussels and turn over the finances and all his affairs to Ned. Hugh was charged with making certain their father held to the bargain, which meant repeated trips to the Continent. At least this last trip had been the final one. Hugh had been summoned back to Brussels because his father had dropped dead after a night of carousing and drinking.

Hugh suffered no grief over his father's death—the man hadn't cared a whit about him or any of the family. His father's death freed him at last.

Now Hugh's independence was again threatened when nearly in his grasp. Only this time it might not be family obligation holding him back.

This time it might be blindness.

Daphne strode immediately from Westleigh's bedchamber through the cottage and out into the garden where beds of red tulips and yellow narcissus ought to have given her cheer.

How could she be calm? She'd counted on Westleigh's family coming to care for him. Who would not want family to nurse them back to health? She'd planned on leaving as soon as a family member arrived. They would never see the elusive Mrs Asher. A mere note would be all they knew of her.

The Westleighs would detest knowing the despised Lady Faville had cared for a family member. Hugh Westleigh would detest it, as well. She'd once tried to steal away Phillipa Westleigh's new husband after all.

And, because her vanity had been injured, she'd heaved a lighted oil lamp against the Masquerade Club's wall. It had shattered, just as her illusions had shattered in that moment. In a flash, though, the curtains and her own skirts had caught fire.

Her hands flew to her burning cheeks. She'd been so afraid. And ashamed! What sort of person does such a thing?

Yes, the Westleighs would hate her, indeed.

She'd been a coward that day, running away after Phillipa had saved her from her burning skirts. She was a coward still. She should simply tell Hugh Westleigh her identity—she should have told him from the beginning—

What would the abbess have said? *Do what is right, my child. You shall never err if you follow the guide of your own conscience. Do always what is right.*

But what happens if one does not know what is right? What is one supposed to do in that event?

Was it right to tell him the truth or better to hide the truth and not upset him?

Daphne paced back and forth. It would only be two weeks until his bandages came off and he'd be on his way. She stopped and placed her hands on her cheeks.

Unless he was blind.

Please, dear God. Let him not be blind!

She shook her head. Who was she to pray?

She, Carter and Monette simply must take the best care of him. Not upset him. Give him the best chance to heal.

Perhaps the dear abbess would intercede with God for

him on Daphne's behalf. And perhaps the abbess would forgive her if she did not tell the truth this time. No real harm in him thinking she was merely Mrs Asher for such a little while. Feeling only slightly guilty, Daphne strolled around to the front of the cottage.

Two young women approached from the road and quickened their pace when they saw her.

'Beg pardon, ma'am. Are you Mrs Asher?' They looked no more than fifteen years, each of them.

'I am Mrs Asher,' she responded.

'We've come looking for work, ma'am,' one said. 'Mr Brill, the agent, told us you might be needing some help in the cottage—'

'We can do whatever you need,' the other broke in. 'We're strong girls. Mr Brill will vouch for us.'

Both were simply dressed and their clothing looked very old and worn. In fact, their gowns hung on them.

'We need work very bad, ma'am,' the first girl said. 'We'll do anything.'

'I am not sure…' Daphne bit her lip. Would it be right to hire maids to work in a house where she would stay for only two weeks?

'Please, Mrs Asher,' the second girl said. 'We can show you how good we work. Give us a chance.'

What difference did it make to her? She had plenty of money to pay them. It was the easiest thing in the world to say yes. Besides, the abbess would say she'd done a good thing.

'Very well, girls,' she said. 'Follow me. If Mrs Pitts approves, you may become our new maids of all work.'

They could deliver the meals to Mr Westleigh. Daphne would be able to avoid him altogether. Then it would not matter who he thought she was.

Chapter Three

Hugh lost his battle to stay awake. He had no idea how long he slept, but he woke again to darkness.

Cursed eyes!

Was it day or night? Was he alone or was someone in the room?

Was *she* here?

He remained still and strained to hear the sounds of someone moving, someone breathing.

It was so quiet.

The hiss of the fireplace; otherwise, silence. Was anyone near? Would they hear him if he called out for help?

Although he'd be damned if he'd call out for help.

Or for water.

His throat was parched with thirst. There must be water somewhere in the room. She must have left some for him.

He climbed out of bed, not as steady on his feet as he might wish. The carpet on the floor was soft and cool on his bare feet. Carefully, he started from right next to the bed, groping—and finding—a side table. He ran his hand over the table's surface. No water. Merely a candlestick—certainly an item for which he had no need.

He groped past the table and bumped into a wooden

chair. He backed away and knocked the table onto the floor. The carpet muffled the sound. No one would be roused by the noise.

Crouching, he felt around for the table, found it and righted it. The candlestick must have rolled away. Useless to search for it anyway.

Moving cautiously again, he made his way past the chair. With the wall as his guide, he inched his way towards the fireplace, feeling the fire's heat grow stronger as he neared. His hand found the mantel. His toes smashed against the hearth.

He backed away and found more chairs and another table upon which there was a book. Another item for which he had no use.

Continuing, he discovered a door. It was a dressing room, smelling of dust, its shelves empty. He closed the door and his fingers felt along the wall until he came to another door. The door to the hallway. He turned the latch and opened the door and felt the change in temperature. But the hallway was silent.

He closed the door again and groped his way back to the bed. On the other side was another table. On the table he found a drinking glass and the water pitcher. He could never pour the water into the glass. He lifted the entire pitcher to his lips and took several gulps of the cool, minty liquid.

Placing the pitcher back on the table, he felt his way back to the bed, but halted. Lying abed like an invalid held no appeal.

He might as well continue his haphazard search of the room.

He found his trunk in one corner, his boots, smelling of bootblack, next to it. He found a rocking chair and a window.

A window! Fresh air. Hugh found the sash, opened the window and felt a cool breeze against his face. On the breeze was the scent of green grass, rich soil and flowers. He stuck his hand out the window and tried to sense whether it was day or night.

Without eyes, he could not tell.

He felt for the rocking chair and turned it towards the window. She must have sat in this rocking chair while in the room; her scent, very faint, clung to it. He lowered himself into it and rocked. The rhythm soothed him. The breeze cooled his skin. And banished the memory of the fire's infernal heat.

He must have dozed. For how long this time? Half awake, half asleep, he became aware of a knock at the door. The door opened. He knew instantly it was not she.

'Sir! You are not abed.' A male voice.

Hugh shook himself awake. 'Who are you?'

'I am Carter, sir. La—Mrs Asher's footman.' The voice did not come closer, so Carter must have remained by the door. 'I came to attend you.'

'I am grateful.' She'd said her footman would come. 'Can you tell me what time it is?'

'Seven, sir,' Carter replied.

'Morning or evening?' Did they not see he could not tell?

'Morning, sir.'

'What day?' Hugh tried not to let his impatience show.

'Oh! You must not realise—' Carter's voice deepened. 'Forgive me—I will explain—it is Friday. We arrived here Wednesday. The day after the fire. You slept most of yesterday. It is Friday morning now.'

He'd lost two days.

'I will assist you, sir. Shave you and whatever else you might require.'

Shave? Hugh scraped his hand against the stubble on his chin. He must have appeared like a ruffian to her.

Carter's voice came closer. 'Unless you would like me to help you back into bed.'

'No.' Hugh forced himself not to snap at the man. It was not Carter's fault he needed the assistance. 'I will not return to bed. Shave me and help me dress, if you would be so good.'

Gentlemen of Hugh's rank customarily employed a valet, but Hugh never did. He had no qualms about borrowing the services of someone else's valet when absolutely necessary, but what he could do for himself, he preferred doing. It made him free to come and go as he wished without having to consider anyone else's needs.

Now, though, he was not free. He was as dependent as a suckling babe.

He submitted to Carter's ministrations with as good grace as he could muster, even though Carter needed to help him with his most basic of needs. He'd do them all without help as soon as he could, he promised himself. After he was shaved, bathed, toileted and dressed, he found his way back to the rocking chair, more fatigued than he would ever admit.

'Thank you, Carter,' he said. 'What of breakfast?' His hunger had returned. 'Will you help me to the breakfast room?'

He sensed Carter backing away. 'I—I believe Mrs Asher preferred you eat here, sir. Your health is fragile, I'm given to understand.'

Hugh refused to be fragile. 'Very well, but tell Mrs Asher I wish to speak with her as soon as it is convenient.'

'Very good, sir.' Carter moved towards the door.

'In fact—' Hugh raised his voice '—tell Mrs Asher that I would like to see the village doctor. I am well able to pay for his services, so let there be no worry over that. I wish to see him today.' And find out, if possible, if he was to be blind or not.

'As you wish, sir.' He imagined Carter bowing. 'Breakfast as well, sir.'

The door closed and the footman's steps receded.

Hugh rose again. It felt better to be dressed, even if he was merely in shirt, trousers and stockings. At least when Mrs Asher returned, he would look more like a gentleman and less like an invalid.

If one could ignore the bandages covering his eyes.

He made his way around the bed. If his memory served him, the table on the other side of the bed, the table he'd knocked down during the night, was where he had eaten the porridge. He found the table again, bumped into the wooden chair again and kicked the lost candlestick with his toe, sending it skittering away.

Nonetheless, he managed to arrange the table and chair for eating. It was a minor matter, but a victory all the same. He was not entirely helpless.

Even so, a lifetime like this would be unbearable.

Daphne had left the two prospective maids in the company of Mrs Pitt after finally sorting out the matter. She'd thought she could simply hand them off to the housekeeper and be done with it, but the woman was shockingly dependent upon Daphne to make even the smallest of decisions, like what their duties should be, whether they should live in the house—yes, they should. Why have maids if they were not around when you needed them? Mrs Pitt also would have offered the girls a pittance for what would be very hard work, tending to the fires, cleaning the house and otherwise seeing to her needs. It was also very clear that they needed new clothes.

And that they were hungry. They both kept eyeing the bread Mrs Pitt had taken from the oven, and neither could pay attention to the discussion. So Daphne told Mrs Pitt to feed them, which led to a long discussion of what to feed them and what to feed Mr Westleigh and how was she— Mrs Pitt—to cook all that food, now that there were two more mouths to feed and two more workers to supervise.

By the time they'd finished, Daphne had given Mrs Pitt permission to hire a cook, a kitchen maid, another footman and two stable boys to help John Coachman. Mr Pitt was sent into the village to speak with some people he and Mrs Pitt thought would be perfect for the jobs, and Monette was getting her cloak and bonnet so she could accompany the girls to the local draper for fabric to make new dresses and aprons.

What fuss. Her husband would have been appalled at her being so bothered by such trivial matters. Even at the convent at Fahr, someone else saw to the food, the clothing, the cleaning.

As tedious as it all was, Daphne walked through the hall with a sense of pride. Her decisions were good ones after all. And she could well afford to pay all the servants even if she stayed here a year instead of two weeks.

As she crossed the hall, Carter descended the stairs.

She smiled up at him. 'How is Mr Westleigh this morning, Carter?'

He reached the final step. 'Much improved, ma'am. He wishes to speak with you.'

Oh, dear. And she wanted to avoid him.

'What about, do you know?' Perhaps he'd changed his mind about contacting his family.

Carter frowned. 'He wants to see a local doctor. I be-

lieve he is most unhappy about being bandaged and confined. He wants to see a doctor immediately.'

It was a reasonable request. He'd been nearly insensi-
ble when the surgeon at Ramsgate examined him. If only
she'd known a few minutes earlier, she could have asked
Mr Pitt to fetch the doctor.

'Could you go to the village and locate the doctor? Or
find Mr Pitt and give him the errand? He left for the village a few minutes ago.'

Carter's brows knit. 'Shall I take Mr Westleigh his
breakfast first, ma'am? I told him it was coming.'

The poor man must be famished. He'd only eaten a bowl
of porridge since they'd arrived here.

She sighed. 'No. I will take him his breakfast. Perhaps
there was something else he wanted to say to me.'

Carter came with her to the kitchen where Mrs Pitt
gave him the doctor's direction and fixed the tray for Mr
Westleigh.

Daphne carried the tray up the stairs and knocked upon
Westleigh's bedchamber door.

'Come in, Carter.' His voice sounded stronger than the
day before.

She opened the door and entered the room, kicking the
door closed behind her.

He was seated at the table and chair where he'd eaten
the porridge, and was dressed in a clean white shirt and
dark brown trousers that showed off his broad shoulders
and lean hips. She swallowed, suddenly remembering his
strong arms carrying her in the inn.

'I can smell the bread from here.' He gestured with his
hand. 'I will eat at the table.'

She crossed the room. 'It is Mrs Asher, not Carter.'

He tensed, as if he'd not liked mistaking her identity,

and stood as a gentleman does when a lady enters the room. 'Good morning,' he said stiffly.

'Please sit,' she responded. 'Carter said you wished to see me, so it is I who brings you breakfast.'

He lowered himself back in the chair. 'I appreciate you coming so quickly.'

She placed the tray of food in front of him. 'I sent Carter to fetch a doctor and we did not wish you to wait. Are you hungry?'

'Ravenous.' He carefully ran his hands over the food.

She'd instructed Mrs Pitts to serve foods he could eat with his hands and spare him the struggle of manoeuvring utensils. They'd settled on warm bread sliced open with melting butter inside, two cooked eggs, cubes of cheese and a pot of tea.

He hesitated.

It made her uncertain. 'I will pour your tea,' she said. 'I remember how you take it, but do, please, eat. You must be very hungry.'

'I hope my manners will not offend.'

Oh, he was merely being polite. 'Have no fear. I am not easily offended.'

How odd of her to say such a thing. At a formal dinner party, she once would have had much to say about poor manners, and she'd often shaken her head at the way some of the lower classes consumed their food. Perhaps she was developing some tolerance, like the abbess had often encouraged her to do.

'I am surprised to see you dressed,' she went on in a conversational tone. 'I thought you would still be in bed.'

'No more bed.' His voice was firm. 'I am well enough to be up.'

She pursed her lips. 'Are you certain? The surgeon in

Ramsgate said you would need time to recuperate. I think he meant you should remain in bed.'

'I think him wrong,' he said stiffly. 'I feel recuperated. Perhaps the village doctor will say I may have my bandages removed and be on my way.' He paused. 'I told Carter I am well able to pay whatever the expense. I intend to compensate you, as well.'

'Money does not concern me. I certainly need no compensation.' She waved a dismissive hand. 'I—I do not know if Carter can produce a doctor this very day, though.'

The village did have a surgeon, Mrs Pitts had said, but he was kept very busy.

Westleigh took a bite of bread, chewed and swallowed it. She could not help but notice the muscles in his neck move with the effort. She touched her own neck.

'Let us hope he can come today,' he said.

He must be as eager to be on his way as she was for him to leave, but should she trust his care to a village doctor? Perhaps she should send for a London physician. She would love to send for the physician her husband had used when he was in town, but that man knew her.

Of course she could simply tell Westleigh now who she was.

She opened her mouth.

But he spoke first. 'Might I have a clock?' he asked. 'A way to keep track of time. I cannot even tell if it is day or night.'

How awful! All sorts of things must be difficult if one was not able to see. How much worse if one would never see again.

She vowed she would leave a large coin in the cup of the next blind beggar she came upon.

'I am so sorry,' she cried. 'I should have thought to provide you a clock. Perhaps I can purchase a watch that chimes. I have seen such watches. You could keep it next to you.'

Although, now that she thought of it, would a small village have such a watch? She'd only seen them in London shops.

'A clock will be sufficient,' he responded. 'And I am well able to pay for it, if there is not a spare one in the house.'

'We'll find you one, do not fear.' There was one on the mantel in the library. She'd have it brought to him immediately.

Or she would have to bring it herself, since she'd sent everyone else away besides Mrs Pitts, who would be much too busy.

'Wait here a moment,' she said, which was a silly thing to say. Where could he go without sight?

She hurried out of the room and ran down the stairs to the library. Carefully she took the clock from the mantel and carried it back to his room.

'I've brought you a clock!' she said as she entered. 'I'll place it on the mantel and we'll make sure Carter winds it for you.'

'I did not mean for you to bring it so quickly, but I am very grateful.' He had finished the food and was feeling for the tea cup.

She walked over and guided his hand to it.

He stilled and his face tilted towards hers.

She wished she could see him, see all his face. She had seen him a few times at the Masquerade Club and had been introduced to him once. It was the only time she could remember speaking to him, and she'd paid little attention.

'Is there anything else?' she murmured. 'Anything else I can do for you?'

He continued to seem as if he was facing her. 'I want to

leave this room,' he said. 'To come and go as I wish. Surely there must be a drawing room or a library or someplace I could sit without disturbing anyone.'

'But how can you? You can't see,' she cried.

He scowled. 'I can walk.'

She feared he would injure himself even more. What would she do then?

'The surgeon at Ramsgate said—' She cut herself off. 'Let us at least wait until another doctor examines you. I would hate to risk your recovery.'

He gulped down the cup of tea.

She leaned closer to pick up the tray.

'Roses,' he said softly.

'I beg your pardon?'

'You smell like roses,' he explained.

She felt her cheeks flush. It delighted her that he'd noticed. It was her favourite scent. She always rinsed herself with rosewater and any perfume she purchased must smell like roses.

'I—I should leave now, unless there is something else I can do—' She bit her lip.

'Nothing.' His voice dipped low. 'I am grateful for the breakfast and the clock. And for sending for the doctor.'

She cleared her throat. 'Let us hope he comes soon.'

Balancing the tray, she exited the room and only then did she realise she'd again not told him who she really was. Maybe when the doctor came, he would indeed say Westleigh was recovered. Maybe he would remove Westleigh's bandages and his eyes would work perfectly and she could have her coachman take him to London this very day.

It was late afternoon before the doctor called at the cottage.

Carter announced him to Daphne as she sat in the drawing room, writing a letter to her man of business, informing him of her arrival in England and her stay at Thurnfield.

She, of course, did not explain *why* she remained at Thurnfield.

She rose at the doctor's entrance. 'Mr Wynne, how good of you to come.'

He was a man of perhaps fifty years, with a rough but kindly appearance. When he saw her, his face lit with surprise, then appreciation. 'Mrs Asher! My word. May—may I welcome you to Thurnfield. You are a very delightful addition, if I may be so bold as to say.'

'Thank you, sir.' Daphne's response was well practised. Men who saw her for the first time often reacted so. In this instance, however, she did not want her beauty to distract the doctor from why he was here. 'I do believe Mr Westleigh is anxious for you to examine him. Carter can take you up to him directly.'

He tapped his lips. 'In a moment. I understand from Mr Carter that you witnessed the injury and the examination by the other surgeon. I think it best I should speak with you first.'

She sat again and gestured to a chair. 'Do sit.'

He lowered himself into the chair and leaned towards her, all ears. And eyes. 'Now. Tell me what happened.'

She relayed the information as succinctly as she could, but he asked several questions about the injury and other surgeon's examination, forcing her to repeat herself.

It was a good thing she had not ordered tea, or the man would never make it up to Westleigh's room.

Her patience frayed. 'I do think you should see Mr Westleigh now, sir. He has been waiting a very long time.'

'Indeed. Indeed.' Mr Wynne took his time rising from his seat. 'You will accompany me? I may need information only you will have.'

She'd just given him all the information she possessed. Several times.

But it seemed expedient to do as he requested, merely to get him to actually see Westleigh, who had waited all day for the man. She rose. 'Come with me.'

Daphne heard the clock in Westleigh's room chime the quarter-hour as she raised her hand to knock.

'Please, come in.' Westleigh sounded impatient.

'Mr Westleigh, it is Mrs Asher,' she said as she opened the door. 'I have brought Mr Wynne, the surgeon, to see you.'

Hugh had been seated in the rocking chair next to the window, which was open to the afternoon breeze. He stood and extended his hand almost in the surgeon's direction. 'Mr Wynne. I have been eager for your arrival.'

Wynne clasped his hand. 'Westleigh. Pleased to meet you. Mrs Asher has told me of your injuries.'

'She has?' His posture stiffened. 'Perhaps you would be so kind as to tell me what she said.'

'I told him you were in a fire,' Daphne responded. 'And that you were hit on the head and your eyes burned. I told him the other surgeon said you were concussed and that your eyes needed to remain bandaged for two weeks.'

'I could have told him that,' Westleigh remarked.

'I agree.' She had not wished to be this involved. Should she tell him the surgeon preferred her company to the duties that called him here?

'A nasty business, eh?' Wynne finally turned his attention to the patient. 'Please do sit and I will bring a chair closer to you.'

Westleigh lowered himself back into the rocking chair and Wynne brought the wooden chair over to him. Daphne stood near to the door.

'Now,' Wynne said, 'tell me—do you have any difficulty breathing?'

Westleigh took a breath. 'No.'

Wynne nodded, but from his bag pulled out a cylindrical tube. 'Best to check, in any event.' He placed one end of the tube on Westleigh's chest, the other against his own ear. 'Breathe deeply for me.'

Westleigh did as requested and the surgeon moved the tube to various locations on his chest.

'Your lungs are clear,' Wynne said. 'Have you experienced any dizziness?'

'None now,' Westleigh answered. 'Not even if I walk. I am quite steady on my feet.'

'Any pain?' the man asked.

Westleigh shrugged. 'My throat feels a bit rough. My head aches still, but not excessively. It is my eyes—my eyes concern me the most. They ache with a dull sort of pain. Again, not excessive. If I try to move my eyelids, however, the pain sharpens a great deal.'

'Best you not move your eyelids.' Wynne chuckled.

Westleigh frowned.

This was not a joking matter to him, Daphne wanted to say.

Wynne leaned forwards. 'Let me have a look at you.'

He placed his fingers on Hugh's head. His fingers looked stubby, but his touch seemed sure.

'It is most remarkable you were not more burned.' Wynne moved his fingers around his head and looked closely at the exposed parts of his face. 'The eyes can get the worst of it even if your skin's damage is superficial. Your hair is singed in places and I cannot see under the bandage, but I suspect you are fairly unscathed.'

Daphne had seen his eyes, though. His eyes had been alarmingly cloudy.

Wynne leaned back. 'I would like to examine under your bandages, but you must promise me something.'

'What is that?' Westleigh asked.

'Keep your eyes closed.' Wynne emphasised each word. 'If you do not keep your eyes closed, you risk further injury and blindness. Do you understand me?'

'I understand.' Westleigh answered in a low voice.

Wynne turned to Daphne. 'Mrs Asher, may we close the window and draw the curtains?'

'Certainly.' She hurried to do as he asked.

Westleigh remained still as Mr Wynne unwound his bandages. He was like a taut string vibrating with tension. The bandages seemed endless, but finally Wynne came down to the two round pieces of cloth that were pressed against Westleigh's eyelids.

'Remember, keep your eyes closed,' he warned.

He removed the last and moved even closer to peer at Westleigh's eyelids. He touched one very gently with his thumb.

Westleigh winced.

'Does that pain you?' Wynne asked.

'Some,' Westleigh responded tightly.

Wynne held the lids closed, but turned to Daphne. 'Will you bring me a lighted candle?'

She took the candlestick from the bedside table and lit it with a taper from the fireplace.

Wynne brought the candle close to Westleigh's face.

Westleigh's eyelids were still red and a yellowish crust clung to his eyelashes. If he did open his eyes now and could see, he'd know instantly who she was, but Daphne thrust that thought aside. He was more important this moment than her pride…and shame.

Westleigh remained like a statue.

'Are you able to see the light?' Wynne asked.

'Yes!' His voice filled with excitement. His eyelids twitched.

'Keep them closed,' Wynne warned again.

'Does that mean I will be able to see?' Westleigh asked.

'I wish I could make that promise.' Wynne leaned back and pulled out more bandages from his leather bag. 'Your eyes need more time for us to be certain. Two weeks, like the other surgeon said. If you want a chance to heal completely, wait the two weeks. There is no infection now, but to open your eyes now—well, I cannot stress how urgent it is that you wait the two weeks. It is your only chance.'

Westleigh's chin set and his head remained erect.

For some silly reason, Daphne felt proud of him for not giving in to emotion.

He might yet be blind.

Chapter Four

Hugh was through with confinement. He was through giving in to his fears. He would see again. He must. He would not sit in one room for two weeks waiting. He'd move around, act as if he could see, no matter how many pieces of furniture he bumped into, no matter what came crashing to the floor. He'd pay for the damages.

But he would not be confined.

Mr Wynne did not require him to remain in bed. The only admonition the surgeon had made was that he was not to remove the bandages over his eyes. Wynne said he'd return in a few days to check him and change the bandages, if necessary. In the meantime, Hugh intended to leave this room.

Wynne also said he could travel, if he wished. He could be in London in one day's coach ride and straight into the suffocating confines of his mother's care.

He'd rather impose on Mrs Asher. Was that ungentlemanly of him? He suspected so, but an unwanted invalid would receive the least fussing and he had no wish to be fussed over. It might cause the lady some annoyance if he did not remain in his room, but he'd go mad otherwise.

Carter knocked and entered the room. 'Do you require anything, sir?'

'Nothing at the moment,' Hugh replied.

'Very good, sir.'

The door sounded as if it was closing and Hugh raised his voice. 'Carter?'

It opened again. 'Yes, sir?'

'What time is dinner to be served?'

'Whenever you desire, sir,' Carter responded.

'I do not wish to cause undue inconvenience,' Hugh countered. 'When is Mrs Asher served dinner? I can wait until she is served, certainly.'

'M'l—' Carter faltered. 'Mrs Asher dines at eight o'clock.'

'Eight o'clock. Splendid. I can be served after she dines.'

'Very good, sir,' Carter said again. The door closed.

Hugh listened for the next chiming of the clock.

Six chimes. Plenty of time for him to prepare.

He groped his way to the corner of the room where he'd discovered his trunk. Opening it, he dug through until he felt smooth, thick fabric, a lapel and buttons.

As he'd hoped. One of his coats, and beneath it, a waist-coat.

He felt around more until his fingers touched the starched linen of a neckcloth. He could tie it blindfolded, could he not? How many neckcloths had he tied himself over the years?

He wrapped the cloth around his neck and created a simple mail-coach knot. Or hoped he had. Next he donned his waistcoat and coat and carried his boots over to the rocking chair. Seated on the chair, he pulled on his boots.

For the first time since the fire, Hugh was fully dressed. Already he felt more like a man.

He made his way confidently to the door.

But missed, touching the wall instead. He ran his hand along the wall until it touched the door. Excitement rushed through him. Would a man released from prison feel this way? Free, but wary, because he did not know what was on the other side.

He took a step out into the hallway and paused again, trying to listen for sounds, searching for the staircase.

This time he could hear sounds coming from below. He must be near the stairs. He stepped forwards carefully and reached the wall. Good. The wall could be his guide. He inched his way along it until he found the banister. His excitement soared.

Hugh laughed. You'd think he'd discovered a breach in the enemy's defences.

He carefully descended the stairs, holding on to the banister. Amazing how uncertain he felt. He'd crept around buildings and other terrains in the dark before without this much apprehension.

Although he could at least see shadows then. Now he could see nothing.

He reached the last step and still kept one hand on the banister. Chances were that the front door to the house was ahead of him, facing the stairway, which meant that the rooms would be to the right, left or behind. Which would be the dining room?

It would have helped if he'd once seen this house, even from the outside.

He took a breath and began walking straight ahead until he, indeed, found the front door. Then, following his strategy for the bedroom, he started to feel himself along the wall.

'What are you doing, sir?' A woman's voice. A village accent. The housekeeper of whom Mrs Asher spoke?

'Are you Mrs Pitts?' he asked.

'Goodness, no, sir,' the voice replied. 'I am Mary, one of the housemaids, sir.'

Mrs Asher had not mentioned housemaids.

'But what are you doing here, sir?' she went on. 'You should be upstairs, should you not? You are recuperating, is that not the way it is?'

'I came downstairs for dinner.' He spoke with a confidence a maid would not question. 'I realise I am early, but if you direct me to the dining room, I would be grateful.'

'It is early for dinner, sir,' she said. 'Would you like to wait in the drawing room? Mrs Asher said we are to announce dinner to her in the drawing room.'

'The drawing room it is, then.' Hugh smiled. 'Can you show me where it is?'

'Oh!' The maid sounded as if she'd just figured out a big puzzle. 'You cannot see and you haven't been there yet! I remember Mrs Asher saying you were taken directly upstairs.'

He heard her approach him.

She touched his arm. 'Come with me.' She led him to the right and through the threshold of the drawing room. 'I think Mrs Asher will be here soon. She and Monette are talking about our new dresses, you see, so I expect she will come here after that.'

'I expect so,' he replied.

'Begging your pardon, sir, I should be about my duties.' She said this with a surprising sense of pride.

'Thank you for your help, Mary.' He did not wish her to leave quite yet. 'I have just one question.'

'Yes, sir?' She sounded very young. And inexperienced. Otherwise she would not talk so much.

'How long have you worked for Mrs Asher?' Because the lady had not informed him of the presence of a housemaid.

'Oh, this is my first day, sir. For me and my sister, Ann. So I must not dawdle.' She paused. 'May I go, sir?'

'By all means.' Were the extra maids hired because of him? 'Thank you again, Mary.'

She gave a nervous little laugh and he heard the door close.

Once again he was in a strange room with no sense of his bearings.

But he was getting used to it. He turned around and listened carefully for the hiss of the fire and the heat of it on his skin. He memorised the location of the fireplace and the location of the doorway. Somewhere in between there would be chairs and other seating. He trod carefully until he found one. When he was still, he also heard the ticking of a clock. Good. He'd keep track of time that way.

The half-hour, then three-quarters chimes sounded.

Shortly after, the door opened and Hugh smelled roses.

'My goodness.' It was Mrs Asher. 'Mr Westleigh, you gave me a start!'

He stood. 'My apologies.'

'What are you doing here?' She did not sound very pleased.

'Carter said dinner was at eight. Since I am not confined to bed, I saw no reason to trouble your servants to wait on me.'

She came closer. 'But Carter did not tell me—'

'I did not consult with him.'

She sounded confused. 'Then how did you get here? From upstairs, I mean.'

He straightened. 'The way of all men, I suppose. I walked.'

'By yourself?'

'Well, I made it to the hall by myself,' he said. 'Mary helped me to the drawing room.'

'Mary?' She sounded confused again. 'Oh. *Mary.* The new maid. That was kind of her.' She paused before saying, 'Do sit, Mr Westleigh.'

He lowered himself back into the chair.

She was a puzzle to him. She'd taken the trouble to bring him into her home to care for him, yet at the same time she seemed displeased at his presence. She was a woman who concealed things, that was certain.

He heard her move about the room.

'Would you like a glass of claret before dinner?' Good manners crept back into her voice.

'I would dearly like a glass of claret.' He missed wine. He missed brandy even more. He wondered if she would have brandy for after dinner.

He heard her open a cabinet and then heard the sound of pouring liquid. She handed the glass to him.

The scent of the claret was pleasure enough. Fruity and spicy, he savoured the aroma before taking a sip. Drinking from a wine glass proved to be quite easy. And the smooth, earthy flavour was a comfort to his sore throat. He felt like gulping.

He heard her sit. 'I understand you just hired Mary and another maid. If that was because of me, you must permit me to bear the expense.' Might as well speak plainly. She might like to conceal, but he favoured being above board.

'The expense is nothing.' She indeed made it sound as if it was a trifle. 'And I did not hire them because of you, not precisely. They needed the work and I thought it would make it easier on everyone to have more help.'

'I should still like to compensate you for the trouble I am causing you.'

'Please say no more about *money.*' She spoke the word as if it left a bad taste on her tongue. 'I detest talk of money. I have well enough money to be a good hostess, you know.

You are here to recuperate and that is what you shall do. The cost of it means nothing to me.'

Why was she so tense?

He tried some humour. 'Are you a wealthy widow, then?'

She was silent for a moment before answering in a serious tone, 'Yes. I am a wealthy widow.'

They drank their claret in such silence Hugh could hear the ticking of the clock and each small rustle of her skirts, but it did not take long for Carter to come to the door to announce dinner.

'Dinner is served, m'l— Oh!' He cut himself off. 'Mr Westleigh! You are here.'

'Mr Westleigh will eat dinner in the dining room with me, Carter.' Mrs Asher made it sound as if nothing was amiss. She must be practised in hiding emotions from servants.

'Very good, ma'am,' Carter said. 'I shall run ahead and set his place.'

Hugh heard Mrs Asher stand, and rose himself, offering her his arm—or hoping he was not merely posturing to the air.

Her fingers curled around his upper arm. 'I'll show you to the dining room.'

He smiled. 'That is a good thing, else I might wander the house bumping into walls.'

'You were very clever making it to the drawing room.' She did not sound annoyed.

Perhaps this was a truce of sorts.

She led him out the door. 'We are crossing the hall. The dining room is on the other side, a mirror to this room. The cottage really has a very simple plan.'

So, coming down the steps, the drawing room was to

the left; the dining room to the right. 'What other rooms are on this floor?'

'A library behind the drawing room,' she began.

He cut her off with a laugh. 'I don't suppose I'll make much use of that.'

Her step faltered. 'Behind the dining room is an anteroom with cupboards for dishes and cutlery and such. From that room there are stairs down to the kitchen and housekeeper's rooms.'

He was able to visualise it. It did not seem like a large home for a wealthy widow, though.

They crossed the threshold to the dining room and she walked with him to what must have been the head of the table.

He heard the chair being pulled out. She released his arm and sat.

Carter came to his side. 'Your chair is here, sir.' He helped him to a seat adjacent to hers.

'Our meal will be rather simple, I'm afraid,' Mrs Asher said. 'Some lamb stew and bread.'

It must have been near because Hugh could smell it. 'It will be perfectly adequate for me. My appetite appears to have returned full force. I am very likely to eat whatever you put before me and demand seconds.'

He heard Carter pour some liquid. A glass of wine, Hugh could tell by its fragrance.

'That is a healthy sign, I suppose,' she said. 'Perhaps tomorrow we shall have fancier fare. We shall have a cook tomorrow. And another footman.'

He frowned. 'You are hiring many new servants.'

'Y-yes.' Her voice cracked. 'Well.' She recovered. 'I just came from a lengthy stay abroad, you see.'

'You are rebuilding your staff?'

'Yes,' she agreed. 'That is it.'

He tilted his head. Why did she always sound as if she had something to hide?

He had no desire to challenge her at the moment, though. Not when she briefly seemed at ease with him.

'I was abroad, as well,' he said instead. 'In Brussels. Were you there?'

'No.' She paused as if there were more for her to conceal. 'In Switzerland.'

'Ah, Switzerland. A place I should like to visit.'

Carter placed a dish in front of him and the aroma of the stew filled his nostrils. 'Here is the stew, sir. I will place the bread on the left for you.'

'Thank you, Carter.' He lifted his head in what he hoped was Mrs Asher's direction. 'It smells quite delicious.'

He could hear her being served, as well. She thanked Carter and his footsteps receded.

'Do eat, Mr Westleigh,' she said.

He felt for the fork first. Spearing meat with the fork seemed the easiest means of getting the food into his mouth. It took him several tries, but he finally succeeded. The lamb was flavourful and tender. Next he managed to spear some potato. Eating so little in the past two days had wreaked havoc on his appetite. It indeed felt like he could not get enough.

'Is it to your liking?' she asked.

He laughed. 'You cannot tell? I am certain I am shovelling it in like an ill-mannered peasant.'

'You are allowed some lack of graces due to your injuries.' His blindness, she meant.

He forced himself to slow down, searching for the bread and tearing off a piece. 'What brought you to Switzerland?' he asked.

'A…' She paused. 'A retreat, you might say.'

He'd heard of spa towns on the Continent, places where a wealthy widow might go for a lengthy recuperation.

Or perhaps to have a child out of wedlock. Was that her secret? She seemed sad enough for such a happenstance. It would explain that air of concealment he sensed in her.

A wave of tenderness towards her washed over him. Women always had a more difficult lot in life. Men seduced women and women paid the price. A child out of wedlock—it made perfect sense.

Daphne toyed with her food, her appetite fleeing under his questions and the impact of his appearance, attired in coat and waistcoat. His coat fit beautifully, accenting his broad shoulders and tapering to his lean waist. He made it difficult to ignore that he was more than an invalid, more than a member of the family who despised her. He was a man, and his presence seemed to fill the room.

He'd paused and she feared he could sense she was staring at him. She averted her gaze, now wishing he would ask her about her retreat in Switzerland, even if she did not know how to tell him her retreat was in a Catholic convent.

He tore off another piece of bread. 'My stay in Brussels was anything but a retreat.'

She breathed a sigh of relief. He was like most men. Wishing to talk about himself.

'Is that so?' she responded politely.

'My time was spent disentangling my father's affairs,' he went on. 'He was living there, you see. And he died there several months ago.'

'I am so sorry.' She felt genuinely sympathetic. She'd not known of the earl's death.

She'd heard the Earl of Westleigh had been living on the Continent. Some scandal associated with the Masquerade Club, she recalled, but she could not remember the details.

In her nights spent in attendance at the club, she'd not paid much attention to anything but her own interests.

'Do not be sorry,' he countered. 'He was the very worst of fathers. The worst of men. Perhaps you've heard of him? The infamous Earl of Westleigh?' He exaggerated his father's name.

'I have heard of him.' He'd been an acquaintance of her late husband's and only a few years older. 'But only his name, really.' It was true. Her husband had not gossiped with her about the people he knew.

'My brother Ned, the new earl, sent me to deal with whatever trouble our father caused. I am glad this was my last trip.'

She did not know what to say to this, so she offered more food. 'Would you like more stew?'

'I would indeed.' He smiled.

He had a nice smile, she thought.

He was also the first person she'd ever met who admitted to not grieving the loss of a family member. Perhaps she wasn't so strange after all, that the deaths of her parents had left her feeling so little emotion. She'd hardly known them. She had regretted that.

'Did you not like Brussels, then?' she asked, just to make conversation.

'It is a beautiful city.' He averted his head. 'But too full of memories for me. When I walk through its streets, all I can think of is Waterloo.'

'You were in the great battle?' All she knew of the battle was what she read in the newspapers that reached Faville.

'Yes.' His voice turned wooden.

She took a big gulp of wine. 'War and battle are not good topics for dinner conversation, are they?'

'Not at all.' He smiled again. 'Tell me about Switzerland. I've seen the Alps from France, but not the other side. Are they as majestically beautiful?'

The Abbey was in a valley. The craggy stone mountaintops of the Alps were not greatly visible there.

'Oh, yes,' she agreed brightly. 'Quite beautiful. It was a lovely place.'

'I should like to travel there.' He laughed. 'I should like to travel anywhere and everywhere. That is what I will do after I report back to the family in London. Travel.'

But he might be blind. What would happen to his dreams of travel then?

'There are many places to see,' she responded conversationally.

They continued though dinner, talking of various places on the Continent where they had travelled. Daphne had seen only the countries through which she travelled to Switzerland and a little of Italy when her husband had taken her there.

The meal was companionable, more pleasant than any meal Daphne could remember in a long time. She enjoyed it far more than she ought, especially considering her resolve to stay away from him.

After dinner, they retired to the drawing room.

'I do not have brandy to offer, I am afraid.' She'd send Carter into the village to procure some the next day, however. 'Would you care for tea?'

'Tea will do.'

He'd been so churlish that morning, but now was agreeable and diverting. She could almost forget that she was Lady Faville and he was a man who would certainly despise her, if he knew.

As they finished their tea, she could see his energy was flagging.

'I believe I shall retire for the night,' she said, saving him the need to admit he was tired.

He smiled. 'Will you escort me upstairs? I am uncertain I will be able to find my room again.'

'It will be my pleasure,' she said.

As they climbed the stairs, he asked, 'What time is breakfast served?'

Goodness. She did not care. 'Whenever you wish.'

'Name a time.'

She ought to check with Mrs Pitts before making a decision. The woman had toiled very hard this day. The new maids had caused her more work and the prospect of hiring more workers had created more anxiety in the poor woman.

What thoughts were these? When had she ever considered the feelings of servants?

'I will send Carter in the morning to help you dress. We will have breakfast ready soon after.'

She left him at his doorway. 'Goodnight, Mr Westleigh. Carter will be up to tend to your needs soon.'

His hand slid down her arm to clasp hers. 'Thank you for a very enjoyable evening.'

Her heart fluttered with pleasure. Appreciation from a gentleman had always gratified her, but did not usually excite such emotion. Not from her husband, certainly. From only one man, the man who'd married Westleigh's sister.

It must merely be the novelty, she thought. She'd been secluded from men for a long time when at the convent. Certainly Hugh Westleigh was the last man on earth who should excite her sensibilities.

She crossed the hallway to the bedchamber opposite Westleigh's. It was smaller than the one she'd given Westleigh, but there was another, even smaller room next to it that was perfect for Monette.

Besides, she'd become used to sleeping in a room in the Abbey even smaller than a maid's room. A cot. A side table. A chest for her clothing. It had been all she needed.

Inside the room, Monette was laying out her nightdress.

She looked up at Daphne, her brows raised. 'Was that Mr Westleigh I heard with you? Carter said he came down on his own for dinner.'

'Yes. I walked with him upstairs.'

'Is he to be up and about, then?' Monette asked.

'Yes. He has no wish to spend time in his room.' Unfortunately.

'That makes you unhappy,' Monette guessed.

Monette was not in Daphne's confidence. In fact, Daphne had told the younger woman very little about her life. She was the widow of a viscount, that was it. Daphne had not told anyone, even the abbess, any more than that. While in the convent, she wore her unhappiness as plainly as the sisters wore their habits, but she'd never explained.

She needed to give some answer, though. 'It makes matters more complicated. No matter what he thinks, he cannot get about on his own.'

Monette folded down the coverlet and bed linens. 'It is good, then, that you have hired more help. There are more of us to tend to him.'

Yes, but Westleigh was her guest, and a hostess did not leave a guest to be entertained by the servants.

'That is so,' she said, there being no reason why Monette should know precisely how difficult it would be for her to spend time with Westleigh.

Spending time with him was like a constant reminder of her lie and of what she was most ashamed.

And now she was also too much aware of him as a man.

Chapter Five

As promised, Carter appeared the next morning in time to ready Hugh for breakfast, and, rather than eating alone, Hugh had company. Mrs Asher breakfasted with him, making polite conversation as if seated with a man who could see. The food was easy for him to eat. He suspected she'd made certain of that.

Her chair scraped against the floor. 'If you will excuse me, Mr Westleigh, I must meet with the housekeeper.'

He stood.

'A new cook and kitchen maid are arriving today,' she explained. 'A new footman, as well. Mr and Mrs Pitts need to involve me in the arrangements, for some reason. Carter will attend to you. He is here to assist you when you are finished eating. Do take your time, though.'

The dining room held no further appeal after she left and Hugh did not remain long. Carter walked with him to the drawing room, although what he would do there, he did not know.

He sat in the same chair as the day before. 'How long have you been with Mrs Asher?' he asked Carter.

'Not long,' the servant replied somewhat hesitantly. 'She hired me right before her travel home.'

'You were in Switzerland?' An odd place to find a footman for hire.

'I was, sir,' Carter responded, but did not explain.

Not that Hugh required an explanation from the poor man. It was merely that Hugh had nothing to do but talk.

'I must beg your leave, sir, to complete my other duties,' Carter said. 'I will return to see if you are in need of anything. Say, in an hour or so?'

'Go, Carter. I shall do very well on my own.' What other choice did he have?

He heard Carter walk towards the door.

'Carter?'

'Yes, sir?' the man answered.

'Could you find me a cane?'

'A cane, sir? Forgive me, sir, I had not noticed you walking with any difficulty.' His voice was distressed.

'No difficulty,' Hugh assured him. 'I merely thought that if I had a cane, I could keep myself from bumping into things. I could walk around without assistance.'

'I see, sir.' The man cleared his throat. 'I will look for a cane for you.'

Carter closed the door and Hugh drummed his fingers on his knee. What the devil was he going to do to pass the time?

He rose and explored the room, treading carefully and trying not to tumble over furniture or break priceless ornaments.

It was a modest drawing room. He found at least three separate seating groups and some cabinetry along the walls. One of the cabinets held the claret. He was tempted to pour himself a glass, but feared he would spill the liquid and stain the carpet. He could drink from the carafe, but that seemed too ill mannered. Besides, he'd just consumed breakfast. It was a little early for imbibing.

He continued through the room and along the wall until finding a window. He knew from opening his window before breakfast that the day was a chilly one for April and to open this one would defeat the fire's battle to warm the room, but he could not resist. The fresh air smelled like freedom.

He took in big gulps of air, as hungry for it as he'd been for his first meal here. But he closed the window again. Nothing was more of a nuisance than a guest who took over and changed a household's entire routine. He was just so extremely tired of being closed inside walls.

But that was his lot for the moment. He ought, at least, to bear it without this constant pitying of himself.

He continued his way around the room.

He found a pianoforte in one corner of the room and ran his fingers down the keys. He pressed one. It sounded a note.

And reminded him of his sister.

How was Phillipa faring? he wondered. Was she still spending long hours at the pianoforte, composing those songs of hers? Was her husband still selling her music? Hugh had heard one of the songs played by the orchestra at Vauxhall Gardens, quite an unusual accomplishment for a well-bred young lady.

Phillipa followed her own desires, no matter the pressure from their mother and the neglect of her father and brothers. Look at the result. She'd married Xavier—a man decent enough to put the whole Westleigh family to shame and well able to provide for her. And she'd just become a mother.

Hugh hoped Phillipa still played music, even though she was now a mother. He'd never given her music much thought—if truth be told, he never gave Phillipa enough thought. With her scarred face, she'd always hidden herself away. And she was seven years younger. He'd been at school, then in the army while she grew up.

He admired her now.

Phillipa's scar, her music, the abominable way everyone had treated her, all freed her from any responsibility to the family. Ned, now the earl, was charged with preserving the family property and good name for coming generations. Hugh had been given the task of family workhorse.

Difficulties emerged at the country estate? Send Hugh to fix them. Papa engaging in bad behaviour again? Dispatch Hugh to set him straight.

All that was at an end. Ned must attend to his property now and their father would no longer trouble anyone. Hugh was free.

Or would be, if his sight returned.

He made a fist and struck the keys of the pianoforte again. The sound was as discordant as his emotions. His freedom was dependent upon his eyes. What if they did not heal?

He straightened. Enough self-pity.

He drummed his fingers on the keyboard and made more pleasant music.

For want of anything else to do, he sat at the pianoforte's bench and felt the keys, hearing his sister's endless scales that echoed through their house for so many years. He found middle C and played the simple C scale, which pretty much exhausted his knowledge of playing.

He played the scale again. And again. And again until his fingers moved smoothly from note to note and the novelty wore off. He tried picking out a tune, an exercise in trial and error, but he kept at it.

He picked out the tune for the military bugle call that signalled the end of the day—or the end of battle.

It brought back memories.

'Do you play, Mr Westleigh?' Mrs Asher's voice came from the doorway.

'Not at all.' He turned. 'You may have heard all the skill I possess.' The extent of his pleasure at having company at last shocked him. 'Are your cooks and maids and footmen all hired?'

'They are.'

She said no more. Moved no more. Her wariness towards him persisted and it puzzled him still.

He turned back to the keyboard. 'Tinkering with the pianoforte is at least something I can do without sight. There seems little else.'

He heard her approach from the rustle of her skirts, knew she'd come close by the scent of roses and the warmth of her body. She excited his senses, but he was unsure whether it was due to the loneliness his lack of sight produced or the fact that she was mysterious and female.

Good God. He must watch himself.

Daphne had resolved to stay away from Westleigh as much as possible, but Carter was busy with the new footman and could not attend him. She should simply ask Westleigh if he needed anything and be on her way, but he'd sounded so…so lonely, it was difficult not to play the hostess.

At least that was what she told herself.

He placed his fingers on the keys. 'See? I can play a scale.'

But he started on the wrong note.

She covered his hand with hers. His hand was large, but with long, strong fingers. She placed one on middle C. 'Try it now.'

He obliged her, then turned and smiled.

She flushed.

It was good he could not see that his smile set her heart to racing. Really, it was nonsensical for her to react so to a man. She'd vowed she would never do so again. Or perhaps she thought she *could* never do so again.

'Do you play?' he asked. 'I am guessing that you do, because you knew how to find C and you have a pianoforte in your drawing room.'

She thought of all the hours of her childhood spent practising scales. 'I learned, of course, but my playing is unexceptional at best.'

Unlike his sister, who had been so skilled Daphne thought she'd played at Covent Garden. Even though her own husband's praise of her skills had been effusive, Daphne had always known he greatly exaggerated.

'What was the tune you played?' she asked, shaking from her mind the guilt she felt about Faville's devotion.

'"The Last Post",' he responded. 'A bugle call signalling the end of the day.'

'Oh, yes.' She did not know much about bugle calls and military matters. 'I have heard it before, of course.'

He picked out the melody again. 'I believe I hit the right keys this time.' He slid over on the bench. 'Your turn. Come sit and play me something.'

She'd not played since her husband had died, she realised, and she did not wish to play now, but it seemed rude of her to refuse.

'Very well.' She sat next to him, realising for the first time how much larger he was than she.

She played the first piece she could think of, 'The Battle of Prague.'

He laughed.

She lifted her hands, her face burning. 'Was it that dreadful?'

He reached for and found her hand. 'No, that is not it at

all. It brought back a memory. My sister played that piece so often, I used to pull out my hair.' He grabbed a fistful of hair and demonstrated.

She pulled her hands away and placed them in her lap. 'Your sister?'

'Lady Phillipa,' he said. 'She loved the pianoforte above all things—until she met her husband, I mean.'

'Oh.' The stab of pain was not nearly what it once might have been. That was not due to Xavier, but her own behaviour; her year at the abbey had done some good.

You will recover, the abbess had assured her. Perhaps she'd made a little progress.

'Please continue playing,' he said.

She wished to flee the room, but her good manners won over. This time she played 'Barbara Allen.'

To her surprise, he began to sing.

'In Scarlet town where I was born,
There was a fair maid dwellin'.
Made every youth cry well-a-day,
Her name was Barb'ra Allen…'

His voice was a pleasing baritone, but anything but smooth. After three stanzas his voice cracked and he stopped. 'Now, I would say *that* was dreadful.'

She had been enjoying it, she realised. 'Is your throat still sore?'

He coughed. 'We shall allow that to be my excuse.'

She'd forgotten her main task. 'Forgive me. I came here to ask if there was anything you needed. Would you perhaps like something to drink?'

'Some water would do nicely.' He coughed again.

'I will see to it.' She rose from the bench and hurried out of the room.

* * *

Damn his throat.

Or his attempt to sing. He'd chased her away, he feared. It seemed as if something always chased her away just as soon as some ease developed between them.

It had felt companionable to sit with her as she played, to converse with her a little. It passed the time. It dissipated his isolation.

The tick, tick, tick of the clock seemed to boom in the room. He found a note on the pianoforte and mimicked the sound. How many notes would lead him to the end of this day? The end of this week? The end of two weeks?

No. Shake that thought away. The way to get through this situation was one minute at a time. Sixty notes. Over and over.

He played randomly, keeping time with the clock until, bored, he switched to picking out the melody of 'Barbara Allen'. Or trying to hunt for the right notes.

Eventually she returned. 'Here we are,' she said with what seemed like forced cheerfulness. 'I thought lemonade might be pleasant for you.'

He lifted a finger. 'Listen to this.'

He picked out the notes.

'Barbara Allen?' she asked uncertainly.

'Correct!' He was pleased she could recognise it. 'And thank you. Lemonade will do very nicely.'

He lifted his hand, again aware that he did not know precisely where she or the glass of lemonade was. She placed it in his hand and he drank it thirstily.

She said, 'I ought to have made certain you had something to drink before leaving you at breakfast. I believe your experiences also gave you a great thirst.'

Indeed. His throat seemed perpetually dry and raw.

'Do not chastise yourself. I am capable of asking for what I need.' However, he hated asking.

He'd even hated asking Carter to find him a cane. At least the cane would make him more self-sufficient, though.

'Of course.' Her placating governess voice was back. 'You must tell me, then, what else you might need, before I take my leave.'

Take her leave? He'd been counting on her helping him pass the time. He might despise being needy, but that did not mean he couldn't be selfish. 'I would like your company for a longer period.'

'My company? What for?' There was the faintest tremble of trepidation in her voice.

'I want to go outside.' He waited, but she said nothing. 'I want to stretch my legs and feel the sun on my face.' She still said nothing. 'If you cannot escort me, perhaps you can send a servant to do it.'

'I will accompany you.' She made it sound like an onerous task. 'Please wait here. I will get my hat and shawl.'

He ought to tell her to return to her tasks. That he would amuse himself in some other way, but time passed more quickly in her company. Besides, he needed a challenge, and solving her mystery was the only challenge available to him. Unless he considered blindness a challenge, and that he refused to do. His blindness was nothing more than a temporary annoyance. Temporary.

In less than a fortnight he would see. He must see.

Daphne hurried up to the maids' quarters, where Monette was measuring Mary and Ann for their new dresses. Daphne had promised to help. Her sewing skills were more decorative than useful, confined to embroidery and needlepoint and other showy arts, but she could stitch a seam if necessary.

'There you are, ma'am,' Monette said cheerfully. 'I am almost ready to cut the fabric.'

Monette had made her own dresses without patterns, copying them from the clothes Daphne had brought with her to the convent. While staying at the convent, Daphne had worn a simple tunic similar to the nuns' habits. Pretty clothes had been part of her vanity.

The maids were brimming with excitement. She'd not thought about maids enjoying pretty clothes just as she had done, not until she'd seen Monette's delight in wearing modern fashions.

The abbess had said to her more than once, *God made us all the same.*

In some ways people were the same, Daphne could agree, but she was always treated differently, even at the convent.

Because of her beauty.

'I cannot help you as I thought,' Daphne said, examining the blue floral print Monette had purchased for the gowns. 'I must entertain Mr Westleigh. He has a desire to take a walk outside.'

'Do not fear, ma'am,' Mary said. 'We can sew and still tend to our chores.' She turned to her sister. 'Can we not, Ann?'

'We can. Oh, yes,' the other girl said agreeably.

'I will help later,' Daphne said.

'Ma'am?' Mary spoke. 'You ought not to be sewing our dresses in any event, if I may be so bold to say. We will finish them.' She turned to Monette. 'Ann and I can finish them, can we not? You will show us what you want?'

Sewing a new dress and tending to maid's chores all in the same day seemed a daunting task to Daphne. She

wondered how much work she'd created for the maids at
Faville House without giving them a single consideration.

'Well, make the dresses your priority today,' she told
them. 'You can tend to the cleaning and other chores tomorrow.'

The three women curtsied. 'Thank you, ma'am,' they
said in unison.

Daphne hurried off to her bedchamber for her bonnet
and shawl, which should do for the cool day. She stopped
in Westleigh's room to get his hat.

Carter was there with the footman, who was to trail
him all day to learn his duties.

'Carter, I am taking Mr Westleigh for a turn in the garden,' she told him. 'Does he have a hat and gloves?'

Carter's eyes widened. 'No, m'l—ma'am. I did not think
of a hat and gloves. He must have lost them.' He turned
to the footman. 'Find Mr Pitts and see if he has a cap the
gentleman might wear.'

'No.' Daphne stopped him. 'Let me see first if he minds
going out without them. Carter, perhaps you or—or—' She
could not think of the new footman's name.

'Toller, ma'am,' he said.

'Toller.' She was ashamed of herself for forgetting. 'Perhaps one of you could go into the village and buy the items
for him.'

'We'll see to it.' Carter crossed the room. 'I do have
something the gentleman asked for.' He lifted a wooden
cane.

'A cane?' She was surprised.

'He said it would help him walk.'

She took it from his hand. 'Thank you. I will take it
to him.'

She left the room and started down the steps, but slowed
her pace.

What happened to her resolve to spend as little time as possible with him? She could have insisted Carter take him for a walk, but then she would have disrupted his instructions to the new footman. And the maids were right. She should not be sewing their clothes for them.

She could not delegate the care of Westleigh to the servants. It was her job as hostess. She could do so without revealing who she was. He still did not need to ever find out who Mrs Asher really was.

Be truthful, especially to yourself, she could hear the abbess say.

Very well. To be truthful, she liked the man's company. No, more than liked his company. All her senses sparked into life when she was near him, in a way she'd never experienced before.

Such a reaction was simply more she must conceal from him. If it was better he never know the truth about who she really was, it was better still that he never know the thrill she felt in his presence.

Chapter Six

'I fear you have no hat or gloves.' Mrs Asher startled Hugh with her entrance. 'Shall I see if you can borrow some?'

'I do not need them.' He'd walk out in nothing but his drawers, if that was the only way.

'We did not even think of them.' She made it sound as if this was important. 'They must have been lost in the fire.'

With his overcoat, some of his money and a change of clothing.

And possibly his sight.

He certainly did not want to dwell on that topic. 'Let us not think of hats and gloves now. I am too eager to stretch my legs and breathe in fresh air.'

'I do have something for you,' she said. 'A cane from Mr Carter.'

She placed it in his hand.

'Good man!' He gripped the handle and tested it. 'I must thank him. This should help me walk around on my own.' He'd seen blind people using canes to feel their way, waving them in front of their feet to warn of obstacles. He tested it in the room.

'Not seeing must be so difficult….' Her voice trailed off.

'None of that.' He extended his hand. 'Come. Show me the way.'

She led him out the front door, holding his arm as if they were walking through Hyde Park. 'There is a step down.'

It felt like flagstone beneath his feet, and he was surprised how insecure it felt to walk into a space without knowing what was ahead. He swept the cane in front of him and it swung free. She held on to him as well, but that gratified him in other ways. The air was crisp and cool and it nourished him. This was not a day to be hesitant or gloomy. This was a day to enjoy the scent of flowers, of a stable nearby, of stone and grass. All cheered him.

They descended the step. 'Tell me what I would see in front of me.'

'There is a walkway,' she responded reassuringly. 'Nothing to trip on.'

'Not what is in front of my feet.' He swept his hand across the vista hidden to him. 'What I would see. I smell the stable. It must be in sight.'

'Oh.' She paused. Had he made her feel foolish? 'There is a stable. Off to the left maybe a hundred yards away. The walkway leads to a road and the stable is several feet away on the road. The road leads past some trees and a field and you can see it reaching a bigger road that leads to the village. You can see the village. It is a mile or two away. There is a church tower rising above the other buildings.'

It could have been a description of anywhere, but it helped him feel grounded.

'What does the stable look like?' he asked.

'It is white stucco, like the cottage.' She turned as if double-checking the cottage's appearance. 'Would you like to walk down the path to the road?'

'That will do.' He did not really care as long as he was stretching his legs.

But they could not move at any great pace. He depended on her support more than he thought he would. His feet faltered a couple of times. She and the cane helped him keep his balance. The only words spoken were her warnings. 'Take heed, there is a puddle. There is a rock.' It made him feel like a cursed invalid.

He forced himself to walk with more confidence, even though he did not know what was in his path.

Perhaps she sensed his frustration. She suddenly made an attempt at conversation. 'Tell me about your family, the ones you refused to allow me to contact.'

His family? He'd already told her about his profligate father. She probably wondered what other horrors his family possessed. 'The others are not like my father.'

'Then why not allow them to be contacted?'

He frowned. Why was she asking? 'Because they would all come running to care for me.'

'And you find that objectionable?' she asked.

She must want to rid herself of his care. 'None would be a good caretaker.' He tried to explain. 'My mother would merely consign me to the role of infant and try to do everything for me. She'd drive me insane in the space of an hour.' He need not mention his mother's lover, now constantly at her side. 'My brother Ned, the new earl, carries the bulk of family responsibility. If he came, he would be neglecting something more important. But worse, he married this empty-headed chit who would be utterly infuriating.' He also did not mention Rhys, his bastard brother. He had no right to ask anything of Rhys. 'Then there is my sister—'

'Your sister?' Her voice tensed.

It was puzzling. 'Phillipa would take good care of me, I am certain. I would not ask her, though. She is busy with the baby.'

'A baby?' Her voice grew soft, but none of the tension in it eased.

He'd forgotten. A baby was the likely reason for her long retreat on the Continent.

'She recently gave birth to a girl.' He was sorry he'd brought this up.

'How nice for your sister.' Mrs Asher's voice turned sad.

He put his arm across her back. 'Is this an unhappy topic for you, Mrs Asher?'

He felt her stiffen. 'No. Why should it be?'

He wanted to ask if she had other children. If not, what a heart-wrenching situation. A childless widow having to give up her illegitimate baby.

He asked a different question. 'Where is your family? Your parents? Sisters or brothers? Do you see them?'

'I have no family.' Her tone hardened.

No other children, then.

He held her tighter. 'Forgive me. I did not know you were so alone.'

She shrugged. 'I am used to it. My parents died a long time ago. As did my husband. There is no one else, really.'

'A long time ago? You make yourself sound as old as Methuselah.' In his mind she was young, but was she?

'I am old,' she said with conviction, avoiding his question.

He halted, dropping his arm from his half embrace. 'I do not believe you.'

'I am,' she insisted.

He hooked the cane around his arm and reached up to her face. He explored her face with his fingers. Her skin was smooth, free of wrinkles, free of blemish. She had high cheekbones, large eyes, a pointed chin. He rubbed her lips with his thumb and felt her sharp intake of breath. Her lips were full. Lush. Moist.

A long sigh escaped her lips and her breath warmed his hand.

His body seized with sudden desire. He leaned closer and felt her tremble.

He caught himself and stepped back. 'You are not as old as Methuselah, that much I can tell.'

She took his arm again. 'I am, though,' she insisted, her voice a bit shrill. 'I am two and thirty.'

He frowned. He was a year older. They were neither of them in the bloom of youth, but neither were they what he would call old. On the other hand, he well knew the feeling of being aged. It came from enduring the horrors of life. The losses. She'd certainly endured losses.

'How old were you when your parents died?' he asked.

This was not the sort of conversation a gentleman should have with a lady, but he preferred talking of something substantial over exchanging inanities about the weather or gossip.

Besides, he wanted to learn about her.

She could always refuse to answer, if she liked.

To his surprise, she did answer. 'I was eighteen. Hardly married a year.'

She'd married so young?

'Poor Papa and Mama,' she went on. 'They never had much of a chance to bask in their triumph.'

'Their triumph?'

She did not speak right away. 'My husband was a wealthy man. It was quite a coup for me to marry him.'

'I wonder that I cannot recall ever hearing his name.' Perhaps her husband was not of society. Or perhaps Hugh had been too busy at war to keep track of the members of the *ton*.

'We did not go to town much,' she said. 'He preferred the country.'

'Tell me about him.' He might as well try to satisfy all of his curiosity.

They walked several steps before she answered. 'My husband was very good to me. My happiness was his greatest concern. Anything I wanted, if it was in his power to provide it, he gave to me.'

Except a child.

Rhys's son and Phillipa's daughter seemed to have sent them both over the moon with happiness. Last he heard from Ned, his wife was obsessed with wanting a child. Hugh had never thought about it for himself. It seemed a part of life to anticipate after one settled down. And he had no intention of settling down.

But she did not know that, did she? What could she know of his situation, if he had a wife or children?

'You never asked me if I was married.' He tried to say this without an accusatory tone.

It took several more steps for her to respond. 'I knew you were not married.'

'How did you know?' He asked, too sharply.

Again she hesitated. 'My husband always received the London papers and I continued receiving them. I—I liked reading about society, the parties, the people. The marriage of a son of Lord Westleigh would have been announced.'

A logical explanation. Still, she was holding something back, something she did not want him to know. Good God. Could it be—?

'Did you know my father, Mrs Asher?' He frowned.

If she'd encountered his father—

Daphne's heart raced. He asked too many questions. Was suspicious of her, as well he should be. She was deceiving him after all.

'No, I did not know your father,' she answered him.

That was the truth. She might have met the man once or twice, in those early days when Faville had taken her to town for the Season, but she didn't remember precisely.

He blew out a breath. 'Good. For a moment I feared he might have misused you. He was entirely capable of such behaviour.'

'But I read of him in the newspapers, of course.' The papers never used full names when spreading scandal and gossip, but everyone knew of whom they wrote.

They passed the stable and two other small buildings whose purpose she did not know. The road was lined with shrubbery, bright green with new leaves. Buttercups and heartsease dotted the lawn beyond. Should she describe them to him? Or would it make it worse to know that spring bloomed all around and he could not see it?

He spoke. 'You never said how long ago your husband died.'

Why must he persist in this interrogation?

She might as well answer. 'A little over three years ago.'

'Three years ago?' His voice rose in surprise. 'I thought you said it was a long time.'

'It seemed like a long time to me.' So much had happened to her since, even if most of it had occurred in her mind and emotions. Her marriage seemed like a dream in comparison.

'How did it happen?' he asked.

'How did what happen?'

He made an exasperated sound. 'Your husband's death.'

'Oh.' Of course. 'He fell from his horse.'

He'd been with her one minute and dead the next. She'd gone through mourning, but had she grieved his loss? She feared not.

What sort of wife did not grieve her husband's death, especially a man who had been good to her?

Faville had always loved her. He'd loved her as a man loved a prized possession or a precious jewel. At the convent she'd realised there had been a man behind all that devotion, a man with his own needs and emotions. He'd given her far more than she'd given him. Instead, she'd filled her head with fantasies of Xavier Campion—husband of this man's sister.

She ought to tell him. Tell him now.

But he would hate her if she did. She could not bear it, knowing a man in her house, under her care, hated her. She hated herself enough.

'Why did you not marry, Mr Westleigh?' she asked brightly. Flirtatiously. Such skills as turning the conversation in the direction she desired were her forte—or had been once.

He answered in a bantering tone. 'I was mostly fighting Napoleon. Not a good time to start a courtship.'

'But the war has been over for years now.'

'I did not sell out until 1818,' he explained. 'Then my brother discovered my father had put our family at the brink of ruin. That certainly did not make me a good marriage prospect.'

She'd had no idea. Gossip about the Westleighs' financial woes had never reached the newspapers. 'The brink of ruin?'

'We were in danger of losing it all. The River Tick was lapping at our toes, you might say. Debt collectors were mere minutes from our door.' He stepped on a rock she'd neglected to warn him about and she had to hold tighter to his arm—his well-muscled arm—so he could catch his balance.

'We should turn around.' They were at the end of the road where it intersected with the road to Thurnfield. When they walked a few steps back towards the house she dropped her flirtatious tone, truly interested now. 'You said you *were* in danger of losing your money. You didn't lose it, then?'

'We were rescued. We scraped together every pound we could get our hands on and convinced our half-brother to run a gaming house for us.' His voice brightened. 'He—Rhysdale—had a brilliant idea. He called the place the Masquerade Club and made it so men and women could gamble there in masks and protect their identity. Ladies are able to attend without risking their reputations.'

Daphne felt the blood drain from her face. How could she have attended the Masquerade Club all those weeks and not have known its connection to the Westleighs?

'Was—is—the gaming house successful?' It must be. When she'd attended, there had always been a crush of people, all throwing away their money to the roll of the dice or a turn of a card.

'Successful beyond our imagining,' he responded. 'The Westleigh fortune is restored and is growing by the day.'

Daphne had never gambled heavily when she'd attended the Masquerade Club. She'd been too obsessed with making Xavier Campion admit he loved her.

But it had not been she whom Xavier loved.

She'd first seen him in a ballroom when she'd been twenty years old. A beautiful young man, the most beautiful young man she had ever seen, the sort of man who'd inspired the Greeks to make statues. His dark hair and skin had been the perfect counterpoint to her pale, blonde beauty. And even his magnetic blue eyes were the equal of hers. She'd thought that meant they were destined to be together, that they were the perfect lovers, an exquisite pair beautifully matched.

But her husband separated them before they became

lovers and Daphne spent years dreaming of a reunion with Xavier. Ten foolish years.

Her head pounded with the memory. Enough of this foolishness. He was nothing but a dream, a fancy. And at the moment she walked beside a very real man, about whom she still knew so little.

'And—and is your half-brother still running this gaming house for you?' she asked to keep him talking.

'Yes, he is.'

She'd heard of Rhysdale, of course. Xavier had been his friend and had managed the gaming house in Rhysdale's absence. Had he known he was a half-brother to the Westleighs?

She glanced at the man beside her, who seemed lost in thought.

Finally he spoke. 'Of all the family, Rhys is the best. Well, he and Phillipa, I suppose.'

Phillipa. Yes. Phillipa. A better woman than Daphne, certainly.

Westleigh went on. 'Rhys was my father's natural son, you see. I grew up despising him, but he saved us when we needed him. He had every reason not to.'

'Do you despise him now?' One could despise a person yet concede his worth at the same time. Was he such a man?

'Not at all,' he responded. 'I hold Rhys in the highest regard. He makes me ashamed of myself.'

They had that in common, then.

'Well, it is what you do today that matters the most,' she said. 'You cannot undo the past, but you can learn from it.' Had not the abbess told her this many times?

'Oh, I have learned from it,' he admitted. 'I don't expect Rhys will change his mind about me, though. We have established a sort of truce, at least, which is more than I deserve.' He smiled ruefully. 'I was horrible to him when we were boys. Taunted him until he'd fight with me. I liked nothing better than a good bout of fisticuffs. I was a wild boy, I'm afraid. Still am.'

'Do you still like fisticuffs?' she asked.

'I wouldn't back down from a fight....' He groaned. 'Listen to me ramble on about myself. Soon I will be confessing to you all the mistakes of my youth.'

'I am not certain our walk will be that long.'

He laughed, a deep and resonant laugh that made her insides flutter. 'I might need all of our two weeks, at least.' His smile turned genuine. 'Never fear. I will not burden you, not with all my sins, in any event.'

Her cheeks burned. She was unaccustomed to making people truly laugh.

His cane caught on a thick root and again she held him tightly until he regained his footing. She'd almost forgotten he could not see.

'Now it is your turn,' he said.

'My turn?'

'To confess the sins of your childhood.' He added, 'Unless you were an obedient, compliant little girl.'

She had certainly not been that. 'I was a trial, I confess.' More painful memories. 'I was not quick to learn things.'

'I do not believe it,' he said. 'You do not strike me as an unintelligent woman.'

They walked on past the out buildings, nearing the stable.

'I suppose I was adequate at my lessons, but I often forgot how to sit properly, how to smile—things like that.'

He shook his head. 'Are you making another jest?'

'No.' She'd said nothing foolish.

Her mother had often chastised her, admonishing her to stand up straight, to walk as if gliding, to smile, to pour tea gracefully, to lean towards a gentleman so her figure showed to best advantage. Her face would only carry her so far, her mother insisted. She must be beautiful *and* affect a pleasing manner. So Daphne had practised being pleasing, over and over, until it had become second nature. The training had borne fruit, too. She'd become betrothed to Viscount Faville in her first Season and married him quickly afterwards.

But she did not want to admit to Westleigh that attributes a gentleman might think natural were really only the result of proper training.

She averted her gaze. 'I was not jesting.'

He blew out a breath. 'I dare say a boy's upbringing differs greatly from a girl's.'

'You should know because of your sister.' Surely Phillipa Westleigh had endured the same training. How much more important it would have been for her.

'I was enough older than my sister to pay little attention,' he said. 'But likely her upbringing was unique. Her face was scarred when she was small. She grew up disfigured.'

Daphne recalled the cruel words she'd spoken to Phillipa at the Masquerade Club and cringed in shame. Now she could only think what it would have been like to have so visible a disfigurement.

'How difficult for her,' she managed.

'I suppose it was.' He pounded the ground ahead of him with the cane. 'In a way it freed her.'

'Freed her?' She did not comprehend.

'She could not be expected to follow the usual course of an earl's daughter. The Marriage Mart and all. Instead, she became an accomplished *pianiste*. Do you know her musical compositions have been performed at Vauxhall and other places?'

What an accomplishment. Phillipa had played beautifully. She'd composed music, as well?

'You sound very proud of your sister.' Daphne envied her. Who had ever been proud of her, except for her marrying well? What had she ever accomplished?

'I am. She does what she wishes to do, no matter what. That is what I will do, as well.' His voice dropped. 'As soon as the bandages are off.'

'You will travel, then. Is that not correct, Mr Westleigh?' They'd spoken of it at dinner.

'Yes.' His voice tightened.

It all depended upon whether or not his eyes healed.

Chapter Seven

After they re-entered the house, Hugh put no further claim on Mrs Asher's time. He asked for the services of the new footman to walk with him around the house. Perhaps if he walked the space enough times, he'd be able to navigate on his own and not disrupt the routine of the servants or Mrs Asher—although if he had his way, he'd commandeer all of her time.

Instead, Toller, the new footman, was placed at his disposal. Toller was a cheerful, chatty young man who seemed perfectly content to walk with Hugh from Hugh's bedchamber, down the stairs, to the drawing room and to the dining room—over and over—all the while telling Hugh about his family, the village, the maids and Mr and Mrs Pitts.

'That Monette is a pretty thing,' Toller went on. 'But I do not suppose I will see much of her, her being a lady's maid and all. She's probably above my touch, in any event.'

Monette, Toller had told him, was Mrs Asher's lady's maid who had come with her from Switzerland. The footman knew nothing else about her, though, and Hugh had not encountered her here—although he'd done once. In the fire.

'What of Mr Asher?' Hugh might as well turn the man's garrulity to matters of which he was truly curious. 'What was he like?'

'Mr Asher?' Toller sounded puzzled. 'I don't rightly know.'

Bad luck. 'Did you come to Thurnfield after he died?'

'I have lived in Thurnfield my whole life,' Toller responded with pride. 'There is nothing I do not know about it.'

'Then how do you not know of Mr Asher?'

'Can't know of him as he was never in Thurnfield,' Toller said. 'At least he never lived here. He might have passed through. Many folks pass through on their way to London.'

'Mr Asher never lived here?'

'Not in Thurnfield,' the footman insisted.

Had she lived separately from her husband? 'How long has Mrs Asher lived here, then?'

'About three days,' Toller answered.

Three days?

Toller kept talking. 'She drove into town looking for somebody to take care of you or someplace she could stay to care for you. Well, the inn was full of people from Ramsgate. There was a fire there, I was told. Maybe the one where you injured your eyes?' He didn't wait for Hugh to answer. 'Anyway, no one wished to take on the charge of caring for a sick man without knowing if he could pay, and you couldn't travel any farther, so Mrs Asher leased the cottage here. The previous tenants were a navy man and his wife. They left about a month ago. The place has been empty since.'

They reached the stairway again.

Hugh rested a hand on the banister. 'Do you mean Mrs

Asher was just passing through? She never meant to live here, then?'

'That I could not say for certain,' Toller replied. 'But Mr Brill, the leasing agent, said she asked for two weeks, but he would not lease for so short a time, so she paid for three months.'

She paid for three months? Why?

And why tell him she lived here?

But did she ever say she lived here? Hugh strained to recall.

He turned his head towards where he thought Toller stood. 'Let us go back upstairs to my room, then I will free you from playing nursemaid.'

'Very well, sir,' Toller said agreeably.

Hugh ascended the stairs with more confidence than when they'd started the practice. He was becoming more accustomed to using the cane. With being unable to see.

At his bedchamber door he thanked the footman. 'This was excellent, Toller. I could not have done it without you. I'm in your debt.'

He'd pay the man a generous vail at the end of his stay. He'd be generous to all the servants, since he was the sole reason they'd been hired, apparently.

Why had Mrs Asher not simply told him she'd taken the house to take care of him? That she'd been required to pay ahead for time she'd not use? Where had she been bound, then? Where was her home?

He was reasonably certain there was no malevolence in her subterfuge, although at first he'd been suspicious of her. She clearly had nothing to gain from assuming his care. All she could gain was his money, but she obviously had money of her own.

Was she simply possessed of a kind heart? Or had she believed she owed it to him because he'd carried her out of the fire? Why, then, not simply order her servants to care for him?

She was a mystery.

She possessed an adept conversational skill that she used to conceal more than she revealed. She swung from the superficial to a hint of deep sadness.

She intrigued him in other ways, as well. Her musical voice, the scent of roses when she was near, her soft hand. Touching her face had been arousing, more arousing than he liked to admit.

He wanted to *see* her, know her, discover what she needed to so carefully hide. Was that the source of her unhappiness? He could not simply ask her. He wanted to know about her life, about her husband. Had she loved him? Had her husband been good to her? Had there been other men besides him? And what had she been doing, travelling alone on the Continent? Was he correct in his guess that she'd hid herself away to have a baby?

He probably had no right to know such personal matters, but he did deserve to know why she had taken such charge of him and gone to all this trouble and expense as a result. He'd discover that much this night. Or at least confront her with what he knew.

That evening Daphne found Westleigh waiting in the drawing room before dinner. Like the night before, she poured him wine. He seemed preoccupied, disturbed. About his blindness, she guessed.

He responded to her efforts at chitchat with an economy of response, although he did accept a second glass of wine. Her mood darkened. Gone was the ease they'd achieved during their walk. Why? She missed it most dreadfully.

Finally Carter announced that dinner was served.

Westleigh took his cane in one hand and stood. He offered her his arm. 'May I escort you in to dinner?'

What was this? The previous night she'd had to carefully lead him to the room.

It sounded like an order, not an invitation, so she took his arm.

He walked almost directly to the door. She guided him to correct his course, else they might have hit the wall.

'Thank you,' he said, his words clipped. 'Tomorrow I will do better.'

'You are doing very well.' She used a placating voice.

He continued to confidently cross the hall to the dining room, although his manner was a bit determined. He led her to the doorway almost as if he could see and found her chair with equal ease.

He pulled it out for her. 'I commandeered Toller to help me learn how to traverse the house. We walked it a number of times until I could envisage the floor plan and not run into furniture.'

'How very clever of you.'

He glowered. 'You need not do that.'

She did not know what he meant. 'Do what?'

'Speak in your governess voice,' he snapped.

Her heart pounded. 'My what?'

'That governess voice, as if you were talking to a schoolboy. You use it often.'

Speak with your heart, the abbess had repeatedly told her. *It is your true voice.* Daphne still did not know what that meant.

'I—I— That is the way I speak.' She did not know any other way.

Except her tone had changed with her last words. Even she could tell it.

'Not always.' Carter and Toller entered and Westleigh stopped talking.

Toller served the soup under Carter's watchful eye.

When they left again, Westleigh dipped his spoon into the soup and carefully lifted it to his mouth.

Not all of it spilled.

She remained silent, but continued to stare at him. His effort to eat normally was heartbreaking to watch, but he managed to finish most of the soup.

No sooner did he put down his spoon than Carter and Toller re-entered carrying the next course. Toller reached for her soup bowl.

Carter stopped him. 'Are you finished, ma'am?'

She'd forgotten to taste it.

She waved a hand. 'Yes. I had no appetite for soup.'

He placed roasted quail on the table, already carved and cut into pieces for Westleigh.

'Some quail, sir?' Carter asked.

Westleigh nodded.

Carter also served small roasted potatoes and apricot fritters, explaining each to Westleigh.

The two servants left the room again.

Would it be the height of poor manners to ask Westleigh what was troubling him, or a neglect of manners to pretend one did not notice?

She took a deep breath. 'Mr Westleigh, what is distressing you?'

He lifted his head as if to look at her. 'Distressing me?'

She nodded, but realised he could not see. 'Your mood is much altered from earlier today when we took that pleasant walk.'

He pushed his fork around his plate until he speared a piece of meat and lifted it to his mouth. The muscles of his neck flexed as he chewed. Had her husband's muscles moved with such suppressed strength? She'd never noticed.

'I did not mean to make you more uncomfortable,' he finally said.

More uncomfortable?

'I am perfectly comfortable, I assure you.' She kept her voice modulated so the tension shaking her insides did not show.

His mouth twisted with scepticism.

She tightened her grip on the stem of her wine glass.

The door opened again. Carter and Toller stood ready to assist them.

'Later,' Westleigh said, so softly she barely heard.

When the dishes and their plates were removed, Daphne turned to Carter. 'Would you serve Mr Westleigh's brandy and the fruit and biscuits with my tea in the drawing room?'

'Yes, m—ma'am.' He waved Toller off to take care of it.

She stood and Westleigh rose as well, taking his cane in hand and walking over to her to offer his arm again.

'Is the cane helping you?' she asked in the most reasonable voice she could muster, because she needed to say something.

His answer was devoid of expression. 'It is. It gives me confidence, even if it be false confidence.'

'False confidence is at least confidence of some sort.' Agreeing with a gentleman was almost a reflex with her. In this case, what she said was certainly true of her, as well. False confidence was all she seemed to possess lately.

One corner of his mouth rose. 'How very wise of you, Mrs Asher.' It was a good mimic of her voice.

He led her out of the dining room without banging into a wall.

She lowered her head. 'Do I truly sound that way?'

His voice softened. 'I exaggerated.' He waved a hand. 'Do not heed me. It is my mood.'

His foul mood, he must mean.

As they crossed the hall she marvelled again—silently—at how well he managed. The drawing-room door was trickier, but she gently guided him and perhaps this time he did not perceive her help.

Toller was just setting down the tea tray. A decanter of brandy and two glasses were already on the table.

'Thank you, Toller,' she said.

He bowed and left.

'Sit, Westleigh,' she said. 'I'll pour your brandy.'

He found the chair he'd sat in before and lowered himself into it. She handed him the glass and eyed the other one for herself.

Why not have some brandy? She'd seen women drink it at the Masquerade Club. She poured herself a generous amount and took a gulp. With much effort she avoided a paroxysm of coughing. His head rose, but he could not possibly know, could he? She made a clatter of pouring tea, just in case.

But it was the brandy she drank.

He inhaled deeply and released his breath slowly. 'I have been trying to puzzle out why you should keep me from learning the truth.'

She felt herself go pale. Had he discovered who she was—?

He pressed on. 'Why did you not tell me?'

'I—I do not know what you mean.' At least she did not know precisely what he meant; only what she feared he meant.

'Someone—I will not say who—told me. In all innocence, I might add. This was not a betrayal of your secrets, but someone who did not know the truth was to be withheld from me.'

She took a relieved sip and, this time, savoured the warmth the brandy created in her chest. Only Monette, Carter, and John Coachman knew who she was and if they had told, it would have been a deliberate betrayal of what she'd asked of them.

'Why, Westleigh—' she put on her most charming voice '—I am at a loss. What truth did I withhold?'

He waved an exasperated hand. 'That you leased this cottage for three months because of me. You gave me the impression you lived here.'

'Did I?' The brandy was making this easier. 'If I did so, it was most unintentionally done.'

He took a gulp of his brandy. 'Please, let us speak without pretence. Why have you gone to so much trouble and expense for me? Taking me from Ramsgate. Leasing this cottage for much longer than needed. Hiring servants for me.'

She stared at him, wishing she could see all his face, wishing she could look into his eyes and gauge how much of the truth to tell.

She finished the contents of her glass and gave a little laugh. 'I assure you, I did not plan to take on so much trouble for you. I thought I would find someone in Ramsgate to take care of you and, failing that, I was certain I would find someone on the road. When that also did not happen, events just seemed to pile on each other.' She poured more brandy in her glass. 'Please believe me that the money is a trifle, as I have told you before. And, like you, no one expected me at any particular time.' There was no one to whom her arrival would matter. 'A delay of two weeks was of no consequence.'

'But the hiring of the servants—' he began.

'That was not for your benefit,' she explained. 'I think we could have done well enough with Monette, Carter and me. And Mr and Mrs Pitts. The others—they seemed to need the work.'

'You hired them without needing them?' He sounded surprised.

'Mary and Ann—the maids—they looked…hungry.' She lifted a shoulder, even though he could not see the gesture. 'It—it felt like the right thing to do and very little trouble to me in the doing of it.' More trouble than she'd bargained for, having to organise everything and make certain they had decent dresses and aprons and caps to wear. 'Then Mrs Pitts knew a cook and others to hire. It seemed easiest just to hire them. Our meal was quite good tonight, was it not?'

'Do they know it is for three months?' The surprise had not left his voice.

'Oh…' Telling him about this made her feel foolish. 'I do not know. We talked in terms of yearly wages, so I suppose that is what I will pay them.'

'Mrs Asher—' Now he sounded scolding.

She was certain the abbess would have approved, but she could hardly tell him that. 'It is my money to do with as I wish.'

'Do you have a man of business? Someone to help you manage such matters as bills and servants?'

She sighed. Dear Mr Everard. She'd written to him that she'd returned to England and would stay a time in Thurnfield. 'Yes. I have a very capable man. He was my husband's man of business and he has continued to help me.'

If anyone knew the whole of her folly with Xavier and Phillipa, it was Mr Everard. He'd remained loyal, even so.

Westleigh stood and, using the cane, paced back and forth. 'Mrs Asher, I do not favour anyone paying for my needs. I do not like that you withheld this information from me. It was one thing for me to accept hospitality at your house, but it is another matter for me to allow you to pay a lease and hire servants.'

'My hiring the servants had nothing to do with you,' she protested.

'You would not have been here to hire them if it had not been for me.' He made his way back to his chair, tapping with his cane to find precisely where it was. He sat again and groped for his brandy glass. He drank it empty.

She reached over and poured him some more. 'Here are some biscuits and candied fruit.' She placed a small plate of the treats next to his glass on the table beside him.

He picked up the glass, but did not sample the other. 'I will pay all these expenses. The cottage and the servants.'

Ridiculous! He could not possibly have as much money as she, considering what he'd shared about his family's recent financial woes. She'd wounded his vanity, though, obviously. Perhaps she possessed too much independence, in his opinion. Men did not like women who displayed too much independence, her mother had taught her.

Although the abbess always told her she must think for herself…

She shook her head. 'Very well, Westleigh. You may pay. We'll make an accounting and you may pay.'

He took another drink of the brandy. 'Good.'

She poured herself a little more and sipped it slowly.

After a time he spoke. 'You need not stay, then.'

She looked at him. 'You wish me to bid you goodnight?'

'No, not at all,' he quickly said. 'I meant, you and your servants need not stay with me any longer. You may go on your way. If I am paying—'

'You wish me to leave?' The brandy made her thinking fuzzy and her emotions raw. The idea he wished to send her away unexpectedly wounded her and she fought back tears.

He frowned and paused before going on. 'I have no right to keep you here. It is not as if I could pay you for your assistance.'

Pay her? 'You certainly cannot!'

She'd wanted to do something for somebody, something unselfish. She wanted to do something for *him*. For restitution—and—and because he needed someone so very much. But here it was, the one time she extended herself for another person, *needed* to extend herself, and he was sending her away.

Hugh had made a muddle of this.

She'd been the one acting under false pretences, so why did he feel so rotten? She sounded as if she'd start weeping. How had the situation turned itself around?

He spoke in low tones. 'Why did you do it, then? Why did you assume care of me in the first place? Me, a stranger. You were not the only one I helped to escape the fire. Someone else would have come to my aid.'

'I cannot explain it.' Her voice turned small, sad and defensive. 'I just could not leave you.' She sighed. 'You are correct, though. You can pay Toller, Mary, Ann and the others to take care of you. You do not need me. I will go if you wish it.'

His chest tightened. Wish it? Her leaving was the last thing he wanted. How was he to bear the darkness without her company? His world had shrunk in his sightlessness, but she filled all the space he had left. For her to leave would plunge him into an abyss.

He'd endure what he must, but the two weeks would be deadly without her.

And something was unfinished between them. He did not know what, and if she left him he would never know.

'I do not wish you to go,' he murmured. 'I simply cannot ask you to stay.'

He heard her pouring more brandy into a glass, not his glass. How much was she drinking?

'Why must this be so complicated?' Her voice was strained with unhappiness. 'If we were friends, you would accept my help without question and without all these noble protestations. If we were acquaintances, you would not question my helping you.'

'If we were friends,' he repeated.

'That is what I said.'

He preferred her irritation to her sadness. 'Then let us be friends. Why should we not be? We have a great basis. I helped you escape a fire and you helped me get care for my wounds.'

'We could be friends?' She said this as if she'd never had a friend in the world.

'Certainly.' At least he'd cheered her. 'You can stay and keep me company. As my friend. And you can be my eyes until mine are working again. I confess, I would feel more secure knowing a friend was looking out for me.'

'Yes…' Her voice turned dreamlike. 'I could help you as a friend. Look out for you.' Her tone changed to one more decided. 'Very well, Mr Westleigh. Let us act as friends.'

He relaxed and finished his second glass of brandy. 'How far should we go in being friends?' he asked. 'Should we pretend we've known each other since childhood and use our given names?'

She giggled, a delightful sound. 'If you wish it.'

'Then you shall call me Hugh from now on.' He smiled. 'No more Mr Westleigh. Agreed?'

'Hugh,' she repeated, making his name sound like a gift. 'I am Daphne, then.'

'Daphne,' he whispered.

Chapter Eight

Hugh heard her rise.

'Oh!' she exclaimed. The chinaware rattled. 'Goodness! I am unsteady.'

He grabbed his cane and stood and immediately she seized his arm. She swayed into him.

'Too much brandy, perhaps?' he said.

She threaded her arm through his. 'You knew I drank some brandy?'

He gestured to his bandages. 'Without my sight, I find my other senses vastly improved. I heard you pour the brandy, which sounded nothing like pouring tea, and I smelled its scent.'

She'd poured herself at least three glasses, which seemed out of character for her.

'I—I did not feel like tea,' she explained, sounding defensive. She released him, but fell against him and again took his arm to steady herself. 'Perhaps I should retire. To bed.'

He held on to her. 'Should I call Carter to assist you?'

'I would rather not have Carter know. I'll be fine if I can get to my room.' She tried to pull away again, but he kept hold of her.

'I'll take you then.' He laughed. 'It will be the blind leading the…jug bitten.'

'I am inebriated?' Her voice rose. 'How is that possible? I drink as much wine to no ill effect.'

'Brandy is stronger.' He walked towards where the door should be. 'Did you not know that?'

He felt her shake her head, her curls brushing his shoulder. 'I never drank it before.'

Why tonight, then?

'Move to the left,' she said. 'You are aiming us to the wall.'

'Blast.' He needed more practice in this room, obviously. He moved to the left. 'Are we heading to the door?'

'Yes.'

He did better crossing the hall with her and finding the stairs. He hooked the cane around his arm and gripped the banister. She gripped him. They made slow and somewhat precarious progress. She leaned on him as if in complete trust of his ability to deliver her safely to her bedchamber door, and he'd be damned if he would fail her.

But he had not practised the way to her door.

When they reached the top of the stairs, he stopped. 'Which way?'

'Mmm.' Was she asleep?

He shook her gently. 'Daphne? You must show me the way to your room.'

'Oh.' She started and paused as if getting her bearings. 'This way.'

She took a step and he followed her direction, although definitely not with the complete trust she'd shown him. With his free hand he used the cane to make certain she was not leading him into pieces of furniture.

Finally she stopped. 'Here it is.'

He felt for the door and found the latch. 'I will leave you here, then.'

She still clung to his arm and rested her head against him. 'Feels nice.'

He eased her arm off and now faced her. 'It does indeed feel nice, Daphne.'

'To be friends,' she mumbled. 'It feels nice to be friends.'

The warmth of her body against his, the scent of roses that always clung to her, her low, brandy-soaked voice all intoxicated him as much as the brandy had intoxicated her. At this moment he did not wish friendship from her, but something more. Something between lovers.

He resisted the impulse, but he did not release her. 'I will bid you a friendly goodnight, then.'

He placed his cane against the wall and searched for her face. Touching her cheek and cupping it in the palm of his hand, he leaned down until he felt her breath on his face. He lowered his face to hers and touched his lips to hers, slightly off-kilter. He quickly made the correction and kissed her as a man kisses a woman when desire surges within him.

'Mmm.' She twined her hands around his neck and gave herself totally to the kiss.

He was acutely aware of her every curve touching his body. His hand could not resist sliding up her side and cupping her breast, her full, high breast. He rubbed his fingers against this treasure and she pressed herself against him, her fingers caressing the back of his neck.

He wanted to take her there in the hallway, plunge himself into her against the door to her bedchamber. She would be willing. Never had a woman seemed more willing.

'Daphne,' he whispered.

Some rational part of him heard footsteps on the stairs.

'Someone is coming.' He eased her away from him. 'We had better say goodnight before we do something two friends might regret.'

'I wouldn't regret it, Hugh!' She tried to renew the embrace.

'Not now.' He pushed her away gently.

The footsteps were coming closer, nearly at the top of the stairs, he guessed. He opened her door and picked up his cane.

'Oh, *madame*!' an accented voice said. 'I—I have come to assist you. If—if I do not disturb you.'

'You must be Monette,' Hugh said. 'I have walked Mrs Asher to her room. She is a bit unsteady.'

He heard Monette rush over to her. '*My lady!* Are you ill?'

'Not ill,' Daphne said. 'Feel wonderful. Am dizzy, though.'

'She drank some brandy,' Hugh explained. 'Without realising the effects.'

'*Je comprends*, sir,' Monette said, sounding very French. 'I will take care of her.'

He felt the two women move past him and walk through the doorway. The door closed behind them and Hugh was left to find his own way back to his bedchamber to await Carter's assistance to ready him for bed.

Sleeping would be difficult this night, he feared.

Daphne rose the next morning humming the tune to 'Barbara Allen'. She laughed at herself. Why was she singing a song of death when she felt so happy?

The previous evening was fuzzy to her, but she remembered their quarrel about money and she remembered that she and Westleigh had made a pact to be friends. It felt wonderful to have a friend, even a temporary one. She so rarely had a friend.

She remembered calling Phillipa Westleigh her friend, but, truly, Daphne had simply been trying to use Phillipa to help in her attempted conquest of Xavier. Daphne had been no friend. She wanted to be different with Hugh—she could call him Hugh now. She wanted to be a good friend.

She had a vision of sharing kisses with him, but that was nonsense. A dream, certainly. She'd dreamed of kissing Hugh, like she used to dream of kissing Xavier. One could not help one's dreams.

One thing was certain. Fantasy must never overpower reason in her relationship with Hugh as it had with Xavier. She would be content—overjoyed—that she and Hugh would spend the next ten days as friends.

Monette entered the room to help Daphne dress. Daphne was tempted to ask for the prettiest of the three dresses she had packed with her. It did not matter what she wore, though, because he could not see her. She did not have to look pretty for him. Imagine! He wanted to be her friend without even knowing what she looked like.

Once ready, she hurried from her room. Hugh was leaving his bedchamber at the same time.

'Good morning,' she said, suddenly reticent to even use his given name. What if he'd changed his mind since the night before?

He smiled and turned in her direction, not quite facing her directly. 'Good morning, Daphne.' His voice was low and deep and warmed her all over. 'Are you bound for breakfast?'

She brightened. 'I am, indeed.'

He offered his arm. 'Would you like to see if I remember how to find the dining room?'

Her fingers wrapped around his muscle. 'It would be my pleasure.'

They descended the stairs together.

'Any ill effects from the brandy?' he asked.

Her head hurt a little, but she was too happy to care. 'None to speak of.'

When they reached the last step, he hesitated. 'Go ahead and lead me. I don't mind floundering on my own, but I would hate to run you into a table or the wall.'

'I will this time,' she responded. 'But you mustn't always act the invalid.'

He smiled again. 'You have surmised it is a role I detest.'

'Oh, yes.' She exaggerated her expression. She did not sound much different than any other time she engaged men in conversation, but inside she felt transformed.

Breakfast was pleasant. It reminded Daphne of those days in her marriage when it seemed as if she made her husband happy.

After breakfast she suggested they take a walk.

They stepped out of the house into a morning as glorious as her mood.

'Tell me what the day is like,' he said as she led him on the same path as the day before. 'Is it as fine as it seems?'

She did not want to answer right away, too acutely aware of all he missed by being unable to see. 'First tell me why you think it fine.'

'Well…' He paused before they stepped onto the road. 'First the air smells of all the wonderful smells of a spring day, of new leaves forming, fresh grass growing, flowers blooming. The sun feels warm on my face. And the birds are making a great deal of noise.' He covered her hand with his. 'Now tell me what you see.'

It had rained the night before and it was as if the rain had scrubbed the landscape into its most presentable appearance. 'First, there is dew on the grass and it sparkles.' Like tiny jewels, she thought. 'There are spring flowers in bloom, in flower beds around the cottage. The sky is very clear. It is that deep, clear blue one does not see very often.'

How many times had her husband compared the colour of her eyes to such a sky? And her hair to the narcissus blooming in the garden? Men always commented on her beauty. This man could not see her, though, and he liked her anyway.

'We're starting on the road now,' she warned him as they walked on.

They approached the stable where John Coachman stood in the door.

'We're near the stable now,' she said. 'My coachman is there.'

The coachman stepped forwards. 'Good morning, ma'am. Good morning, Mr Westleigh. I'd say you look a sight better than when I saw you last.'

Hugh stopped and extended his hand, but the coachman was too far away to reach it. He strode over to accept Hugh's grip.

'You assisted me,' Hugh said. 'I thank you.'

He coloured. ''Twas nothing, sir.'

'You know my name.' Hugh released his hand. 'What is yours?'

It had not occurred to Daphne to introduce them.

'I go by John Coachman, mostly,' the man replied.

Hugh nodded. 'My father always called our coachmen John Coachman. My mother always knew their Christian names, their wives' names and the names of all of their children. She also knew precisely how they should raise their children and how they should conduct every aspect of their lives.'

Daphne knew none of those things. When she'd sent for John Coachman to meet her in Ramsgate, had she taken him away from his family? She'd certainly never given it a thought.

Her coachman gave Hugh a toothy grin. 'Not married, nor have any children.' He winked. 'That I know of.'

Hugh sobered. 'We'd better not pursue that conversation, not with your employer standing here.'

The coachman darted her an anxious look.

'What is your name?' she asked, feeling ashamed of herself. 'I am sorry I never learned it.'

'Oh, John Coachman does well enough,' he responded. Rather kindly, she thought. 'But, if you would like the real thing, it is Henry Smith.'

'I'll call you Smith from now on, then.' The sounds of voices came from inside the stable. She glanced towards them. 'How are the stable boys working out?'

Smith glanced back, too, a pleased expression on his face. 'They leave me nothing to do. They are good workers, ma'am.'

At least she'd eased his load a bit. 'You must enjoy some leisure, then, Smith. Take some time for yourself.'

His eyes widened. 'Thank you, ma'am.'

She took Hugh's arm again and they continued on their walk.

'I ought to have known his name,' she murmured.

He touched her hand again. 'My mother's style was always to insinuate herself into everyone's business, whether they were family or servants. Not everyone adopts such a style.'

She knew a little about Monette's life. Monette had been the daughter of English parents who'd lived in Switzerland. She'd also been orphaned at an early age, with no relatives to take her in. The convent had given her a home, but she was never meant for that life. Daphne had given her a different choice.

Of Carter she only knew he had been stranded in Switzerland without employment. Now she wondered about his story, as well.

She thought about the servants at Faville House, about how little she knew of their lives, and of the servants at the estate in Vadley, the house and property her husband had left her and where she had spent so little time. How would the servants feel about her return? she wondered. Would they be dreading it?

His voice broke into her reverie. 'A penny for your thoughts,' he said. 'Or whatever the rate is for a wealthy widow.'

'I was thinking of my servants at home,' she answered honestly. 'Of whether they would welcome my return.'

'How long have you been away?' he asked.

'More than two years.' She'd spent only a few months in the house in Vadley after the new Viscount Faville had taken possession of Faville House. He was the son of her husband's cousin whose wife had been eager for her to leave.

'You've been two years in Switzerland?'

She guided him around a rut in the road. 'Almost.'

If he was more curious about her stay in Switzerland, he did not say so. The sound of horse's hooves in the distance seemed to distract him.

'Someone riding this way?' Hugh asked.

Daphne turned to see. 'No, one of the stablemen is leading one of the horses. They are going in the opposite direction from us.'

'Which reminds me.' His tone was light. 'Was the hiring of the stable workers more of your charitable efforts?'

'I suppose so.' She furrowed her brow. 'Was I so terribly foolish?'

He pulled her closer to him. 'I think you were terribly generous.'

She felt like weeping at the compliment. At the same time, her senses soared at his closeness. 'You could not see them, but the new maids were so very thin and very eager. How could I say no? And then Mr and Mrs Pitts came up with the idea for hiring the others.' She considered this. 'I wonder if there are many people needing work so urgently.'

'There are many former soldiers out of work, now that the war is over,' he responded. 'And with the Corn Laws there are a lot of hungry people.'

Feed the poor.

One day she had helped the nuns give out bread to needy people. The looks of hunger on their faces had rendered them grotesque. An empty belly was a pain she'd never experienced.

'What is one to do?' she wondered aloud.

'You've done well enough,' he responded.

She jostled him. 'But you are paying, remember? Except I will pay the stable boys. I insist upon it.'

Another stable boy led another horse out of the stable.

'Lord, I miss riding.' His voice turned wistful. 'I do not suppose you have a riding horse in that stable? I'd be tempted to have one of those workers take me out riding.'

'Only the carriage horses.' But Daphne smiled. Surely there were riding horses to procure in the village. Perhaps John Coachman—*Smith*, she meant—would not mind his leisure interrupted to make riding possible for Hugh.

For her friend.

* * *

The very next day after breakfast when she and Hugh, complete with new hat and gloves, walked towards the stables, she remarked, 'Oh, there is Smith again.'

'Morning, ma'am. Mr Westleigh,' Smith responded.

'Good morning, Smith,' Hugh greeted cheerfully. He inhaled. 'Do you have a horse with you?'

'I do indeed, sir.' Smith grinned. 'And one of the boys is here, as well. Henry.'

'Hello, Henry,' Hugh said.

Daphne smiled at the young man mounted on a horse and staring open-mouthed at her. Somehow she was glad Hugh could not see the boy's reaction.

'This may sound daft.' A corner of Hugh's mouth lifted in a half smile. 'But may I pet the horse?'

'I'll do you one better, sir.' Smith pulled the horse forwards. 'How about you take a ride with Henry here.'

It was Hugh's turn to be open-mouthed. 'You are jesting.'

'It is no jest.' Daphne pushed him forwards. 'Mr Pitts found us two riding horses. One for you and one for Henry, so he can accompany you.'

Hugh turned back to her, shaking his head, but speechless.

'Enjoy yourself,' she said. 'Smith was told this horse will not dump you in a hedge.'

He laughed. 'That is a good thing.'

Smith brought the horse to him and Hugh patted the animal.

'I'll help you mount, sir.' Smith guided him to the stirrup, but Hugh mounted easily as soon as his foot was in it.

Smith touched his hat and walked back into the stable.

Daphne stood and watched Hugh ride away, straight backed and confident, as if he was free of the bandages.

Her heart soared with joy. Was it always this way when one did something to make another so happy? This was a gift better than any she'd ever received.

Chapter Nine

What were the odds Hugh would find any recuperation enjoyable, especially this one?

For the past four days he'd ridden in the mornings before breakfast, starting the day feeling free and unfettered by the bandages covering his eyes. Afterwards, he shared pleasant breakfasts with Daphne and they spent most of the rest of the days together. Taking walks. Playing the pianoforte. Talking. In the afternoon and evenings she sometimes read the London newspapers to him or books about exotic places, places he intended to visit and see for himself. They shared dinner and afterwards retired to the drawing room where he sipped brandy and she drank tea. That she seemed happy gratified him more than he could say.

She didn't pour herself brandy, though. Did not repeat that release of restraint that had led to the kiss he could not put out of his mind. His senses burned for her; otherwise the time was idyllic.

This morning was no different. He and Daphne walked together to the stable where Henry waited with his horse. Hugh bid Daphne goodbye and he and Henry set off. There was a field nearby where they could give the horses their heads and race at exhilarating speed.

This was Hugh's favourite time, a time he forgot the bandages on his eyes. He merely savoured the wind in his face and the power of the horse beneath him. He'd galloped like this through cannon and musket smoke in the war. This was not so different—except perhaps that no cannon or musket fired at him. He and the horse were familiar with the field now. Hugh knew how long before the horse would slow and they would progress at a milder pace through some brush.

But now he was flying free. Life was good.

The next moment, the horse balked and stumbled back. Hugh pitched forwards, his face hitting the horse's neck and loosening his bandages and pushing them askew. He managed to hold on to the horse, but in his struggle, he did the unthinkable.

He opened his eyes.

He saw nothing but the white of the loosened bandages. A stab of pain lanced both eyes and he immediately shut them again as he found his seat and pulled on the reins to steady the horse. The pain persisted until finally subsiding into an ache reminiscent of the first two days of his injury. He repositioned the bandages as best he could, but he'd injured his eyes again. He was certain of it.

He heard Henry's horse approach. 'Are you hurt, sir? You almost took a tumble.'

'Not hurt,' Hugh said. At least, not hurt in the way Henry meant. 'Merely shaken. Do you know what happened?'

'Something spooked the mare,' Henry said. 'Didn't see what it was.'

'Well.' Hugh's breathing almost returned to normal. 'No harm done. Let's keep on.' He didn't want to turn back. Didn't want to admit to himself that everything he hoped for might be lost.

* * *

By the end of the ride Hugh had composed himself. Mr Wynne was due to call this very day. He'd change the bandages and they'd again be tight. Until then Hugh must simply remember to keep his lids closed. Maybe Wynne would tell him he was still on the mend. Maybe he had not done terrible harm.

He managed to act normally during breakfast. Daphne needn't know he might have ruined all her efforts at taking care of him.

'I must go into the village this morning,' Daphne told him. 'Monette asked me to accompany her. I've neglected her of late.'

'You've neglected your lady's maid?' This was indeed an odd statement.

'She is not accustomed to being in England.' Daphne explained, sounding embarrassed. 'Nor to being around so many people.'

So many people? In a village?

'Besides, I think there is something on her mind,' she went on. 'There is nothing like a nice walk to help loosen tongues.'

He must be careful not to agree to a walk with her today, then.

'I should be back by the time Mr Wynne calls,' she added.

He was due in the afternoon.

'I'll find some way to amuse myself.' Hugh would probably sit in his bedchamber and worry, but she need not know that.

She was gone most of the day, which was just as well. Hugh heard her voice outside as she returned. He left his rocking chair to make his way down the stairs.

'There you are, Hugh!' she said brightly.

Were her cheeks flushed from the exercise and fresh air? he wondered. Would he ever see such a sight?

'Welcome back.' He made himself sound cheerful. 'Are you there as well, Monette?'

'I am, sir,' the maid answered shyly.

'Did you ladies find much to look at in the village?' he asked.

'We had a delightful time,' Daphne answered. 'We had tea in a very nice tea shop and we browsed through all the stores we could find.'

'Browsed? Do not tell me you did not find something to purchase? I do not believe my mother ever merely browsed in a store in her life.'

'We purchased some fabric for Monette and a few other things. Some lovely marzipan from a confectioner. We should have that with tea later.'

Marzipan was typically formed into fancy shapes and colours, to appear like fruits and vegetables. It was a confection that was better to see than to eat.

Would he ever see it? 'That sounds quite nice.'

'I trust Mr Wynne did not call early?' Daphne said.

He could hear the handling of packages wrapped in paper. 'He sent a message that he would arrive late.' More waiting. At least Daphne would be a distraction.

Hugh reached the bottom step.

'Pardon, sir.' Monette passed by him.

He felt Daphne walk near. 'Were you bound for the drawing room? I will join you shortly. I must change. My skirts are full of dirt from the road.'

He nodded, knowing she could see, even if he could not.

It pleased him to hear the sound of pleasure in her voice from a simple walk to village shops. So often he felt sadness around her, even as they were entertaining themselves at the pianoforte or taking a walk or reading. Maybe he was the reason, if spending a day away from him lightened her spirits.

Blast. He was acting gloomy. The least he could do was avoid inflicting his low mood on her.

He made his way to the drawing room and distracted himself at the pianoforte by playing the scales and chords she'd taught him.

It did help to pass the time. It seemed only a few minutes before she came in the room, saying, 'Carter will bring us tea. You can taste the marzipan.' She walked over and stood behind him. 'You are improving very quickly. I am astonished.'

He made himself laugh. 'Not as astonished as I am.'

'Do you wish to keep practising? Do you want another lesson?' Her scent wafted around him.

'No.' He placed his hands in his lap. 'Why don't you read to me a little?'

'Should we continue with *The Annual Register*?' she asked.

'Yes. *The Annual Register*.' They'd found an old Annual Register from 1808. Among the usual topics covered in *The Annual Register*, like politics, finance and notable world and local events, were chronicles of travels, places he'd like to see for himself. *See* for himself—if he could see.

'Banks of the Mississippi from Mr Ashe's *Travels in America*,' she began.

'Mr Ashe?' he interrupted. 'A relation of yours?'

She did not answer for a moment. 'Ashe. Asher. Two different names.' Her voice was stiff.

'Of course.' He'd been trying to make a joke even though he did not feel like joking. 'Proceed.'

She cleared her throat. '"In many respects the Mississippi is far inferior to the Ohio. The Mississippi is one continued scene of terrific grandeur…'"

While she read, Hugh drummed his fingers on the arm of his chair and only half listened. It was Wynne he wanted. Let the man finally show up and get the bad news over with.

Wynne did not arrive until near the dinner hour. 'So sorry to be late,' he said as he bustled into the room. 'Busy day today.' He paused. 'It is delightful seeing you again, Mrs Asher. I hope I find you in good health?'

'I am in excellent health, thank you, sir. I would offer you tea, but Mr Westleigh has been waiting a long time.' Daphne spoke as if she was the hostess of a London ball, but her voice was edged with impatience. The tea was tepid now in any event.

'It would be a pleasure to partake of tea in your company, my dear lady, but alas, I am not at liberty today.' The surgeon sounded mournful. 'I hope you will renew the invitation at a later time. Today, I fear I must not tarry. I have another patient to see before I shall be free to return home to my dinner.'

'I do understand, Mr Wynne,' Daphne responded. 'You must tend to your patients and your family, of course.'

Hugh heard the sound of a strap being unfastened. 'How have you fared, Mr Westleigh?' Had Wynne finally been able to tear his attention away from Daphne so as to tend to his patient? 'You have kept your eyes closed, I trust.'

'I opened them today.' There, it was out. 'I closed them right away, but I did open them.'

'Hugh!' Daphne cried.

'The bandages came loose when I was riding and my eyes opened before I could think about it.' He sounded as if he were making excuses.

'You were riding?' Wynne sounded incredulous.

'Not alone,' Hugh assured him.

'Hmmph.' The surgeon clearly disapproved. 'When you opened your eyes, did you experience pain?'

'A sharp pain, yes.' And the ache persisted. There was more he'd noticed. 'I can feel my eyes move under my lids a great deal when I want to look at something, but they have remained closed except for that one instance.' Now it hurt every time his eyes moved.

'Well—' Wynne sighed as if all was lost '—let us take a look.'

His hand cupped the bandages on Hugh's head and lifted them off rather than unwinding them. Amazing how light-headed Hugh felt with the bandages gone. His lids fluttered.

'Keep them closed.' Wynne briefly touched Hugh's eye-lids to still them.

Through his closed lids, Hugh saw nothing.

He felt the warmth of a candle come near. 'Do you see the light?' Wynne asked.

Daphne must have had the candle ready.

'I see light,' Hugh responded, but no better than during that first examination.

The candle moved away, and Wynne's fingers touched his eyelids again. 'Your lids have healed very nicely, Westleigh. I see no signs of infection.' He felt the man back away and heard him rummage in his bag. 'I'm going to apply a salve to your eyes and bandage them up again.'

The salve felt cool and the new bandages clean. Wynne wound the cloth tightly around Hugh's head. 'I dare say you have re-injured the eyes, though. The pain you felt confirms that. We may hope they heal again, but we will not know until another week goes by.'

He rummaged in his bag again and Hugh heard him rebuckle the straps. 'I must take my leave.' Hugh heard Daphne's skirts and presumed she'd stood, as well. 'I regret not being able to spend more time, my dear,' Wynne said.

'You are a very busy man,' Daphne replied.

He heard them walking to the door. Wynne had told him nothing encouraging. He'd been too busy making himself pleasing to Daphne.

That was unfair. Wynne had examined him equally as carefully as he had the first time. Hugh had not expected good news. He had no choice but to wait.

And hope he kept his eyes closed. And hope he healed.

Daphne saw Mr Wynne to the door and hurried back to the drawing room. 'Hugh!' She rushed over to him. 'Why did you not tell me?'

He shrugged. 'I do not know. I suppose it would have made it seem real.'

She knelt in front of him and took his hands. 'You must be worried.'

'I cannot deny it.'

He leaned towards her and she rested her forehead against his. 'You poor man.'

He inhaled and she leaned back. What was she thinking? Acting so intimately with a man. He was her friend. He was a Westleigh. She must expect nothing of him.

Carter knocked on the door. 'Dinner, ma'am.'

She squeezed Hugh's hand and pulled him to his feet. 'Come. You must be hungry.'

During the meal she tried to cheer him up and she guessed he tried to pretend it was working, but the prospect of his blindness shrouded them.

After dinner, back in the drawing room, she poured

him a glass of brandy, and a little for herself, just to warm herself and to calm the emotions she sensed inside him.

'Shall I continue reading from *The Annual Register*?' It was not the book she would have chosen for her own entertainment, but it interested him and might distract him from his worry.

'Certainly, if you like,' he responded without enthusiasm.

She refilled his glass, adding more for herself, as well.

Opening the book, she found the place where she'd left off. 'We were about to begin the part about the price of gold in Abyssinia.'

He made no comment.

'"Price of gold,"' she began. '"Gold at a medium, sells for ten pataka each wakea, or ten derims, salt…"' The words meant little to her but they lulled her as she read about the price of gold, about weights and measures, about servants' wages, about how they made beer and finally about marriage. 'It sometimes happens that the husband and wife mutually, without any cause of ill will, agree to part. In this case the effects brought by the wife are united with the sum stipulated by the husband, then divided into equal shares of which the parties take each one, and return to their former places of abode.' She stopped reading. 'Oh, my.' Had she read correctly? 'What do you think of that?'

'Of what?'

'Of what I just read.' She scanned the words again to be certain. 'In Abyssinia, a husband and wife can end their marriage by mutual agreement. They divide their agreed-upon settlements and that is it.' She could not believe this. 'And their church sanctions it.'

He turned to face in her direction. 'Daphne, why does this interest you?'

She could not answer him. 'No reason.'

'You have read of all sorts of odd things,' he pointed out. 'Why did this one interest you?'

'I do not know.' More truthfully she did not wish to say. 'I suppose it is because it is such a shameful and difficult thing to get a divorce in England.'

He lowered his voice. 'Did you wish for a divorce from your husband, Daphne?'

Her stomach flipped. Her response was shrill. 'No. Of course not.' She had not wished that, had she?

He lifted his glass to his lips. 'Tell me about your husband, Daphne. About your marriage.'

Tell him? That her husband was good to her, that he indulged her, but even so, she had never been a good wife to him?

She swivelled towards Hugh. 'I—I—' She twisted her skirt with her hands. How she felt about her marriage did her no credit at all. 'Would you still consider me your friend if I told you I did not wish to talk about this?'

'Of course.' His spine stiffened and he took another sip of brandy.

As did she. 'Please understand, Hugh. I cannot talk about my marriage any more than you can talk about your eyes.'

He stood. 'You are correct. I do not wish to talk about my eyes, although there is not much to talk about. I will either be blind or not.' He searched for and picked up his cane. 'I am going to retire. I'm not very good company for you tonight.'

She rose, too, and put a hand on his arm. 'Please do not be angry with me, Hugh. Please. I want this time between us to be—to be—free of any past. Heedless of any future. I want to enjoy being friends now, while we are here.'

'I am not angry with you, Daphne.' He turned to her, but could not see to face her directly. He placed his hand over hers. 'I hope sometime you will trust me enough to tell me what it is that makes you so sad, but you are correct that tonight is not the night. I need to get myself in order first.'

His fingers, long and strong, wrapped around hers. The gesture brought tears to her eyes. No one touched her any more. No one held her, not since the abbess had once enfolded her in her arms. Daphne, sobbing like a wounded child, had clung to the old woman as if the abbess had been her last hold on forgiveness. She wished she could be held now. She wished Hugh could hold her and comfort her, but she didn't deserve his embrace, not after wronging his family and deceiving him.

To her surprise, he released her fingers and slid his hands up her arms, to her shoulders, her neck, her face. His palms were warm and gentle against her cheeks, and his touch roused her like no man's touch had ever done before.

His cane fell to the floor and he cupped her face with both hands. 'I wish I could see you,' he murmured.

He'd never touch her if he could see her, she knew. This might be her only chance to receive the comfort for which she yearned. There was no resisting it.

His thumbs stroked the tender skin of her cheeks, and she felt as if the imprint of his touch would remain for ever with her. But she wanted—needed—more. Her body quivered with need. With desire. She wanted something more precious than comfort. She wanted Hugh.

Wrapping her arms around his neck, she rose on tiptoe and urged his head lower. His lips were so near she tasted the brandy on his breath. She trembled with desire, but feared closing the gap between them. Perhaps he meant only to comfort her. Perhaps he did not want her at all.

He held her face more firmly, and the thrill of it radiated throughout her body. He guided her face still closer until his lips took possession of hers with a need all their own.

Her body ignited with passion, passion for this man. She thought she might perish if she could not feel his bare skin against hers, to join her body with his. She wanted him more than she'd ever wanted any man. Even her husband.

Even Xavier.

This was new to her. Irresistible. It would do no harm to make love to him, would it?

He pulled away from her. 'I had best say goodnight.' He lowered himself to search for his cane.

Shaken and bereft, she crouched down to retrieve it for him, her head close to his. 'Hugh?' She touched his arm.

He found her face again for one more caress, even more gentle than before. 'Goodnight, Daphne.'

Tears rolled down her cheeks as he straightened and walked away from her. Why had he stopped? He wanted her as well, did he not?

After he left, she sat a long time, thinking, trying to calm herself, trying to talk herself out of needing him.

Chapter Ten

The clock in Hugh's room chimed the hour. He counted each chime. One...two... Ten...eleven...twelve. Midnight.

Even though Carter had readied him for bed two hours ago, even though the man had left him with a bottle of brandy, Hugh remained awake, drinking and rocking.

At least night evened the odds. In darkness no one could see.

Who was he fooling? He heard the hiss of coal in the grate. The glow from the fireplace would give a person with eyes enough light to make out the furniture in the room. Eyes that worked, that was.

If he wished to be completely honest with himself, he'd admit what was really keeping him awake.

Daphne.

His thoughts were consumed by her. A second kiss with a promise of passion equal to the first had done it. He'd counted how many times she poured herself brandy. Only three times and all had been short, not enough to explain her response to him. No, she'd chosen this kiss with a clear mind.

Had he gone too far? He'd meant only to touch her. Hadn't he?

His masculine urges were surging, unleashed by that kiss. She was not far, a few steps away. He could find his way. By God, he believed he could find his way without his cane, without feeling for the walls. She drew him so strongly he did not need the glow of coals or a lamp in the hallway.

To bed a widow was not a scandalous matter, but all he could think of was that he would risk creating another child she would need to give up. For all her cool manner to him at first, it was now clear she was a passionate woman whose desires could be easily aroused. The responsibility was his to keep in control of his baser needs. How long could he restrain himself? Even if he decided to behave himself now, could he resist trying for another kiss later? Every moment with her would be one of decision.

To bed her or not.

He burned to feel her bare body beneath him. To fill his palms with her breasts and rub her nipples against his skin. He wanted to bury himself inside her and bring her to pleasure at the same moment of his release.

He took a swig of brandy, not bothering with a glass.

What he ought to do was get himself to London, put himself in the suffocating care of his mother and endure it for a week. Or longer, if his eyes could not heal. If his eyes could not heal, what other choice would he have? It had been unfair of him to impose himself on Daphne, especially since he'd prevented her from proceeding on her way. Wherever that may be.

He drank again and let the liquor burn down his throat into his chest.

Carter could make the arrangements for him. Hire a carriage. It was not even a day's journey.

He heard the door open. Might as well ask the man now before he lost his nerve. 'Carter?'

The scent of roses reached his nostrils. 'It is not Carter.'

He stood. 'Daphne. What are you doing here?' Good God. He wore nothing but his drawers. 'I'm not decent.'

She remained near the door. 'Neither am I.'

'Why, then—?' he began.

She stopped him. 'Don't speak.' He felt her move closer to him, felt the heat of her when she came near. 'I—I felt so unhappy when you left me tonight.'

She was close enough to touch and he wanted to touch her. 'I had to leave you, Daphne. And you should leave me now.'

'I was thinking,' Her scent, her voice, her nearness, intoxicated him. 'I am a widow and widows have certain licence.'

But she was also a woman and women conceived children.

'We are close, are we not?' she said. 'Why can we not be close in—in a physical way, as well?'

'There are risks, Daphne.'

'No one will know.' Her voice rose. 'Except the servants, of course. Monette and Carter would never gossip, I can assure you, and we'll be leaving the others. They will not care what we do.' She put her hands on his bare shoulders.

His resolve could stand only so much. 'There are other risks, as you well know.'

'I do not care.' Her fingers played in the hair at the nape of his neck. 'Please, Hugh? We have only one week. Can we not spend it truly together?'

One week. Or perhaps one night. Maybe he could risk one night. He could still leave for London in the morning. One chance to love her. Could he turn it down?

Her hands slipped down to his chest. 'After one week

you will be off on your travels and I will return to my home.'

'Or I'll be blind,' he said.

She threw her arms around him and pressed herself close to him. 'Do not say you will be blind. You will see. You must see. You must do all those things that make you happy at last. Life cannot be that unfair to you.'

She could not be wearing anything but a nightdress. One thin piece of fabric between them. He was aroused, painfully so.

'I can feel that you want me, Hugh,' she whispered. 'Make love to me.'

He could not refuse.

He lifted her into his arms and carried her to the bed. He knew just how many steps it took to reach it. 'Are you certain, Daphne?'

She reached for him, clasping his arm as if she had the strength to pull him onto the bed. 'I am very certain.'

Daphne's heart beat so rapidly she thought her chest would burst. She had brazenly offered seduction to Xavier more than once, but this was different and she did not know why. She only knew that she'd break into a million shards if she did not soon feel Hugh's hands upon her skin.

He stood at the side of the bed, removing his drawers while she pulled her nightdress over her head. When she tossed it aside, it brushed against his arm.

He caught it and held the fabric in his hand. 'I wish I could see you.'

'I just want you to touch me.' She reached for him, impatient to have him next to her on the bed. On top of her. Inside her. 'Look at me with your hands.'

He climbed on the bed, kneeling over her, her legs between his. His hands touched her lightly, making their way to her head. His fingers ran through her loose hair, like one might run hands through cool water. He combed through the length of it, reaching its ends and exploring the feel of it.

'Your hair is longer than I thought,' he said. 'With some curl. What colour is it?'

She hesitated to say. He could not possibly identify her by hair colour alone, could he? Many women had her hair colour. 'Blonde.' She cleared her throat. 'It is blonde.'

'As I imagined it to be.' He played with her hair, twisting it around his hands, threading it through his fingers, creating sensation that flooded through her.

He explored her face, as he'd done once before, but this time his fingers were reverent, stroking each contour as if he were sculpting her himself out of pliant clay. Could he feel what other men saw with their eyes? Would her face matter to him? She did not want it to matter to him. Or perhaps she did. She wanted him to admire her, did she not?

Tears of confusion sprang to her eyes. Oh, dear! How would she explain tears at such a moment? How could she tell him she did not wish to be beautiful for him, merely loved?

Luckily his hands moved to stroke her neck and trace the contours of her ears. She blinked away the tears and savoured the lovely sensations his fingers created. He slid his hands down farther, reaching her breasts, stroking, tracing around her nipples. Her back arched in response. His hands had been gentle in their exploration, but now she felt their strength as he pressed her flesh more firmly, again taking possession as he'd done with the kiss.

She flared with need. A moan escaped her lips and her body ached for him. Her hands grasped him, kneading his skin, not so much exploring him as urging him to keep touching her, to keep filling her with need.

His hands slid farther, pressing against her rib cage, reaching her waist and spanning it with his fingers as if measuring. Yes, she knew her breasts were full, her waist narrow, and her bottom fleshy enough to please a man. How often had she been told of it?

'Does it matter to you, how I am shaped?' she asked, her voice tinged with both annoyance and gratification.

'Matter?' He swept his hands up and down her torso. 'This is the only way I can see you.'

She did care how he perceived her, she realised. 'Do— do I please you?'

He leaned down and possessed her lips, his kiss long and dizzying. Her muscles melted like butter left too close to the oven.

'You please me very much, Daphne,' he murmured, still touching his lips to hers. 'You have pleased me since the moment I first woke in this room.'

Her spirits soared. He could not have known anything of her appearance then, not even by touch, and still she pleased him. A memory flashed. Of her husband undressing her like a doll and looking at her, admiration glowing in his eyes.

No. She did not want to think of her husband at this moment. She wanted to think only of this night, of this man. Of Hugh. She could seek happiness for a week, could she not? A week with Hugh should be enough to last a lifetime.

He splayed his fingers over her abdomen. She slid hers down his back. Everywhere she touched was firm muscle. How thrilling to think of that masculine power beneath his skin. The light in the room was dim, a mere glow from the fireplace, but it was enough to reveal his magnificence. She could not help but compare him with Xavier, who she'd imagined to be at the peak of masculine perfection.

Hugh was not perfection, but there was glory in his rough-edged manliness.

Enough exploring, she wanted to scream. *Take me now.*

She arched her back and pulled one of his hands down to where she ached for him.

Pleasure me, she wanted to say, but she'd never before spoken such wanton words.

She did not have to tell him. His fingers touched her with exquisite intimacy, exciting her even more acutely. Fevered cries escaped her lips, and she writhed in the glory of his touching, stroking, building need and pushing it to the breaking point.

She could keep silent no longer. 'Please, now, Hugh. Now.' She pressed his buttocks and scraped lightly with her fingernails. 'Now, Hugh.'

But first he leaned down and kissed her again, moving his tongue until her mouth opened to him. His tongue was warm and wet and tasted of brandy. When he broke the kiss, he thrust into her and her exhilaration flared. She liked that he was not gentle, not careful. He was assured, skilled. He knew her body was slick and ready for him.

He moved with equal skill and control, just the right cadence to calm her need, but to allow it to rebuild slowly, like an avalanche she'd witnessed once when visiting the mountains in Switzerland. It started slow, building and building until everything in its path was consumed by it and swept along.

She was swept along, almost giddy at the wonder of the journey.

When his control broke, she was enveloped by the wildness of it, his animal growls, his abandon, until the pleasure burst inside her and he thrust one final, frenzied time. He'd spilled his seed inside her, his gift, the part of him that was now part of her.

He exhaled a long breath, and his weight grew heavy on top of her for a moment before he rolled to her side and nestled her against him. 'Daphne,' he murmured.

Words swirled inside her, words of wonder and thanks and joy, but she could not speak them. She kissed him instead, a long, lingering, tender kiss into which she put all she could not say.

They made love again. And again. Until finally sated and satisfied, she lay next to him, bare skin to bare skin, enjoying the mere fact of his breathing, the soft sound of his heartbeat.

Hugh felt as if his bones had melted like candle wax. Not an essence of tension remained inside him. He was where he most wished to be.

Next to her.

'Daphne, Daphne,' he murmured. 'Nothing could ever be better than that.'

'Mmm,' she said, which he took as agreement.

He knew she'd experienced as much passion as he. He knew she relished it equally as much, but before he could help it, the past crept in. Had it been that magnificent with her husband? If so, what a lucky man. Had it been like that with other men?

She sighed, a contented, satisfied sound. 'I always had the sense there was more.' She snuggled closer to him. 'Now I know for certain.'

Was she reading his thoughts now? 'Do not tell me you have never experienced the like of this with a man before?'

'Like this?' She laughed a soft, near-silent laugh. 'No.'

It made no sense. She'd been created for lovemaking. How could he believe that no man had ever discovered that before? Had her husband been a fool? The other men, as well?

'My husband was the only other man I've bedded.'

Were their thoughts joined as well as their bodies and souls? Even after making love to her once, Hugh felt a part of her and she, a part of him.

Hugh stroked her glorious hair. The finest silk threads could never feel as luxurious. 'Your husband—?' he began to ask. He'd all but promised he would not ask about her husband again, but he'd also assumed there had been someone else. If she had not gone to Switzerland to wait out a pregnancy and to give up a baby, then why had she gone?

'My husband was older,' she went on. 'Twice my age and more. A vital man, even so. I was very young when he married me. Barely seventeen. It was a very advantageous match for me. He was wealthy and of greater status. His—his lovemaking was—' she paused '—different.'

He frowned. 'Were you unhappy?' Was that the unhappiness he sensed in her?

'Unhappy?' She seemed to consider this. 'No, not unhappy. Just young and foolish and filled with silly ideas.'

He thought her so serious a person. 'Silly ideas? I do not believe you.'

'Oh, yes.' Her tone turned sad. 'I had very foolish notions.'

He rose up on one elbow, wishing he could look down on her. 'What sort of foolish notions?'

She paused again before finally saying, 'I was quite indulged, but I wanted what I could not and should not have. It took me a long while to accept that I should be content with what I have been given.'

There had been another man; he knew it. 'Was it another man, then?'

Again she paused. 'Yes. Once, but not really. I mean, nothing came of it.'

Hugh wanted to know everything. He wanted to put it all right somehow.

'What about children?' he could not help but ask.

'I was not blessed with children.' She sounded sad, but not unduly so. 'Perhaps that was best.'

No children? He'd been wrong, indeed. 'Why best?'

She took a deep breath. 'I would not have made a good mother.'

He lay back down again and hugged her to him. 'Of course you would have made a good mother. Think what a good nurse you have been for me.'

He felt her shrug. 'Well, not then, at least.'

He kissed her temple. 'Tell me about then.' He wanted to understand. To soothe whatever pain she'd endured.

She moved from his grasp and sat up. 'Oh, I do not wish to think of the past. I only want to think about now.'

He reached for her, found her and lifted her on top of him. Straddling him, she leaned down to kiss him, a long impassioned kiss that aroused him once more.

'Well, I am quite pleased with right now,' he told her. 'And I will be more pleased if you consent to make love with me one more time.'

She laughed. He wanted to hear her laugh for ever. 'I shall do as you command.'

'As I ask,' he corrected. 'I do not command.' He positioned her on top of him and slid inside her.

She moved, as perfectly as he could wish, in a rhythm that matched him as if they were created for each other. Only one thing could make the moment better. If he could see her. Gaze upon her, feast his eyes. God knew his eyes were hungry for the sight of her.

She moved faster, more urgently, seeking her own pleasure at the exact moment his need increased. That she became so easily aroused by him aroused him further, until sensation and need overtook him.

She cried out and at the moment of her release, his came, an explosion of sensation equal to the pleasure they'd already shared.

She collapsed on top of him, as he'd done, only her weight was a trifle. He held her there, moving his hands over her skin, enjoying the smooth, slightly damp contours of her body.

'I stand corrected,' he murmured, his lips touching her hair. 'I said nothing could be better than the last time, but this was equal to it. Better, even.' He ran his fingers through her hair. 'Nothing quite matches making love to you, Daphne.'

She released a satisfied breath. 'I thought you would have shared such pleasure with many women.'

It was his turn to laugh. 'Not as many as you would expect. Never as gratifying.'

She nestled by his side again and was silent for so long he thought her asleep. He felt himself drifting towards that state, as well.

'Did you ever think yourself in love, Hugh?' she asked.

'No.' He'd experienced a youthful infatuation or two, but never as a man. 'I was too busy, I suppose. Being an officer and then tending to family matters.' That was the easy answer. He suspected his choices had been affected by his mother's unhappiness and the fact that his father had been a thorough reprobate.

'I dare say many officers found reasons to marry in that period of time.' Her voice turned sad. 'And afterwards you could have married for money.'

It was what she had done, was it not? He could not imagine himself doing the same.

'Enough of this topic.' The last thing he wanted was to

make her sad. 'We all do what seems best at the time. Is that not correct?'

'I suppose so,' she said uncertainly.

'I know so.'

He held her beside him and gradually felt her muscles relax and her breathing turn even. What could be more pleasant than this, feeling the warmth of her skin against his?

When she woke in the morning, would she regret this intimacy? Would he? There was no one to be hurt in it, was there? Especially now he knew there had been no child.

Would she ever tell him the true reason she had been in Switzerland? It did not matter. Nothing mattered except loving her. Making love to her had changed everything. He no longer planned on having Carter arrange a carriage ride home for him. He planned on enjoying this week with her. He wanted to spend every week with her in such enjoyment.

The thought surprised him. He did not wish to settle down, to stay in one place, to be beholden to another person, but what better adventure could there be than spending each day with her, forging a life together? Maybe they could travel together. He could think of no travelling companion he could desire more. Even more than travel, though, he wanted merely to be with her. He was certain of it. He'd actually mused that he'd enjoyed his recuperation because of her. When his bandages came off and he became whole again, think how much better being with her could be.

If his eyes healed, that was. That was the larger question. He might end this week blind. Could he really ask her to spend her life with him, if he was permanently impaired and dependent? She would do it, he'd wager. She had gone to all this trouble for him when he was a stranger to her. She would do even more for a lover.

Or a husband.

Hugh tried to imagine living in endless darkness as an invalid. What kind of man, or part man, would blindness make him? He'd have nothing to offer her. He'd merely take, take, take.

In a week, he would know. What was a week to wait? One thing was certain, he would spend this week loving her and enjoying their time together to the full. If luck would truly be with him, the bandages would come off and he'd open his eyes to the sight of her face.

Then his future would be certain. He'd ask her to share it with him and he was certain she'd say yes.

Chapter Eleven

The next week proved to be the most beautiful week of Daphne's life, but finally it was at an end. Today was her last day with Hugh. The knowledge that this was her last day with him was like walking around with a dagger in her heart, a dagger she could neither remove nor reveal.

The week had been extraordinarily wonderful and acutely agonising.

Their lovemaking had shredded any barriers between them. She'd never felt as close to anyone in her life as she felt to Hugh. He was a part of her now. He would always be a part of her.

But in a short time she would leave him.

It was all arranged.

Monette, Carter and Smith the coachman were in her confidence, but Carter pursed his lips whenever she mentioned her plan and Monette looked mournful. She'd also told Toller, because she needed his assistance and she wanted someone familiar to Hugh to remain with him when the bandages came off. Toller was also tasked with handing Hugh—or reading to him—her letter of farewell.

She'd arranged for Mr Wynne to call after breakfast, although Hugh thought it would be in the afternoon.

After dressing, Daphne came down to the dining room and waited for Hugh. She stared at the buffet table without appetite. She would have to force food down when Hugh sat with her, or he would notice and wonder why she was not eating.

Why could she simply not tell him who she was, which she should have done in the beginning?

She could not bring herself to do it. Better he think she left for some mysterious reason than that the despised Lady Faville had deceived him the whole time.

The abbess had been correct about lies. They grew worse with time. If at the beginning she had told him she was Lady Faville, not Mrs Asher, he probably would have left for London immediately and this past week would never have happened.

No, she would never regret this week with him. She'd learned so many lessons she could not have learned otherwise. She'd learned that she could love unselfishly, that another person's well-being could mean everything and her well-being nothing. She'd learned that joy came from managing some kind gesture to Hugh. Like helping him to ride. Like reading to him, playing the pianoforte for him. She learned that lovemaking could be glorious when pleasure was mutually shared and when two people loved each other.

Daphne also learned one more thing, perhaps the most important of all. She learned a man could love her for herself and not merely for the beauty of her face or the shape of her figure. She would for ever be grateful to Hugh for that gift.

What had she given him in return? Lies. Deceit. Would she be able to live with herself for it?

She hoped—and prayed—that Hugh would be rewarded

for what he'd done for her. She prayed he would open his
eyes and see.

Even if he would never see her.

She heard the tapping of his cane as he approached.
May this be the last day he would need the cane! She
quickly wiped her eyes and blew her nose into a handkerchief and placed a smile on her face, ready to play her
part one last time.

Hugh had ridden that morning. He'd galloped over the
fields, heedless of the risk he'd open his eyes. What difference would it make now? Today he would either be
blind or not.

He could not pretend to be free of anxiety. He wanted
so badly to be whole for her, to not have to wrestle with
the issue of whether he could stay with her or not.

The whole cottage seemed to have caught his nerves.
The very air felt different. Tense with waiting. At breakfast he could tell Daphne was putting on a cheerful front.
She spoke with her governess voice, always a sign she was
feeling other emotions than she was willing to reveal. After
breakfast she excused herself to tend to some servant matter. He retired to the drawing room to practise his scales.

Instead, he played 'The Last Post', which he now could
play without hesitation. Its mournful notes seemed fore-
boding. The other tune he knew by memory was 'Barbara
Allen', but it, too, was depressing. He didn't want to think
of loss—the potential loss of his sight.

Daphne should have taught him a happy tune.

There was a knock on the door and Toller's voice said,
'Mr Wynne is here, sir.'

'Wynne?' The surgeon was early. 'Find Mrs Asher and
ask her to come immediately. I'll see Wynne here.'

'Yes, sir.' Toller sounded tense.

Hugh was touched that even the servants were worried for him.

He moved to his usual chair in the drawing room, where he had been sitting when Wynne had called before.

The surgeon bustled in. 'Good morning, Westleigh.' He paused. 'Mrs Asher is not here today?'

'I've sent for her,' Hugh said. 'You've come early.'

The surgeon unbuckled the straps of his bag. 'Sometimes I cannot help being late.'

Hugh did not try to make sense of that. 'Did you wish to wait for Mrs Asher?'

'Well…' Wynne sounded tempted. 'I would be delighted to see her, but I cannot stay long.'

'Pardon, sir.' Toller entered the room again. 'I cannot find Mrs Asher.'

'You do not say.' Wynne was obviously disappointed. 'We might as well get started. I imagine you are anxious to know what's what.'

Hugh was disappointed, as well. He had counted on her being with him. 'Yes, proceed.' Perhaps it would be for the best, though. If the removal of the bandages went as he feared, she would not witness his despair.

Hugh sat in a chair and Wynne pulled up another to face him. He rummaged in his bag and Hugh heard the blades of the scissors open and close. Wynne snipped the bandage at the back of his head and started to unwind it.

'Keep your eyes closed, now,' the surgeon cautioned. 'Toller, would you close the curtains? We don't want any bright light.'

Hugh heard Toller attending to the task.

Wynne placed his fingers on the pieces of cloth covering each of Hugh's eyes and unwound the last of the bandage that held them in place. 'Now keep them closed. I'm going to take these last bandages off and examine your eyes first.'

Hugh kept his eyes closed with difficulty. He could feel his eyes darting behind his lids. Was that a good or a bad sign?

Wynne lifted his lids slightly. 'All good so far.'

Hugh saw light from the slit beneath his eyelids. Seeing light was not the same as having vision, though.

Wynne took a breath. 'Now slowly open your lids. If there is pain,' he added quickly, 'close them again.'

Hugh carefully lifted his eyelids, the first time he'd done so deliberately in a fortnight. There was pain, but not like when he'd opened his eyes before. This pain was more akin to staring into the sun. Everything was blurred. He blinked and tried again. This time he saw shapes. Another blink and the shapes took on a more exact form.

He stared into the weathered face of an older man and laughed. 'I can see. Wynne.' He pointed to him, as if to prove it.

The older man's face creased into a smile. 'Bravo!'

Hugh turned to a tall, skinny young man standing to his right. 'Toller!'

Toller grinned. 'That I am, sir.'

Wynne gathered up the old bandages and set them aside. He placed the steel scissors in his bag, a worn black leather satchel. 'Mind that you do not strain your eyes, young man. Stay out of strong sunlight for a few days. Don't read too much. Rest your eyes often. Work up to normal use gradually.' He touched Hugh's face. 'You have a few burn marks, but those might fade in time.'

Hugh glanced around the room. The decor was plain and a little worn. The chairs were upholstered in green and the curtains matched them. He knew precisely where to look for the pianoforte, for the cabinet that held the brandy. 'It is just good to see.'

Wynne stood. 'I must go. Give my best to Mrs Asher.'

It had taken no time at all. After hours, days of anticipation.

Hugh walked Wynne out of the room into the hall. The walls of the hall were all oak wainscoting. The front door was oak as well, as was the stairway and the door to the dining room.

Toller handed Wynne his hat and gloves, and Hugh walked him to the door. 'Thank you again, Wynne.' He reached into his pocket and placed coins into the man's hand.

Wynne handed the coins back to him. 'Mrs Asher already sent payment. Quite as generous as she is beautiful.'

She was beautiful? Hugh had known so. He'd felt her beauty under his fingertips. Soon he would see for himself.

He opened the door and Wynne gave a little wave and strode off.

Hugh turned to Toller. 'I must find Mrs Asher.'

He could hardly contain his excitement. He would surprise her, take her in his arms, ask her to marry him.

Toller frowned. 'She's not here, Mr Westleigh.' He handed Hugh a folded and sealed note.

Hugh gave him a puzzled look, broke the seal and unfolded the paper. The handwriting was neat and precise with a decorative flourish to some letters, just as he would have expected her handwriting to look.

Dearest Hugh,

If you are reading this, then my heart soars for you.
If not, words cannot express how very sorry I am. I

am gone. I cannot explain the reason, except to tell
you it is for the best. It is no use to try to find me.

There is no Mrs Asher. I am not who I said I was.
The only truth about me is how dearly I came to love
you. I thank you for the most glorious week of my
life. I shall live the rest of my life on its memory.

Forget me and be happy.

My enduring love remains with you for ever.
Daphne

The air whooshed from Hugh's lungs, as if he'd fallen
from a great height. He'd plunged, all right. From the highest joy to the deepest anguish.

She was gone?

No. Impossible.

He rubbed his eyes and read the letter again. What good
was seeing now, if he must read these words? There was
no mistaking it. She was gone.

He glanced over to Toller, despair creeping through his
body like a venomous snake.

'Does she tell you she has left, sir?' Toller asked, distress written on his face. 'She, Mr Carter and Miss Monette
left in their carriage—'

Hugh would have heard a carriage. Unless it waited for
her at some distance. She'd deliberately fooled him.

Toller went on. 'She wrote letters for Mr and Mrs Pitts,
for Mary and Ann and the stable boys. She left us all with
pay to cover two years instead of two weeks. That is all I
know, sir. We are to help you in whatever way you need.
You may stay here as long as you like, because we're all
paid for two years.'

How generous of her. Why so generous to them when
she'd robbed him of what he'd needed most?

'Thank you, Toller,' Hugh managed, although it felt as if his insides had been eviscerated. 'I—I will let you know if I need anything.' What he needed most had left him. Vanished.

And he did not even know what she looked like.

Toller bowed and left the hall.

Hugh glanced around him, but sight was no comfort. He felt as disorientated as when he'd first woken in this house. His hand gripped her letter. He lifted it and read the words again:

The only truth about me is how dearly I came to love you. I thank you for the most glorious week of my life. I shall live the rest of my life on its memory.

Pretty words, but surely as false as the story she'd told him from the start. Was any of it true? Love. It was not love to lie, to leave with no goodbye, with no explanation.

His chest ached and he cried out, a frustrated, helpless, angry sound.

There was more than one way to be blind. She'd blinded him to the truth of her. Deliberately. She'd made a fool of him, pretending at love.

His fist crumpled the paper.

Curse her! He did not even know who she was.

Chapter Twelve

The next day was overcast with grey clouds that threatened showers, but Hugh was determined to leave. Even Wynne's warning to rest his eyes would not stop him. He unpacked his greatcoat and arranged to have his trunk shipped to his mother's house in London. He purchased the horse he'd been riding for nearly two weeks and settled generous vails on the cottage servants. Daphne, if that was her name, was not the only one who could be generous.

With one last look at the place he'd been unable to see, he bid the servants goodbye and mounted the horse. Let it rain, let the heavens pour down on him, he did not care. He wanted to be away from this place. He needed the open road. He needed the air. He needed freedom. A carriage would close him in like a coffin and trap him with his own thoughts.

London was less than a day's ride away, but he took it slowly, not changing horses, instead sticking with his old equine friend, who had offered him such essential diversion when he'd needed it. *She* had arranged that diversion. How was he to make sense of that?

Hugh wanted the miles to strip away memories of the cottage in Thurnfield, but that was futile. The memories would never fade. The memories flooded his mind, repeating over and over, and if he stopped them, the questions rushed in. Why had she deceived him? What sort of woman would do such a thing? Had she merely been toying with him? Seduce the blind man. Make him think it is his idea and convince him he is a great lover. Then what? And why? Why do that? Why make herself a part of him, then strip herself away? Would it have made a difference if he'd not regained his sight? Had Toller been given two letters, one for each situation?

No. She'd known the whole time she would leave.

Curse the woman.

She might as well have sliced him with a sabre. The ache inside him began to burn white-hot. It was good that he could not go in search of her. His anger seethed so strongly, who knew what he would do?

Anger was preferable to the sheer despair of losing her.

His mind and his emotions had spun in circles as the horse plodded steadily forwards. By the time he neared the shores of the Thames and spied the dome of St Paul's Cathedral, he'd made some decisions. First, he would not say anything to his family about the fire or Daphne or his recuperation. There was no reason they should know any of it. He'd say he came directly from Brussels. If they noticed any burn marks on his face, he'd tell them he came too close to some flames, which was true. Second, he'd cut himself loose from the family and book passage to… somewhere. He'd continue on his original plan to travel the world and do anything he damned well pleased.

Hugh crossed the Thames and made his way to Mayfair. Riding past the familiar buildings on familiar streets gave him more comfort than he would have guessed. He rode on Piccadilly, passing near the Masquerade Club.

He was half tempted to drop in to see how it was going, but his eyes were aching from the strain of riding all day. He continued on to the family stable at Brooks Mews and gave charge of the horse to the Westleigh stablemen, trying not to remember Daphne's stablemen, workers she'd had no need to hire.

He walked the short distance to Davies Street and, finding the door locked, sounded the knocker.

Mason, the butler, opened the door. 'Why, Mr Hugh! Did we know you were to arrive today?'

Hugh suspected there would be a scramble to make certain his room was ready. 'I didn't send word, I'm afraid. But do not fuss for me.'

'Oh, your mother would want your room properly prepared.' Mason peeked out the door. 'No luggage?'

Hugh lifted the satchel he'd carried with a change of clothing. 'My trunk is being shipped.' He stepped into the hall. 'Is my mother at home?'

Mason took the satchel from Hugh's hand. 'I believe she and General Hensen are in the drawing room.'

The ever-present General Hensen, his mother's lover. 'I'll go in and let her know I'm home.'

He glanced around the hall, at the portraits that hung on the walls and thought of a smaller, wainscoted hall he'd known only by feel until yesterday. He walked to his mother's drawing room, gave a quick knock and entered the room.

His mother and the general were seated together on a sofa, looking into a kaleidoscope. Both looked up.

'Hugh!' His mother's face lit up in a smile and, to his surprise, Hugh felt uncommonly glad to see her. She might act the tyrant at times, but, to be fair to her, it was always on behalf of her children.

General Hensen helped her to her feet. 'How nice this is, eh, Honoria?'

His mother hurried over to him and waited for his kiss on the cheek. 'Mother. General. Yes, here I am, back from Brussels.'

The general shook his hand. 'It is good you are back, safe and sound.'

'I am so glad to see you, but you look a fright.' His mother touched his face. 'What happened here?' Of course she would notice the burn marks.

He shrugged away from her touch. 'Nothing of consequence. Some cinders blew in my face.'

She pursed her lips. 'You ought to be more careful, Hugh. Fire is nothing to trifle with.'

As well he knew. He'd run into an inferno after all.

The general chuckled. 'Now, Honoria. He is not two years old. Hugh is a man who has fought in war.'

Hugh wanted to dislike a man who took his mother to bed, but Hensen was a decent sort and good to her. Hugh laughed at himself. He was not unlike Hensen. He'd been bedding a widow, too.

If she'd really been a widow. She might have lied about that, too.

He stepped away from his mother and looked down at himself. His clothes were damp and mud splattered. 'You are quite right, Mama. I am not fit for company at the present moment. I merely wanted to inform you of my arrival.' *And to see you,* he thought, *because I feared I might never see you again.* 'I must change out of these clothes.'

'Yes, do,' His mother settled back in her chair.

He bowed and turned to the door.

His mother's voice followed him. 'So fortunate you have come today. We have a family dinner tonight.'

A family dinner? He'd hoped to have a day or two in

relative peace, if peace and his mother could coexist in the same house.

He turned back to her. 'Who is coming?'

She beamed. 'All of them!'

Hugh washed off the dirt of the road and unpacked clean clothes to wear, but his eyes ached so much all he wanted to do was close them. Clad only in his drawers, he lay on the bed. Best he rest his eyes for a few moments. Wynne had told him not to exert himself.

Next thing he knew, Higgley, his mother's footman, knocked on the door. 'Almost dinnertime,' Higgley said. 'Your mother sent me up here to assist you.'

Hugh groaned as he sat up. 'I must have fallen asleep.' Not that it had helped his eyes. They still ached.

Higgley went straight to the clothing he'd laid out. He handed Hugh a shirt.

'Tell me what is happening in the family, Higgley.' Hugh pulled his arms through the sleeves. 'Anything I should know?'

Hugh had grown up with Higgley. They were nearly the same age and had played together as boys. Since Higgley had come to work for the Westleighs, he and Hugh had a bargain. Higgley would tell Hugh whatever family secrets he discovered and Hugh would never betray him for it. Plus he always found a way to slip Higgley a few extra coins or see he received a special privilege or two.

The footman brushed off Hugh's waistcoat. 'Nothing of consequence, to my knowledge. General Hensen is here much of the time, but I am certain that is no surprise to you.'

It was certainly no surprise.

'What about my brother and his wife? What news of them?' Hugh buttoned his breeches.

'The earl is very busy, of course, it being his first year in the Lords. The countess is finally increasing, which is a good thing, because your mother was becoming impatient. I take it the countess was none too happy that your sister and Mrs Rhysdale bore children and she hadn't.' Higgley enjoyed talking about the family.

He was like Toller in that way. Hugh thought he might miss Toller. He'd missed Higgley, he realised. He'd missed the comfort of home.

'How are your parents?' Hugh asked. Higgley's parents had also worked for the family. They'd been pensioned off some years ago and lived in a small house near the village. They would have been among the many people connected to the Westleigh estate who would have suffered if Hugh and Ned had not found a way to restore the family fortune.

'Doing very well,' Higgley answered. 'My mother thinks her flower bed the equal of any around Westleigh House and my father claims to have the best kitchen garden in the county.'

Hugh asked about other members of Higgley's family while Hugh buttoned his waistcoat and was helped into his coat. The familiarity of it soothed him. He allowed Higgley to tie his neckcloth, although it was something he usually did for himself. After he finished dressing, Hugh ran a brush through his hair and put on his shoes.

He left his bedchamber and descended the stairs. A memory flashed of the fiery staircase at the inn, of carrying Daphne to safety. He closed his eyes and compared walking down these steps to descending the stairs at the cottage in Thurnfield.

He opened his eyes. Forget this!

The sound of laughter came from the drawing room. The family had gathered, obviously. Hugh forgot his desire to be alone and his wish to rest. He hurried to enter the room.

'Hugh!' His brother Ned saw him first and immediately strode over to shake his hand. Ned's brow was etched with lines and he looked weary, as if assuming the family title had automatically aged him.

Before Hugh could get out even a word of greeting to Ned, his sister, Phillipa, rushed over with a huge smile and sparkling eyes. Her scar still marked her face, but it had not been the first thing he'd noticed about her. The first thing he'd noticed had been her happiness.

'Phillipa, you look beautiful,' he exclaimed. It must be the first time he'd ever said those words to her. He kissed her cheek, the cheek with the scar, and then simply gave her a hug. 'Beautiful.'

She laughed.

Her husband, Xavier, a longtime family friend, stood behind her. 'Motherhood agrees with her, does it not?'

Yes. She was all softness and womanliness, no longer the little girl he used to ignore.

He released her and shook her husband's hand. 'Xavier. Good to see you.'

'You must call on us soon,' Xavier said. 'And meet our little girl. She is the image of your sister.' The man was nearly bursting with pride.

'I will. I will.' He could spare enough time to visit his sister before travelling.

Hugh spied his half-brother, Rhys, and his wife, Celia, holding back. The next person he must greet was Ned's wife, Adele, who happened to also be Celia's stepdaughter. Protocol demanded he greet a countess before his bastard brother. 'Adele, you look lovely, as well.'

She giggled at the compliment, her blonde curls bobbing. To his surprise, a wave of fondness for her washed over him. He could forgive her for being a silly chit. She was young, perhaps not yet twenty. Besides, she adored his brother. Even now she gazed at Ned as if he were Zeus.

Had his week with Daphne turned him sentimental? Or had it been her abandonment that made it so comforting to be in the company of people who cared about him?

Hugh took both Adele's hands in his and stepped back to give her an approving look. 'You look different somehow. A lovely difference.' He knew the reason, thanks to Higgley.

She blushed and leaned forwards conspiratorially. 'That is because I am increasing. We are going to have a baby!'

'Is that not delightful news?' His mother's voice reached from several feet away. Stood to reason she'd heard everything. Nothing got past her.

Even that filled him with tenderness. 'Delightful, indeed.' He squeezed both Adele's hands and smiled. 'Very wonderful news. I am as happy as I can be for you.'

He meant it. Having a child would mean a great deal to Adele.

Once he'd imagined that Daphne had to give up a child—but then, he'd been mistaken in everything about her, why not that, as well?

He mentally shook himself again and kissed Adele on the cheek before releasing her to her husband. Ned put his arm around her. Their mother called the two over to where she was conversing with the general, and dutiful son Ned immediately went over to see what their mother wanted.

Hugh crossed the room to greet Rhys and Celia. 'Rhys.' He extended his hand.

Rhys shook it. 'Hugh.'

Theirs was an uneasy relationship, entirely Hugh's fault. As a boy Hugh had hated to think of his father siring a bastard son, betraying his mother like that. Hugh had taken it out on Rhys. He'd been monstrous, picking fights with Rhys every time he saw him. Now his admiration for his base-born brother was vast. As he'd told Daphne.

Blast! Why did everything remind him of her?

He turned to Rhys's wife, Celia, who had once been a baron's widow. He gave her a kiss on the cheek. 'How is my third sister faring?'

She returned a mocking look. 'I am waiting for my compliment.'

He tilted his head, not certain he'd heard her correctly.

She laughed. 'Well, Phillipa is beautiful. Adele is lovely—both of which are true, but where is my compliment?'

He pretended to eye her from head to toe. She was not the fashion in beauty. Too tall. Too thin. But her features shone with intelligence. She was the sort of woman who became more beautiful the longer you spent with her. In fact, she'd once been the sort of woman of whom one took little notice, but no longer. Love had transformed her.

'You are peerless,' he said.

She laughed again and threaded her arm through her husband's. 'That will do nicely.'

Hugh smiled back and turned to survey all his family. His eyes pained him, his muscles felt fatigued from riding half the day and the ache inside him persisted as his emotions continued to wage war. His anger was as raw as seared flesh, such a contrast to the loving joy surrounding him, the joy he'd briefly thought within his grasp, the joy that had evaporated like a mist.

His family was faring well. That helped ease his discontent.

Conversation at dinner covered discussion of children, Parliament, the Masquerade Club, Rhys's steam-engine factories and Xavier's shops. Ned and their mother wanted to hear details of the disentangling of their father's affairs in Brussels, what Hugh had done and how much he'd needed to spend. No one asked Hugh about his own affairs. They rarely did, he suddenly realised, but this evening he was grateful. This evening he did not wish to speak of his own affairs—his brief liaison with Daphne.

Dessert was served. Baskets of cakes, bowls of fruit and, most distracting to Hugh, dishes of marzipan. Mason and Higgley poured champagne. When they were finished, General Hensen stood.

He held his glass of champagne. 'Your mother and I have an announcement.'

Conversation ceased.

He gazed down at her and reached for her hand. 'I want you all to know that your mother has made me the happiest man on earth. She has consented to marry me.'

'Ooooh.' Adele clapped her hands in delight. 'That is such happy news.'

Ned frowned. 'When do you plan to marry? A year has not yet gone by. You must not marry before waiting the full year of mourning, Mama. The family must not be subjected to more scandal.' Ned was the arbiter of everything correct in the family. In that sense he was the direct opposite of their father.

None the less, their mother tossed Ned an annoyed look. 'Of course we will wait a year. We decided to announce our betrothal now, though, so we may be seen together without talk.'

Hugh suspected there had already been plenty of talk, but why not seize happiness when it was offered? 'If this makes you happy, Mother, it is good news,' he told her.

She gave Hensen a loving look. 'It makes me very happy.'

'I propose a toast.' Hensen raised his glass. 'To your mother. May she never regret saying yes. May I succeed in making her every day happy.'

Congratulations and good wishes broke out from everyone. They'd always been united in support of their mother's happiness—unless she was telling them how to live. She'd been appalling to Phillipa in that regard. Cruel, even. Amazing that Phillipa appeared to have forgiven her.

They ate cakes and drank champagne and soon the ladies retired to the drawing room. Hensen went with them. Mason poured brandy for Hugh, Ned and Rhys. Higgley removed the baskets of cake, but left the fruit and marzipan.

Hugh took two pieces of marzipan, one shaped like a strawberry, the other like a pear, and rolled them in his fingers. The scent of the confection and of the brandy brought him back to the cottage drawing room and evenings he and Daphne had shared.

Damnation! Could he never stop thinking of her?

'I am glad we are all here.' Rhys's voice broke Hugh's reverie. 'Because I want to discuss the Masquerade Club. I must give it up. You see, I need to spend too much time at the factories now. I've asked Xavier to take it over, but he cannot.'

'I wish I could assist you.' Xavier looked regretful. 'Time simply won't permit.' He was too busy investing in shops and employing out-of-work soldiers.

'This cannot be.' Ned's eyes darted around in panic. 'We cannot give it up now. We still need the revenue. We are not yet on firm footing. One bad crop and we'll be under again.'

Rhys shook his head. 'I cannot run the place any longer. I simply cannot. As it is now I never see Celia or the children.'

'I cannot do it.' Ned's voice grew strident. 'Not only

would it be unseemly for a peer to run a gaming house, but I am already buried in estate matters and Parliament. And now with the baby coming—' He broke off and turned his gaze on Hugh. 'You must do it, Hugh.'

'Oh, no. Not me.' Hugh put up a hand. He'd already devoted the years since the war to family needs. 'I have other plans.'

'What plans?' Ned demanded. 'What could be more important than preserving the family fortune and ensuring the well-being of our people?'

Put that way, travel seemed a petty ambition.

'You must help us. There is no one else.' Ned shifted in his chair.

'You know enough about the business now,' Xavier added. 'It will not be difficult.'

'You may always consult me,' Rhys added. 'I certainly can be available to advise you on the running of the place.'

'And if Rhys is out of town, I will assist you,' Xavier added. 'I can do that much.'

'You must do it, Hugh,' Ned insisted, his legs shaking nervously. 'You are the only one of us at liberty to take it on.'

'But—' Hugh began.

Ned cut him off. 'Meet with me tomorrow and I'll show you the ledgers. We cannot abandon the club now, not when solvency remains at stake. I'll prove to you how our situation stands. Our father's latest business in Brussels managed to cost us a great deal, as you well know. It has put stress on the finances.' His voice turned despairing. 'You must do this, Hugh.'

Hugh closed his eyes and sipped his brandy, but that only brought him back to peaceful evenings in the cottage with Daphne. He blinked and scanned the three pairs of eyes anxiously staring at him.

What was the use? He would be unhappy on his travels, thinking he'd abandoned his family in their time of need. He certainly knew the pain of being abandoned. Besides, what did any of it matter? He might as well be unhappy in London. He might as well make his family happy, even if he could not be.

He blinked again and sipped more brandy. 'Very well. I will do it.'

Chapter Thirteen

Daphne stared at the calendar and realised it had been exactly one month since she'd left Hugh. It was remarkable to think so much time had passed and she'd managed to endure it without falling into complete despair.

She thought of him much too often. Wondering where he was. On some ship bound for a distant shore? Or in a carriage on the Continent on a more tried and true course? Would he travel through the valley in Switzerland? Would he pass by the whitewashed walls of Fahr Abbey?

Wherever he was, she wished him happy. She hoped he had forgotten her.

She pulled up the sleeve of her robe and tapped her finger on the desk. Sitting in her bedchamber sipping a cup of chocolate, not yet dressed, she reviewed her list for the day. She'd begun creating lists of tasks to accomplish each day. It helped to make her busy. If she did not fill her day with several things she must accomplish, she was at the mercy of that ever-lurking despair.

'Good advice, my dear, dear abbess,' she said aloud. The abbess had often told her that busy hands were happy hands. *Happy* was too much to hope for in Daphne's case. Daphne no longer aspired to happiness.

Instead, she resolved to do good works, starting with her own property. Her husband had left her this small estate in Vadley in lieu of a dower house. When he died and his second cousin's son had inherited Faville House, she'd come here to wait out her grieving period before searching for Xavier. This estate had not been home then, but now she was determined to make it so.

The day after she arrived in Vadley, she'd sent for Mr Quigg, the estate manager, and asked him to take her on a tour. She wanted to meet all her tenants and employees and learn their names, like Hugh had said of his mother, Lady Westleigh.

To her shock, she'd found tenant cottages in need of repair, hungry children and struggling people. Her husband's financial arrangements for this estate had not accounted for the current difficult economic times. Or perhaps that had been her fault. She'd been the one responsible since her husband's death. In any event, not enough money had been allotted for the tenants and workers to live comfortably and to have enough food for their children. The bank that managed his money, now hers, had ignored the manager's request for more revenue. Had she ignored the man, as well?

Stinging with still more guilt, Daphne had immediately sent a letter to the bank, via her man of business, approving the funds.

The money was released and improvements were underway, but her man of business was travelling to Vadley to discuss the matter with her. He was expected to arrive today.

Dear Mr Everard. He'd been so devoted and she had taken such advantage of him. He'd escorted her to the Masquerade Club almost every night when she'd been in pursuit of Xavier. She dreaded his arrival. Seeing him again would remind her of how badly she'd behaved.

To think, if she'd not behaved so badly, she and Hugh might have remained together. She dropped her head into her hands.

But then they would not have met.

Trust God's plan, the abbess had told her. Many times.

There was a knock on the door and Monette entered. 'Good morning, my lady. Are you ready to dress?'

Daphne stood. 'I suppose I had better do so.'

Monette brought her a blue-madras day dress and helped her into it. When Monette stood in front of Daphne to straighten out the skirt, Daphne noticed her eyes were red. 'Monette! Have you been weeping?'

Fat tears immediately brimmed on the young woman's lids. 'Perhaps a little, my lady.'

Daphne felt her own tears, the ones that were never far from the surface, sting her eyes. 'Whatever is distressing you, Monette? You must tell me.'

Monette wiped her eyes with her apron. 'I—I am missing someone. That is all.'

The young woman had changed her whole life. Daphne could understand that it would be sometimes difficult. 'You are missing Fahr? Some of the nuns in the Abbey? I miss them, too.'

Monette shook her head. 'It is not the nuns—I mean—I do miss them, but I did not want to be there. It does not make me cry to not see them.'

'Who, then?' Had there been someone in Switzerland who'd been important to her?

'I—I am homesick for the cottage. The people there. I liked it there.' She stifled a sob.

'I liked it there, too,' Daphne said, her voice low, the ache inside her growing.

Monette gestured for Daphne to sit at the dressing table. She stood behind Daphne and combed out her hair. 'How do you endure being away from Mr Westleigh? I mean—I know—you—you—were lovers. How did you bear leaving him?'

The dagger always in Daphne's heart twisted. 'I told you that I had to leave. He could not know who I was.'

'I know, but you did not wish to leave him, did you?' Monette arranged Daphne's hair into a simple knot.

'No.' Daphne's throat tightened. 'I did not wish to leave him. I had to. It was for the best.'

Monette stuck pins in her hair.

Daphne glanced up at Monette's reflection in the mirror. 'But you are not weeping for Mr Westleigh.'

The maid coloured. 'No.' She stepped back, her head bowed. 'It is Toller I miss the most.'

'Toller?' Daphne had had no idea.

'We became friends.' Monette glanced up at her. 'Remember when we went to the village together and I asked you about women and men?'

'I remember.' She'd thought Monette, who'd grown up amongst celibate women, had been trying to figure out Daphne's relationship with Hugh.

'I was talking about Toller. I liked him very much, but in a different way than I liked Mary and Ann.'

'I see.' She understood that *different* way only too well.

'And I miss him!' Monette burst into tears.

Daphne left her chair and held the maid in her arms, like the abbess had once held her. What else did she know of comforting? 'There, there.' She felt as if Monette's pain were hers. It was all she could do to keep from weeping herself.

'I wish Toller were here!' Monette wailed.

'I could send for him.' The words were out of her mouth

before she even thought of them. 'I could send a letter to Thurnfield and ask if he would like to come work for me here. Would you like that?'

Monette pulled away, a huge smile on her face. 'Oh, yes!'

Daphne walked over to her bureau and pulled out a handkerchief. She handed it to Monette. 'I will write the letter this very day.'

Daphne finished the letter to Toller, posting it in care of Mr Brill, the leasing agent in Thurnfield, who she knew would put it into the young man's hands.

She soon heard a carriage. No doubt Everard had arrived.

She stood and straightened her spine. She could face him, this man she'd so misused. If she could face the pain of leaving Hugh, she could face anything.

Carter soon announced him and Everard walked in the drawing room.

'My lady.' His voice cracked. 'It—it is a privilege to call on you.'

She extended her hand to him. 'Everard. I am delighted to see you.' It was not precisely true, but she'd not forgotten how to sound sincere.

He took her hand and merely squeezed her fingers.

Carter waited at the door.

'Would you bring some tea, Carter?' She turned to Everard. 'Or do you wish to rest from your journey?'

'I would be grateful for tea,' he replied. 'I will rest later at the inn.'

'The inn?' She signalled Carter to bring the tea. 'I will not hear of it. You must stay here. I have a room ready for you.'

'Here?' Everard looked about, as if the drawing room

were where he would be sleeping. 'I do not wish to put you to any trouble on my behalf.'

'Nonsense!' she retorted. 'You will be no trouble and it will make conducting our business so much easier.'

'Very well.' He bowed. 'I do thank you.'

She asked questions about his health and he asked about hers and she wondered when he would start to scold her for lavishing so much of her capital on improvements for the tenants and the workers.

He waited until they settled down with tea. 'As you know, there was great concern about your decision to deplete your capital.'

'I hardly depleted it,' she countered.

'Forgive me.' He inclined his head. 'An unfortunate choice of words. Diminish, I meant. I fear you might not comprehend how these matters work. Once you spend the capital, you cannot get it back. It is best to leave the capital in the four per cents and other investments and live on the income.'

'I do understand, Everard.' She continued to use her charming voice. 'But a great deal of money was required, and I still have plenty in the investments, do I not? One would still call me a wealthy widow, would they not?'

'You do have plenty of capital,' he admitted. 'But it is imperative that you do not pull it out for frivolous spending.'

'For improvements to the farm buildings?' She made herself laugh. 'Is property not the best investment?' She smiled and looked directly into his eyes. 'My husband always said so.'

He blushed and noisily stirred his tea. 'You know I dislike countering your judgement in any way, my dear lady, but after your husband died, I pledged to make certain your welfare was protected in all ways.'

It was her turn to feel the heat of shame tinge her cheeks. The man was devoted to her. It was why he'd agreed to accompany her to the Masquerade Club. It had not occurred to her that he would see her purpose in any manner different than her own. She'd assumed she and Xavier should be together because they made such a pretty-looking couple. Everard must have thought her foolish and frivolous, and she had behaved shabbily by making the poor man come with her night after night. She'd never considered that he must have had to work during the day.

She lowered her gaze and dropped her charming voice. 'I am very grateful to you for it.'

He pulled at his neckcloth. 'As you can imagine, I was quite concerned about your travel to the Continent and your—your extended stay in Switzerland—'

He'd known she'd stayed in a convent. He had written concerned letters to her to return to society, as well as letters pertaining to business, of course. She'd written back, assuring him that she was doing well and trusting him to take care of matters in her absence. He'd been the only person with whom she'd corresponded.

'My stay in Switzerland was good for me,' she told him.

He looked embarrassed again. 'I have no doubt...' He quickly drank some tea.

She handed him a plate of biscuits. 'If you are up to it after our tea, I will have Mr Quigg, my estate manager, take you on a tour of the property and show you where the money is being spent, then we can discuss the matter further.'

She knew he would not refuse. Everard never refused anything she asked of him.

Daphne did not see Everard again until dinner.

After the soup was served, she asked in her charming

tone, 'So what did you think of how my money is being spent?'

He slurped soup from his spoon before answering, 'I cannot argue with what you have done except to say you might have been a bit extravagant.'

She lifted a disapproving brow. 'Oh?'

He sputtered. 'I mean—I confess to being surprised at your exceptional generosity to your workers and tenants. You might have confined your spending to essential re-pairs only, and you need not have lowered the rents and increased the salaries.'

In other words, he valued money over the comfort of those people on whom the prosperity of the estate de-pended. Once she might have agreed—or, rather, she would not have given the people one moment of thought.

She dipped her spoon into her soup. 'What did Mr Quigg say about it?'

He lifted his shoulders. 'He spoke with ebullience about all that you have done, saying it was a long time coming.' He frowned. 'But I must be concerned for your welfare. You must not give your fortune away.'

Why not? So far, being generous had helped her feel she'd atoned for her selfishness. She'd never experienced that sort of satisfaction purchasing jewels or clothing or any such thing. And he had never scolded her for throw-ing away her money at the gaming tables of the Masquer-ade Club.

But to argue this point with Everard would certainly distress him. Discussing the Masquerade Club would dis-tress her.

She favoured him with one of her most amiable smiles. 'If you will but indulge me these whims from time to time, I promise you, I will trust you to warn me if I ever spend too much.'

He flushed. 'I am ever your faithful servant.'

Carter and a footman—named Finn, Daphne had learned—served the next course and she and Everard spoke in more detail about the improvements. Everard did not presume to do anything but praise the work she had approved, and the time passed more pleasantly.

When the apple tart was served and more wine poured and the conversation about the estate exhausted, Daphne groped for other topics to discuss. 'What of you, Mr Everard? Tell me how you are faring. What is happening in your life?'

'Me?' He flushed again. 'I am doing well enough. Business is tolerably good.'

'I am delighted to hear it.' She'd not thought of it before. He must have other clients to assist. She knew very little of him, she realised. 'And—and do you have family? I suddenly am aware that I do not know. I am sorry for never asking before.'

His eyes widened in surprise. 'Why should you ask, my lady?' He sipped his wine. 'But, as a matter of fact, I have taken a wife in this last year.'

'You are married?' She loved the idea that this sweet man might have found the happiness that escaped her. 'How wonderful for you! Tell me about your wife.'

He answered in a serious tone. 'She comes from a good family. Her father is in banking and that is how we met.'

'No,' she scolded. 'Tell me about *her*! Is she pretty? Is she accomplished?' Goodness. Those were Daphne's own qualities. They might have made her a desirable wife, if not a very good person.

He lifted his gaze to her. 'She is not beautiful like you.'

Oh, dear. Certainly she did not intend to go in that direction.

She waved a dismissive hand. 'But is she pretty?'

*Do you love her? Do you love her as I have loved Hugh,
with every inch of your body and soul?*

He glanced away. 'I think her very handsome and sensible.'

Poor Mrs Everard.

She made herself smile again. 'I am very happy for you.'

In fact, she should give him a raise in salary. If he was
supporting a wife now, he could use a raise. That idea comforted her. It was another good deed she could perform.

But she feared being taken into further confidence about
Everard's marriage, since he described his wife as handsome and sensible. 'Tell me news of London,' she asked
instead.

To her surprise, his countenance became very serious.
'I quite understand.'

He understood she wished to change the subject? Why
this intensity?

'I do not know very much, you understand, merely what
I have heard people say and what has been written in the
newspapers.' He drained the remainder of his wine down
his throat.

Goodness. She was merely hoping for general gossip
or what debates were consuming Parliament or what was
being performed at the Royal Opera House.

Carter and Finn removed their dishes and put a fresh
cloth on the table. Fruit and biscuits appeared and port
wine was poured.

Everard continued after the food was served. 'The
gentleman of whom you wish I would speak—' did he
mean Xavier? No, she did not wish him to speak of Xavier
'—did marry the Earl of Westleigh's daughter—'

'Yes, I knew this,' she broke in.

His brows rose. 'He no longer runs the club. Did you
know that? Rhysdale returned to run it. People say your

gentleman has turned into a shop owner, but I do not know the truth of that.'

She had no right to care what Xavier did. She had no right to even speak of him. 'I—I gather the Masquerade Club was repaired at my expense?'

'Oh, yes.' He chewed on a biscuit. 'It is as prosperous as ever, they say, although the masked *pianiste* does not play there anymore.'

Of course not. She was married and bore a child.

'That is excellent,' she said too brightly.

'Although I read just the other week that the new Lord Westleigh's younger brother has taken over the managing of the club. Apparently the Westleighs were partners in the enterprise all along.'

Daphne felt as if the air had been knocked out of her lungs. 'Younger brother?' she managed. Her heart beat faster.

Hugh!

He nodded and took a sip of port. 'The old Lord Westleigh, the scandalous one, died suddenly and his older son inherited. Did you know of that?'

With difficulty she kept a pleasant expression on her face. 'Yes. I heard of that.'

He prattled on. 'So when I said the new Lord Westleigh, I meant the older son. The younger son recently returned from the Continent. Their father left his affairs in a terrible mess and the younger son was sent to settle them.' He picked up another biscuit. 'So when I said younger brother, I meant it is Hugh Westleigh who now manages the Masquerade Club.'

Hugh.

Her mind raced the whole evening, thinking of him. She barely made it through tea in the drawing room after dinner and was relieved to be free of the obligation to make conversation when she noticed Mr Everard tiring.

'Dear Mr Everard.' She could at least hide her swirl of emotions behind charm. 'I hope you will forgive me. I am greatly fatigued and would beg you excuse me for the night.'

The relief on his face was immediate. 'Yes. Yes. I will retire, as well. I must head back to London in the morning.' He stood and offered his hand to help her stand.

She accepted it, but kept her distance from him as they walked out of the drawing room into the hall.

When he reached the stairs, she stepped back. 'I must speak with my housekeeper for a minute, so I will bid you goodnight here.' It was not true, of course.

He looked relieved again. 'Goodnight, my lady.' He spoke formally and bowed correctly. That reassured her.

'Goodnight, sir.' She released a breath and turned to the door of the servants' wing, but did not open it. Instead, she leaned against the wall and waited, listening to his footsteps recede as he mounted the stairs.

Hugh.

She was free to think of him again.

Tears stung her eyes. *Hugh, you are not blind!* He could not be blind. If he was blind, how would he be able to manage a gaming house where the job was to watch everything and everyone? *But why are you not on some exciting voyage somewhere?* What happened to change his plans?

She closed her eyes and remembered the Masquerade Club. She imagined him there walking through the rooms like Xavier had done, speaking to the patrons, watching everything. He would look magnificent in formal clothes, circulating among guests both masked and unmasked. She could not imagine his face precisely. She could only remember him bandaged.

If she saw him she would know him, though. She'd recognised him during the fire after all. But she longed to gaze at him at length, see every detail, discover the colour of his eyes, reassure herself that he was indeed as strong and robust as she remembered. If she only had a chance to memorise all of him, she'd hold that memory for the rest of her days.

Her heart started pounding. The Masquerade Club was the one place she could see him! It was perhaps the only place she could see him.

At the Masquerade Club she could wear a mask. Nobody would know her.

It felt like her heart would burst, she was so excited. She opened the door and hurried down the servants' staircase in search of Carter.

Mr Everard would have company on the road to London.

The next morning Daphne made certain she was at breakfast with Mr Everard.

When he entered the breakfast room, set up in a sunny sitting room not far from the formal dining room, he looked pleased. 'My lady, I did not expect to see you about so early.'

She smiled at him. 'I wanted to be certain to see you first thing.'

The man blushed.

She went on. 'You see, I have decided to go to London, as well. Just for a few days. So you do not have to take the public coach. You may ride with my maid and me.'

His brows rose. 'You are travelling to London? This is sudden.'

'Indeed, it is very impulsive, I admit.' She fluttered her eyes. 'Please choose your food. I hope Cook has prepared something you will like.'

He filled his plate from the sideboard and sat in a chair across from hers. 'Please do not feel compelled to time your travel around my need. I do not mind the public coach.'

She nibbled on a piece of toasted bread and raspberry jam. 'It is no trouble to me at all.'

The footman Finn attended them and poured Everard a cup of hot tea.

He nodded his thanks and turned to Daphne again. 'If I travel ahead of you, I can make certain your house is ready to receive you.'

'It is not necessary,' she assured him. 'I have already dispatched a messenger. We will not require much on arrival.'

He frowned. 'My lady, why the urgency to visit London?'

'No urgency.' Except she could not bear to wait. She was convinced that seeing Hugh vital, fit and sighted would finally settle the unrest inside her. 'I—I merely discovered that I had a great desire to visit London after hearing you speak of it and it seemed silly to send you in a public coach when we could use my carriage.'

His gaze turned sceptical. 'My lady, may I speak with frankness?'

She was certain she did not wish to hear this, but she nodded. 'Of course.'

'Did my speaking of—of that certain gentleman in London precipitate this decision?' His voice was concerned. 'Because I must advise you not to attempt a meeting with him.'

A certain gentleman, yes. But not Xavier. 'Not at all, Mr Everard. I have no plans to attempt a meeting with him.' In fact, if she thought he would be in attendance at the gaming house, she would hesitate to go there, even masked. He'd recognise her at once, even with a mask.

There was a knock on the door and Monette entered, looking very distressed. 'Forgive the interruption, my lady, but I cannot find the masks you wished me to pack. They were not in the drawer in your wardrobe.'

Monette's timing was unfortunate. Daphne had not intended to inform Everard of her plans to visit the Masquerade Club. 'Perhaps the masks are in a trunk. Have one of the maids show you where the trunks are stored, but do not fuss too much. We can purchase what we need in London.' Her old masks would need to be altered anyway. She wanted her whole face covered so that there was no chance anyone would recognise her.

'Yes, m'lady.' Monette curtsied and left the room again.

Mr Everard gaped at Daphne. 'You cannot mean to attend the Masquerade Club!'

'Do not fret, Everard,' she said in her charming voice. 'I wish only to make certain all the repairs were made and that the rooms are restored to their previous condition.'

'I would be honoured to perform that task for you,' he said. 'You were asked not to return to the club, if you recall.'

'I know.' How mortifying to be forbidden to return to a place because of your bad behaviour. 'That is why I plan to be well masked. I wish only to see what I would come to see.' Hugh. She would come to see Hugh.

'I cannot dissuade you?' he asked in a hopeless tone.

She returned a most pleasing smile. 'Please do not worry over me. I promise I will be on my best behaviour.'

He sighed. 'Then I will accompany you, of course.'

She did not want him there! 'You certainly will not!' Her voice turned sharp. She softened it. 'If you come with me, we are almost certain to be recognised. You must not come.'

'I cannot allow you to attend there alone,' he insisted.

She waved a hand. 'I will make other arrangements. A servant can come with me.'

Two hours later they were ready to depart. The carriage waited in front of the house, Smith at the reins and a stable boy seated at his side. Carter would ride on top of the carriage with them. Everard, Monette and Daphne would ride inside.

Monette was last to leave the house, looking as if she was bound for the gallows rather than taking what ought to be an exciting trip for her.

Daphne took a basket of food from Monette's hand. 'Goodness, Monette. Do not worry so. We can purchase anything we forgot. One can purchase anything in London.'

'It is not that, my lady,' her maid said in mournful tones. 'It is about Toller. We won't be here if he sends a letter.'

She patted the girl's arm. 'I wrote to Toller when I wrote to the housekeeper in London. I asked him to contact us there.'

Monette looked only a little more hopeful.

Daphne leaned closer to her. 'I promise we will not leave London until we hear from Toller. Will that please you?'

The maid burst into a smile. 'Very much, my lady!'

Carter helped Daphne and Monette into the carriage. Everard entered last, and soon they were on their way. Everard took the rear-facing seat. Monette shared the other seat with Daphne. As soon as they were on the road, Daphne closed her eyes and leaned her head against the deep red velvet upholstery of the seat. The trip would take seven hours at the most. They would reach London in daylight, but she'd be exhausted by the time they arrived at the London town house her husband had left her. She must wait until tomorrow night to go to the Masquerade Club.

And then she would see Hugh.

Chapter Fourteen

Daphne stood at the door of the Masquerade Club, her heart in her throat. Carter accompanied her, and she'd arranged for Smith to pick them up in the carriage in two hours.

Two hours. Too brief a time to see Hugh again, but she dared not risk much more lest she call too much attention to herself. She'd chosen her most demure dress, in deep blue, and a black mask. She and Monette had added black satin to the mask, covering almost her whole face, just to be certain she would be unrecognisable. Carter was also masked and seemed perfectly comfortable with the idea of visiting a gaming house.

But that was something to enquire about another time.

Carter sounded the knocker and the door opened. The footman attending the door was the same man who had been there two years before. Cummings. She must remember not to call him by name.

'We have come to gamble,' she told him. 'May we come in?'

Cummings nodded and stepped aside. Carter took off his hat and gloves as if he were a proper gentleman and handed them to Cummings.

Daphne removed her cloak. 'What do we do next?'

Cummings peered at her, too closely, she felt. 'See the cashier.' He pointed to a door off the hall that was ajar.

She took Carter's arm and they walked together to the door and entered the room. The cashier was also the same man who had been there before. MacEvoy. He passed out mother-of-pearl gaming counters to a gentleman ahead of them.

The gentleman, an older man, glanced at Daphne, smiled and bowed. 'Good evening, ma'am.'

Another man she remembered.

'Sir Reginald at your service, ma'am.' The man's glance scanned her from head to toe. 'Do let me know if I may be of assistance to you.'

Daphne inclined her head. 'Thank you, sir.' She had no intention of asking anyone for assistance.

MacEvoy cleared his throat. 'Ma'am? Sir? Perhaps you have not been here before? Step up to the table and I will tell you how the house works.' He spoke quickly. 'Masked gamblers must not wager beyond the amount of counters they purchase or win. Masked gamblers are not permitted to sign vouchers. You may not incur debt to the house or to another patron unless you are unmasked and your identity verified. Each patron must know who borrowed from them and who owes them money. Is that clear to you?'

'It is.' Daphne had understood two years ago, as well.

Carter stepped forwards and purchased the counters for them. While he double-checked the number MacEvoy gave them, Daphne noticed MacEvoy staring at her.

'Are you certain you have never been here before?' he asked.

'Never,' Carter answered truthfully. 'Where is the gaming room?'

MacEvoy gestured with his hand. 'Right off the hall. Follow the sounds.'

They walked out of the room, and Daphne released a relieved breath. She'd obviously seemed familiar to Cummings and MacEvoy. She had been a frequent visitor during that summer two years ago and had made a spectacle of herself in so doing. Hugh had certainly seen her a few of those times. He and the others would have known her as Lady Faville then.

Carter handed her half the counters. 'I truly may gamble with these?' he asked, displaying his portion on his open palm.

'You may indeed,' Daphne answered. 'And keep the winnings. Enjoy yourself, Carter. There is no need for you to stay at my side. Just be ready to leave in two hours.'

'Yes, m'lady.'

They entered the gaming room and it was as if Daphne had never left. The card tables were still arranged throughout the room, filled with four people playing whist, or two concentrating on piquet. At the back of the room and along the side of one wall were the faro, hazard and *vingt-et-un* tables. All were crowded with gamblers. Most of the men did not wear masks, but many of the women did. The hum of their combined voices filled the room, along with the shuffling of cards and tossing of dice.

Daphne scanned the room. 'Do you see him?' she asked Carter.

Carter knew she'd come to see Hugh. He also surveyed the scene. 'I do not.'

What if Hugh was not here tonight? To come all this way and not see him would be agony.

'Go and gamble, Carter.' She shooed him off. 'I'll just take a turn around the room before playing a little hazard or something.'

Carter nodded and strode off.

Daphne strolled through the tables, trying not to look as though she was searching for one certain person. As she passed, both men and women took notice of her. Once it would have pleased her for heads to turn wherever she went, but tonight she wanted to blend into the walls. Carter quickly found a card game and began expertly shuffling the cards. He looked as if he was in his element.

She wandered over to the faro table, thinking she ought to make the appearance of gambling, as well. She glanced over to the croupier, a pretty young woman, who was about to start another round.

'Place your bets, ladies and gentlemen,' the croupier called out. Daphne remembered her name was Belinda. She'd handled the hazard table before.

Daphne placed two counters on number seven, the number of days she and Hugh had so intimately shared together.

Belinda popped a card from the faro box. 'Ten.' The first card was the losing one.

All the gamblers who had placed their counters on the number ten groaned as Belinda collected them for the house.

She popped out a second card from the box. This would be the winning one. 'Seven!'

Daphne smiled. Her lucky number.

She scooped up her winnings, but left two counters on number seven. There were three more sevens in the deck of cards after all. She might win more.

She glanced up at Belinda, but riveted her gaze on the man who'd come to stand next to the croupier.

Hugh!

Her insides fluttered with excitement. A face she'd only glanced at in her past now loomed more important than anything else. His looks were not perfection, but were ruggedly handsome. The shadow of dark beard made him look rakish. She stared at his eyes. Even from across the table she could see they were brown. Large brown eyes with thick brows above them. She nearly laughed in delight as his eyes darted here and there, watching the room even as he conversed with Belinda.

He could see!

She'd known he could see, of course, but witnessing it made it all seem real. Her purpose in coming here was satisfied.

If only it were enough. She yearned to touch him. Trace his brows with her thumb. Comb back his unruly dark locks with her fingers. Cup his face in her hands, like he'd once done to hers. It was impossible. She must be content with gazing upon him.

Belinda popped another card from the faro box. 'Seven!'

Daphne won again. All eyes, including Hugh's, swung her way as she collected her winnings, but his interest in her seemed impersonal. A few gentlemen placed counters on number seven and she let her original two counters ride. It truly did not matter to her if she won. In fact, she'd prefer losing, because losing would benefit the Westleighs and thereby benefit Hugh. Besides, her debt to the family could never be completely repaid after she'd almost burnt down this building and risked so many lives.

'Luck is with you, ma'am,' a voice at her elbow said. She turned to see Lord Sanvers standing next to her. Sanvers had been in the fire at Ramsgate. He'd spoken to her that night. He'd seen her tend to Hugh.

'Yes. Luck,' she responded, her heart pounding.

He could not possibly recognise her, could he?

She waited at the faro table until she lost her two counters and was happy to move away from the attention. She wandered over to a hazard table, keeping Hugh in sight. He'd not given her another glance, but Lord Sanvers followed her.

'I have not seen you here before, have I?' he asked. 'I am Lord Sanvers. Are you alone?'

What an impertinent question. 'I am not here alone, sir. Are you?' She'd intended to sound dampening, but her voice was too accustomed to being pleasing.

He flushed with pleasure. 'I am quite alone and would be grateful for company.'

'Oh, dear.' She was eager to shed him. 'I must look for my escort. If you will excuse me, sir?'

She hurried away, sorry to give up sight of Hugh. She'd retire to the supper room for a few moments. She did want to see it before leaving, as she'd told Everard, to make certain it had been restored to its former beauty. She left the room and climbed the stairs to the supper room.

As she crossed the threshold, she saw immediately that it remained very much in the style of the Brothers Adam. Pale walls. Decorative plasterwork. Phillipa Westleigh's pianoforte still stood in the same place. She could half-imagine the masked Phillipa seated on its bench, playing and singing and totally anonymous. Daphne had enjoyed listening to her perform.

A footman, another familiar face, approached her, carrying a tray. 'Some wine, ma'am?'

She took a glass and walked over to the buffet. It was on a table like this that the lamp had stood, the lamp that Daphne had thrown against the wall in a fit of temper. She closed her eyes and remembered the curtains aflame, spots of fire on the carpet, her skirts aflame.

She shuddered at the memory.

'Ah, there you are.' It was Sanvers again. 'May I help fix a plate for you?'

* * *

Hugh noticed Sanvers talking to the woman who'd won at faro. The woman walked off and Sanvers, the lecherous old roué, followed. Women patrons who were masked typically were not at the Masquerade Club for seduction, but to gamble. If this woman found the man's attentions unwelcome, she might not return to lose money another day. It was part of Hugh's job to see women guests were not so bothered.

Neither Sanvers nor the woman remained in the game room, and Hugh guessed the woman might have fled to the supper room. He walked up the stairs and entered the room, immediately spying the woman and Sanvers at the buffet. It was still difficult to tell if she was flattered by or objected to Sanvers' attentions.

He watched her draw away from the man, a sure sign his instincts had been correct. Hugh crossed the room to where two men and another woman also stood selecting food. Hugh approached casually, as if about to join them.

He overheard Sanvers. 'Would you do the honour of sharing my table, *madame*?'

Hugh caught a whiff of roses and froze. He closed his eyes and inhaled the scent again.

He heard her reply. 'It was kind of you to ask, sir, but no, I prefer to be alone.'

The scent. That voice.

'A lovely lady such as yourself ought not to be alone,' Sanvers persisted.

'Surely no harm will come to me here,' she retorted. 'And surely a gentleman such as yourself will respect a lady's wishes.'

There was no mistake. The one person he expected never to see was here.

Hugh opened his eyes. 'Pardon me, Sanvers.'

His limbs trembled as he stepped between Sanvers and the woman.

Her eyes widened.

Hugh seized her arm. 'I must speak with this lady.' Hugh pulled her away. 'Come with me.'

He did not even know by what name to call her. His grip was firm, but she did not attempt to pull away. Together they crossed the room and stepped into the hallway where they were alone.

It was only then she spoke. 'What is this, sir?' she demanded, using the governess voice he remembered so clearly.

He was not about to confront her there. 'Come upstairs.'

He held her arm while climbing the stairs that led to Rhys's private rooms. Hugh had moved into them when he took over the management of the house, an arrangement he preferred over living with his mother…and her lover.

He escorted her into the drawing room and shut the door.

'Who are you to treat a woman so?' she demanded.

'Come now, Daphne, or whatever your name is. You, at least, know who I am, which gives you an advantage. I demand to know what you are doing here.' He released her, but stood between her and the closed door.

'I came here to gamble. Is that not what one does at a gambling house?' She straightened her spine. 'You speak as if you think I should know you.'

Did she think he would fall for her protestation of innocence? 'Take off the mask, Daphne.' His whole body coursed with rage, but even so, his eyes ached to see her at last.

She folded her arms across her chest. 'No. I came to this club because I can wear a mask. I will not take it off for anyone. Not even you, sir.'

'Not even me?' He advanced on her and she backed away. 'So you admit knowing me?'

She retreated until he backed her against a wall. 'I admit nothing.'

He made a cage of his arms. 'What is your reason for coming here? Was it for more amusement at my expense? To watch me and believe yourself safe from my knowing who you were? Or was there some other plan? Had there always been some other plan?'

She seemed small and vulnerable next to him. Ironic that when his eyes were bandaged he'd been the one who'd depended upon her strength. He remembered holding her in his arms. He remembered exploring her with his touch. For a brief moment he closed his eyes again and felt her scent, her warmth, envelop him.

He opened them again to glare down at her.

'I—I merely wanted to—to attend here,' she rasped. 'No one was supposed to know.'

He leaned down to her, inches from her masked face, so close he felt her breath against his lips. 'There was much I was not supposed to know.'

'Leave it that way, Hugh,' she whispered. 'Please. Let me leave now and I promise you will never see or hear from me again.'

'Allow you to leave?' He shook his head. 'You want to walk out again without any explanation? Did what passed between us not give me the right to an explanation, at least? Or was that a lie, as well? Were you deceiving me then, when we were in bed together?'

Her gaze reached his. 'Not everything was a deception.' She glanced away. 'But it is best we leave it at that.'

Her eyes were the blue of cloudless spring day and her lips the pink of her rose scent. He longed to see all of her.

'Best for who?' he countered. 'Do not presume to know

what is best for me. Take off your mask. Show me your face and tell me who you really are. You owe me that.'

She pushed against his chest. 'No. Please let me go, Hugh!'

Her touch inflamed him. His arms encircled her and pressed her against him. She struggled only for a moment before melting against him. 'Hugh. Hugh.'

They remained in an embrace, clinging to each other as if clinging to a cliff. His arms slid down her back and he ground her against him, where he was instantly hard for her. He found her lips, demanding a taste of her, a taste for which he'd felt starved since she'd left him. His kiss was urgent and angry and full of need.

She gasped beneath this onslaught, but met him with matched intensity. Her hands cupped his face, holding him in the kiss as urgent sounds came from deep in her throat.

He wanted no barriers between them. No secrets. No deceptions. No cloth.

He reached up and pulled off her mask.

She let out a cry and pushed him away. He stared at her, his body still throbbing with desire for her, his breath still coming fast. The ache inside him shattered like shards of glass, slicing him to pieces.

He knew her! By God, he knew her!

He spat out her name. 'Lady Faville.'

There was no mistaking her. Smooth, alabaster skin with a natural blush to her cheeks. Full mouth. Huge blue eyes fringed with long dark lashes. Hair the colour of spun gold. Tantalising curves. Anyone in London would know her. She knew he'd know her.

Could her deception be any crueller? This was a thousand times worse than being played for a fool. She'd known the connection between them from the start.

How had she dared hide her identity from him, knowing all the while it would matter to him? His mortification at her hands was complete.

Blast! Now even the memory of their time together was tainted. He could not even cling to a delusion that being with him had meant anything to her. He lost her all over again.

This time he lost the illusion of her.

Daphne felt tears sting her eyes and she ached with anguish. 'I told you. I told you it would be better to leave my mask in place.'

The mask was still in his hand. She snatched it away, but did not attempt to put it back on. What was the use now?

'All this while.' He laughed drily. 'Lady Faville.' He said her name like a curse.

She waved a hand and put more space between them. 'I comprehend. I was forbidden to come here. I will not come again.'

He continued to glare at her.

She lifted her chin. 'I assure you I will not burn this place down, if that is your fear. In fact, I will leave now so you will know I can do no harm.' She started for the door.

He seized her arm. 'You are not leaving yet. Do no harm, you say.' His face was stiff with anger. 'You have already done harm—more than enough.' He tightened his grip. 'You are not leaving until you give me an explanation.'

His grip hurt, but she'd never let that show. 'Is it not obvious, Hugh?'

'Not to me.' He released her, but his gaze pinned her in place. 'Was this a new trick to play on my family? Some kind of revenge on Xavier?'

'Neither.' She collapsed into a nearby chair, trying to resist the impulse to cover her face. It was too late for that now. 'I have no defence, Hugh. I deceived you terribly and I should never have come here. It was just another foolish whim.'

He planted himself in front of her, looking even more imposing than when she'd been standing. 'Foolish whim? You spent two weeks pretending to be someone else, when you knew all along I would know you. You shared my bed, knowing! How am I to feel learning who you are now?'

'It was a terrible thing to do to you.' What else could she say?

Her heart was breaking. Rather, it was being slashed to shreds by the dagger that had taken up residence there. She rose from the chair, but he did not back away. He stood too close to her, assaulting her with the memory of his arms around her, his body flush against hers.

And now he despised her, as she always knew he would.

'I will go now,' she said in a low voice. 'I promise I will not return.'

She took a step, but he seized her arm again. 'You promise? Have you not proved the quality of your promises?'

She was reasonably certain that she had never promised him anything, but what good would it do to argue that point with him? 'It does not matter if you believe me or not. Even if I desired to return, you would recognise me, obviously, so I would be foolish to attempt it, would I not?'

He leaned closer to her and whispered in her ear, 'You probably knew I would recognise you this time.'

But she hadn't. It had never occurred to her that he could tell who she was by any other means but sight.

She stepped back. 'I was fully masked. At worst someone might have guessed Lady Faville had returned, but you never saw Mrs Asher. I never imagined you would know it was me.'

His eyes bore into her; their gleam heightened her

senses. 'I knew you in other ways, Daphne.' He blinked and his eyes grew hard again. 'It is Daphne, is it not, Lady Faville? Or was that a lie, too?'

She cleared her throat. 'I was Daphne Asher before I was Lady Faville.'

He smirked. 'Oh, just a little lie, then.'

Or a very childish desire to be mere Daphne Asher again. 'Yes. A little lie.'

The clock on the mantelpiece chimed twice, startling them both.

Two o'clock. 'I must leave, Hugh. My carriage is coming to pick me up.'

He stepped back. She managed to walk to the door even though her feet felt gelatinous. She could not help but glance back for one last look at him. He stood with arms akimbo, glaring at her. She swallowed the tears that finally fell from her eyes as she reached the door and opened it. Once in the hallway, she stopped to tie the mask onto her face again. Her hair and clothing were mussed, but she did not care. For most people here, she was merely a masked lady come to gamble, and if anyone else guessed who she was, they'd never know she'd briefly been Daphne Asher again.

She descended the stairs, where Lord Sanvers lingered on the landing like a hunter waiting for his prey. Must she deal with him again?

'What the devil was that all about?' he asked, his voice amused. Likely he thought it a trifle.

To her it was like a mountain falling on top of her. 'Nothing for you to know, sir.'

She passed by without looking at him and continued to the hall.

Carter waited for her there. He did not ask her any questions. 'I will cash in your counters, m'lady.'

'Thank you, Carter.' She fished in her reticule for the counters and handed them to him.

The hall servant—Cummings—stood nearby.

'Would you please bring us our things?' she asked him.

He nodded and disappeared into the cloakroom. Daphne stared vacantly at the door. All she wanted was to leave this house. There would be plenty of time for regret later. Now she could add coming here, revealing herself to Hugh, to her long list of regrets.

She heard Cummings come back and turned, ready to take her cloak from his arm.

Hugh descended the stairs. She'd not expected him to follow her.

'I'll help the lady with her cloak, Cummings,' he said. He must wish to make certain she truly left the premises; it was the only explanation.

Cummings handed him her cloak and he walked over to her. She endured the bittersweet sensation of Hugh's hands upon her shoulders as he draped the cloak around her.

'Who escorted you?' he asked her, his voice low enough so only she could hear. 'No other men, indeed. Another lie, I suppose?'

She did not turn. 'It was Carter.'

He released a surprised breath.

Carter, still masked, emerged from the cashier's office and took a step back when he spied Hugh standing next to her. Bless Carter; he did nothing more to betray his identity. He handed her a purse filled with coin.

'We will settle it later,' she told him.

Carter nodded.

Hugh approached him, a sceptical look on his handsome, angry face. 'Carter?'

Carter nodded. 'Sir.'

'We must go,' Daphne said. 'The carriage…' The least

she could do was spare Carter from being interrogated by Hugh as he'd interrogated her.

Cummings handed Carter his hat and gloves. He put them on and walked to the door, opening it for Daphne. To her dismay, Hugh took her arm and walked out the door with her. He stood with them on the pavement where the carriage was to pick them up. Carter stepped a few paces away, giving Daphne privacy she did not want.

'I suppose it is Smith coming to pick you up,' Hugh remarked. 'Assuming your servants were not using fictitious names, as well.'

'All of the names were real,' she retorted. 'Including mine.' She squared her shoulders. 'Why are you out here, Hugh? To make certain I leave as I said I would?'

'Perhaps I find it difficult to be certain of anything you say.'

She lifted a shoulder. 'Of course. I cannot blame you for that.' It was the consequence of not telling the truth. Trust once betrayed was difficult to earn back, if even possible to earn back.

They stood in silence for what seemed an eternity to Daphne, but must have only been a few minutes. Smith finally drove up in the carriage. He warily nodded to Hugh.

'Smith.' Hugh nodded back.

Carter hurried over to open the carriage door and let down the steps. He waited for Daphne.

'Goodnight, Hugh,' Daphne murmured.

By the rushlight of the doorway, he looked very handsome, very mysterious. Very angry. She stifled a sob. She'd wanted one more look at him. This would certainly be the last one.

Hugh walked with her to the carriage door and helped her climb inside, but said nothing. He nodded to Carter, who entered the carriage after her.

When Smith pulled away, Daphne turned around to get the very last glimpse of Hugh, still framed in the light, now no more than a silhouette.

Carter sat opposite her in the rear-facing seat, taking off his mask immediately, although he kept silent and left her to her thoughts. Dear, dear Carter. His intent was to be kind, she was certain, but at this moment, she felt too much agony to be left alone. She needed a friend, even if he was her servant.

'He recognised me, Carter,' she said. 'He heard me speak and he recognised me.'

'So I gathered, m'lady.'

'It never occurred to me that he could recognise me by my voice. I never intended to be so close to him.' She reached behind her head and untied her mask. 'He was so angry.'

'I am sorry, m'lady.' Carter sounded genuinely sympathetic.

'I should never have come.' She rubbed her forehead. 'We should have stayed in Vadley.'

'It is done now,' he said. 'Some good will come of it, you will see.'

She glanced at him in surprise. Such words might have come from the mouth of the abbess.

She smiled. 'Thank you, Carter. You comfort me.' She felt the coin purse in her lap. 'I won a little. Did you?'

The corner of his mouth turned up. 'I did all right.'

'You are no stranger to cards, are you, Carter?' She lifted the purse.

He frowned. 'I hope that does not distress you, m'lady.'

'Not at all,' she said. Perhaps someday she would ask him more about that. Might it have had something to do with finding him penniless and jobless in Fahr? 'I am glad you won.'

Perhaps that was the only good that was meant to come out of this night.

Chapter Fifteen

Hugh watched Daphne's carriage until it disappeared around the corner of St James's Street. His insides were churning with rage and confusion. Why had she come here?

She'd given him no answers. He knew little more than the day she'd left him. He knew only that she was Lady Faville and that she had pretended to be someone else. But why? Why deceive him?

He'd known Lady Faville only to nod a greeting to. He'd seen her a few times at the Masquerade Club in the days she'd been pursuing Xavier. That very pursuit had prevented Hugh from joining the ranks of her many admirers. She'd wanted Xavier and had no concern for whom she hurt in the process. He'd learned later it had been his sister who was hurt.

And that final act. Attempting to burn down the club. What would have happened to his family if she'd succeeded? The Westleighs would have drowned in the River Tick, that was what.

Hugh shook his head. He'd been staring at an empty street. She was gone and he did believe she would not be back.

But why had she come? Apparently not to speak to
him. To see the Masquerade Club again? It made no sense.

He walked back to the gaming house door.

Why, she might have been in London all this time without him knowing. Had he read anything about Lady Faville being in town? He could not remember, but she might
have been mentioned a hundred times. He rarely read that
part of the newspaper.

Forget this. Forget *her.*

He opened the door and re-entered the hall. Cummings
stood there, as if at attention. He'd been in Rhys's regiment, Hugh recalled, not that he talked of it. Cummings
rarely talked at all.

Cummings's brows rose. 'Lady Faville?'

Hugh was surprised the man guessed. 'Yes.'

'Thought so,' Cummings said. 'Needed a second look.'

In his month managing the Masquerade Club, Hugh
had become pretty good at guessing the identities of the
masked patrons. He was nothing to Cummings and Mac-
Evoy, though. Those two knew everyone. They also could
spy a card shark within a couple of minutes.

'Well.' Hugh blew out a breath. 'She won't be back.'

Cummings's brows rose again.

Let him be sceptical. Hugh knew she would not be back.

He headed for the game room. *Forget her,* he told himself again. It was time to perform his duties.

Daphne sat at her dressing table already dressed for bed.
All that waited was Monette to remove the pins from her
hair and brush it smooth so she could put it in a plait. At
the moment Daphne despised looking at her own reflection, but she could not expect Monette to understand that.
So she sat in front of the glass as she did every night. This
dressing table was her most ornate, with two side mirrors

and dozens of compartments for her creams and tints and hairpins and combs. And her rosewater scent.

'Was he really very angry at you?' Monette asked as she pulled out pins.

'I knew he would be.' The pain of it shot through her again. 'I knew he would be angry to discover I was Lady Faville.'

Monette untwisted a coil of hair. 'That is why you did not tell him before, is it not?'

'Yes.' She'd been correct that he would both despise her for being Lady Faville and for not telling him who she was. There was no winning. She'd made him pay a high price for those glorious two weeks.

Monette took out the last pin and Daphne's blonde hair tumbled to her shoulders. She glanced at Monette in the mirror. The maid's lips were pursed and her brows knitted.

'Monette, these are my troubles, not yours. Do not let it distress you.' Daphne had enough on her conscience already.

'It is not that, m'lady.' Monette brushed her hair. 'I mean. I am distressed for you. I do not want you to be unhappy, but—' She clamped her lips shut and brushed with more vigour.

'But what, Monette?' Daphne asked.

It took several strokes of the brush before Monette answered her. 'It is just that— Are we returning to Vadley now?'

Daphne understood. 'You are worried that I will order us all back to Vadley as quickly as I sent us to London.'

Monette nodded.

Daphne continued, 'And you are worried that Toller will send a letter here and that we will miss it.'

Monette stared at Daphne's image in the glass and nodded again.

There was nothing more Daphne wished to do than run back to Vadley and make herself busy again. She did not care if it took her entire fortune, she wanted to do so many good works that she would not have a moment to think about herself.

Or about Hugh.

She reached back and squeezed Monette's hand reassuringly. 'Do not worry. We will wait here for word of Toller. I promised you that you would see London. Perhaps we will take in some of the sights while we are waiting. There is much we could do here. Order new livery for the footmen, new dresses for the maids. We must think of what the house in Vadley needs and purchase it here. One can find anything in the shops of London.' She'd make herself so busy in London that she would not have time to think of him.

Monette smiled. 'I would like that, my lady. The part about Toller I would like the most.'

Daphne smiled in return. 'I know. We will wait to hear from him and, if he wishes to come, we will wait for him to arrive here.'

After her terrible behaviour with Xavier and Hugh's sister, Mr Everard had encouraged her to remove to the Continent until society forgot the whole episode. She'd stayed away two years. Was that enough time? She had no intention of attending parties or the theatre, but would she be given the cut if the *beau monde* encountered her shopping at Floris or consuming an ice at Gunter's?

She must not care about matters such as this. She must instead try to make reparation for being vain and selfish and wicked to people who deserved none of her nonsense.

And now she needed to do something to make up for deceiving Hugh. Not directly, though. She must never seek to see him again.

Monette put Daphne's hair into a plait.

She bid the maid goodnight and climbed into her bed. When Monette closed the door behind her, Daphne extinguished her lamp and lay in the darkness, staring at the glow from her fireplace. How was she to sleep? She wanted to weep, but what good would weeping do?

Instead, she closed her eyes and tried to remember Hugh's face, especially his dark brown eyes that so burned with anger at her. How would those eyes appear during lovemaking? She again felt his hands exploring her body, touching her face, joining his body to hers. She remembered the ecstasy of her release, of sharing the blissful moment with him.

She'd live on these memories. What other choice did she have?

When morning came Daphne forced herself to eat some toast and jam for breakfast. She feared offending her London cook's efforts to please her with kippers, veal pie and baked eggs, but toast was all she could manage. She was sipping a cup of tea when Carter entered, looking again like a servant, not a masked gambler.

'Mr Everard, m'lady,' Carter announced.

'Everard? Here? So early?' It was ten in the morning, too early for callers.

'Yes, m'lady. He is eager to speak with you, he says.'

She'd hardly slept, still felt near tears and was not in the mood for callers. 'Very well. Tell him to join me here.'

A moment later he entered and immediately bowed. 'My lady.'

'Good morning, Everard.' She managed a smile and a bright voice. 'Do serve yourself some breakfast from the sideboard. I insist.' Perhaps his appetite would gratify Cook's desire to please.

'As you wish, ma'am.' He bowed again, piled food on his plate and sat down opposite her.

Daphne poured him tea. 'To what do I owe the honour of your visit?'

He had already put a forkful of food in his mouth and held up a finger to signal he would answer after he swallowed. 'I was concerned about your intention to go to the Masquerade Club last night, as you know. I simply wished to make certain nothing went amiss for you.' He speared a piece of veal from the pie. 'I hope you do not think it improper of me to be concerned.'

She did think he took too much of an interest in her affairs, but it was her own fault for manipulating him into escorting her to the Masquerade Club night after night two years ago.

'Not at all,' she said. 'But you must not be so concerned about me. You have much more important matters to tend to, I am sure.'

He placed his fork down on his plate and gave her a direct look. 'Nothing is more important than your well-being, my lady.'

She must do what she could about this devotion to her. 'Nonsense.' She took a sip of tea. 'As you can see, I am well. How is your wife? She is fortunate indeed to have a husband who concerns himself with the welfare of others.'

'My wife?' He sounded as if he'd forgotten the woman. 'She is in good health.'

'I am so glad to hear it. I should like to meet her some time.' She took a bite of toast.

'You would?' He tackled more of the food on his plate.

Did she really wish to meet Mrs Everard? It would be

a nice gesture, she supposed. 'Of course I would. Why would I not?'

He devoured yet another forkful of food before asking, 'Did you find everything satisfactory at the Masquerade Club?'

Her stomach fluttered at the mention of the club, but she put on a pleased expression. 'Oh, yes. I was so happy to see it looking so unharmed. The supper room was as lovely as always.'

He took a gulp of tea. 'Then you will not go back?'

She glanced down at the table. 'I will not go back.'

He looked relieved. 'Is there any service I may render while you are in town?'

She made herself smile. 'You may pay my bills. I intend to do some shopping while we are here.' She sounded like the old Daphne, even to herself, although this time she could think of nothing she wished to buy for herself.

She wondered if there were items she could purchase for the tenants. Perhaps she ought to send a letter to Mr Quigg. The estate manager would know what they might need. Perhaps some furniture. Furniture was so expensive. The tenants might like a nice bureau or a chest or something. Who could not use a pretty chest?

'Do you know of any good furniture shops?' she asked him.

'Furniture shops?'

'Oh, not fine furniture shops, but some that might be appropriate for an ordinary household.'

He looked very puzzled. 'I cannot think offhand, but I will make enquiries, if you like.'

'That would be so good of you,' she said.

If she kept very busy, shopping for her servants and her tenants, she might not think of Hugh so often and she might not always feel this despair so acutely.

* * *

Hugh stumbled out of bed with a colossal headache. No doubt the bottle of brandy he'd consumed after closing the Masquerade Club had done the damage. He was half tempted to drink down another. Better to remain in a stupor than to remember. He walked over to the mantel clock and read the time. Ten minutes to noon. Why was he up so early?

Because even the brandy did not help him sleep. His mind whirled with thoughts of Daphne. He felt fresh rage at her for leaving him, for deceiving him, and a deep painful ache of desire for her that even his anger could not eliminate.

Daphne had returned to him for one more deception, one more trick, and was this not the biggest and best of all her tricks? She'd known him all along. She'd been the bane of his family for a time, nearly ruining his sister's happiness and almost burning down this building.

Why had she done it? Why had she deceived him from the beginning and why had she returned? Apparently she'd not planned to make herself known to him. Why?

He'd allowed her to slip through his fingers again without answering any of these questions. Well, this time she would not get away with it. Now he knew who she was, he could discover where she lived. In fact, he probably had the information in the Masquerade Club records. She would have wanted Xavier to know where she lived; she probably had provided the location of her town residence.

He rummaged through the cabinets in the bedchamber and in the drawing room until he found another bottle of brandy. He drank enough to calm the headache, even though it burned his stomach. He poured water from the ewer into the basin and washed, shaved and dressed before going below and looking for some breakfast.

He found MacEvoy at the breakfast table, as well.

'I counted our take from last night,' MacEvoy said.

'How did we do?' Hugh asked, although the success of the Masquerade Club was not at the forefront of his mind this morning.

'Better than the previous night,' MacEvoy said, 'by about two hundred pounds.'

'Well done.' That was a very tidy sum.

When Hugh and Ned first convinced Rhys to run the club for them, Rhys took half the profits, but now that he'd given up the management, his share dropped to one quarter. Hugh would receive the other quarter, and half still went to repay the Westleigh estate. At least, if this rate continued he'd come out of this latest family task with a fortune.

'Yes, indeed,' admitted MacEvoy. 'The club is still doing well.' He sounded surprised.

Hugh supposed Cummings and MacEvoy and the croupiers did not expect him to be as successful as Rhys. Hugh figured that Rhys had built the foundation and there was not much he could do to weaken it. The idea of being able to gamble masked was still a popular one.

One of the kitchen maids brought in Hugh's breakfast and he made himself eat, knowing it would sooth his brandy-burnt stomach. There was also a welcome pot of coffee on the table.

Hugh poured himself a cup. 'I have a favour to ask.'

MacEvoy looked up warily from his plate. 'What is it?'

'See if you have Lady Faville's location in the records.'

MacEvoy nodded knowingly. 'So that was the lady, eh? I suspected as much. Why did she come back? Was she looking for Campion?' Campion was Xavier's surname.

She'd been obsessed by Xavier before; Hugh feared she still was.

'I do not know why she returned,' he answered Mac-
Evoy. 'But I intend to find out.'

MacEvoy gave him an approving look. 'Good idea.
Make certain she keeps to her bargain and never returns
here.' He turned thoughtful. 'Although with Campion busy
with his shops, there's really no reason for her to come
back.'

Somehow that did not appease Hugh.

After breakfast, MacEvoy checked the records and
found the location of Daphne's town house. Hugh immediately set off to call upon her.

She resided in Mayfair, but where else would Lady
Faville reside? Her house was on Hereford Street, a few
streets from Grosvenor Square and near the corner of Hyde
Park that bordered Oxford Street. From the Masquerade
Club near St James's Street, it was a little over a mile. Hugh
welcomed the walk. He'd been spending too much time
in darkness, watching people play cards and dice. Even
though the nightlife suited his recent gloom, the sun and
fresh spring air made him feel more alive than he had felt
in over a month.

Or was it the prospect of seeing Daphne again that
roused him?

Perhaps anger was a step up from gloom. He refused to
believe that anything but anger prompted him to make this
visit. He wanted answers, answers she'd cleverly avoided
giving him. This time he would not leave until he knew
precisely why she had returned to the Masquerade Club.
If Lady Faville planned more mischief for his family, he
would nip it in the bud right now.

While he'd tossed and turned in his bed that morning,
one thought had consumed him, and it was not the notion

that she'd come to the Masquerade Club looking for him. It was that she'd come looking for Xavier.

Apparently she'd held her obsession with him for ten years. What made him think it was over now? Or had been over even when she'd been with him in the cottage? What other reason than Xavier would have made her come back? She might not have known Xavier was rarely at the club now that Hugh had taken over its management.

If she was really pining for his brother-in-law, what had been her meaning in making love to him?

He passed Berkeley Square and walked down Mount Street to Park Lane, which bordered the park. He needed to smell trees thick with new leaves, spring grass and flowers. Scent had become so much more important to him, a vestige of his two weeks of blindness.

He turned onto Hereford and found the house easily. With no hesitation, he strode up to the door and sounded the knocker.

A footman opened the door and broke out into a smile of recognition before composing his face again. 'Mr Westleigh.'

'Carter?' This was Hugh's first glimpse of Carter's face. The man had been masked at the Masquerade Club. Hugh returned the man's smile. 'Believe me when I tell you it is good to see you.'

Carter grinned again. 'I am delighted you can tell me so, sir.' He stepped aside to allow Hugh to enter. 'Have you come to see—?' The man shut his mouth and looked perplexed, probably not knowing which name his mistress wished him to use.

'I have come to see Lady Faville.'

Carter bowed. 'Allow me to see if she is receiving callers.' Carter's voice was comfortingly familiar.

He escorted Hugh to the drawing room and, leaving the door open, left him there to find Daphne.

The room was dominated by a full-length portrait of Daphne—or rather, Lady Faville—her expression too cool and remote to be the Daphne he thought he'd known. Hugh closed his eyes and remembered the cottage drawing room, which he'd learned to navigate without sight. He turned away before opening his eyes again. This room was larger, more formal and feminine than the cottage's furniture had turned out to be. This room was decorated in fine brocades and velvets in shades of ivory and blue, no doubt to reflect the blue of her eyes. There was no pianoforte in this room, which somehow made it seem cooler, more impersonal, not warm and comfortable like the cottage had been.

Perhaps this room suited the cool beauty of the portrait, whose appearance was always calculated to turn heads. At least, that had been his impression of Lady Faville. That was not the same woman he'd known in the cottage. He closed his eyes and remembered her, the sound of her voice, her scent, the warmth of her skin. That Daphne had not been real, but a fabrication based on her lies and his need. To know her as Lady Faville could only make it easier to forget the illusion she'd been.

He heard a swish of skirts behind him and her voice. 'Hugh?'

Daphne stood in the doorway. Or rather, Lady Faville stood there. Her gleaming blonde hair was pulled away from her face into a simple knot and the rose-coloured dress she wore accented her flawless skin and matched the pink of her full lips. This paragon of beauty, so cool and flawless, was, indeed, not the Daphne he'd known.

'Why have you come here, Hugh?' She'd not moved from the doorway, as if she was afraid to enter the room.

'We have unfinished business, you and I.' He stared her in the eye. 'I would speak with you.'

She blinked and glanced behind her. Looking for an escape? But she closed the door and took a step closer to him. 'I have apologised for coming to the Masquerade Club. I will not come there again.'

'As you said.' His voice sounded bitter. 'But that is not why I have come.'

'What more can be said?' She lifted her chin regally.

There was no reason to mince words. 'I want to know why you came in the first place.'

She clasped her hands together. 'I—I wanted to see the place.'

'See the place?' He gave a dry laugh. 'Do not play me for a fool. Again.'

Her eyes flashed. 'Then why did you think I came there?'

He glared at her. 'To find Xavier.'

'Xavier?' She acted surprised.

'Xavier,' he repeated. 'You remember him. Xavier Campion? My sister's husband? The man you lusted after for weeks—years. You planned to break up his marriage, if you recall.'

She lowered her gaze to the floor. 'That was a long time ago.' She raised her eyes again and her expression was like ice. 'Surely you have not come here simply to point out my past failings. I assure you I am well acquainted with them.'

'I want to know if you came to the Masquerade Club to see Xavier.'

She stepped towards one of the chairs and placed her hands, delicate and long fingered, on the back of it. 'You took the trouble to call upon me merely to ask me that?' Her voice rose in pitch. 'You want only to know that I will not further trouble your family?'

That was not the only reason. He wanted to know how deep her deception had been in those two weeks he'd been blind. He wanted to know if she was still as obsessed by Xavier as she'd been before. If so, what had he, Hugh, meant to her?

He moved closer, standing behind her, close enough for her scent to reach his nostrils. Her scent matched the rose of her dress.

'I will cause no more trouble, Hugh,' she said, her voice weary.

That did not answer his question. 'I am to believe you? You made other promises and broke them. You've told other lies.'

'Yes,' she admitted. 'But whether you believe me or not, I will trouble you and your family no further.'

He scoffed. 'Maybe you cannot return to the Masquerade Club, because now you know even a mask cannot disguise you from me, but how do I know you are not plotting some other mischief?'

'You cannot know.' She shook her head. 'I mean, I ask only that you believe me this time.'

Believe her? 'I am to believe you do not have some other mischief to wreak upon my family?'

'Yes, because I do not.' Her voice turned very quiet. 'I mean none of you any harm at all.'

He strode up to her and held her by her shoulders. 'Then tell me why you came. If not to start that business with my sister's husband again, then why?'

It was a mistake to come so close to her, to touch her. His body was drawn to her like a magnet to metal.

She made no effort to pull away. Instead, she looked up into his face. 'Would you believe me if I told you I came to see you?'

His senses heightened at her words and her nearness. It hurt to look at her; she was that beautiful.

'I would not believe it,' he managed.

She took a breath and it felt as if she'd robbed him of air. 'Well, I did come to see you. I wanted to look at you without bandages, to see for myself that you were not blind. When I left the cottage, I did not know if you would be blind or not.'

'If you'd cared so much, Daphne—' he released her '—you never would have left.'

She stepped away from him. 'If I'd stayed, you would have discovered who I was.'

His voice dipped low. 'I would have discovered how seriously you deceived me, you mean.'

'Yes,' she agreed again. 'That is what I mean.'

Had he meant that much to her that she needed to see him healed? Wait. He must not fall for more deception. 'How did you even know I was at the Masquerade Club?'

She paused before answering, 'Mr Everard, my man of business, told me.'

Her man of business? Hugh knew that Lady Faville's man of business had met with Rhys and Xavier to arrange the compensation for the damage to the Masquerade Club.

'Your man of business told you I was at the club and that was why you came there?'

She nodded.

He could not believe her. If he'd been that important to her, she would not have deceived him. She would not have left him. 'You came to assure yourself that I was not blind and not to see Xavier?'

She turned her head away. 'Yes.'

Was she jesting? 'Your man of business would have mentioned a blind gambling-club manager. There cannot be so many of those in London. When he spoke of me, surely you knew then I was not blind. Why come to see it?'

Her shoulders slumped and she retreated to the fireplace. 'It does no good to banter back and forth. You cannot believe me and I cannot convince you. Suffice to say I will not bother you again, Hugh. I do promise that.' Her voice cracked. 'Please leave me now.'

He crossed the room and turned her around to face him. 'Not before you tell me why you lied to me! Why did you not tell me you were Lady Faville? Why did you let me think—think you were someone else? That our time together meant something else?'

Her eyes glittered with unspent tears and she trembled beneath his touch. Instead of pulling away and slapping him across the face as he deserved for such roughshod behaviour, she reached up and touched his cheek.

'I am so sorry, Hugh,' she whispered.

Her voice was like her whispers in bed. He could resist no more. He crushed his lips against hers. Closing his eyes, he brought back the Daphne he loved, warm and soft and real.

Daphne threw her arms around him and kissed him back, starved for his touch, the feel of his lips. He tasted wonderful, so familiar, so masculine. She held him in the kiss by burying her fingers in his hair, savouring the feel of his thick, dark, unruly hair no longer covered by bandages. The heat of his body inflamed her and she could think of nothing but joining with him again.

In the month they'd been apart it was if she'd been torn in two. She needed him to be whole again, to give her life some kind of meaning. She clutched at him with a desperation that matched his own. He backed her to a *chaise longue* near the fireplace, and her need was too great to wait upon removing clothes. She undid the buttons of his trousers while he pulled up her skirts. Suddenly she was beneath him, pulling him to her, opening herself to him. It was madness, but a glorious derangement, this urgent need to make love to him, to again share the ecstasy of a passionate release.

They freed themselves of enough clothing, and he thrust into her, his power so exhilarating that she thought she would weep for the pleasure of it. She rose to meet him in a frenzied, desperate rush that was unlike any of their past lovemaking. Never had her need for him risen so quickly, become so violently intense.

She clutched at him, fearful something would yank him away, like a sailor swept from his ship in a storm. This storm was of their own making, Daphne thought, but she felt as helpless as if it had come from the wind.

She felt the sensations inside her grow more intense, building with each rhythmic thrust. Did he realise what his body did to her? Did his need drive him higher and higher, harder and harder? Suddenly she reached the precipice and his seed exploded inside her. She cried out as her own release came and she quivered beneath him in waves and waves of supreme pleasure.

A moment later, it was over. They plummeted quickly from the highest peak straight to the deepest reality.

He lay atop her only briefly before standing, looking alarmed. She made an attempt at covering herself with her skirts when he fumbled through his pockets and handed her his handkerchief. It was a kindness she didn't expect after such an animalistic coupling. He glanced at her, but quickly turned away to button his trousers and straighten the rest of his clothes.

'Did I hurt you, Daphne?' He faced her again.

She shook her head, but felt a tear escape her eyes and run down her cheek.

He leaned down and gently wiped it away with his thumb. 'I am sorry for that.'

Her brows knitted. 'Sorry?' Had he regretted this?

'I should not have treated you so. It was not well done of me at all.'

Was he ashamed? 'Then why—?' She could not get the words out.

'Why?' He blew out a breath. 'I honestly do not know why. Your beauty—?'

Her beauty.

The dagger inside Daphne's heart twisted.

Of course. Acclaimed beauty, Lady Faville. What man did not want her?

Besides her husband, she'd allowed no man in her bed. Except Hugh. Even though he despised her for causing trouble for his family and lying to him, he'd made love to her beauty.

And she'd allowed it.

She'd wanted it. She'd wanted nothing more.

Except perhaps that he make love to Daphne, a woman he couldn't see.

She glanced around the room. The curtains were open and sunlight streamed in. Anyone walking by might have seen them on the *chaise*. Her cheeks burned at the thought.

'I must go,' he said.

She managed to stand and to smooth her skirts. 'Yes. Go.' He'd walk out the door, out of her life, and she feared all the shopping and good works in the world would not be enough to take away the pain of that.

He nodded and crossed the room to the door. She could not take her eyes off him. Tears still stung, but she refused to let him see her cry. There was plenty of time for weeping in the middle of the night.

He reached the door and opened it. Her breathing quickened. This was the end.

He turned around. 'Daphne?'

Her heart pounded. 'Yes?'

He waved a hand, erasing whatever it was he'd been about to say. He crossed the threshold and walked out.

She watched until he disappeared in the hall. He said a word or two to Carter and the front door opened and closed. She hurried over to one of the windows and watched him step onto the pavement.

As he passed by the window, he turned and saw her there. Their gazes caught for a moment before he continued walking and was soon out of sight.

She looked down at her hand. She still clutched his handkerchief, all that she had left of him. Hurrying out of the room, she climbed the stairs to her bedchamber and washed the small piece of linen. When it dried, she'd put it in a special place and keep it always.

Chapter Sixteen

After one last glance at Daphne through the window, Hugh turned away and strode quickly down the pavement. The sight of her disconcerted him. It wasn't that he'd formed a clear vision of her when his eyes were bandaged. It was seeing her as Lady Faville that sparked a whole set of disparate emotions.

The Daphne of his imagination had never been Lady Faville.

Hugh chose the bustle of Oxford Street rather than retrace his steps through Mayfair. He walked at a brisk pace, needing to put as much distance between himself and Lady Faville as possible.

No matter who she was in reality, he'd behaved appallingly towards her, coupling with her in such a lustful frenzy. Where had been his control? His gentlemanly respect? Never before had he moved with such desire for a woman.

One look at her revealed how he'd upset her. How could he have taken her with such swift need? It was just that, for a moment, that brief moment of lovemaking, he'd thought he'd found her again.

He turned onto Bond Street and pushed past the street

vendors, crossing sweepers and other pedestrians. He passed a jewellery shop and almost collided with a gentleman coming out the door.

'Hugh!' It was his brother Ned.

Hugh, in no mood to speak to anyone, mumbled a greeting.

'I've not seen you in over a fortnight. I keep meaning to stop in the club…' Ned looked apologetic.

'All is well there,' Hugh assured him.

'Where are you headed?' Ned did not wait for Hugh to answer. 'Have you time? Come with me to White's. We'll have a drink.' His eyes pleaded for Hugh to say yes.

How could Hugh refuse?

Ned began talking right away. 'I had no idea what work it would be to sit in the Lords, about the complexity of decisions to be made. The Poor Relief Bill. Usury laws. Timber duties. Not to mention the budget and preparing for the coronation.' He took a breath. 'I do not see how Father did it.'

'I suspect he shirked his Parliamentary duties as he did all the rest,' Hugh responded.

'I suspect you are correct,' Ned admitted. 'But to me, it all seems too important to neglect.'

Ned was the best sort of man to own a title. He strove always to do his duty, to do what was good and right. He was the opposite of their father, as a matter of fact. To an annoying degree, sometimes.

Ned talked of the various bills on which he had to vote, seeking Hugh's approval of his decisions all the way to White's. He continued talking as they sat down and ordered glasses of claret. Hugh noticed several members in the gaming room, deep in their cards. He recognised some of the gentlemen and expected to see them at the Masquerade Club that night. Did they not take Parliamentary duties as seriously as Ned, or were they working on gaining support for their various positions? There was more than one way to achieve a result.

'How is your wife?' Hugh asked when Ned stopped talking long enough to take a sip of his wine.

'Adele?' Ned's expression softened. 'She fares very well, except in the morning. She cannot keep food down in the morning. It is common amongst women when they are increasing, she assures me.'

Hugh thought of Daphne, never having children. He'd been certain it had made her sad. Had it made Lady Faville sad? He could not stop thinking of them as two separate people. He could not stop thinking of her at all, not even under the deluge of Ned's words.

He asked Ned about the rest of the family. Their mother. Phillipa. Rhys.

Ned asked about the Masquerade Club, detailed questions about its profits, the expenditures Hugh had incurred. They debated the necessities of new dice and new packs of cards, items that Hugh insisted upon. Rhys had instilled in him the importance of assuring the patrons that the games were honest. New dice, new cards were a part of that.

By the time the clock struck the hour for the second time, Ned jumped to his feet. 'Gads. I must be off. Adele is expecting me.'

Hugh rose more slowly, but followed Ned back out to the street.

Ned shook his hand, clasping his arm at the same time. 'So good to see you, Hugh. I promise to stop by the Masquerade Club the first chance I get. In the meantime, if you need me for anything, you have but to ask.'

Hugh had no doubt that Ned would drop everything and come if Hugh needed him, although he was self-absorbed enough to neglect enquiring about anything of Hugh's life besides the Masquerade Club. Nothing besides the task assigned to him.

Would he have told Ned about Daphne if Ned had asked? He doubted it.

Hugh watched his brother hurry down the street and disappear in the crowd of pedestrians. With nothing better to do, he turned to walk the short distance back to the Masquerade Club.

That night Rhys and Xavier visited the Masquerade Club. After greeting the workers and the patrons who frequented the club, they sat down with Hugh in a corner of the supper room. In front of them were plates laden with food and bottles of wine. Hugh poured them each a glass.

Rhys tasted the food and nodded appreciatively. 'I see Cook is still up to her old standards. I'd forgotten how good the food could be.'

Hugh also appreciated her and made certain she knew it. She was the widow of one of the men in Rhys and Xavier's regiment and was intensely loyal to both men.

'I've had no problems to speak of,' Hugh told them. 'Do you see any?'

Xavier's gaze wandered to the pianoforte. He grinned. 'You are missing the masked *pianiste*.' His wife, Phillipa, the woman so wronged by Daphne, had increased the crowds at the club the few weeks she'd performed.

Hugh made himself smile back. 'Perhaps she will return? Are her nights free?'

Xavier's expression turned sly. 'Her nights are very occupied, I am afraid.'

Hugh regarded the man discreetly. Xavier was indeed very handsome. The gazes of women in the supper room often turned his way. With his thick, dark, poetically unruly hair, manly features and startling blue eyes, it was no wonder Daphne had been enamoured of him. They would have made a very handsome couple.

Hugh shook that thought away.

At least Xavier was a decent man. In fact, Hugh suspected his appearance meant nothing to him. The opinion of others meant nothing to him. He'd defied society's expectations of the son of an aristocrat and invested his money in shops. If he stank of trade, as the saying went, then the women in the room liked the smell.

Hugh asked about Phillipa and the baby and went on to ask about the shops.

'I have ten of them now.' Xavier straightened. 'The furniture shop is doing the best. There's a good market for good furniture at moderate prices. I prefer enterprises that require manufacture. We can employ more workers that way. I added a pianoforte maker recently.'

'A former soldier knew how to make pianofortes?' Rhys asked.

Xavier mainly hired out-of-work former soldiers.

'No.' Xavier sipped his wine. 'The man who made Phillipa's pianoforte was in danger of going out of business. He agreed to train some former soldiers in the trade.'

Xavier's benevolence reminded Hugh of Daphne's generous overpayment of the cottage servants.

He shook himself. He needed to change this subject. 'Rhys, how are your interests faring?'

Rhys was heavily invested in the manufacture of steam engines. 'We are seeking to improve designs all the time, but some of our machines have started selling to factories and mines. You know there is a steam locomotive operating between Stockton and Darlington. I am certain there will be more in the future.'

Hugh shrugged. 'This is another form of gambling, is it not?'

Their father had disowned his bastard son, Rhys, after his mother died. He'd been a mere lad who learned to survive by gambling.

Rhys nodded. 'It is indeed, but more exciting than the turn of a card. More useful, too.'

Xavier saw one of his brothers enter the supper room and excused himself to go and speak to him.

After he'd left the table, Hugh asked Rhys, 'Have you found a life that suits you, then?' Hugh might have been hateful to Rhys when they were boys, but now all he wanted was for Rhys to do well.

Rhys glanced away and back, his eyes warm and intense. 'I have more than I could ever have dreamed of possessing.' He took a bite of food. 'And I do not mean money.'

Hugh met his gaze. 'You have a wife and children.'

'A family,' Rhys said, his voice low.

'We are your family as well, Rhys,' Hugh added in the same tone. 'We Westleighs. I know I did not always think that way, but my mind has changed.'

Rhys maintained the mood. 'People can change. I certainly have.'

Could they? Could people truly change? Or were their characters forged at birth? Did circumstances foster certain traits to come to the fore and others to be hidden? He and Rhys had hated each other since boyhood, until Hugh saw him for the decent, strong, compassionate man he was. Had always been, Hugh suspected. Perhaps as a boy, Hugh had only seen Rhys's facade, a tough ruffian always up for a fight.

Was Lady Faville the facade or was Daphne?

He knew he must find out.

When Xavier returned to his seat, Hugh asked him, 'Where is this pianoforte shop of yours?'

'Why?' Xavier asked.

Hugh pierced a piece of cold beef with his fork. 'I may be wishing to purchase one.'

Xavier gestured to the instrument sitting idle in the supper room. 'You have a pianoforte right here. Or do you mean this for someone else?'

'Yes. Someone else.' He was not ready to say who, but they had spent many a pleasant hour seated together on the bench of the pianoforte in the cottage. Maybe the gift would at least convey his gratitude to her for tending to his care those two weeks. And his apology for ill using her this day.

Maybe it would give him an excuse to see her again.

It was no difficulty for Daphne to rise early the next morning. She had hardly slept at all. It seemed as if only in the privacy of her bedroom, late at night, could she free the grief that wreaked havoc inside her during the day. The darkness took away all reminders of who and where she was. What remained were her emotions, which she dared not release during the day.

The previous day had not been at all busy enough to distract her, although she'd done her best. Monette needed distracting, as well. The girl fretted that they would not have a reply from Toller or that he would decide to remain in Thurnfield.

For want of anything better to do, Daphne and Monette had gone through several trunks stored in the attic. She'd packed away so many clothes, so many pairs of shoes, gloves, hats, cloaks. How shameful of her to pack away items that might make others happy or be of good use to them. What Monette did not want, Daphne offered to the maids and the kitchen staff. When they were all through sorting and selecting, what remained they could sell on Petticoat Lane.

But digging through memories had not been the easiest way to endure the day. Over and over Daphne had been compelled to face the woman she'd been, the woman she feared she could never escape.

But this morning dawned a new day and she had a new resolve. Today she would show Monette London's shops. Give the young woman some pleasure, some adventure. Oh, perhaps not adventure like Hugh had once talked about, but certainly sights Monette had never seen. Nothing could compare to the vast array of London's shops.

She was nearly through breakfast when Carter entered the room. 'Mr Everard calls again, my lady.'

'Everard?' He'd just called the day before. She feared he was forming an attachment that would simply hurt everyone. 'I suppose you must tell him I'll see him here.'

A moment later he appeared in the doorway. 'Good morning, my lady.' He bowed.

'Good morning, sir.' She tried not to sound too curt, but also not too inviting. 'You are back to see me so soon. I do hope nothing is amiss.'

'Not at all. Not at all.' He remained in the doorway.

She sighed inwardly. 'Do come in and have something to eat, if you'd like. I confess I do not have a great deal of time as I am going out very soon, but tell me why you have come.'

'Some tea, perhaps,' he said as he sat.

She poured him some tea.

He took a grateful sip. 'I come only to inform you that I have done what you wished of me.'

What had she asked of him? She could recall nothing.

She waited and eventually he continued, 'You asked me for recommendations for furniture shops.'

'Oh, yes.' But a note bearing the names of the shops would have sufficed.

'I am not well versed in such matters, but I have arranged for someone who is quite knowledgeable to call upon you.' He looked quite pleased with himself.

Daphne did not want callers, although she supposed she could not hide from all society for ever. Who would Everard send? 'Who is it who will call upon me?'

'My wife.'

His wife? The poor creature. What was Daphne to do with a visit from his wife?

She caught herself. It would be a kindness to receive his wife. She would be kind to the young woman.

She made herself smile. 'How lovely.'

'She purchased most of the items in our residence and has a good eye for quality at a fair price. I could think of no better person to advise you.' He paused. 'And you did say you wished to meet her.'

'I did, did I not?' She took a bite of toast. 'I suppose she could call on me this afternoon. I will certainly be at home after two o'clock.'

He stood. 'I shall make certain she knows this. She will not fail you, my lady.' He bowed. 'I fear I must take my leave. With your permission, of course.'

'Of course,' she said somewhat gratefully. 'Good day to you, sir.'

Shortly after Mr Everard left, Daphne set out with Monette to show her the shops and distract her from the fact that they had not yet heard from Toller. They started on Oxford Street, it being so close, and visited linen draper after linen draper. In one, Monette found a blue muslin that was just a shade deeper than Daphne's eyes. She begged Daphne to purchase it and allow her to make a gown for Daphne from it, in repayment for Daphne's generosity to her.

It was a hard decision to make. She did not need a new gown. Had she not the day before given away countless gowns? But she was forced this time to admit that accepting Monette's gift was the most generous act she could make at the moment.

They explored hat shops, glove shops and jewellery shops. Daphne had several pieces of fine jewellery locked away, expensive gifts from her late husband, which she'd not worn since leaving London for the Continent two years ago. She certainly had not needed jewels in the abbey. It surprised her how little she had missed them.

They stopped in a clock shop. On the shelf, among grander pieces, was a clock in a porcelain case that might have been a twin to the one she'd placed in Hugh's bedchamber in the cottage. Swallowing tears, she purchased it and arranged for it to be sent to her town house.

They bought Dutch biscuits from a street vendor and savoured the sweet and spicy taste. As they finished the last crumbs, they passed a sheet-music shop.

'I want to look in here.' Daphne opened the door and entered the shop.

Monette followed her.

The proprietor approached. 'May I be of assistance, ma'am?' His look of admiration was familiar.

'I hope you may assist, sir,' she responded. 'I am looking for music for the pianoforte written by a lady.'

'A lady?' His brows rose. 'Do you know the name of the lady or of the piece?'

She smiled. 'I do not. I suspect she has written the music anonymously.'

He tapped his finger against his lips. 'I have an idea.'

He let her to a file of music sheets and riffled through them, pulling out one. 'Perhaps this one?'

She took it from his hand and read that it was a sonatina by Lady Songstress. Her heart beat faster. Lady Songstress had been the name she'd given to Phillipa Westleigh when she'd known her only as the masked *pianiste* at the Masquerade Club.

Daphne's throat tightened. Had she been a better person, Lady Songstress might have been a friend.

'Yes,' she told the proprietor. 'This is it exactly. Are there other compositions by Lady Songstress?'

He found three others, one quite new. A lullaby.

'I will buy them all.' It was at least something she could do for Phillipa. It would honour her music.

'My lady?' Monette touched her sleeve. 'You do not have a pianoforte here. What will you do with this music?'

Daphne had not thought about playing the music, but would that not be the best way to respect Phillipa's talent?

She turned to the store proprietor. 'Is there a pianoforte shop you might recommend?'

'Indeed there is,' he responded. 'Near here on Duke Street.'

She made her purchases and she and Monette left.

'Are you going to buy a pianoforte?' Monette asked.

Daphne smiled. 'I believe I will.' Playing music would be another way to pass the time.

And to remember when she and Hugh played music together.

They found the pianoforte shop and entered. The shop had several instruments on display. The clerk was busy talking to three gentlemen, so Daphne and Monette walked around, looking at simple pianofortes, ornate ones, even a small one that could be carried from place to place. The clerk broke away from his conversation and approached Daphne.

He flushed when he looked upon her face. 'Are you interested in a pianoforte, my lady?'

'I am indeed,' she said.

When she spoke, the three gentlemen turned and Daphne felt the air leave her lungs.

It was the new Lord Westleigh, Xavier—and Hugh.

Hugh felt both his brother Ned and Xavier stiffen when they saw her. She looked equally as shocked, but more than that, she looked vulnerable. How would Ned and Xavier react? Even in front of the pianoforte clerk and her maid, a cut would wound her.

He stepped towards her and bowed. 'Good morning, ma'am. Daphne.' He could not help calling her by name. 'You are planning to purchase a pianoforte?'

She darted a glance at Xavier and Ned before answering. 'Yes. I—I do not have one and I am lately interested in playing again.' She held out a large envelope. 'I purchased some music.'

'Did you?' He extended his hand. 'May I see?'

She turned paler, hesitating before handing over the packet. He glanced inside. His head snapped up, catching her gaze, when he saw what she had purchased. Phillipa's music.

'I—I was interested in this composer. I wanted to give my support,' she explained.

What was he to make of the fact that she'd purchased his sister's compositions? He glanced back at Xavier. Had it been because of Xavier?

Ned gazed at her as if she was a pariah. Xavier looked on guard. Both reactions annoyed him. Was there a need to be cruel to her? 'Xavier, Lady Faville has come to purchase one of your pianofortes. Ned, you remember Lady Faville, do you not?'

Ned inclined his head to her, but did not speak.

Xavier stepped forwards. 'Did you know this was one

of my shops?' His words might have sounded polite to
the clerk and Monette, but Hugh suspected both Ned and
Daphne sensed the sharp edge to them.

Daphne looked genuinely surprised. 'I had no idea of it.'

Monette edged closer to her.

Hugh nodded to the young maid. 'How are you,
Monette?'

'Very well, sir,' she replied shyly, her eyes wandering to Xavier. 'We—we just learned of this place at the
music shop.'

Brave girl to defend her mistress in front of an earl and
son of an earl. Although she would not know that.

He handed the envelope back to Daphne and their fingers touched. She flushed. 'I did not know,' she said just
loud enough for Hugh to hear.

He nodded slightly and turned to the clerk. 'Do you
have a recommendation for the lady? Which do you feel
would suit her best?'

The man snapped back from gazing upon her. 'You
might try them for sound. All are manufactured to the
highest standards, but their sound will differ slightly.' He
pressed the keys of the nearest instruments.

Hugh could hear a difference.

The clerk cleared his throat and continued. 'Or perhaps the decor of the cabinets will matter more to you.'
He walked over to one that was painted with pink roses,
its corners edged in gilt. 'This would be a fine addition
to any room.'

'I—I prefer one that is less flamboyant.' She turned to
one that was plainly styled. It was quite like the one at the
cottage, although obviously of higher quality. 'This one.
You may prepare the bill of sale and have the instrument
sent to my residence.' She gave him the direction to her
town house.

The clerk looked to Xavier.

'Yes, Mr Ball. You may do that for Lady Faville,' Xavier said.

'Yes, sir.' He walked over to the counter and pulled out a book to prepare the bill of sale.

Xavier turned to Daphne. 'I did not know you were in town.'

She darted a glance at him, but did not sustain it. 'Yes. We have come to do shopping.'

Monette spoke up again. 'My lady is showing me all the shops.'

Ned broke in with a sarcastic tone. 'The shops?'

Daphne turned to him. 'That is all. I have no other plans. Although we might visit some of the special sights. The Tower. Westminster Abbey. The Egyptian Hall…' Her voice faded as if she feared she'd said too much.

She glanced at Xavier again.

What was she thinking at seeing Xavier again? Hugh wondered. Had she really not known this was his shop? It seemed too coincidental.

Although how could she have known Xavier would be at the shop? Investors did not spend a great deal of time in their shops. Did Lord George Cavendish patrol the Burlington Arcade like one of his beadles? Indeed not. How would she even have known Xavier owned such shops? From Mr Everard, perhaps, if there was some way that man might have known of it.

It made more sense that she would want to show Monette London. She'd brought the girl from Switzerland and treated her more like a younger sister than a lady's maid.

The clerk returned with the bill of sale.

'You will be paid promptly after the instrument is delivered,' Daphne told him. She turned to Ned and Xavier.

'Good day, gentlemen.' She gave Hugh a direct gaze. 'Hugh.'

He walked with her to the door and opened it for her. 'Enjoy your music, Daphne. Monette.'

When he closed the door again the clerk excused himself and went to the back of the shop.

Ned turned on Hugh. 'What was that all about, Hugh? You acted as if Lady Faville was an old friend of yours.' Ned shot daggers at him. 'Let me remind you that she nearly ruined us.'

'I did not know she was in London,' Xavier said, as if he talking only to himself. 'God knows I want no more trouble with her. I won't have Phillipa hurt again.'

'Trouble.' Ned laughed drily. 'That is what she is. You know that, Hugh. Have you lost your senses?'

He had lost his senses with her, but it would be no use trying to explain why to his brother. 'No more than you, Ned,' Hugh shot back. 'There is certainly no reason to discuss this with you.'

Ned glared at him. 'I think there is every reason to discuss her with me.'

'I am acquainted with Lady Faville,' Hugh admitted. 'But she is hardly the terror you make her out to be.'

'I suppose you met her in Brussels,' Ned scoffed. 'It was said she ran off to the Continent. Were you one of her conquests over there? You stayed a long time. Perhaps not all your time was spent tending to our father's affairs.'

'You know nothing of it, Ned.' Hugh raised his voice, his anger reaching boiling point. 'If you did not trust me to take care of things in Brussels, maybe you should have gone yourself. Cleaned up the mess yourself.'

'You cannot speak to me in that fashion!' Ned countered, his face red.

'Why? Because you own the title? Remember, I'm your

brother. I've seen you without your Parliamentary robes. And it has been a long time since you could best me in at fisticuffs.' He wished Ned would challenge him right now. He'd relish punching him in his aristocratic nose.

Xavier stepped between the two of them. 'Enough. You don't have to scrap like a couple of schoolboys. Lady Faville is my problem, if she is anyone's.' He faced Hugh. 'Are you going to buy a pianoforte?'

Hugh shook his head. 'Not today. I've changed my mind.'

'Very well,' Xavier said. 'I'm leaving. I need to tell Phillipa about Lady Faville being in London.'

'Do not tell her,' Ned protested. 'It will upset her.'

'Not as much as keeping it a secret from her.' He called to Mr Ball that he was leaving, gave Ned and Hugh one more annoyed look and left the shop.

Hugh started for the door, as well.

Ned was at his heels. 'Promise me you will have nothing more to do with Lady Faville.'

'Promise you?' Hugh laughed as he walked out of the shop. 'Why not simply trust me to do the right thing?'

He strode away from his brother and did not look back. At the moment he was too angry at Ned to deal with him a moment longer.

Chapter Seventeen

Daphne walked so briskly, Monette had difficulty keeping up with her. She stopped and waited. 'I am sorry, Monette. I simply must return home.'

'Yes, *madame*,' Monette said, out of breath. 'It upset you to see Mr Westleigh. I am sorry for you.'

'It—it surprised me, is all. I did not expect it.' She had not expected to ever see him again.

He'd been civil to her, even kind. That made the pain greater. Had he been as rude as his brother, her anger might have blocked out the ache of losing him all over again.

'Who were the other gentlemen? They were so angry at you, I think,' Monette asked. 'One man was very handsome. I have never seen a man so—so handsome.'

Another surprise. Seeing Hugh had so completely overshadowed the sight of Xavier that she'd no emotion to spare for him. It simply had not mattered to her to see Xavier again. She'd never truly known him, merely the superficial fantasy of him she'd created herself.

She'd known Hugh, though. Intimately. She knew his character, his determination, his strength.

She answered Monette, 'The handsome man is married

to Mr Westleigh's sister and the other man is Mr Westleigh's brother, Lord Westleigh.'

Monette's eyes widened. '*Lord* Westleigh?'

'He is an earl.'

'*Mon Dieu,*' Monette murmured.

They retraced their steps on Oxford Street and returned to the town house. When they walked in the door, Daphne said, 'I will be quite myself again, Monette. I simply need some solitude for a little while.'

Monette nodded.

Daphne forced herself to climb the steps at a normal pace. When she entered her bedchamber, she realised she was still clutching the envelope containing the music sheets. She dropped it on a table, pulled off her gloves and hat and pressed her hands against her temple.

Calm yourself, she scolded. It is very unlikely she would see Hugh again, even if she went out. It was merely a terrible coincidence this time. She hurried over to her bureau drawer and pulled out his handkerchief, all clean and folded.

She held it in her hands and flopped into a rocking chair. She gazed out the window while she rocked, but she did not see the blue sky or the green trees. She was consumed by the memory of his fingers brushing against hers, by the kind look in his eyes. Of course, he'd appeared puzzled when he'd seen what music she'd purchased. Why had she done such a thing? She could have purchased any music. What was he to think of her selecting Phillipa's music?

She could barely remember what Xavier had said. There was not even a vestige of her former infatuation.

Hugh's brother's anger had been very evident. She'd expected such a reaction from a Westleigh. She deserved it. The surprise had been Hugh's defence of her. At least it

felt like he'd defended her, practically forcing his brother
to be civil. Why had he done such a thing?

Her mind whirled in circles for the next hour and always wound up in the same bleak place.

There was a knock on the door and Monette peeked into
the room. 'Mrs Everard has come to call.'

Daphne had completely forgotten about Mrs Everard.

She rose wearily. 'I must see her.'

'Wait.' Monette touched her gown. 'Do you not wish
me to help you change? One of your morning gowns is
ready for you.'

Daphne looked down at herself. She supposed her skirts
were a bit soiled from the street. 'Might we simply brush
off the dirt? I hate to keep her waiting long.' Truly she
wanted to be done with this interview, regretting she'd
ever said anything to put Mrs Everard in this position of
having to call upon her social superior.

Monette quickly brushed the hem of her skirt. 'You
must let me dress your hair,' she said when finished.

Daphne glanced in her mirror. Her hair was coming
loose of its pins, strands escaping from the knot atop her
head.

She sat at her dressing table and allowed Monette to
make her hair presentable, although it might have done
just as well to cover it with a cap.

Daphne was certainly not looking forward to this interview, but poor Mrs Everard was in a worse position.
Daphne could not greet her with this gloomy mood. The
woman would likely think her presence to be the cause.

She'd make herself friendly and cheerful. She'd been
trained to do so no matter how she felt inside. For so many
years she'd performed the task so well, she'd forgotten
how to feel.

No longer.

Monette tied Daphne's hair with a ribbon, and her curls fell around her face as if it all had been carefully arranged.

Daphne stood and straightened her spine. 'Thank you, Monette,' she remembered to say. 'I do look a great deal neater.'

She left her room and descended the stairs, placing a smile on her face and stuffing all other emotions deep inside. With her social facade erected, she entered the drawing room, where Mrs Everard stood staring at Daphne's portrait so prominently displayed.

She really ought to have it replaced by some nice landscape.

'Mrs Everard?'

The woman turned and quickly composed her unhappy face into an expression of politeness. She curtsied.

Daphne approached her with hand extended. 'I am Lady Faville.' She glanced at her portrait. 'As you have undoubtedly guessed.' She shook the woman's hand. 'I am so sorry to have kept you waiting. Especially when it was so kind of you to come.'

Mrs Everard's handshake was very tentative. 'Ma'am' was all she said.

Daphne took her arm and led her to a set of chairs near the fireplace. 'Do sit.' She gave Mrs Everard a chair that did not face her portrait. One Lady Faville was enough for the woman to deal with.

Daphne had always known she was prettier than most women. Her mother certainly had told her so from the time she was in leading strings. It had been the abbess who helped her understand how much a barrier her beauty could be. She'd realised, though, that the biggest barrier had been one she created herself. She'd been the one who'd not looked beyond a person's physical appearance.

She smiled at her guest. 'I've ordered tea. It should be here any minute.'

Mrs Everard's gaze did not quite meet Daphne's. 'You ought not to have gone to so much trouble for me,'

Mrs Everard was young, perhaps no more than twenty. She was pleasant looking, but plain, although with a little effort she might actually be pretty. Her hair was a nondescript brown, pulled away from her face and covered by her bonnet. Her dress was well cut and well sewn, but it was an unadorned grey, the colour of a dreary day. Her eyes were an identical shade of grey, but Daphne suspected they would brighten with colour if she chose to wear rich greens or blues. Daphne could think of three gowns in her wardrobe that would look lovely on the young woman. Would Mrs Everard accept them? she wondered.

Daphne exclaimed, 'Gracious! It is no trouble to serve tea. And it will make our visit more cosy, will it not?'

The young woman's eyes flashed. 'As you wish.'

Mrs Everard was angry about the visit! Daphne had not seen it at first, thinking her merely uncomfortable, but Mrs Everard resented being here, Daphne would wager.

The tea arrived, carried in by one of the London footmen. Daphne resolved to learn his name.

'Thank you,' she said as he placed the tray on the table between the two ladies.

He left the room.

Daphne lifted a tea cup. 'How do you take it?'

Mrs Everard removed her gloves and placed them in her lap. 'A little milk will do.'

It stood to reason she would not want sugar. There was no sweetness in her manner at all, but the unguarded expression of her face suggested her acerbity was meant entirely for Daphne. Such a reaction, to dislike her for her looks, was as familiar to Daphne as being liked for them.

She poured the tea and handed the cup to Mrs Everard. The silence between them stretched until Daphne was considering making the weather a topic of conversation.

'My husband talks of you a great deal,' her guest finally said.

Ah, jealousy. Daphne lifted her cup to her lips. 'Does he?'

Mrs Everard nodded. 'He has talked of nothing else, I believe, since your letter arrived that you were returning to England.'

Daphne knew how dangerous jealousy could be. It had nearly caused her to burn down a building. 'He takes his duties very seriously.'

'Too seriously, some might say.' Mrs Everard lifted her cup, but did not take a sip. 'I believe he frets more over your finances than he does over our own.'

Daphne laughed a little, trying to make light of it. 'I cannot see why he should.'

The woman's eyes flashed again. 'Can you not?'

Oh, dear. She must tread very carefully. She took another sip and took on a thoughtful expression. 'Perhaps your husband has more trust in your management of money than he does mine. He spoke in such a complimentary manner of that very thing when he called this morning.'

Mrs Everard's gaze shot back to Daphne's. 'He called on you this morning?'

Oh, dear. 'Very briefly,' Daphne quickly assured her. 'Merely to make certain I would be home to receive your call, so you did not exert yourself for no purpose.'

The young woman's brows knitted as if she had not considered that possibility. Of course, Daphne feared the visit from Everard had been mostly to indulge his infatuation. How could she convince him that an infatuation was nothing but fantasy?

Daphne went on. 'I asked your husband for the name of a good cabinet maker and he spoke of you as the expert in that area. I understand from him that you have very nicely decorated your home at the most reasonable cost.'

Mrs Everard swept a gaze over the room. 'What need have you of furniture, especially furniture of modest cost?'

Maybe if she pretended to take Mrs Everard into her confidence, the young woman would become more at ease. She'd tried such a tactic with Phillipa Westleigh once upon a time, when she'd pretended to herself they'd been friends.

It would be so nice to have a woman friend. Not this woman, though. Mrs Everard hated her without knowing her, hated her by sight alone.

Daphne leaned towards her. 'I will tell you why I wish to buy furniture, but you must promise to say nothing to your husband.'

Mrs Everard returned a wary look. 'I am not in the habit of keeping secrets from my husband.'

Spoken like a newly married woman, indeed. Daphne waved a dismissive hand. 'Oh, but this is a matter only of importance to me. You see, I recently authorised the repair of my tenants' cottages and I thought it would be a nice gift to all of them if I would buy them each a piece of furniture.' She took a sip of tea. 'What do you think? I thought perhaps a bureau for each family would be best. And some nice wooden chests for the farm and stable workers.'

Mrs Everard spilled some of her tea into the saucer. 'You are purchasing furniture for your tenants?'

'And the workers,' Daphne added. 'So I need good sturdy furniture, but I want it to be well made and pleasant to look at, too.' She gave Mrs Everard another thoughtful look. 'I do think everyone enjoys pretty things no matter what their circumstances.'

'I see.' Mrs Everard took her first sip of tea. 'Why would you do such a thing?'

To atone for never giving such people any thought her whole life, she could say. 'Call it a whim,' she said instead.

'Well.' Mrs Everard placed her tea cup back on the table and opened the strings of her reticule. She took out a piece of paper and handed it to Daphne. 'Here is the name of a cabinet maker in Cheapside.'

Daphne read from the paper. 'Jeffers Cabinetry.' She smiled. 'Thank you so much for this! I am so greatly indebted to you.'

Mrs Everard picked up a glove and put it on. 'If you would forgive me, I must leave. I have taken up too much of your time already.'

Daphne stood. 'Nonsense. It has been delightful to meet you.'

Mrs Everard rose, putting on her second glove. She started to walk away, but stopped and turned to Daphne. 'One thing more.' She looked Daphne directly in the eye. 'My husband is unnaturally attached to you.' She glanced from Daphne to her portrait and back. 'A woman like you must—must exert an undue influence on men. I would ask that you release my husband from your clutches.' Her eyes flickered with pain. 'He is all that I have.'

She turned to leave, but Daphne put a hand on her arm. 'I am fond of your husband, but he is my man of business. Nothing more. I wish you both happiness in your marriage.'

Mrs Everard moved out of Daphne's grasp. 'You outshine me. He cannot even see me when you are near.'

Daphne wanted to tell her she would not be around for long. Toller should be in touch any day now. If there was one thing today had taught her, it was that she should not come to town. Here she only made people unhappy.

She walked Mrs Everard to the door. The footman, whose name she did not know, stood in the doorway about to knock.

'Another caller, my lady,' he said. 'Mr Westleigh.'

Hugh?

Her heart flew into her throat.

Mrs Everard's head cocked in recognition, but she could not know of Hugh. More likely she knew of Phillipa Westleigh. Perhaps even her foolish husband had told that whole story.

No wonder the poor woman feared she would steal her husband.

'Mr Westleigh may come in,' Daphne said to the footman. To Mrs Everard she said, 'Thank you so much for coming and for bringing me such an excellent recommendation. Please do not worry over the rest.'

Mrs Everard avoided looking at her and simply followed the footman back to the hall.

The woman in grey glanced at Hugh as she passed him in the hall. She did not seem the sort who would call upon Lady Faville.

'Lady Faville will see you in the drawing room, sir,' the footman said, gesturing to the doorway to the room where Hugh had been the day before, where he had made love to Daphne.

He nodded politely to the woman in grey and crossed the hall to the drawing room.

Daphne stood waiting for him. 'Hugh, come in.'

He inclined his head in the direction of the hall. 'Did I interrupt?'

She shook her head. 'She was just leaving.' Her brow knitted. 'Is—is this about the pianoforte shop? I give you my word I did not know anything of Xavier's connection to the shop. If I had known, I would have gone to a different place.'

She wore the same green-and-white-striped walking dress she'd worn earlier, only her hair was a loose cascade of blonde curls tied with a ribbon high on her head. Her expression was not the cool perfection of her portrait, but seemed wounded and sad.

He remembered their frenzied lovemaking in this room. Was she still reeling from that assault or was encountering Xavier responsible?

Or the lady in grey?

In any event, she was on the defensive.

And he with her. 'Why did you purchase my sister's music?' he said, forgoing niceties.

She flinched at his words. 'I felt I owed it to her. It was the least I could do.'

Owed it to her?

She went on, 'I also enjoyed her music when she performed.'

'And you bought a pianoforte so you could play her music?' Was that not a bit much?

She glanced away. 'I purchased the pianoforte because I do not have one here. As you know, it helps one pass the time.'

'Do you need help passing time in London during the Season?' Usually a lady received more invitations than she could accept.

Her lashes fluttered before she gazed at him again. 'I am not attending social events.' She brushed a curl off her forehead. 'Not that I expect any invitations.'

He frowned. 'No invitations?' Had her scandal with Xavier and the Masquerade Club damaged her reputation to that extent? Surely someone would want such a beautiful creature in their ballroom.

'I did not announce my arrival in town.'

Then why had she come?

She stepped away from him and faced the window, the same window through which he'd glimpsed her the previous day when he'd had no intention of seeing her again. 'I am only staying a few days, but I promise you, any encounter with you or—or your family will be a happenstance, like today. I say again, I do not wish to trouble your family.'

But she troubled him. He closed his eyes and caught her scent of roses. His hands itched to hold her again. His body yearned to join with hers. The anger that had once burned as hot as the inn's fire now merely smouldered in a corner, nearly forgotten. Much hotter had been his need to protect her from his brother's rudeness to her in the pianoforte shop.

'You are in town only for a few days?' He tried to make his voice sound as if this did not greatly disappoint him. 'May I call upon you while you are here?'

She whirled around. 'Call upon me!'

'Start over. Become acquainted. You with the new manager of a gambling club, me, with Daphne, Lady Faville, a woman I do not believe I know.'

'I—I do not know what to say.' Her voice was little more than a whisper.

'Say you will walk with me in the park. Right now.' Why not? They'd enjoyed walks together when he'd been blind.

She stared at him.

He averted his gaze. 'I promise to be a gentleman. I will not repeat yesterday's appalling behaviour.'

He looked back at her and could read only puzzlement in her expression. 'A walk? Like old times?' he pressed. 'It is early. The park should not be crowded yet.'

It was not yet three o'clock. The fashionable hour for being seen in the park came at four o'clock.

He lowered his voice. 'Daphne?'

She swept a curl off her forehead. 'Just give me a moment to get my hat and gloves.'

Daphne rushed up to her bedchamber, her heart racing with pleasure. He'd said he wanted to spend time with her. To take a walk with her.

Perhaps it would feel a little like the walks they'd taken at the cottage, only this time he could see. She could take his arm and he could lead her, not the other way around. And she could see his whole face, all his expressions, nothing blocked by bandages.

Even if it lasted only the few days she was here in London, it was more than she'd ever dreamed.

Monette was in her room, folding her laundered undergarments. She looked up, all bright eyes, when Daphne entered the room. 'My lady, there is a letter for you!'

'A letter? But I am in a hurry.' She rushed up to Monette and clasped her hands. 'Mr Westleigh has called and invited me for a walk!'

Monette seemed to force a smile. 'Oh, that is so nice for you.'

Daphne peered closer at her. 'Something is troubling you. Tell me what it is.'

Monette turned away. 'Oh, it is nothing that cannot wait. You must hurry.' Her tone was flat.

Daphne persisted. 'What is it?'

Monette glanced towards the table near the door. 'The letter.'

'Oh.' Understanding dawned. 'Is it from Toller?'

Monette cheered. 'I believe so. Would—would you please open it? See what he says?'

Daphne strode over to the table and picked up the letter. 'It is from Thurnfield!' She broke the seal, unfolded the paper and read aloud, '"Dear Lady Faville."' She had explained to Toller her true identity. '"I most gratefully accept your offer of employment. I will travel to London in four days' time and will anticipate returning to your employ with great pleasure. Yours respectfully, Toller."'

She looked up.

Monette beamed. 'He writes a pretty letter.'

'He does indeed,' Daphne agreed.

'He will be here in four days' time!' Her voice rose in excitement.

'In three days' time, Monette,' Daphne said. 'The letter is dated yesterday.'

Monette flung herself into Daphne's arms and hugged her tightly. 'Oh, thank you, *madame*. Thank you!'

Daphne's spirits soared. She'd done something good.

Monette released her. 'But you must hurry! Mr Westleigh is waiting for you.' She ran to a drawer and pulled out a fresh pair of gloves. Her expression turned worried. 'He is not angry at you, is he?'

Daphne grinned. 'No, he is not angry. So I am happy, too.'

She reached for the hat she'd worn earlier, but Monette stopped her. 'No. No. Wear a prettier one.' She went into the closet and brought out a bonnet trimmed in silk flowers with a thick satin ribbon to tie under her chin. Monette put the bonnet on Daphne's head and fussed with the bow. She helped her into the spencer that matched her walking dress. 'There, you look very pretty now.'

Daphne gave her a quick hug. 'Thank you, Monette!'

She rushed out of the room and down the stairs.

Hugh stood at the foot of the stairs, waiting for her, his hat in his hands. She'd seen similar admiring looks on countless men's faces, but seeing it on Hugh was an entirely new thrill. It mattered to her that he admired her. She wanted his admiration for her character, as well.

It was something for which she would strive. Even if she never saw him again, it could be like a little test—*would Hugh think well of me for this?*

He put his hat on his head and offered her his arm. 'Shall we go?'

She nodded, liking him all the better for not prosing on about her beauty.

The footman opened the door and they left the town house.

They had only to cross Park Lane to reach the Cumberland Gate to Hyde Park. They chose a path that led to the Serpentine. It might not have been the fashionable hour, but there were other people in the park. Governesses with children in tow. Clerks and shop girls taking a quick respite. A few gentlemen with fancy-dressed women who were likely not their wives.

'It is not as quiet as the cottage in Thurnfield, is it?' Daphne remarked.

'It was not quiet there,' Hugh said. 'Although I might not have heard all the noises, had my eyes not been bandaged.'

She held his arm tighter. 'Those must have been difficult days.'

'Difficult,' he agreed. He stopped and lifted her chin up with a finger. 'Difficult, but happy. I do not regret a moment of it.'

'Truly?' She was surprised.

He started walking again. 'Only the end,' he murmured. 'When you were gone.'

She lowered her head. 'I made so many mistakes. I should have told you who I was that first day.'

'Why didn't you?' he asked.

'I was cowardly.'

'Cowardly?' He sounded surprised.

She'd promised she would be honest with him. 'I knew you would hate me. I did not want to face that. Oh, I did not want you to be forced to accept care from someone who had been such a torment to your family, but mostly I did not want to face being disliked.'

He squeezed her hand. 'Instead, you wound up being nursemaid and costing yourself a lot of money.'

'Not a lot of money,' she said. 'At first I thought it would only be for a day or two. It didn't seem like such a bad thing to pretend I was not Lady Faville for a day or two. But then—'

He interrupted. 'But then I refused to have my family contacted and you were stuck with me.'

'But you also became my friend,' she added. 'I did not want to spoil having a friend.'

She glanced up into his face. His expression was puzzled, but full of sympathy. How rare, to be looked upon with sympathy.

Likely she did not deserve it. 'A wise woman once told me that even little lies grow big. That is why one should not lie. I knew that and still I did it.'

They came upon a patch of spring flowers and discussed the variety of each. She was no better than he at naming flowers. Perhaps she would add gardening to the list of activities to pursue when she returned to the country.

'I should tell you that Toller is coming to work for me,' she said later. 'He is coming in a few days.'

'Toller?' His brows rose. 'I am surprised. He seemed so very attached to Thurnfield.'

She smiled. 'I think he is rather attached to a Swiss lady's maid.'

'Ah.' He laughed. 'I take it you do not really need another footman, but you hired him anyway.'

She felt her face turn red. 'One can always use another footman.'

Hugh glanced down at the woman walking beside him, blushing at his suggestion that she'd hire a footman to please her lady's maid. Was this the same woman who'd pursued Xavier so relentlessly? Xavier said it had been because she thought they would have made a handsome couple.

And so they would, a contrast of dark and light, the handsome man and beautiful woman.

He walked in silence for a while, unable to forget her past and unable to reconcile her with the woman she seemed to be now.

He finally spoke. 'What was it like for you to see Xavier again? I assume the pianoforte shop was the first time you'd seen him.'

She did not answer right away. 'I felt I deserved his anger and suspicion.'

That was not the answer he sought. 'You were unrelenting in your pursuit of him two years ago. Was that all you felt?'

'I felt sorry he had to encounter me. I am certain he would have preferred never seeing me again.' She said this without any tone of resentment.

He stopped and made her face him. 'Daphne, what I want to know is, do you still want him? Did that attraction you had for him return?'

She turned away while he spoke, but slowly lifted her gaze to his. 'No. That left me a long time ago. After the fire. The fire I caused, I mean.'

He believed her. He was unsure how long it would

last, but at this moment he was entirely certain she spoke the truth.

'Daphne,' he whispered, wanting more than anything to touch his lips to hers and feel their warmth, their singular taste.

She glanced around and stepped away. They were in plain view and there were people who would see.

He smiled and leaned down to her ear. 'Perhaps later.'

The colour rose in her face again, making her even more beautiful than she'd been a minute before.

'We should walk,' she said.

They continued on the path and were halfway to the Serpentine when Hugh spotted another couple walking in their direction.

'Blast.'

'What is it?' she asked.

'My mother and General Hensen.' Of all the luck. His mother would be walking in the park at this same moment.

'General Hensen? I remember him from the Masquerade Club.'

They were still some distance away, but close enough to recognise faces. His mother had seen him, he was certain. He was equally certain she had noticed Daphne.

'We do not wish to encounter my mother, however,' he said. Ned had been rude enough to Daphne. There was no telling how his mother would behave. 'Let's turn here and leave by the Grosvenor Gate.'

They could do so without looking as if they were fleeing. Which they were.

'I understand,' Daphne said. 'You do not wish to be seen with me.'

She was correct. He did not wish to explain something he did not understand himself, and his mother would demand an explanation of why he was strolling through Hyde Park with Lady Faville.

Their camaraderie disappeared. After spying his mother, it seemed to Daphne that all Hugh wanted was to take her home and be rid of her.

The dagger twisted in her heart again, but she understood. His mother would hate her. What other choice would a mother have?

If only Daphne could shut out her past and its consequences. If only she could truly emerge as Daphne Asher and start anew, then perhaps she would have a chance to be with Hugh.

He walked her to her door.

She offered her hand to shake. 'Goodbye, Hugh.' It seemed she was always saying goodbye to him.

He took her hand, but pulled her into an embrace. 'I am sorry our walk was cut short,' he said. 'May I call upon you tomorrow?'

Her eyes widened. 'Call upon me?' She would see him again? 'Yes. Yes. Of course.'

He leaned down and lightly kissed her on the lips.

Chapter Eighteen

By the time Hugh returned to the Masquerade Club, the message was waiting for him. From his mother. Summoning him to dinner.

He was not fooled. She'd seen him with Daphne.

He might skip dinner, send his regrets, spend these next few days with Daphne and leave the family out of it, but that seemed a cowardly thing to do. He'd face his mother and explain.

If he could.

He arrived at the appointed hour and was ushered in to the drawing room. To his surprise, Ned and Adele were there, with Xavier and Phillipa. So this was to be a family meeting? Family pressure.

He glanced from one to the other. 'What? No Rhys and Celia? Or are they not family enough?' More likely they would inject some sanity into the situation to which his mother would object.

'Rhys had to leave town,' Xavier said. 'What is this about, Hugh? None of us knows.'

Hugh crossed the room and poured himself a glass of

claret from a crystal carafe on the side table. 'I expect we will find out soon enough.'

A short time later, his mother entered the room on the arm of General Hensen. 'So good of all of you to come.' She glanced at Adele. 'Are you feeling well, my dear?'

'Mostly,' Adele responded. 'Well enough to attend the opera with you and the general, I am sure.' The opera was the big entertainment of the evening, after which the Masquerade Club would flood with more patrons.

His mother smiled. 'Excellent.' Her gaze rested on Hugh for a moment, but she addressed them all. 'I am so glad you could come, because this seems to be a family matter we should discuss together.'

'What is it, Mother?' Ned asked.

She turned to Hugh. 'Tell them, Hugh.'

He did not waver. 'Tell them what, Mother?' He knew precisely what she meant.

She lowered herself into a wing-back chair, as regal as a queen on her throne. 'Do not play coy with me, Hugh,' she scolded. 'Tell them who you were with in the park today.'

He took a sip of his wine. 'You tell them, Mother. I expect you will imbue the story with more drama than I.'

She narrowed her eyes at him and turned to the others. 'The general and I saw Hugh walking in the park with Lady Faville.'

'Lady Faville?' Adele piped up. 'Isn't she the one who tried to burn down the Masquerade Club?'

'It was not quite like that, Adele,' Phillipa said.

'Hugh!' Ned turned on him. 'You sought out her company when you knew I wanted you to have nothing to do with her?'

'It was not for you to tell me what to do,' Hugh shot back.

Ned straightened in outrage. 'As head of this family, I dare say it was my concern.'

His mother gave Ned an approving look, but her expression turned stern when she addressed Hugh again. 'Why you were with that woman, Hugh?'

He glared at her. 'What if I told you I was courting her?'

'Courting her?' his mother cried.

'Are you mad?' Ned took an angry step towards him.

'I did not realise you knew her,' his sister said, her voice tight, but absent of Ned's and their mother's outrage. She, over all of them, was entitled to be outraged.

He had no wish to hurt her. 'I became acquainted with her before returning to London,' he responded.

He was still not ready to share the whole story. In fact, he much preferred his family's typical uninterest in his affairs.

'Oh, yes, Xavier said she had been on the Continent.' Phillipa glanced at her husband. 'He also said you saw her at one of his shops today.'

Ned pointed to Xavier. 'She has come back to try to ruin our sister's marriage, you mark my words.'

Xavier raised both hands. 'I want nothing to do with her.'

'She is dangerous!' Ned insisted.

What right had he to judge her?

His mother broke in. 'She is not the sort of woman we would desire to be a part of our family, so courting her is out of the question.'

Hugh had forgotten. Ned had inherited his priggish behaviour from their mother.

She went on. 'I presume you were merely taunting us with the idea of courting her, but Ned is correct. She is dangerous. We managed to keep the whole affair of the fire out of the newspapers, but there is no telling what new scandal she might bring upon the family. If she is currying your favour, Hugh, undoubtedly it is so she can contrive to be near Xavier.'

'Are you certain, Honoria?' the general asked. Brave man. 'She seemed a charming woman to me when I met her years ago.'

His mother gave him a quelling look.

'Remember, she nearly destroyed the Masquerade Club,' Ned told him. 'Where would the family be if she had succeeded?'

'I absolutely forbid you to see that woman!' his mother said. 'Think of what talk there would be. Think of how dangerous it would be to give her such access to Xavier. It will ruin Phillipa's happiness.'

Hugh turned to Phillipa. 'Do you think she seeks access to Xavier?'

She shrugged. 'I do not know what to think, but I certainly believe it is possible that is her motive—'

Xavier broke in. 'No matter what, she will not ruin Phillipa's happiness, because I will not allow that to happen.' He took Phillipa's hand in his. 'I caution you, Hugh. Daphne has a way of using her charm to get what she wants. She can play a role quite convincingly.'

'See?' Ned broke in. 'She is duplicitous.'

His family's worries were ones that hid deep inside him, Hugh had to admit. At the same time, he yearned for the Daphne he'd known at the cottage, the Daphne who had looked so vulnerable at the piano shop and who had walked with him in the park this afternoon. The more his family spoke against that Daphne and told him what he must do, the more Hugh chafed at their words.

He put down his glass. 'Was there any other reason for summoning me here?' he asked his mother.

'This is enough of a reason.' His mother sniffed.

Mason, the butler, who undoubtedly had been listening to the whole exchange, knocked on the door. 'Dinner is served, my lady.'

His mother rose. 'Thank you, Mason.'

The butler bowed and was about to leave.

Hugh stopped him. 'Mason, would you get my hat and gloves? I am not staying.'

'Not staying?' His mother's eyes flashed.

He walked over to her and grasped her hand. 'I know you mean well, Mother, but you must not dictate our lives.' He turned to his brother. 'You neither, Ned. I cannot stay.'

He strode to the door.

Ned reached it first and spoke quietly so only he could hear. 'I don't mean to dictate, Hugh. I—I do not wish to see you or the family hurt. Is—is that not my role?'

Hugh had forgotten that Ned was still learning to be the Earl of Westleigh, but too many emotions warred inside him to be charitable to his brother at the moment.

His voice softened, though. 'Say no more, Ned.'

He left the room. Mason waited in the hall with his hat and gloves. He took them and walked out the door.

He was two houses away when he heard a voice behind him. 'Hugh!'

It was Phillipa.

She caught up with him. 'Are you all right?'

He nodded. 'We did worse to you when Mother tried to force you to do what she wanted and Ned and I did not protect you.' He looked into her eyes. 'I am sorry for it.'

She waved her hand. 'That is all past.'

He expected her to press him about Daphne, but she did not.

He put an arm around her. 'It is chilly out here. You should go back.' He walked with her, but paused at the door. 'She bought your music, Phillipa. Before she went to the pianoforte shop.'

Her brows rose. 'My music?'

'She said she owed it to you.'

'That seems odd.' She peered at him. 'I feel I must say something, but I do not wish to influence you one way or the other.'

He stiffened.

'Back at the Masquerade Club, when I was masked and she called me Lady Songstress, I sometimes thought she truly wanted to be friends, but it was so hard to tell, because she tended to be whatever people expected her to be. And she expected people to be whatever she wanted them to be. Xavier never gave her the least encouragement, but she truly believed he would be hers, because she was beautiful and she wanted it. When she discovered he loved me, a scarred woman, it shocked her.'

'And she started the fire,' he added.

'She set herself on fire, too,' she told him. 'Did you know that? Her skirts caught fire and she was so terribly frightened. It was far worse for her than for Xavier and me.'

Poor Daphne. No wonder she'd been terrified when the inn caught fire.

She patted his cheek. 'I cannot forgive her, I'm afraid, but, for what it is worth, my dear brother, I sometimes felt sorry for her.'

'Sorry for her?' His brows rose.

She shrugged. 'She seemed pitiful to me, sometimes.'

He leaned forwards and kissed the scar that ran from the corner of her eye almost to the edge of her lips. 'Thank you, my dear sister.'

She went back inside and he set off again, walking the short few streets to the Masquerade Club off St James's Street. When he entered the club, the delicious odour of

Cook's fare for the night reached his nostrils. Cummings, MacEvoy and some of the croupiers were all busy setting up. They would open at eleven, but the place would only fill after society's events were over and people with more money than sense came to seek the excitement of the gaming tables.

He thought of walking in the park that day in the fresh air, with the scent of green grass, spring flowers and leaf-filled trees wafting around him. To remain in the closed, lamp-lit rooms of the gaming house seemed akin to the prison of his former blindness.

MacEvoy approached him. 'Everything is ready, Mr Westleigh, or almost so. We've replaced the faro box with a new one that does not stick. The cards come out one at a time. We tested it.' He went on detailing a dozen other matters that he and the others had seen to, matters that now seemed inconsequential to Hugh.

That itch to be free returned with great intensity. 'MacEvoy, tell me, can you run the house without me tonight?'

MacEvoy nodded. 'Certainly. We've done so before on occasion. I'll walk the floor and one of the croupiers can act as clerk.' He indeed acted as if the request was nothing.

'Good.' He put his hat back on his head. 'I will be off, then. Likely I will see you tomorrow.'

MacEvoy did not even seem concerned where Hugh might spend the night. 'Right. See you tomorrow. All will be taken care of here.'

Where was Hugh to spend the night? At the moment, he cared for nothing but being free to walk wherever he pleased. No obligations. No dictates. No destinations.

He stepped back out into the evening air. In moments it would be dark, but he did not care. He wanted only to empty his mind, to set aside his family's voices and his own doubts. He wanted to shut his eyes to visions of Daphne—warm, loving Daphne and cool, conniving Daphne. He walked up Bond Street where shops remained open and the pavements were nearly as crowded as daytime. When he crossed onto Oxford Street, though, he knew where he was heading.

To Daphne's house.

He wanted to be with her in spite of his family's warnings, his own doubts. When he was with her, none of that mattered.

He reached her door and knocked.

Carter answered. 'Mr Westleigh!'

'I know it is unforgivably late, Carter, but would you ask if Lady Faville will see me?'

'She is in the drawing room awaiting dinner,' he said. 'One moment, please.'

Hugh stopped him. 'Wait, Carter. Might I go in unannounced?'

The footman thought a moment. 'I suppose you might.'

Hugh did not give him a chance to change his mind. He gave him his hat and gloves and crossed the hall to the drawing room. When he opened the door, her back was turned. Probably thinking it was Carter, she did not turn around right away.

'Daphne?'

She whirled around. 'Hugh!'

He could not find words to speak.

'What is wrong?' she asked.

'I come from my mother's house. She gathered the family to tell me not to see you again.'

She flinched, as if stung. 'Then you should not be here, should you?'

Why had he put that burden on her? It was cruel. He closed the distance between them and wrapped his arms around her and spoke the truth. 'I realised there was nowhere else I wanted to be.'

He lowered his lips to hers and kissed her as though he'd been starved of her kiss for too long. She flung her arms around his neck and gave herself to the kiss, melting against him.

When he finally took a breath he said, 'May I stay with you?'

'For dinner?' she responded. 'Of course you may.'

'Not for dinner,' he murmured, his lips still on hers. 'For tonight.'

Hugh woke to Daphne's warm body nestled against him, her golden hair splayed across his chest. He swept it back so he could see her face. In dawn's first glimmer she appeared like a Raphael Madonna, heavenly in her beauty.

What a change to gaze upon her now. He could hardly remember seeing the despised Lady Faville when he'd first unmasked her. Now she was Daphne, warm and giving and kind, words he would never have used to describe her when she'd glided through the Masquerade Club trying to make Xavier desire her.

She stirred and opened her eyes. Her eyes, gazing into his, reflected wonder and yearning.

The yearning he understood. His body flared with need for her, need to join her in lovemaking once more, this time in daylight, this time when he could see her as well as touch her, hear her, taste her lips, be enveloped by her rose scent.

He pulled the bed linens aside and rose above her, gazing at her smooth creamy skin, her full breasts, her narrow waist. Her hair fell upon her shoulders and on the pillow like a golden halo. He gazed upon her face that now resembled his Daphne, the woman with whom he made love in a cottage in Thurnfield.

His eyes were open now, in more ways than one. He loved her no matter who she'd once been. He loved the woman she was at this moment, a woman ready to give herself to him. He covered her with his body and kissed her, joining his tongue with hers, mingling their tastes. Breaking from the kiss, he entered her. The sensation of her body closing around him increased his arousal, and he wanted to savour the moment for as long as he could.

He moved in slow, languid strokes, relishing the quickening of her breathing, the rise of her hips to meet him. He could increase her pleasure by moving slowly, letting their passion build like smouldering ash can build into a raging fire. They'd originally come together in fire—let this be a blaze to meld them together for ever. He never wanted to lose this.

Daphne was the answer to his wanderlust. It was not travel he needed, but a place like this, with her, where every moment was an adventure.

His joy fanned the flames and he moved faster, revelling in the heat they created, letting it burn away all thought, leaving only emotion and sensation. Building. Building. Building.

To release.

He let out a primal sound and she cried out, her own climax joining with his. This was what he wanted. To be hers. To be forged together by the heat of their passion.

Hugh's muscles relaxed and he lay beside Daphne again. 'I should get dressed. Your maid will be in to tend the fire in a moment. Perhaps I should not be here.'

She held on to him. 'I do not want you to leave.'

He pulled her into another kiss. 'I do not want to leave you. Ever.' He sat up and gazed down at her, excitement invigorating him again. 'Travel with me, Daphne. Let us go somewhere else in the world, just you and me—and whomever of the servants you want to bring along. We could travel to Paris. Or Rome. Or Venice. We could sail to America. Or India. Wherever you wish.'

She rose as well, and wrapped the linens around her. 'What about your family? The Masquerade Club?'

'I have devoted enough of my life to my family's needs.' He took her face in his hands. 'Tell me you will come with me. Tell me you will marry me.'

Her eyes widened. 'Marry you?'

He released her. 'Yes. Marry.'

She leaned towards him. 'Hugh, I cannot marry you. Your family despises me, and rightfully so.'

'They do not know you as I do.' His high spirits fell more sensibly to earth. 'But give them no thought. I cannot live my life merely to please them.' He moved around her and embraced her from behind. 'I want to be with you, Daphne. Say you will marry me.'

Her muscles were taut and she was silent for several tortuous seconds. Finally she said, 'I want to, Hugh.' She sighed and gave herself to his embrace. 'Very well. I will marry you, because I cannot bear not to.'

He twisted around and kissed her again, a joyous kiss that threatened to arouse him all over again. Instead, he released her and bounded from the bed. 'I'll dress and be off for now. Let me see what I can do about covering the Masquerade Club. It is still my family's livelihood.'

She stiffened again. 'And if you do not find a way to deal with the Masquerade Club?'

He leaned down and brushed a kiss on her lips. 'I will.'

He put on his clothes, hoping they did not appear too wrinkled from lying in a heap on the floor all night.

Daphne rose from the bed and tied his neckcloth into a quite decent knot.

With one more kiss he said goodbye. 'I'll be back this evening or I will get word to you, never fear.'

Chapter Nineteen

Daphne felt as if she were floating on clouds as Monette helped her dress and arranged her hair.

Monette smiled at her. 'You do not need to tell me why you are so happy, my lady. We know that Mr Westleigh shared your bed last night.'

Daphne grinned. 'I am not saying he did.'

'There is not much about a house a servant does not know.'

Daphne gave her an amused glance. 'You sound as if you have been in service your whole life, Monette, instead of a few short months.'

The girl sobered. 'The abbey was not much different than a house in that way. We always knew the secrets.' She nodded decisively. 'I prefer being a lady's maid, though, because soon I will have a man, too, when Toller comes.'

Daphne stilled her hand. 'Monette, you must not bed Toller, not unless he marries you. It is different for me. I was a married lady, but you are a maiden and you must guard your maidenhood until a man marries you.'

Monette's brow furrowed. 'But I can have kisses, can I not?'

The role of duenna was new to Daphne. 'You may have

kisses, but you must be very careful that there is nothing more.' A thought struck her. 'Monette, do you know what takes place between a man and woman? A man and wife, I mean.'

'I know, *madame*,' Monette assured her. 'The novices talked about it all the time. And we watched the animals, you know.'

'It is a little different than what animals do.' Daphne's heart filled with fondness—and anxiety—for the maid. Was this how it felt to be a mother? She felt very protective. In fact, she must have a good talk with Toller when he came. She would not see Monette misused or hurt, not by anyone.

When Daphne walked down to breakfast, Mr Everard was waiting in the hall and Carter stood at the foot of the stairs.

'Mr Everard wishes to speak with you, m'lady,' Carter said with a barely detectable disapproving glance at the man.

She nodded her agreement and turned to Everard. 'Come in to breakfast and tell me why you are here again.'

'I do apologise, my lady.' He bowed. 'I will take up very little of your time.'

He followed her in to the breakfast room. She went directly to the sideboard and selected a slice of ham and some cheese.

'Do help yourself,' she told him.

'I will not stay so long.' He did not choose food this time, but rather paced the room. 'I fear my effort to assist you by sending my wife with her recommendations for cabinet makers has had unforeseen consequences.'

Something so dire? She sat and poured herself some tea. 'What consequences?'

'My wife believes I have—have an attachment to you that is beyond—beyond what a man of my position ought to have.' His wife was obviously more astute than he, if he did not see what was readily apparent. 'She thought it a contrivance that I sent her here and not a true need on your part.'

'Mr Everard, I did not ask you to call or to send your wife. That was your doing. You cannot blame her for finding it a strange matter.'

He rubbed his forehead. 'Yes. Yes. I know. It was a grave error.'

'I hope you apologised to her.'

He paced again. 'I did. Many times, but she thinks I see her as plain and dull in comparison to you….' He paused and shook his head. 'Of course, there is no comparison to you. I mean, I do not compare you with my wife—'

And Daphne would wager he didn't tell his wife she was beautiful or skilled or valued in any way.

He looked thoughtful. 'Perhaps I have talked of you too much. Of—of your affairs. Your financial affairs, I mean.' He seemed to reconsider that. 'Not that I divulge details, for that matter. I merely talk of my work, you see.'

How much had he told his wife about her? Had he told her of her time at the Masquerade Club? Did his wife know her as a woman who had tried to break up marriages? If so, no wonder the poor woman worried.

'Mr Everard, if your wife is concerned about your attachment to me, you should not call upon me so frequently, but only if there is a matter of great importance.'

'This is of great importance,' he wailed. 'I cannot have a wife who threatens to leave me.'

'I do not have the power to influence your wife.' His wife was clearly among the many people who despised her.

'But I beg you will do me one service.' She feared he

would go down on his knees. 'It will not be difficult and you will benefit as well, I promise.'

Her egg was getting cold. 'What can I possibly do?'

He leaned towards her, his hands folded as if in supplication. 'Write her a letter. Implore her to meet you at the cabinet-maker's shop. Say you need her to advise you what to buy.'

What could it hurt? Perhaps Mrs Everard would know better what furniture would suit her tenants. Besides, she'd used Everard shamelessly two years before. She could at least humour him in this way. She had no illusions, though, that writing this letter and forcing this meeting would suddenly make Mrs Everard cease to despise and be jealous of her.

'Very well,' she said. 'I will do it, but you must do something for me and you must promise.'

His face turned worshipful. 'I will do anything you ask, my lady. I always have.'

She spoke to him as if he were a child using what Hugh called her governess voice. 'You must never talk about me to your wife. You must tell her once a day that she is beautiful. You must thank her every day for the kindnesses she does for you, even if you think them ordinary, like planning meals, seeing to your laundry or the cleaning of the house.'

His brows knitted. 'That is what you wish?'

She nodded emphatically. 'And you must encourage her to purchase pretty gowns and pretty hats, and if she has a pretty dress made for herself, you must tell her she looks lovely in it.'

These were all things her husband had done, she realised, things that had flattered her vanity, but she'd learned later that she'd needed other things more.

'And talk with her,' she went on. 'Ask her opinion. Ask

what is important to her.' Until the abbess—and Hugh—
no one had ever asked what was important to Daphne.

Everard looked very sceptical.

'Promise me or I will not write your letter or meet your
wife at the cabinet maker.' She spoke this like a stern governess.

'I will do it,' Everard said in a desperate voice. Unfortunate that he could not hear the wisdom in what she said,
but perhaps he'd realise when he experienced the results.

'Ask Carter for pen and ink and I will write your letter.'

He rushed out to do her bidding.

When the time came she would order the carriage and
ask Smith to drive her and Carter to Cheapside, to Jeffers
Cabinetry Shop. She hoped she would not miss Hugh if
he called while she was away. She must leave word for
him to wait for her.

That afternoon, Hugh sat in the gaming room with
MacEvoy, Cummings and some of the croupiers, seeking
their opinion about running the gaming house without him.
No one saw any difficulties. A monthly visit from a member of the family would be sufficient, MacEvoy thought,
to ensure the place was being run in a manner that suited
them. Perhaps they could find a gentleman to stand in for
him, someone like Sir Reginald, who was a frequent visitor to the club, but who could use some additional funds.

Hugh could not wait to present the plan to the family.
They would have to accept it, because he was declaring
himself free of the obligation.

The door to the gaming room opened and Xavier
stepped in.

'Xavier! Come in.' Hugh waved his arm. 'I want you
to hear what we've been discussing.'

Xavier nodded to everyone. 'Good to see you all.' He

frowned at Hugh. 'May I speak with you alone first, Hugh? Out in the hall?'

Hugh stood. 'Of course.'

Something was wrong. Was it to do with a member of the family?

To his surprise, Phillipa waited in the hall. They stepped away from the gaming room door.

'What is it?' Hugh asked, his alarm growing. 'Is someone ill? Injured?'

'Nothing like that,' Phillipa assured him.

Xavier pulled a paper from his pocket. 'I received this a little while ago. We thought you should see it.'

Hugh took the paper from his hand and immediately recognised the handwriting. He'd been handed a similar note at the cottage and had read it enough times to be familiar with the script.

Would you be so good as to join me at Jeffers Cabinetry Shop at three o'clock this afternoon? After our meeting yesterday, I realised that I greatly need you and no one else to settle my plan.

Please set aside any misunderstandings and do me the honour of keeping this appointment.

Yours, etc,
Daphne, Lady Faville

Hugh crushed the note in his hand.

'A boy delivered it to me a short time ago,' Xavier explained. 'He told us a lady paid him to do it.'

Phillipa touched Hugh's arm. 'I am so sorry, Hugh.'

Hugh's throat grew tight. 'No.'

Daphne set up a meeting with Xavier? What had happened? Had she started thinking of Xavier after Hugh had left her that morning? Or had she already planned a meeting with Xavier even before he proposed marriage to her? Ned might have been right all along. Maybe Hugh had fallen into a trap intended only to allow her to be close to Xavier. Was that the *plan* she wished to *settle* with him?

A sabre's thrust could not be more painful than this betrayal. Hugh had been fooled by her once, when she'd played Mrs Asher, now he'd been fooled again.

'What time is it?' he asked.

Xavier pulled out a pocket watch. 'It is twenty past three.'

He quickly gathered his hat and gloves. 'She may still be there. I am going to meet her.'

Daphne was not surprised that Everard's wife did not show up at the furniture shop. In fact, she was relieved. She could happily select her tenants' gifts without any unpleasantness to intrude. On this day that Hugh had asked her to marry him, she wanted only happiness.

She loved the cabinetry shop. She sensed it was a happy place with happy workers. The pieces they made were skilfully done, using good timber. Mr Jeffers, the proprietor, a rather frightening-looking man with a scar on his face, was friendly and obviously very proud of his shop's work. He was more than delighted when she ordered ten oak-banded bureaus for her tenants and a dozen pine coffers for the stable and farm workers.

She and Mr Jeffers had just finished the transaction when the shop door opened.

Daphne looked over and broke into a surprised smile. 'Hugh!'

But the look he returned to her was like a knife. 'Surprised to see me, Daphne?'

Behind him walked in Xavier and his wife.

'Mr Campion!' Jeffers started towards him.

Xavier gestured for him to stay back, and Jeffers disappeared behind the curtain that separated the workroom from the store.

Daphne's heart pounded with anxiety. Something was amiss, something terrible. Carter must have sensed it, too, because he moved from where he waited in the background to Daphne's side.

She glanced from Hugh to Xavier to Phillipa. 'I do not understand.'

Hugh looked at her as if she were an infestation. He handed her a crumpled paper.

She glanced at it. 'But this is— How did you get this?'

'From Xavier, obviously,' Hugh said, his voice rough.

'How did Xavier—?' She handed the letter back to Hugh. 'I did not send this!'

He came closer to her, his eyes burning like fire. 'It is your handwriting, Daphne.'

'I do not know how to explain it,' she said. She'd sent the note to Mrs Everard.

Hugh huffed. 'Do not make an attempt to explain. I will not believe you.'

Daphne's legs weakened. She clutched Carter's arm, needing to steady herself. 'I did not send this to Xavier!' She glanced at Xavier. 'I do not know where you live.'

'You knew of my shop,' Xavier countered. 'You could learn of my residence, as well.'

'Your shop?' He owned this shop as well as a pianoforte shop?

It felt as if the walls were falling in on her, like the walls of the inn had fallen in from the fire. Hugh would never believe she'd not known this was Xavier's shop.

Everard's wife must have known. But would it not be even more unbelievable to say that the wife of her man of business must have set this up? It was no use. He would never believe her.

No one would ever believe the beautiful Lady Faville would ever change. She'd once made a fool of herself over the incredibly handsome Xavier Campion, and no one would ever think that she no longer cared for him. Xavier was not the man who mattered to her.

Hugh mattered.

She gripped Carter's arm. 'It is no use,' she whispered to herself, but she made herself look Hugh in the eye. 'I misled you once. I made you think I was someone I wasn't, but I never lied to you then and I will not lie to you now. I did not arrange a meeting with Xavier. I am nothing but ashamed of that time. I spent two years trying to change, and I have changed.' She summoned all her remaining strength and rose to her full height. 'What I cannot change is what other people think of me.' She took a breath. 'I cannot change your mind, Hugh.'

He blinked and lost the red rage that had tinged his face.

She turned to Carter. 'Let us take our leave, Carter.'

'Yes, m'lady,' he responded, giving her something solid to hold on to while her world shattered into little pieces.

Carter escorted her outside to where Smith waited with the carriage and helped her inside. Before he closed the door and climbed onto his seat on the outside, he touched her hand. 'Some things we've done never go away, m'lady, but we move on anyway, do we not?'

He sounded as if he knew firsthand of what he spoke.

She tried to smile. 'We move on.'

The coach pulled away and Daphne tried to stitch herself back together. She needed to move on. There never had been a chance that she and Hugh could be together. Her past would always separate them. No more trying. He was a beautiful memory. Proof she could truly love a man. Proof she could feel real emotions, real joy, real despair.

By the time the coach reached her town house, she'd regained a modicum of composure. She could stand. She could walk. She could speak.

She could move on.

As soon as they entered the hall, Monette ran up to her. 'My lady! My lady! Look who is here! Toller has come a day early.'

Toller stepped forwards. 'M'lady. I hope you approve of my coming early. I was able to settle my affairs in Thurnfield more quickly than I'd anticipated.'

Daphne put on a smile. She would not ruin Monette's happiness with her grief. 'I am so happy to see you, Toller. You have arrived at the perfect time. Now we can leave for Vadley tomorrow.' She turned to Carter. 'Will you arrange it, Carter? Toller can help you.'

'We are leaving London so soon?' Monette sounded disappointed.

Daphne felt a twinge of guilt. 'We'll come back again later, but I need to return to Vadley.'

'What of Mr Westleigh?' Monette asked.

'He knows.' Daphne's voice lowered. 'He knows.'

Hugh knew she would be gone.

Chapter Twenty

He'd recovered nicely, Hugh thought. He'd thrown himself into his duties at the Masquerade Club, abandoning the idea of leaving it. After the club closed at night, what did it matter that he consumed too much brandy in order to get to sleep?

He ignored the nearly daily summons from his mother. He saw no one outside of the club. In fact, he rarely went outside. The Season flourished without him. The preparations for the king's coronation created extra excitement, but what had that to do with him?

A good week went by. Daphne, he was certain, had returned to her country house, wherever that was located. He'd never bothered to discover where she lived and now it was of no importance. No importance at all.

This evening he opened the door to the supper room and walked in to make certain all was ready for the night ahead. He'd taken to checking things two or three times—to help the days go by more quickly. This evening he stared at the pianoforte, idle since his sister had stopped performing. Having a performer in this room had been a good idea. Phillipa had drawn more people to the gaming house simply to hear her. Surely there was another songstress who could be hired to play?

He sat down at the bench and closed his eyes. As he had done once before, he picked out the notes of 'The Last Post'.

He turned away and rose from the bench. He strode from the room and wondered if there was any brandy left in the bottle he'd left in the drawing room.

Before he could climb the stairs, Cummings approached him. 'Captain Rhysdale to see you.' Rhys was always Captain to Cummings.

'Where?' Hugh asked.

'Hall,' Cummings said.

If Hugh had heard Rhys was back in town, he'd forgotten. He'd had notes from Ned and Phillipa as well as their mother, but he'd paid them little heed.

When he reached the hall, he saw Rhys was still wearing his hat and gloves.

Before Hugh could say anything, Cummings handed him his own hat and gloves.

'Come with me, Hugh,' Rhys ordered.

Hugh held up his hands. 'I cannot, Rhys. I need to get ready for tonight.'

'No, you do not,' Rhys said. 'MacEvoy and Cummings will see to it. We have been summoned by your mother and I am charged with making certain you answer her call this time.'

'I am not going.'

'Yes, you are.' Rhys placed the hat on Hugh's head. 'Do not make me fight you.'

Hugh grimaced. 'I'd rather like to fight someone.'

Rhys pulled him out the door. 'I can still beat you.'

'*I* can still beat *you*,' Hugh countered, but it wasn't

worth the effort. He had to face his family eventually, so why not now?

At least Rhys did not ask any questions as they made the short walk to the Westleigh town house. Xavier must have told Rhys about Daphne and the note. Hugh suspected all the family knew the whole story.

Not the whole story. None of them knew he'd shared her bed. None of them knew she'd nursed him through blindness. He held those memories for himself alone.

When he and Rhys reached the town house and walked into his mother's drawing room, the rest of the family was there. His mother. The general. Ned and Adele, who was thickening around the waist. Xavier and Phillipa, looking sympathetic. Celia, alert and not about to miss a thing. His mother had obviously issued an edict that they were not to talk to him about Daphne, because they hardly talked to him at all. They asked him nothing he couldn't answer in one or two syllables.

Through dinner, he had more appetite for the wine than the food. The conversation washed over him, and a second after, he could not recall what was said. He watched his family as if they were exotic animals on display at the Tower, an entirely different species. He'd felt that way once before when they'd tried to convince him that Daphne was not to be trusted.

Of course, they'd been right.

Although how did the passionate nights he and Daphne shared fit into the picture they created of her? That was like a piece to an entirely different puzzle.

After dinner, they retired to the drawing room, where Hugh sat with a glass of brandy, which he refilled each time he emptied it.

Hugh's mother pulled out a letter. 'Adele, dear, I received a letter from your grandmother. I entirely forgot to tell you. Shall I read it?'

'Oh, please do!' Adele cried with an enthusiasm that made Hugh wince.

His mother lifted up the letter, making a big show of it. 'It begins "Dear Honoria"—I do not know why she becomes so familiar, using my given name like that. Imagine. "Dear Honoria."'

Hugh sat up straight. *Dear Honoria...*

Something he'd not considered before this moment struck him like a hammer to anvil.

'A salutation.' His voice came out louder than he'd intended and everyone gawked at him. He turned to Xavier. 'It did not have a salutation, did it?'

Xavier looked at him as if he'd gone mad. 'What did not have a salutation?'

His mother pursed her lips. 'Really, Hugh. You do not say a word all evening, then you interrupt with nonsense.'

'It is not nonsense.' He rose from the chair and walked over to where Xavier stood. 'The letter you received from Daphne. It did not have a salutation.'

Xavier looked puzzled, but said, 'I do not believe it did.'

Phillipa broke in. 'I know it did not have a salutation. I remember thinking it odd at the time, but what does that matter?'

Hugh felt as if a fog in his brain had suddenly cleared. 'It means the letter might not have been for Xavier.' He tapped his lips with his fingers. 'Tell me, did that note two years ago have a salutation?'

Xavier obviously knew precisely which note he meant—the one Daphne sent asking him to meet her in the supper room at the Masquerade Club. Xavier shook his head. 'I do not recall.'

'I remember,' Phillipa broke in. 'I remember every word of it. It began "My dear Xavier..."'

Hugh stabbed the air with his finger. 'So why would she not start this letter the same way?'

What a fool he'd been. He'd seen what he was led to expect. That she'd wanted a liaison with Xavier. But what if the letter had not been intended for Xavier at all?

'She wrote the letter to someone else, someone who cut off the salutation.' Hugh was sure of this. The pieces fit perfectly now.

'Hugh.' Ned threw up his arms. 'You have taken leave of your senses again. That woman was after Xavier.'

'I agree with Ned,' Adele piped up, as if Adele's opinion carried any weight with Hugh.

Ned went on. 'You know what the woman was like.'

'*Was* like,' Hugh emphasised. '*Was* like. She changed. She is not the woman she was then.'

'Utter nonsense!' his mother cried.

The general wisely remained silent.

Hugh turned back to Xavier, as if his mother had never spoken. 'It was a note she sent to someone else.'

Xavier looked unconvinced. 'It seems like such an elaborate hoax, then, for her to send someone the note, for them to cut out the salutation and then know to send it to me. Why would a person do such a thing?'

'I do not know why,' Hugh admitted. 'I only know they did it.'

Xavier shook his head again. 'The only sensible explanation is that it was sent by her.'

Rhys joined the conversation. 'Hugh's version is possible, though.'

'There is one way to find out,' Celia said. 'Go to her. Ask her. Hear what she has to say.'

Things he had never done.

'You are right, Celia,' Hugh admitted, though his spirits dropped. 'There is only one problem.'

'And that is?' Celia asked.

Hugh met her eyes. 'She is gone.'

Hugh rode the horse he'd purchased in Thurnfield, the horse Daphne had arranged for him to ride while there, the one he'd ridden when he made his solitary way back to London after Daphne left him. This time, however, Hugh rode towards her.

It had been an easy matter to find where she'd gone. He simply tracked down Everard, her man of business. To Hugh's surprise, finding Everard also solved the mystery of the note. Daphne had written the note to Everard's wife, who knew from her husband of Daphne's past infatuation with Xavier. Mrs Everard had cut off the salutation and sent the note to Xavier, hoping to make trouble for Daphne. Mrs Everard had done so out of jealousy, which made perfect sense to Hugh.

At least Everard did not seem to know of Hugh's relationship with Daphne, and Hugh did not enlighten him. He offered no explanation of why he needed to contact Daphne, but Everard told him her country house was in Vadley, near Basingstoke, a long day's ride from London.

It was late afternoon by the time Hugh reached the village. He stopped at the public room of the inn for some refreshment and to ask directions to the house.

The publican took a fancy to him and chatted a great deal about Lady Faville.

'She was not a favourite here when she first came, let me tell you,' the man said. 'I do not care how beautiful she was, she thought nothing of making her servants' lives difficult with her demands, but no more. Now they say she's made improvements in the cottages and she's raised all the wages.' He went on to detail her other good deeds and poured another tankard of ale for Hugh. 'Are you a friend of hers?'

'I am,' Hugh replied. He intended to be a faithful friend from now on.

Armed with directions and the publican's good wishes, Hugh rode to Daphne's house, reached its gates and made his way down its tree-lined private drive to the large brownstone Jacobean house that stood at its end. When he reached the front entrance, he dismounted and sounded the knocker.

Toller opened the door. 'Mr Westleigh!'

Hugh smiled. 'Toller. I am surprised, but pleased to see you here.'

Toller grinned. 'Mrs Asher—Lady Faville, I mean— offered me a position.'

Another good deed. 'Is she in?' he asked. 'Would you see if she will receive me?'

Toller shook his head. 'She is out visiting the tenants, I think. You could wait for her in the drawing room.'

He could not bear waiting. 'Might I catch up to her where she is?'

'Surprise her? That would be a treat, wouldn't it?' Toller directed him to where the tenants' cottages would be found.

Hugh was soon back on his horse and hopeful it would not take long to find her.

He spied her from a distance, at first unsure if it was indeed her. She wore a dress so simple it could have belonged to one of the tenants. It was covered by a white apron and she carried a large basket. Her face was shaded by a wide-brimmed straw hat. He approached slowly and saw the moment she recognised him.

He dismounted. 'Do you see what horse this is?'

'Yes.' She stroked the animal's head.

The soft light of late afternoon illuminated her face and tinged it with colour. The blue of her eyes rivalled the sky's hue. He did not think he'd ever seen her more beautiful.

Her expression, though, was guarded. 'Why did you come here, Hugh?'

He realised she'd had to ask him that question several times before when it seemed they had parted, but he'd come back to her. 'This time, to apologise.'

She started walking again. 'To apologise.'

He fell in step with her, leading his horse. 'For not listening to you. Not believing you. I was wrong.'

'It does not matter,' she said without emotion.

'What do you mean, it does not matter?' He was filled with emotion. Joy at seeing her. Regret for his behaviour. Fear that she would not forgive him.

'I mean, it does not change things.' She sounded sad.

'I have come back to you, Daphne.' Had he missed his chance? His heart pounded. 'To ask your forgiveness. I have held on to the past. Listened to my family. Let both blind me. But I see clearly now. I want to start over. I want to be with you.'

She stopped and looked up at him, her eyes filled with pain. 'I am reconciled with this. The past is always with me, always there to come between us.' She reached up as if to touch him, but withdrew her hand. 'We've tried, but the past always comes back. I cannot change what I've done. I can never change it and it will always come between us.'

An ache grew deep within him. 'But you have changed. Even the publican at the inn knows this.'

She started walking again. 'Yes, I have changed, and I

do not wish to ever be the woman I was. But that woman is still part of me. What she did, I still must pay for.' She glanced at him. 'Your family will never forgive me, nor should they.'

'Blast it, Daphne. If your behaviour was unforgivable, then mine must be, too.' He walked a few steps before halting. 'I do not care about your past and I intend never to repeat mine.' She tried to walk away, but he took hold of her arm. 'I want to be with you. I asked you to marry me once and you said yes. I renew that proposal. Marry me and let us live together. Forget the rest of it.'

Daphne searched his face, his dear face. She looked into his eyes, gazing so intently at her, and rejoiced again that he could see, remembering how it had been for him to be bandaged and blind, groping tentatively with a cane.

She wanted to be with him more than anything, but they'd come this far before and everything had shattered. Could she bear it another time?

'What of your family, Hugh? Will they not disown you?' She had no family. How much worse might it be to have family and have them not acknowledge you?

He held her firmly by the shoulders. 'They may. Or they may change, as well. That is up to them. I only know that it feels like agony to have lost you, and I am not willing to choose my family over you.'

She glanced away. 'I do not know.'

He forced her to look at him again. 'I love you, Daphne. If you need time, I understand. But let me court you. I'll take rooms nearby. Give me a chance to prove to you that I've changed, that I believe in you. Completely.'

She gazed back at him. 'But I do not want to travel, Hugh. I want to stay here. There is so much to do here.

With a little effort, I could really help the people who work for me. I could make their lives so much easier.'

He grinned. 'I think you are saying yes.' He picked her up and whirled her around. The horse caught wind of the excitement and whinnied. When he set her down again, he still held her. 'No travel.' He kissed her. 'We'll stay wherever you wish to be. I have found what I was searching for in you.'

He leaned down and placed his lips on hers. She flung her arms around him and held him in the kiss. He wanted it never to end. What a marvel. What a miracle. She loved him.

And he loved her back will all his heart and soul.

Epilogue

They arranged for the banns to be read right away in the parish church in Vadley and St George's in Hanover Square. Daphne did not make Hugh take rooms nearby, but rather welcomed him into her home and her bed for a blissful wait until they could speak their vows before God and witnesses.

Hugh had written to his family as soon as he knew the exact day of their wedding ceremony. It pained him that none of them responded to the invitation, because he wanted to share his happiness with them. He refused to let them diminish his joy, though. He'd not been happier than during these four weeks and only expected his happiness to grow.

He could no longer see the cool, perfect beauty that Daphne had once been. Now he noticed only her warmth and kindness. It made her more beautiful in his eyes.

Their wedding day was becoming a bigger celebration than he thought it could ever be, because the whole village seemed to want to celebrate the day with her. It made him happy that others could see in her what he now saw.

He laughed aloud. He was no longer blind.

* * *

The wedding day arrived and he was banished from her bedchamber while she dressed in a new gown. He walked to the church with Mr Quigg, her estate manager, a man who had nothing but good things to say about her. Quigg had agreed to stand up with him at the wedding, for want of anyone else to do it. People had already gathered, and he greeted those he'd met before and was introduced to those he hadn't. He and Quigg entered the church and the vicar strode up to speak with them.

While they were speaking, the arrival of carriages sounded from outside and Hugh assumed Daphne had arrived. The doors from the vestibule opened, but it was not Daphne, nor anyone from the house.

Down the aisle strode Hugh's mother and the general, followed by Ned and Adele, Phillipa and Xavier, Rhys and Celia. His family. They had all come.

He bounded down to them, kissing his mother, Phillipa and the wives, hugging his brothers and shaking hands with Xavier. Moved more than he could ever remember, he stepped back. 'You've come.'

'Of course we've come,' his mother retorted. She did not sound precisely happy, but she was here. 'We are family.'

He quickly introduced them to the vicar, who made certain they were seated in an honoured place at the front.

Hugh turned to Quigg. 'Do you mind? I want my brothers to stand up with me, now that they are here.'

'I do not mind at all,' the man said, smiling.

'Will you, Ned? Rhys?' Hugh asked.

Ned's smile looked forced, but he nodded. 'I will, if you wish it.'

Rhys peered at Hugh. 'Are you certain you want me, as well?'

Hugh smiled. 'I want both my brothers.'

They were all sorted out when another carriage was heard, as well as cheering and clapping. A man stepped in. 'The bride has arrived.'

More of the villagers and Daphne's servants and workers came in and took seats. The organ started to play, and Hugh saw Phillipa take Xavier's arm and place her cheek against his shoulder. The doors opened again and Monette walked up the aisle to take her place by the altar.

What would his mother think of that? Hugh wondered. Daphne's lady's maid was to be her witness and Carter, now her butler, would give her away.

Then Daphne appeared in the doorway and Hugh forgot about anything but her.

She wore a simple blue dress with tiers of blue lace at the hem and sleeves and a matching hat and veil covering her face. The dress, which might not compare with one made by a mantua maker in Mayfair, had been lovingly designed and sewn by Monette. It allowed Daphne's happiness and beauty to shine through.

She stopped when she saw Ned and Rhys standing beside Hugh. He smiled and gestured to where his mother and the others were sitting.

Daphne broke away from Carter and walked over to them, grasping their hands. 'I am honoured and grateful you have come,' she said. She paused in front of Xavier and Phillipa. 'I—I have no words.'

Phillipa, looking pale, accepted her hand. 'Best wishes.'

Xavier nodded stiffly.

Daphne glanced towards Hugh.

She returned to Carter, but before coming to Hugh's side at the altar, she greeted Ned and Rhys, thanking them, as well.

Finally, she came to Hugh, and the vicar began, 'Dearly beloved…'

* * *

Later, at the hastily organised wedding breakfast with the family, Daphne sat next to Hugh, too happy to eat. Somewhere in the house, governesses and nannies were seeing that Rhys and Phillipa's children were fed and entertained. Outside, the villagers were celebrating with food and wine. The family conversed together as if this was a family dinner. Or at least how Daphne imagined a meal with a large family might be.

She reached for Hugh's hand under the table.

He grasped it and squeezed. 'What do you think, Daphne?'

She gazed up towards the ceiling. 'I think somewhere in heaven there is an abbess who is smiling down at me and saying, "Did I not tell you so?"'

He looked puzzled, but leaned forwards and kissed her anyway.

Daphne laughed for the joy of it.

* * * * *

JOIN US ON SOCIAL MEDIA!

Stay up to date with our latest releases, author news and gossip, special offers and discounts, and all the behind-the-scenes action from Mills & Boon...

 millsandboon

 millsandboonuk

 millsandboon

It might just be true love...